THE
PRINCESS
SCOUT

HENRY VOGEL

Published in the United States of America by Rampant Loon Press, an imprint of Rampant Loon Media LLC, P.O. Box 111, Lake Elmo, Minnesota 55042. "Rampant Loon Press" and the Rampant Loon colophon are trademarks of Rampant Loon Media LLC.

www.rampantloonmedia.com

Cover by Miblart.com

ISBN: 978-1-958333-22-8 (ebook)

ISBN: 978-1-958333-21-1 (paperback)

ISBN: 978-1-958333-20-4 (hardcover)

First publication: March, 2024

In memory of my wife, Audrey. She was my Callan, my Jade, my Michelle, my Elise, my everything. I don't know how I will go on without her.

YOU IDIOT

Dear Diary,

    Many people believe I should hate being the second-born child of the royal heir. That I should resent my big brother for being the next in line to the throne behind Mom. Yeah, Rob gets to follow in Mom's footsteps, and will rule the Kingdom of Mordan someday. But that doesn't bother me. Because, when I turned eighteen, I got to follow in Dad's footsteps.

    I got to attend the Scout Academy!

    There are also those who don't think I belong here. That I only got into the academy because David Rice—the man I call 'Dad'—is the Academy's most famous graduate. That Dad pulled strings and called in favors to get his only daughter admitted. Those people obviously don't know Dad. They don't believe I worked my butt off preparing for the Academy entrance exams. And they really don't believe I aced the exam!

    But I did. I kept working my butt off throughout my plebe year at the Academy, too. And all that hard work paid off when they posted class rankings at the end of the year. Out of over four hundred plebes, my name appeared third on the list. That meant I earned a berth on the Cadet Cruise. One of five reserved for plebes. Sophomores get fifteen berths, and all juniors and seniors get a berth.

    That's why I'm sharing a cramped room with five other girls, sitting on my narrow bunk, and writing in my diary for the first time in ages. I'm sorry I ignored you, Diary, but you wouldn't believe how busy I've been since the ship left Draconis two weeks ago.

There are over a thousand people on this ship, counting instructors and cadets, and the only ones I outrank are the fourth and fifth ranked plebes. Instructors order me around during my duty shifts. Upperclassmen order me around when my duty shifts end. I sleep the rest of the time. It took me two weeks to learn the ship's routines well enough to evade everyone looking for a plebe to order around. That includes my bunkmates, who are juniors and seniors. But, for once, they're all on duty while I'm off duty.

So I can hide in my bunk and finally have time to write. But where do I start?

And... that's when the ship's alarm sounded.

Above the din of the alarm, the ship-wide intercom broadcast the captain's voice. "Abandon ship! All personnel to their assigned lifepod. Repeat, abandon ship!"

Yeah, sure. This is the fourth 'abandon ship' alarm since the cruise began. But I knew better than to dawdle. The instructors expect us to report to our lifepod within sixty seconds, and they punished everyone assigned to a lifepod if all six cadets assigned to a pod weren't seated and ready for launch at the end of that time.

I knew that all too well, since my pod received punishment duty after two of the three previous drills. Not because of me. But that didn't stop some of the cattier upperclassmen from blaming the Princess Scout—my not-so-beloved nickname, among a certain group of cadets—for the failures of others assigned to my pod.

Those thoughts ran through my mind as I hurried to my assigned pod. I ducked into it less than thirty seconds after the alarm sounded. And I had the pod all to myself. Surprise, surprise. I'd bet anything my upper class podmates were about to get me punished. Again.

Then everything changed.

Over the intercom, the captain called, "Cadets, board the nearest lifepod. Repeat, board the nearest lifepod. Lifepods launch in fifteen seconds. This is not a drill."

A white-faced upper class cadet dove into my pod. As she scrambled for a seat, I yelled, "To anyone nearby, we have lots of space in this pod! Hurry!"

I heard feet pounding down the corridor. But the hatch slid shut before they reached it, and our lifepod launched with just the two of us aboard.

The other cadet and I stared at each other, our eyes wide and our mouths agape. My heart pounded so hard I thought it might break one of my ribs.

"Did I hear that right?" the other girl asked. "Not a drill?"

I nodded. "I heard it, too."

"Do you have any idea what happened?"

"Not a clue. I was in my bunk, off duty."

"Yeah, but you're..." The other girl looked at the deck, and her voice trailed off.

"I'm *what*?"

"You know."

I did know, but I said, "No, I don't know. I'm just a plebe, so I obviously need an upperclassman to explain it to me."

"You're... *her*."

"Her who?"

"Quit acting stupid," she snapped.

"I'm not the one suggesting someone on the bridge crew took the time to call a mere plebe in the middle of a ship-wide emergency."

"Everyone knows the Princess Scout isn't a *mere* anything."

"Just like everyone knows," I made air quotes with my fingers, "I didn't earn my spot at the Academy. That I only got in because my father is David Rice."

The other girl met my eyes. "You said it, not me."

"You implied it. You just didn't have the guts to come out and say it."

The other girl opened her mouth for a reply, then shut it. She closed her eyes, took a deep breath, and said, "I'm sorry. My brain overloaded and stopped working after everything that's happened in the last few minutes." She took another deep breath. "Let's start again. I'm Cadet Sergeant Christine Montide."

I flashed a quick smile as a peace offering. "I'm Cadet Fourth Class Anne Villas. And I'm as much on edge as you are."

"Then let's follow standard lifepod procedures until we can get our emotions under control."

"Deal. What are your orders, Sergeant Montide?"

"Let's drop rank for right now. Just call me Chris."

"Only if you'll call me Anne."

"Okay, Anne. So, are you better with sensors or navigation?"

I shrugged. "I'm in the top two in the plebe class at both."

"You take sensors, then. Feed the readings to me at navigation, so I can figure out what system we're in."

I moved to the sensor controls and got started. It only took a moment to find the Academy cruiser, more than one hundred lifepods, and a nearby planet. I fed data to Chris at the nav station, but also passed along the information the nav station couldn't use.

"We're about three million clicks from a human-habitable planet, Chris. I'm not picking up any broadcasts from the planet, nor any other signs of a colony. But the Academy cruiser and the lifepods are all heading for the planet."

"Wait," Chris said, "the *cruiser* is heading for the planet?"

"Yes."

"Then why have us abandon ship?"

"I don't know. I'm a plebe, remember?"

Chris waved off my comment. "I wonder if that was this year's Big Surprise?"

"The what?" I asked.

"Big Surprise. The Academy decided the Cadet Cruise had become too predicable. Ten years ago, they started inventing a surprise event to keep us cadets on our toes. I heard the cadets had to rebuild an engine last year. Maybe they pretended the ship had a catastrophic failure this year." Chris frowned. "I sure wouldn't want to be a cadet who didn't make it into a lifepod!"

"No kidding." I thought of the punishment those poor souls had to look forward to from the instructors, and shivered. "Back to the sensors. Our pod is the one farthest from the planet, and we're falling farther behind by the minute."

"That's okay. We've got plenty of oxygen and supplies. Let's give this star system a thorough examination, compose a detailed message for the messenger drone, and impress the instructors with our thoroughness." Chris glanced at me. "Sound good?"

"Sounds good," I said.

I kept taking sensor readings and feeding data to Chris for five more hours. By the time she called a halt to it, the cruiser and the other pods had already landed on the planet. "Chris, are you sure we won't get in trouble for coming in so far behind everyone else?"

"I don't think so, and it's not like we can't justify the extra time we spent taking readings." Chris leaned back and stretched. "The navigation charts have hardly any info on this system, but what little they have tells me we don't want to spend much time on that planet. It's hot and humid, and I'll bet cadets will get really uncomfortable waiting for the cruiser to locate their lifepod and pick them up."

"Which we can avoid," I added, "by coming in last. All we have to do is land our pod right next to the cruiser, right?"

Chris grinned. "Exactly!"

My eyes darted back to the sensor screen as an alarm warbled. My blood ran cold when I saw the sensor readings.

"What is it?" Chris asked.

"An uncharted wormhole just opened in front of us," I said.

Fifteen seconds later, our lifepod entered the wormhole. Chris and I were headed God only knew where. And no one from the Academy even knew we were gone.

Numb, I watched the sensor readings drop to zero across all the sensor's bands. That only happens inside wormholes. But in case it was due to a sensor malfunction, I looked out the lifepod's lone viewport. The splotchy gray only found within a wormhole filled the port.

"You *idiot*!"

I turned from the viewport and looked at Chris. "What?"

"And to think I started believing your whole Poor Pitiful Princess routine!" Chris turned her eyes up. "God, what was I thinking?"

"I don't understand. What are you—"

"You had me believing you really were among the top two sensor operators in the plebe class." Chris turned an icy glare on me and leaned closer. "Until idiot you completely overlooked a wormhole that was directly in front of us!"

I inherited more than my looks from Mom. I got her temper, too. I ignited my version of Mom's Princess Glare, a white-hot gaze she uses to cow even the most intransigent men and women. My glare isn't as good as hers yet, but it's getting there. "In case you hadn't noticed, this is life-pod, *not* a fully equipped Scout ship. The pod's sensors only cover the basic bands."

Chris pulled back, as if driven back by the heat from my glare. But that was her only concession to it. "What's your point, plebe?"

"Wormholes only show up on the Theta band." I leaned in. "Four bands aren't included in the basic sensor suite. Want to take a wild guess at one of those four bands?"

"Theta. I know," Chris said. "So what?"

"*So what?*" I threw my hands up. "How, oh so brilliant Cadet Sergeant, do I get a reading for a band that isn't included in the sensor suite?"

"You combine the Sigma and Omega bands, plebe." Chris folded her arms across her chest and smirked. "It's rough and nowhere near the granularity of a real Theta band scan, but it will detect a nearby wormhole."

I opened my mouth for a retort. Closed it again, considered Chris's suggestion, and gave a slow nod. "Yeah... I can see how that would work."

"Then why didn't you do it?"

I rolled my eyes. "Maybe because this is the first time anyone has ever suggested that technique to me?"

"It's common knowledge. How can you *not* know it?" Chris feigned the sudden arrival of an idea. "Oh, right, because you're the Princess Scout! Common knowledge is for commoners, right? At home, do you keep common people nearby just so they can share their common knowledge with you? I bet common sense is something else you—"

"When did you learn the technique?" I asked.

"I don't know. I've known it, like, forever."

"Who taught it to you?"

"My father. He's an independent trader, and can't afford anything but a basic sensor suite. He learned all the tricks to wring as much information from them as possible. And then he taught them to me."

"Maybe if he got a job teaching at the Scout Academy, *I* could have learned that, too. Instead, I learned how to handle the *Scout* sensor suite." I leaned back, folded my arms across my chest, and mimicked Chris's smug expression. "You know, the one that covers the Theta band and is installed in every Scout ship?"

Chris's expression slipped. "But everyone in my plebe class knew the trick by the end of the year."

"Did they learn it from the instructor, or did you tell them about it?"

"Um..." Chris closed her eyes, scrubbed a hand over her face, and sighed. "It was me."

My parents taught me to be graceful in victory, and this struck me as a good time to follow their advice. I mean, Chris and I were going to spend a lot of hours cooped up together in the lifepod. So I extended an olive branch. "Then it's too bad my plebe class doesn't have someone as knowledgeable as you in it."

Chris's lips spread in a wan smile. "Don't you mean someone as pigheaded as me?"

"Nah. The plebe class has plenty of pigheads. But none of them knew anything useful before they got to the Academy." I offered a sly grin. "I mean, they *must* be a bunch of idiots if a pampered twit like the Princess Scout finished the year as the third-ranked plebe. Right?"

Chris's smile widened into something more genuine, but she didn't concur with my self-deprecating remark. So I changed the subject.

"Besides, the wormhole isn't a big deal, right? We just have to wait until we come out the other side, then turn around, and go through it again."

"You idiot." Chris's smile took any sting from her remark. "Lifepods just have glorified maneuvering thrusters. You can land on a planet with them easily enough. But it would take a week to counteract the pod's momentum, reverse course, and return to the wormhole."

"Oh."

"That's why all lifepods have a messenger drone. We'll record a message and send it back through the wormhole."

"How long do you think it will take for the Cadet cruiser to pick up the drone's beacon?"

Chris furrowed her brow. "I don't know. It depends on how long they take to realize we're missing."

"So we might be stuck in this lifepod for a while?"

"Maybe. But we have plenty of oxygen and supplies. We'll be fine."

On that positive note, Chris set a wormhole exit alarm, turned the pod's lights down, and we stretched out for a nap.

The alarm sounded four hours later. Followed immediately by a collision warning.

COLLISION

C hris leapt for the lifepod's simplified piloting controls, and my eyes locked onto the sensor screen. My heart skipped a beat when I saw the source of the alarm. The wormhole had snared an asteroid almost as big as the lifepod, and drawn it right into our path.

"Hard starboard!" I yelled. "Hard starboard! Hard starboard!"

Chris wrapped her right hand around the lifepod's joystick and shoved it as far to starboard as it would go. Her left hand danced over the controls, coaxing maximum power from the pod's meager thrusters.

I watched the asteroid's course and fought down rising panic. "Harder starboard! Inclination thirty-one degrees."

"Roger," Chris said, as she slid the joystick up.

The pod continued its glacial course change. Slowly, ever so slowly, it swung away from the asteroid's path. The lifepod nosed away from a head on collision, but we weren't in the clear yet. And sensor readings made it clear we wouldn't get clear.

"Brace for port side impact," I said.

Chris braced herself as best she could without releasing the joystick. "Copy."

I eyeballed the asteroid's likely point of impact. Right on the messenger drone launch tube. As if the last fifteen seconds hadn't been bad enough already. I made a snap decision, launched the drone, and then took a death grip on the sensor control panel.

With a grinding crunch, the asteroid smashed into the lifepod. An ear-splitting shriek followed as the asteroid scraped down the port side of the pod. The impact threw me from my seat and across the small cabin. I smacked into the starboard bulkhead. My head rang from the impact, but I fought against the disorientation and checked on Chris.

Despite being thrown about by the impact, Chris somehow held onto the joystick. Even as her left hand flailed for a secure hold, her right jerked the stick, fighting to maintain control of the lifepod. I wrapped my right arm around her waist, my left arm around the back of the pilot's chair, and did my best to hold her in place.

Chris's concentration never wavered from the piloting controls. Free from worrying about securing herself, she worked the controls with both hands. After what felt like hours, but was probably only a minute, she reduced the lifepod's collision-induced tumble to a wobble. She'd eventually need to counter the wobble, but we could tolerate that long enough to take stock of our situation.

"Thanks for bracing me." Chris released the joystick and turned my way. Her gaze flicked over my shoulder, to the bulkhead I'd hit, and her eyes widened. "You're bleeding!"

I followed her gaze and spotted a bright red splotch on the otherwise immaculate white bulkhead. I touched the back of my head and winced. "Ouch."

"Sit." Chris backed her order with a gentle shove into the pilot's seat. She grabbed the pod's first aid kit and began examining the back of my head. "Hold still. I'll be as gentle as possible."

Chris was true to her word, but I couldn't stop my sharp intakes of breath as she cleaned the wound. Finally, she sprayed the area with something that numbed the wound.

As the pain faded, I could finally think about other things. Like a high-pitched sound that just barely registered. "Um, Chris? Do you hear a whistling sound, or is that something I got from banging my head?"

Chris stopped what she was doing and listened. "No, Anne. I hear it, too."

I slid into the seat before the sensors and called up the lifepod's damage control system. Big, pulsing red letters filled the screen.

HULL INTEGRITY COMPROMISED

The whistling was the sound of the lifepod's atmosphere leaking into space.

I dismissed the hull integrity warning with a quick tap and opened Damage Control. Flashing red lights highlighted dozens of systems requiring repairs. Solid red lights—far too many of them—highlighted systems damaged beyond repair.

Chris looked over my shoulder and muttered, "Holy crap."

"Tell me about it." I expanded the life support display and felt my heart sink at all the pulsing alerts. "That's a lot of leaks."

"Eight." Immediately after Chris spoke, another alert came to life. She closed her eyes. "Nine."

She gave herself a little shake, straightened, drew a deep breath, and said, "Record a message for the drone, and then launch it. I doubt the cadet cruiser will pick up the drone's signal in time to rescue us, but you never know."

I scrolled through the damage reports. Without looking up, I said, "I already launched the drone."

"You *what*?"

"Launched the drone. Its launch tube was right in the middle of the asteroid's likely point of impact."

"Anne, please tell me you recorded a message before you launched it."

"It was a split second decision, Chris. There wasn't time."

"Then why launch it at all?" Chris rolled her eyes and growled, "Seriously, your freaking highness, why even launch the drone without a message? What's the point?"

"Because the drone carries this lifepod's ID code."

"But that's all it will broadcast. What good will the ID do?"

"It'll tell our instructors that our lifepod isn't lost on the planet, for one thing. And—"

Chris interrupted. "This is your assigned lifepod, right?" I nodded, and she continued, "So, you're hoping they'll come running to rescue the Princess Scout?"

"I'm *hoping* they'll track back along the drone's path and find the wormhole," I snapped. "Maybe they'll even find the asteroid that hit us. It should have pieces of our lifepod embedded in it. That will tell them we're in big trouble. And then, yes, I pray they come running to rescue *us*."

Chris was quiet for a moment, then said, "I'm sorry."

I glared at Chris over my shoulder. "I worked my butt off to get to the Academy. Hearing cadets whisper that I only got in because Daddy and Mommy made the Academy admit me pisses me off. Knowing other cadets—cadets like *you*, Chris—believe the whispers hurts more than I can say."

"I'm sorry," Chris repeated.

I wasn't quite ready to let her off the hook this time. "Did you go on the cadet cruise as a plebe?" Chris blinked rapidly and shook her head. Still angry, I plunged on. "What about when you were a sophomore? Did you go on the cruise then?"

"No," Chris whispered.

"So, I not only belong at the Academy, I belong there more than you."

Chris turned away and scrubbed a hand across her eyes. My anger broke.

I forced gentleness into my voice. "That last bit I said? It's not true, Chris. But hearing it hurts, doesn't it?"

Chris kept her back to me, sniffed once, and nodded.

I checked the sensor screen. The sensors were still gathering data on the unknown star system where the wormhole dumped us. Sensors can't work faster than the speed of light, so it might take another hour before we knew what was out there.

I rose, went to the back of the lifepod, and opened the supply locker. I rummaged behind the food, water, blankets, and stuff like that, and found the pod's patch kit. The patches weren't designed for the damage we had, but anything we could do to slow the leaks gave us that much more chance of rescue.

Without speaking, Chris pulled a patch from the kit and began searching for a leak. Over the next forty minutes, we fully repaired four leaks and slowed three more. We couldn't find the other two leaks—the worst ones, naturally—and assumed they were behind the control panels.

I stood, stretched my sore back, and glanced at the sensor screen. I blinked, rubbed my eyes, and gave another look. The screen report remained the same.

"Chris?"

"What?"

"Take a look at the sensor screen. I am reading that right, aren't I? It's not my imagination?"

Chris glanced at the sensors, and her eyes widened. "No, I see it too."

The sensor screen displayed a map of the star system. It showed a yellow dwarf star, similar to the star my home world of Aashla orbited. Three red-colored planets—red for extreme heat—orbited much too close to it to support human life. Two blue-colored icy planets orbited too far from the star for our needs. But between those extremes, right in the middle of the Goldilocks Zone, orbited a green-colored planet.

Green for an oxygen-nitrogen atmosphere.

Green for human habitable.

Green for hope.

Green for life.

Chris returned to the pilot's chair and started plotting a course for the green world.

I returned to the Damage Control screen, called up life support, and said, "After our repairs, we have about sixteen hours of oxygen left."

Chris gave a vague nod and kept working on the course. After the two longest minutes of my life, Chris activated her course. The lifepod's thrusters activated, and the pod began the journey to the green world.

Chris looked up from the controls. "It's going to be close."

"How close?"

"Five minutes, give or take."

"Five minutes before our oxygen runs out?"

She shook her head. "After."

Chris's pronouncement hung in the air as I came to grips with it. I forced an optimistic tone into my voice and said, "Five minutes? That's not too long, right?"

"It's long enough," Chris said.

"But we won't die if we go that long without oxygen, will we?"

"Probably not, but we'll pass out." She closed her eyes and leaned her head back. "That's assuming we haven't already passed out from the carbon dioxide buildup."

"Won't the scrubbers remove that?"

"And replace it with what? Our oxygen reserves will be gone by then, leaked into space."

"But when we land on the planet, we can just open the hatch."

"How? We'll be unconscious, remember?" Chris's voice hardened. "Face facts, Anne. If the lifepod's navigation and life support calculations are accurate—and they *are*—we're going to land on a human-habitable world, and die of asphyxiation surrounded by air that would save our lives."

"My parents found themselves in tough spots before I was born, and even a few after. They survived because they never gave up. If I learned one thing from—"

"This is real life, Anne, not some action vid fairy tale!"

My temper spiked at Chris's tone, but I knew yelling wouldn't help, and it would use more of our precious oxygen. I slowly counted to ten, then said, "It was real life when my parents won through against enormous odds, Chris. The vids came later, and they're mostly accurate."

Chris gave a dismissive wave with her left hand. "Yeah, right."

"I watched them after I got to the Academy," I said. "The dialogue was way off from the way Mom and Dad talk. But the vids got the major points right."

"Sure." Chris looked me in the eye. "The Academy installs implants at the beginning of the second year. But you already have yours, right?"

The change of conversational tack caught me off guard, but I said, "Yeah. No one can go on the Cadet Cruise without one. The five of us at the top of the plebe class got our implants installed early, so we could come."

"And is Boost activated?"

"Yes." I lifted my chin a little. "We even got a crash course on Boost training."

"Including all the warnings?" Chris asked.

"Yes, though Dad gave me more thorough warnings about Boosting after the Academy accepted me."

"Yeah? What did the famous David Rice tell his only daughter about Boosting?"

"That the initial flood of stored adrenaline from the implant felt euphoric. That the enhanced strength and speed I'd get from Boost would make me feel invincible. But his most dire warnings dealt with over Boosting—the damage it could do to my body and the risk of Boost burnout."

"I heard the same thing at the beginning of Boost training. They even threw in vids and images of four Scouts who suffered Boost burnout. One guy managed to Boost for five minutes before he died. The other three didn't last that long."

"Okay... Where are you going with this?"

"You say the vids about your parents are mostly accurate," Chris said, "but those same vids had a scene where your father Boosted for something like eight minutes, and he *didn't* burnout."

This time, I was ready when Chris changed tack and returned to the original subject. "You're right. *That* part isn't accurate." Chris opened her mouth to speak, but I pressed on. "Dad really Boosted for thirteen minutes."

Chris closed her mouth. Then she opened it again and said, "Wha—?"

"The vid director cut it from thirteen minutes to eight, because she didn't think anyone would believe the real number."

"Thirteen minutes of Boost? You can't be serious?"

"Dad's heart stopped when he cut Boost. Mom said it took ten minutes to get it beating again." I drew a deep breath and returned to my original subject. "But the real reason I brought up my parents is because they never gave up. They'd have been dead a dozen times over, if they had. That's why I say there has to be something *we* can do to survive this."

Chris stared at me for a moment, flashed a rueful smile, and asked, "Is your entire family as obnoxiously optimistic as you?"

"If you think I'm bad, you ought to meet Rob." Chris furrowed her brow, so I added, "Prince Rob, second in line, behind Mom, for grand-daddy's throne. You know, my big brother?"

"I forgot you had a brother," Chris said. A thoughtful expression crossed her face. "If we survive this and get rescued, will I get to meet him?"

"Him, and my parents, too."

"And is he, um, anywhere near as handsome as you are gorgeous?"

I resisted the urge to sigh as the subject of my family's looks came up. Like it always does. "If anything, Rob's more handsome. I'm the ugly duck of the family."

Chris's eyes widened. "No way that's true! You're the most beautiful girl anyone at the Academy has ever met."

I heaved the sigh I resisted a few seconds before. "Just once, I wish someone would tell me I'm the *smartest* girl they ever met."

"You *are* smart, Anne. It's just that people have to get to know you before they can figure that out. But people can see your beauty at a glance."

"Yeah, and too many people stop with the glance. They never see *me*, just my looks."

"Won't the same thing happen to me if I meet your super cute brother? Won't he take one look at me and recognize that he's way out of my league?"

I shook my head. "Rob knows what it's like to be judged solely on his looks, too. He'll take the time to get to know you."

Chris flashed a shy smile. "And if we somehow survive this, you swear you'll introduce me to him?"

"We take family seriously, on Aashla. Rob will insist on meeting the girl who helped his baby sister survive." I cocked my head and gave Chris an appraising look. "I think he'll like you."

Chris grinned. "Thanks for giving me extra incentive."

"Extra incentive to do what?"

"Survive, of course! I mean, it would be a shame if your gorgeous brother missed out on the opportunity to meet me."

"I'm glad I could be of service," I said.

That's when the sensor console beeped, alerting us it had completed its analysis of the unknown system. I thought we already knew everything we needed to know about the system, but I glanced at the sensor screen, anyway.

My eyes widened. "Hey Chris, you know that human-habitable world?"

"The one we're going to? What about it?"

"The sensors picked up radio waves coming from it."

Chris turned her attention to the console. "Say what?"

"Now we have even more reason to survive our landing," I said. "Because it looks like our human-habitable world is already human-habited!"

LEAKING LIFE

Chris and I stared at each other in mute astonishment. For, I don't know, something like the twentieth time since our lifepod launched.

Then I blinked, gave my head a thought-clearing shake, and bent over the pod's control board. "Let me see if the lifepod's comm can pick up any of the radio signals."

"Good idea," Chris said. "If we can find a continuous news broadcast, maybe we can collect enough language data for our implant translation routines to decipher the local language and starting teaching it to us."

My fingers tapped and slid over the comm screen. Distance weakened the radio signals, and it took me five frustrating minutes before I isolated one that was all speech. I spent another few minutes filtering static and boosting the incoming signal, but we finally had a strong, urgent male voice coming from the comm speaker.

The comm analyzed the voice, and I reported its findings. "The comm reports a ninety-nine percent chance he's human."

"You know what this means, Anne?"

"It's a lost colony."

"Right, and *we* discovered it."

"By accident."

Chris waved off my comment. "Something like half of all lost colony encounters are accidental. But do you know what this makes us?"

"No."

"We're the first cadets in the history of the Scout Corp to discover a lost colony. We're going to be written up in history books!" The excitement faded from Chris's expression. "Which won't matter to us if we die in this lifepod."

"Yeah. Have you come up with any brilliant ideas to keep us alive long enough to land and open the pod?"

"Not yet. What assumptions did you make when you calculated how long our oxygen will last?"

I waved a hand at the life support console. "I went straight by the book. Us being as inactive as possible. Preferably sleeping through most of the trip."

"I'd have done the same. I guess we'd better relax as best we can." Chris sighed. "It's going to be a long, boring sixteen-hour trip, if we can't sleep for most of it."

I worked my seat's controls and laid it all the way back. I stretched out and said, "Lifepod, dim the lights."

As the light faded in the little cabin, Chris added, "Lifepod, in fifteen hours and fifty minutes, sound an alarm and return the lights to operational brightness."

I closed my eyes and tried stilling my thoughts. Instead, my brain kicked into high gear. Images of my family and home filled my mind.

Dad smiled at me, his eyes filled with pride as I prepared to board the shuttle to start my trip to the Scout Academy. Next to him, Mom's eyes reflected that same pride. But it shared space with worry. And after everything she and Dad went through before Rob and I were born, she had reason for concern. A Scout's life isn't safe and can be downright dangerous.

Like now. But I pushed that thought aside and dove back into my memories.

Rob hugged me. "I know you're going to do us proud, baby sister."

"I'll do my best." I blinked back tears and returned his hug. "Scritch Spice for me, while I'm gone, Rob."

Rob laughed. "I'll try, but she's your cat and doesn't like me nearly as much as she likes you."

I wondered what Spice would think if I died in this lifepod? Would she wonder why I'd abandoned her forever? Would she think I no longer loved her? That she'd done something to drive me off? Or, equally distressing, would she just forget about me and pick someone else to love?

It's crazy, worrying about a cat's feelings instead of the grief my death would bring to my parents and Rob. But emotions go in baffling directions in times of stress. And my eyes filled with tears at the thought of what my cat would feel if I died.

I thought I'd kept my feelings to myself, but I must have made some sound. Chris's hand grasped mine, and she said, "We're going to survive this."

I sniffed and wiped my free hand across my eyes. "How?"

"I don't know," Chris said. "But we will."

"What makes you so certain?"

"We're Scouts, Anne. It's what we do." Chris was quiet for a moment, then added, "Besides, you're the daughter of David freaking Rice. Surviving against all odds is built into your DNA."

I squeezed Chris's hand. I won't say my fears vanished, but they receded. My whirling mind gradually stilled, and sleep overtook me.

The instructors on the Cadet Cruise ran us cadets ragged. From day one, most cadets suffered from sleep deprivation. Add in the stress Chris and I suffered during our way-too-eventful lifepod journey, and I felt certain I would have no problem sleeping away the sixteen hour trip to the lost colony. Only, I didn't.

I awoke after six hours. It took my exhausted brain a couple of minutes to remember where I was—on a doomed lifepod. And what I was doing—hoping I wouldn't die from lack of oxygen before we landed on the green world. I opened my eyes and glanced at Chris. I saw tear tracks on her cheeks and almost reached out to her. But she wore a relaxed expression, and her chest rose and fell in the rhythm of sleep. Rather than risk waking her and letting our tear-inducing reality crash back into her mind, I clasped my hands together and tried to think of something we could do to improve the long odds against our survival. But I think people hate facing harsh realities so much, we evolved minds that turn away from dreadful outcomes. I spent less than a minute searching for a solution to our dilemma before my mind drifted off the subject.

My attention turned to the radio signal from the planet. A different voice issued from our comm unit. There must have been a shift change or something.

No one person could broadcast twenty-four hours a day. Or however long days were on the voice's planet.

Because only Earth had a twenty-four-hour day. My home of Aashla had a twenty-six hour day. Draconis, home planet to the Scout Academy, had a twenty-four and a half hour day. My internal clock took three weeks to adjust to the time difference.

My attention turned back to the radio broadcast, and I wondered how much progress my implant's translation routine made while I slept. I tried accessing the translation, but it was locked. Still working on it, I guess.

And mentioning working, I forced my mind back to the problem of surviving the pod's landing. But a couple of minutes later, I wondered if Chris and I would meet any noble, handsome guys on the planet. I mean, Dad became a Scout so he could search the galaxy for his spacebabe. Okay, that wasn't his *only* reason for entering the Academy, or even a major reason. But it was a reason. And my parents met when Dad crash landed on Aashla.

If it worked out for Dad, maybe it would work out for me, too, right? Would I find my future husband—my... spacebeau? Yeah, spacebeau worked. Would I find a spacebeau on the planet, just waiting for me to drop into his life? Maybe with a friend for Chris?

And that brought my mind back around to surviving long enough to breathe the planet's atmosphere. Which I wasn't spending enough time thinking about. So, I bent my attention in that direction.

Until it slipped from my control and wandered off topic again.

My mind spun around and around like that for a couple of hours. Then I drifted off to sleep again.

I dreamed of the lifepod's landing on the planet. Well, of *a* lifepod's landing. Because the one in my dream bore no resemblance to our real lifepod. The dream lifepod was more like an aircar, with windows surrounding two seats in which Chris and I sprawled, artfully unconscious.

A pair of sleeping beauties awaiting their spacebeaus. As the dream lifepod settled onto the planet, two handsome men peered at us through the ridiculous windows. At the sight of us, hammers miraculously appeared in their hands. The spacebeaus smashed the windows, and cool, life-supporting air poured into the lifepod. My spacebeau gently lifted me from the pod, drew my lips towards his, and...

The alarm Chris set nearly sixteen hours before went off.

A dull pain pounded in my head as I raised eyelids that felt as if they each weighed a ton. Then I lay there and looked up at a gleaming bulkhead while my brain struggled to pull free of the dream.

From the corner of my eye, I saw Chris stand. She moved slowly into view, as if she had difficulty walking. Chris shook her head, winced, and leaned over the sensor screen next to me. Her brow furrowed, as if she couldn't figure out the reading.

I sat up and looked at the screen, too. I felt as if it held important information, but I couldn't figure out what.

Chris reached out and tapped a screen reading. "Atmosphere. In."

Oh, yeah. The sensor detected a thin atmosphere outside the lifepod. It wasn't thick enough to sustain us, since the lifepod was thousands of meters above the planet. But a thin atmosphere beat what little air was left inside the lifepod.

Vestiges of my dream still hung in the back of my mind. I looked at the bulkhead next to me, searching for the controls to lower the windows in the dream lifepod. That would let the carbon dioxide-filled air out, and we'd get some oxygen. Right? And more as the pod neared the planet's surface.

But the real pod had no controls to lower windows. Or windows. Or any other way to open the lifepod to the atmosphere outside.

From the back of my mind, a bolt of pure inspiration burst. "Leaks! Chris, leaks."

Chris slowly turned her head and focused on me. "What?"

"Leaks." I struggled from my reclining seat. Chris watched me as I stumbled to the tool cabinet and pulled a small pry bar from it. I turned to a patch I'd hastily installed over a leak and attacked it with the pry bar. "Life!"

I shoved the pointed end of the bar under one edge of the patch, worked it deeper, and pried. The patch peeled away. The re-opened leak hissed loudly.

Chris got the idea and followed my lead. Soon, the sound of hissing filled the cabin. Sixteen hours ago, it was the sound of death. Could it be the sound of life now?

Chris sagged to her knees, her body oxygen starved. I found myself next to her on the floor. Darkness filled my mind, and I lost consciousness.

Someone groaned.

Not me.

Fabric slid against fabric.

Another groan.

Still not me.

The sound of a tentative step.

Another step.

Someone fell against a bulkhead.

Electronic chirping from a control pad.

Soft mechanical whirring.

Cool wind flowed around me.

Bright light lanced through my closed eyelids.

A hand shook my shoulder.

"Anne?"

I batted at the hand on my shoulder. It didn't go away.

"Come on, Anne. Wake up!"

Someone groaned.

Me, this time.

"Anne!" The voice sharpened. "Get your ass in gear, plebe!"

My head pounded.

Hands grabbed my hands and pulled.

"No."

My voice.

I struggled to open my eyes.

A silhouette leaned over me.

"Thank God!" the silhouette said.

I lost the struggle and my eyelids slid shut.

"No, you don't, Anne!"

The hands dragged me to my feet.

A shoulder slid under one arm.

We lurched towards the blinding light.

"We're almost there," not-me said.

A step. Two. Three. Cool air enveloped me. Dad would have called the air crisp.

I opened my eyes again. It was easier this time. Concerned hazel eyes stared into mine. I blinked, focused, and finally recognized Chris. I found the strength to raise my right hand to my forehead. "Yes, ma'am."

Confusion replaced the concern in Chris's eyes. "What?"

"This plebe's ass is in gear, ma'am."

"Oh, right." Chris smiled. "Well done, plebe. Do you know who I am?"

"Cadet Sergeant Christine Montide."

"Right. Do you know who *you* are?"

"Her Royal Highness Princess Anne Megan Karen Heidi Tisha Erin Courtney Stephanie Villas. AKA Cadet Fourth Class Anne Villas. AKA the Princess Scout."

"Right, again." Chris lowered me to the ground. "Sit here while I get water from our supplies."

A minute later, she pressed a bottle into my hand. "Drink."

As I did, the fog of oxygen deprivation lifted from my brain. My eyes adjusted to the bright sunlight, and I finally took a moment to look at the surrounding countryside.

The lifepod's autopilot landed us on the side of a hill, in a small meadow surrounded by strange, twisting trees with red leaves. The cool temperature and the crimson foliage suggested autumn. Or it would on my home world of Aashla, or on Draconis, home of the Scout Academy. Who knew what it meant on this planet? For all I knew, this was the height of summer and leaves were usually red.

The tall meadow grass, really a mixture of at least half-a-dozen different grasses, was green, which made the argument for autumn more compelling. But I recognized several varieties as Earth-native grass found on most human settled worlds. The grass wouldn't tell me anything about native tree coloring.

I filed that away for later investigation. Much later. Or maybe never, considering our situation.

My gaze wandered beyond our little meadow. More low hills surrounded us, all mostly covered by red-leafed trees. I couldn't see any towns or settlements, or even any human-built dwellings. A town would stand out from the tree cover, but I thought houses would be a different matter. So I turned my gaze to the horizon and looked for other signs of humanity.

Such as the narrow column of smoke rising from beyond the nearest hills. I pointed to it and said, "I think we should go that way, Chris."

Chris shaded her eyes and peered in that direction. "Good eye, Anne."

"This plebe strives to please, ma'am."

Chris rolled her eyes. "You can stop with *this plebe* bit. I only said that to get your attention."

I kept a straight face. "Of course, ma'am. This plebe follows all lawful orders."

Chris punched my arm. "Say *this plebe* one more time, and your nose gets the next punch."

I cocked an eyebrow at her. "On Aashla, striking a member of the royal family is a criminal offense."

"Then it's lucky for me we're not on Aashla, isn't it?" Chris turned back to the pod. "Let's pack all the survival supplies and take them with us."

"There's enough stuff in there for six people. That's going to make for heavy loads."

Chris shrugged. "Better to have it and not need it."

She left the other half of the saying unspoken. But I couldn't argue with her point. I joined her inside the lifepod and began stuffing as many supplies into one survival backpack as I could. I ended up using two packs, as did Chris. We exited the pod, and then Chris did something unexpected. She closed the lifepod's hatch, slid aside a door covering the pod's maintenance controls, and activated its internal decontamination routine.

I caught Chris's eye. "Why did you do that?"

"We can't hide the lifepod, but running decon will hide our numbers."

"By destroying all the physical evidence we were ever in the pod?"

Chris nodded. "Even if this colony doesn't have DNA analyzing technology, our fingerprints would tell whoever finds the pod that it only carried two people."

Chris slung one pack on her back, one in front, took her bearings on the narrow smoke column, and set off across the meadow. I followed suit, trying to figure out why Chris was acting so paranoid. We'd only walked twenty meters when we heard a roaring sound. It came from the sky, but echoed around the hills. I scanned the sky for the source of the roar without success. But Chris spotted it.

She pointed into the sky. "There."

Even with her hand guiding my gaze, it took me a minute to find what she saw. That was because the object looked tiny and moved incredibly fast. As we watched, it changed course and swung our way. Within seconds, the small dot in the sky grew into some kind of aircraft.

"Run," Chris said, and took off towards the nearby forest.

I didn't know why she wanted to avoid detection by whoever piloted the aircraft, but I assumed it was the same paranoia that made her decontaminate the lifepod. I ran after Chris. Twenty seconds later, we hunkered down behind a tree. Five seconds after that, the aircraft thundered over the meadow, no more than fifty meters above it.

"Military," Chris said.

"How can you tell?"

"The Academy's third year curriculum includes a class on primitive vehicles, including air and water craft. That thing ticks all the boxes for a military aircraft."

"Okay, but why run from it? On Aashla, the military performs search and rescue operations all the time."

"It's the same almost everywhere," Chris said. "But another third-year course taught me a Scout should only make contact with lost colonists after... well, *scouting* the populace. It helps avoid misunderstandings."

"They know we're here. I mean, the lifepod is a dead giveaway, right?"

"They know *someone* is here," Chris corrected. "But I still want to know more about these people before I try talking to them."

"You're the senior cadet," I said. "But what if these lost colonists have infrared detection systems? They'll find us, even if we try hiding in the forest."

"Good point." Chris opened the pack on her chest and rummaged around inside. "Pull out a chameleon cloth and wrap it around yourself."

Chris followed her own instructions and immediately faded into the background. She left her face uncovered so I could easily see her, but I had to concentrate to pick the rest of her out from the surrounding countryside. I followed Chris's lead, and then we set off towards the distant column of smoke.

ON THE RUN

The loud, fast aircraft—Chris told me it was called a jet airplane —kept making low-altitude passes over the meadow and the lifepod. Meanwhile, we worked our way deeper into the forest of twisting, red-leafed trees that surrounded the meadow. But we ran into our first snag less than ten meters from the meadow's edge. Literally.

Chris suddenly stopped walking. Her chameleon cloth so thoroughly hid her from view, I almost walked into her before I realized she wasn't moving.

"I'm caught," Chris said. We were alone, so she couldn't mean that someone spotted her. But she added, "I snagged my chameleon cloth on something. Can you free it?"

I knelt, caught the hem of her cloth, and gently tugged on it. I felt resistance from a snag, pulled from a different angle, and felt the resistance again. Both tugs gave me an idea where to find the snag. A moment later, I freed her cloth from a ground-hugging thorned plant. After that, we re-wrapped our cloths, so they didn't brush the ground.

"We're already showing our faces," I said. "Isn't it risky showing our feet, too?"

"Yes, but we'll never get anywhere if we have to stop for snags every ten or fifteen meters. If we stay alert, we should hear searchers before they can spot our faces or feet."

"And we cover ourselves completely if searchers come our way?"

"Right."

We kept heading downhill, and the going was easier without the chameleon cloths dragging on the ground. We'd been hiking for about twenty minutes, when a new sound joined the ever-present roar of the jet. The new noise was even louder than the jet, and had a strange, staccato quality to it. Like the jet's roar before it, the choppy growl echoed through the hills. With the red foliage blocking most of the sky, we didn't try looking for the sound's source. But it grew louder.

"That sounds familiar," I said. "It's like the sound an airship's propellers make."

"You're talking about the lighter-than-air ships from your home world?"

"Yes."

Through the leaves, we caught glimpses of something large moving through the air. It moved far slower than the jet, but faster than any airship I'd ever seen back home. And this aircraft was too small for a lighter-than-air craft. The thing passed right over us, and the noise became so loud I felt it as much as I heard it. It had two rapidly spinning propellers, but they spun horizontally, not vertically. I'd never seen anything like it.

"It's a hello copter," Chris said. Then her brow furrowed. "No, that's not quite right. Let me check my implant." Chris's eyes lost focus as she queried her implant. They refocused ten seconds later. "Helicopter. That's the name."

"I like hello copter better," I said. "*Hello* sounds a lot friendlier than *heli*."

"Regardless of the name, we have to assume it's not friendly." Chris stared at me until I nodded in agreement. Then she said, "A helicopter is like a primitive aircar. Unlike the jet, it can land in the meadow. And the one that just flew overhead looks big enough to hold around a hundred soldiers."

"You think this forest is about to get a lot more crowded?"

"Yes. And the farther we get from whoever is in that helicopter, the better I'll feel."

"It's going to be hard to run and keep ourselves wrapped with the chameleon cloth at the same time." I let the cloth slide off my head and looked back towards the meadow. The trees blocked my view of it, but it sounded as if the helicopter had stopped over the meadow. "If that thing *is* carrying soldiers, and if they're anything like the soldiers back on Aashla, it's going to take them a while to unload and get organized."

"Don't forget the lifepod." Chris pulled her chameleon cloth off and stuffed it in her backpack. "They'll waste time with it before they begin searching."

I stowed my chameleon cloth, too. Then Chris and I started running downhill. We kept our pace to a jog, which we could keep up for an hour or more, due to Academy training. But running through wild countryside is much harder than running around the Academy's track. Plus, we each carried two packs. The one on our backs stayed in place well enough, but the one over our chests slipped, slid, and threw off our balance. But we managed well enough to reach the bottom of the hill fifteen minutes later.

We stopped next to a wide, shallow stream, and drank water from our bottles. Chris looked back along our path. "Do you think we left a trail someone could follow?"

"If they have someone with the right training, or a good hunter, yeah." I turned my attention to the stream. "But if we wade upstream for a hundred meters, it'll slow trackers down."

"Why upstream?"

"It's harder than going downstream." I shrugged. "It might not help, but it won't hurt."

Chris put away her water bottle. "Then let's get going."

Our official-issue Academy boots were supposed to be waterproof. And they were, much to my surprise. The stream never got more than calf-deep as we sloshed our way upstream.

We wasted a few minutes looking for an easy place to climb the far bank. When we didn't find one, Chris picked the best spot she could find, grabbed a branch that extended over the stream, and hauled herself out of the stream. She set her feet, released the branch, and reached for a higher handhold.

Her weight was too much for the steep bank. The small soil ledge under her feet crumbled, and Chris fell a meter back into the stream. Her left foot landed wrong, overextended, and it collapsed out from under her. Chris cried out in pain and fell back into the stream. She sat up, her uniform soaked through, and cradled her ankle.

"I think I sprained it," she said.

A shout sounded from up the hill we'd just descended. I felt certain someone searching for us had just discovered our trail.

I waded over to Chris and helped her stand up. "Can you put any weight on your left foot at all?"

"I'll try." She lowered her foot and gingerly put weight on it. Chris sucked breath through gritted teeth. Her face screwed up in agony, and she immediately shifted her weight back to her right foot. "It's no good. I think my boot is the only reason it's not broken."

More shouts echoed from the hill we'd just descended. Worse, we heard the air chopping sound made by the helicopter. I had to assume it was joining the search for us.

I scanned the stream bank for a place where I could help Chris climb from the stream. But Chris had already chosen the easiest spot in sight, and it hadn't worked out well for her. Worse, I felt Chris shiver as her soaked uniform and the cool air of the hills drew warmth from her body.

I made a snap decision, turned my back to Chris, and hunched over. "Climb on."

"Are you crazy, Anne? If you try carrying me up that bank, we'll both end up soaked and injured. Take your time climbing and then toss me a rope."

"Don't argue, Chris. You can't stand by yourself, and pulling you up the bank with a rope will leave tracks the worst tracker in the galaxy could follow."

"But how can you—?"

"I'm David Rice's daughter, Chris. How do you think?"

Her mouth formed a silent O of comprehension. Chris gave a decisive nod, wrapped her arms around my neck, and hopped with her good leg. I caught her legs and pulled her higher on my back. "Hold on."

Chris's arms tightened, though she was careful to avoid choking me. "Ready."

I took a deep breath. Released it. And sent a one-word command to my implant.

Boost!

Stored adrenaline flooded my body and washed away my fatigue.

Time slowed. My senses sharpened. My strength multiplied. I took a step towards the bank and leapt. My bound carried me up and over the stream bank's lip.

Puddles and damp ground appeared beneath me. I'd leave deep footprints if I landed there. I took advantage of my heightened reflexes, released my hold on Chris's right leg, and grabbed a low-hanging branch. It couldn't hold our combined weight for long, but I prayed it wouldn't snap and leave a sign we'd passed this way.

As I'd hoped, the branch bent instead of snapping. I held onto the branch long enough to reverse my downward trajectory. Then I swung my legs forward and released the branch. We arched over the damp ground and landed next to the trunk of the tree that supplied the branch.

I spent three precious seconds getting my footing. The last thing we needed was for both of us to end up hobbled. I cast a glance over my shoulder at the branch. It still bobbed wildly from my swing, but I didn't see any cracks in it. I hadn't even torn any leaves from the branch.

Now that we were safely out of the stream and clear of the damp ground beside it, I almost dropped Boost. But I knew I had nearly a minute left before my implant's safety protocols cut Boost. I could use the extra strength to carry Chris as far from the stream as possible. Then I could find a place for us to hide, get Chris out of her wet clothes, and see to her ankle.

Chris let her arms relax while I insured my footing. I said, "Hold on again."

Chris's arms tightened again, and I ran into the forest. Boost let me avoid leaving footprints by bounding from tree root to tree root.

"You should drop Boost, Anne."

"Soon."

"*Now!* Boost is only for emergencies. You got us out of the stream, so the emergency is over.."

As if in response to Chris's claim, the jet airplane roared overhead, and the *whup whup* of the helicopter drew ever closer.

I queried my remaining Boost time from my implant. "Thirty more seconds."

Chris leaned her head against my right shoulder and sighed. "Thirty seconds. But no more!"

I knew Boost caused my buoyant mood, but grinned anyway. "This plebe hears and obeys."

True to my word, I let my implant cut Boost thirty seconds later. Despite the rough terrain and the uphill slope, I'd carried Chris over two hundred meters from the stream. All without leaving tracks.

The fatigue Boost held at bay washed over me as soon as my implant cut Boost. I knew that was coming, but I'd underestimated how much I'd pushed myself while Boosting. Chris felt twice as heavy as she had when I picked her up in the stream. Without thinking, I sagged against a tree.

"Are you okay, Anne?"

"Yeah. Just need a minute to catch my breath."

"You need more than a minute." Chris's head turned left and right. She pointed with her right arm. "Can you get us under that tree with the low-hanging branches? They're too low for the soldiers looking for us to walk under, and we can rig both chameleon cloths to camouflage us."

I put all the confidence I could muster into my voice. "Sure, Chris. No problem."

It was a problem. When we got to the tree's edge, I had to put Chris down. She scooted with her good leg while I half-dragged her. We got her under the tree, but she left a trail of displaced leaves and branches in her wake. I propped her against the trunk, then went out and did my best to obscure her trail.

On fingertips and toes, I crawled back under the tree. Then I spent the next five minutes rigging a curtain around us using all of our chameleon cloths. When Chris and I were both satisfied with the curtain, I propped my back against the tree and let my muscles turn to jelly.

Chris pressed a water bottle against my lips. "Drink."

I did. And then I ate the survival ration bar she handed me. Then I said, "I should take a look at your ankle and help you change clothes."

"You need rest first. My ankle isn't going anywhere, and I don't have any spare clothes. Neither do you."

"Oh, yeah." I still wanted to check Chris's ankle, but I didn't have the energy. "Okay."

I closed my eyes and dropped into a light doze. A loud, nearby voice drew me back to full awareness.

"Hey, Sarge?" A young man's voice, less than ten meters from us. "I think I have something over here."

"Whatcha got?" An older man's voice, accompanied by the crackle of leaves as he moved towards our hiding place.

The young man spoke again. "See those leaves, Sarge? They tried to cover it up, but someone or something got dragged under it."

I desperately wished chameleon cloths let those inside see what was going on outside. We could see shadows beyond the cloth, but that was it. One of those shadows stood still while a larger one moved to join it.

"That the tree you talkin' 'bout, Garcia?" the older man asked.

"Yeah, Sarge." Garcia's shadow raised an arm, pointing. "See how the leaves are mussed up right there?"

"Maybe sorta. But there ain't nothing under that tree."

"Not now, Sarge, but something *was* there."

"So?"

"So I could crawl under there and see if I can spot something else."

I shook my head and prayed Sarge would refuse the suggestion. Chris's head shook slowly, too, and I guessed she was praying at least as hard as I was.

"You sure you ain't grabbing at straws? We ain't seen nothing since that stream." Sarge's shadow shifted. "I still ain't sure that little bit o' stream bank didn't just collapse on its own."

"The captain sent me with you because I'm the best tracker in the company. But that doesn't matter if you won't listen to me, Sarge."

The sergeant's shadow straightened, and his tone sharpened. "That's Sergeant Gibbs, to you. I been soldierin' longer'n you been alive, boy, so don't think you get to tell me how to do my job. You got that?"

"I'm sorry, Sarge. I mean Sergeant, but—"

A burst of static interrupted Garcia. Sarge's shadow moved again as he raised something big and blocky to his head. "This is Tracker One, sir. Go ahead."

The blocky thing must have been some kind of comm, because a voice emerged from the static. "The engineers finally got that amy landing craft open."

Chris looked at me and mouthed, "Amy?"

I shrugged, and we turned our attention back to the shadow play outside our hiding place.

The voice continued, "The craft held six, repeat six, invaders."

Chris and I exchanged wide-eyed looks when the voice called us invaders.

Sarge's shadow shifted nervously. "I only got three men with me, sir. If them amies ambush us—"

"I know, Gibbs," the voice said. "Have you found anything?"

"Garcia tracked 'em right good till we got to a stream at the bottom of your hill. He spotted two more signs that something passed. One on the stream bank and t'other a couple of hundred meters up the next hill."

"Is Garcia sure amies made those two marks?"

Shadow Sarge shifted. "Whatcha got to say, Garcia?"

"I... Maybe?" Shadow Garcia's head swiveled back and forth, like he was scanning the forest for a possible attack. "And maybe we ought to have more men with us before we find the amies."

"Sir?" Sarge said. "Garcia ain't positive. It ain't his place to decide how many men we got with us. Mine, neither. But I agree with Garcia."

"As do I, Gibbs," the voice said. "Return to the stream and await reinforcements."

"Yes, sir. Tracker One out." Sarge's shadow returned the bulky comm to his belt. "You heard the captain. Back to the stream."

Leaves crackled as the two shadows in front of us faded away. I heard two more men moving behind us. The noise of their passage faded over the next two minutes and then vanished entirely. I waited another minute before I let myself take a deep breath.

"That was close," Chris whispered.

I matched her volume. "Yeah. But what the heck is an *amy*? And why do they think we're invading? Even if there *were* six of us, we couldn't even invade a village, much less an entire planet!" A sudden thought occurred to me. "And why could we understand them? They weren't speaking Gal Base."

"Our implants absorbed sixteen hours of broadcasts from the planet. That's way more than the translation routine needs. Our implants probably finished teaching us the language before we landed. But this is the first time we've heard someone talking since then. As for the rest," Chris shrugged. "Your guess is as good as mine."

Without the stress of discovery clouding my judgment, I realized

Chris was shivering. "Let's get you out of those wet clothes, Chris. I can wrap a blanket around you."

She shook her head. "Not yet. We should find a new hiding place before Sarge comes back with more men."

I'd been so busy puzzling over amies and invasions that thought hadn't even entered my mind. But Chris was right. "Should we give them a few more minutes?"

"I want to, but my ankle is going to slow us down. So, we'd better get moving."

I took down our chameleon cloth curtain, stuffed all but one cloth in a backpack, gave that one to Chris, lugged the packs out from under the tree, and then went back for Chris. Since we'd be moving out—*with* the branches, instead of against them—I made Chris climb on my back. Then I crawled out from under the tree, again using only my fingers and toes. That was much harder to do while carrying Chris, but it left most of the leaves undisturbed.

Chris got off my back so I could stand, then she slung three packs on her back. I hung the fourth over my chest, then bent over so Chris could climb onto my back. I wrapped my arms around her legs, balanced her as best I could, and set off uphill. Away from Sarge and his tracking party.

Once I found my footing, Chris draped her chameleon cloth over us. The camouflage wasn't as good as it had been when we each had our own cloth, but it was much better than nothing.

We kept an ear out for the sound of Sarge and his men returning. The helicopter kept flying around overhead, though, which made it all but impossible to hear anything else. Worse, several more helicopters arrived. The new ones were much smaller. What we saw of them through the foliage suggested they could only hold five or six men, but their size meant they could land in clearings too small for the huge helicopter that brought the soldiers.

After thirty long minutes of hopping from tree root to tree root, fighting for balance that came naturally when I Boosted, and ignoring the burn building in my legs, arms, and back, I crested the hill.

Chris's left arm pointed down the hill. "Look."

I set my feet, and only then looked up. Smoke rose from a house at the bottom of the hill, maybe half a kilometer away. Chris desperately needed shelter from the cooling air, not to mention first aid for her ankle. The smoke meant someone was home, so we couldn't just sneak into the house. But I spotted a second, larger roof to the right of the house.

A barn.

Not as good as a house, but a lot better than hiding under a tree. With the chameleon cloths to hide us, surely we could take shelter in the barn.

"Barn," I gasped.

"Good idea," Chris said. "You sound tired. Do you need to rest?"

"This plebe can make it, ma'am!"

Chris gave a humorless laugh as I started down the hill towards the barn.

Chris need never know, but it took everything I had just to keep going. I kept my head down, put one foot in front of the other, and never stopped moving. I knew if I stopped to rest, I'd never get myself moving again.

Breath rasped my throat

Fire consumed my muscles.

My feet radiated pain.

Sweat stung my eyes.

Time lost all meaning.

I turned my mind away from my suffering and to everything my parents went through before I was born. If they could do everything they did, I could do something as simple as walking down a hill.

Just take a step.

Take another.

And another.

Keep going.

Don't—

Chris hissed my ear, "Anne? You're at the edge of the forest. Stop and let me look around."

I blinked sweat from my eyes and realized I'd almost stumbled out into the open. I'd stayed on course, at least. The barn door was twenty meters away, across a hard-packed yard with scattered patches of green grass. Better, it stood open. The house sat fifty or sixty meters from the barn. And no one was in sight.

I heard a helicopter in the distance and headed this way. Not ideal, but...

"Should I go or wait for the helicopter to pass?" I asked.

"Go," Chris said. "You have *got* to rest."

I gave a nod and stumbled into the open. Twenty meters never seemed so far. I moved in a shuffle across the yard and slowly drew nearer the open barn door.

"Hurry!" Chris urged. "The helicopter is getting closer."

I nodded and shuffled faster. Closer. Finally, I passed through the door and into the deep shadow of the barn. And stopped short.

An old man stood five meters away, his chin propped on a rake handle and staring straight at us.

FUSS AND BOTHER

I wondered how the old man saw Chris and me, since a chameleon cloth covered us. Exhaustion slowed my thinking. Because we had our faces uncovered, so we could see where we were going. What the man thought of the two girls' faces floating before him, I couldn't guess.

From over my shoulder, Chris blurted, "We won't hurt you!"

Age-whitened eyebrows arched over brown, grandfatherly eyes. A smile tugged at the corners of his lips. "That's good to know, miss." He caught my eye and pointed to a bench against the wall to my left. "You better sit down before you fall down."

I staggered to the bench. Chris dropped the chameleon cloth she'd held wrapped around us, then she slid from my back. Chris put too much weight on her left foot, gasped in pain, and dropped onto the bench. I felt incredibly light without the weight of Chris and her three backpacks. I sidestepped so I wouldn't sit on Chris, and then collapsed on the bench.

The helicopter we'd heard earlier *whupped* by overhead, so low the barn vibrated as it passed. The old man looked at the barn's roof and turned his head, tracking the helicopter's passage by ear. He dropped his rake and strode over to us, his eyes switching back and forth between Chris and me.

He stopped before us, and he eyed Chris with concern. "You look half-frozen, girl! What are you doing wandering these hills in wet clothes at this time of year?" The old man waved off his own question. "Never mind. Have you got dry clothes in those packs?"

Chris and I both shook our heads.

He *tsked*. "How about blankets?"

"Yes, sir," we answered in unison.

"Then you need to get out of those clothes and wrap up in a blanket or two." The kind eyes shifted to me. "I don't think I've ever seen a girl as worn out as you. Will you be able to help your friend undress?" A gentle smile lit his face. "I can help her, if you can't. But if you two are anything like my granddaughter, you don't want an old geezer like me seeing you in your underwear."

I know *I* wouldn't want that, so assumed Chris would feel the same. "I can help her, sir."

The man nodded once. "I'll leave you to it." He turned towards the barn door. "My granddaughter left some work clothes up here after her last visit. I think some of her stuff will fit you."

Another helicopter passed low over the house. Or maybe it was the same one. Who knew?

The old man pointed up. "Is all that fuss and bother for you two?"

I wanted to lie, but I felt certain the old man would see right through me if I tried. Besides, he felt trustworthy. "Yes, sir."

He nodded absently and kicked at the chameleon cloth puddled at our feet. "Did you steal this camouflage thing from a top secret lab, or something? Because I've never seen anything like it before."

"No, sir. The chameleon cloth belongs to us."

"Did you break any laws? I'm not harboring dangerous criminals, am I?"

I looked him right in the eye. "No, sir."

He held my gaze for a moment, gave a decisive nod, and headed for the barn door. Over his shoulder, he said, "If you hear any voices except mine, cover yourselves up in that... What did you call it? Chameleon cloth?"

"That's right, sir. And we will."

The old man looked out the barn door and then turned back for his rake. He brandished it as he returned to the door. "You left tracks across my yard, girl. I'll take care of them first and then get the clothes."

He pulled the big barn door shut behind him.

I immediately pulled a blanket from my backpack, then turned to Chris. Her shaking fingers fumbled at her cadet uniform's fastenings. I pushed her hands aside, ignored my fatigue, and helped her out of her coat, blouse, and trousers. Unsurprisingly, Chris's underwear was as wet as the rest of her clothes. I stripped her underwear off and wrapped the light, heat retentive blanket around her.

I dug into my pack again and pulled out a towel. I dried her face and hair, and then held the blanket around Chris while she rubbed the towel over her damp skin. By the time Chris was more or less dry, she'd stopped shivering.

"Better?" I asked.

"A lot warmer," Chris said. "But my ankle is throbbing."

"We've got half-a-dozen medical nanite injectors. One injection would repair your sprain in just a few minutes."

Chris shook her head. "Not yet. We don't know what medical care is like on this planet, or even if they'll give it to us. It's not like we've gotten what you'd call a warm reception."

The distant sound of an approaching helicopter emphasized Chris's comment.

"Yeah, though the old man has been kind."

Chris leaned her head back and closed her eyes. "For all we know, he's on the comm to the local military base right now."

"I don't think so."

"You trust him?"

"Yes."

"Why?"

I shrugged. "Call it a gut feel."

Chris sighed. "I hope you're right."

We fell silent. The only sound came from the helicopter. Chris and I waited for it to roar over the barn. But the noise slowed, stopped almost directly overhead, and then grew louder.

The helicopter was landing right outside the barn.

"We've got to hide!" Even though Chris spoke at normal volume, I barely heard her over the clatter of the helicopter's engine. She pushed herself to her feet, clutching the blanket around her and favoring her sprained left ankle, and pointed to an empty corner stall. "Over there."

I looked at the bench where she'd been sitting. Her wet clothes had left a damp water stain in the shape of Chris's backside. I caught Chris's arm and stopped her from hobbling away. "Sit back down, Chris. We have to hide here."

Chris frowned at me. "Why on whatever planet we're on would we do that?"

I pointed to the water stain on the bench. "Because then the soldiers would see that. They know we went through the stream. It's not a huge leap to guess one of us fell in."

Chris gave a reluctant nod and dropped back onto the bench. "It's too bad. We could have burrowed under the straw in the stall. With the chameleon cloth and straw piled over us—"

"We'd still have been found." I bent over and grabbed the chameleon cloth Chris dropped at our feet when we sat on the bench. "Anyone searching this barn will check any straw pile large enough to hide a person."

Chris thought for a second and then nodded. "Sorry. I wasn't thinking."

I scooted right next to Chris, draped the chameleon cloth over us, and began tucking it under and around us. "Don't let it get to you. I only thought of it because my brother and I used to play hide and seek in the palace stables. I learned early that straw piles make bad hiding places."

Outside, the helicopter's engine wound down. One man's voice rose above its noise. "Betts? Find the owner of this place. Martello? You and Walsh search that barn."

Three voices responded, "Yes, sir!"

I whispered in Chris's ear, "Is the chameleon cloth tucked in all around you?"

She nodded. Then we heard the barn door creak as it swung open. Two sets of footsteps sounded as Martello and Walsh entered.

One man snorted with disgust. "What's that awful smell?"

"What's the matter?" The other man's voice held what I thought was probably a country twang. "Can't stand the aroma of horses?"

"Are you crazy, Walsh? That's a stink, not an aroma."

"Wrong again, city boy. A stink is what you get on the trash-piled streets of Struphis." Walsh took a breath deep enough that I heard it over the still-decreasing engine noise. "But horses? Man, that's the aroma of home."

"Yeah, right," Martello muttered. "What do you know about searching barns, country boy?"

"Start at one end, search every stall, and poke through the straw."

Chris drooped a bit when she heard what Walsh said.

"Hey," Martello said, "did you see something move over there?"

"Are you getting spooked, Martello? It's just a bench."

"But I thought I saw something move just now."

"Probably just a rat," Walsh's voice began moving, probably towards the back corner stall. "You can check it out. Just be careful. Country rats make city rats look small and cuddly."

Martello was still for the longest three seconds of my life. Then I heard his footsteps as he followed Walsh.

I slid my right hand over her left hand and gave it a gentle squeeze.

Walsh and Martello performed a methodical search, though Martello made Walsh search all the occupied stalls. The soldiers searched every part of the barn's ground floor, except for the area where Chris and I huddled beneath the chameleon cloth. They had just ascended to the loft when someone else entered the barn.

The soldier who gave orders earlier said, "You worked in this barn all afternoon?"

"Ayup." The old man's voice held a drawl that wasn't there before, and his vocabulary and syntax changed, too. "Tha's what I done said."

"What were you doing?"

"Whatcha think, Mister... Whatcha say yer name was, agin?"

"*Lieutenant* Watts."

"Wayul, mister Lieutenant Watts, I was mucking out them stalls. Tha's why yer boys in this here barn didn't have to poke through dung, along wit' the straw."

Walsh called from the loft. "Me and Martello are much obliged for that, sir!"

"Din't do it fer you," the old man said, "but you's welcome, anywho."

Lieutenant Watts raised his voice, drawing attention back to him. "And, uh, mucking this barn took you all afternoon?"

"Ayup. It be a big barn, I be a old man, and I ain't so spry no more."

"So you didn't see anything?"

"Nothing you'n yer fancy helicopter be lookin' fer."

Suspicion tinged Watts' voice. "How do you know what we're looking for?"

"Don't know, don't care. But less'n you be lookin' fer what comes outta the backend of a horse, I didn't see nothing to interest the likes of you."

"You didn't see any people who didn't look like they belonged here?" Watts asked.

"You mean, 'sides you an' yer boys?"

"Yes." From Watts's tone of voice, I imagined him grinding his teeth. "Besides us."

"Nup. Din't see nobody."

"Well, if you see anyone like that—anyone *besides* the soldiers searching these hills—you call the number on this card. Is that clear?"

"Ayup, mister Lieutenant Watts." The old man paused for a moment, then asked, "Them folks you lookin' fer. They be dangerous?"

"It's an invasion, old man," Watts snapped. "What do you think?"

"Invasion? Here? We ain't nowhere near the sea. You sayin' a buncha soldiers from Plausen flew right through that air force my taxes pay fer?"

"I didn't say they were mere foreign invaders."

The old man was silent for three seconds, then whispered, "You don' mean? Nuh. Can't be. Not... amies?"

"I can neither confirm nor deny your assumption," Watts said. "Just be on your guard." Watts raised his voice. "Martello? Walsh? You done up there?"

"Yes, sir," Martello said.

"Then get back to the copter. We still have four more houses to search."

"Mister Lieutenant?" the old man asked.

"What?"

"If'n it be a invasion, you oughta leave one of them soldiers with me. I be all alone, here."

"I can't spare any men. You'll have to make do on your own."

"I got kin livin' 'bout a hour drive away. How's about I get some of them up here to help me?"

"We've got the roads blocked. Nobody goes in or out."

"But if'n I had my grandson here, maybe we'd catch some of them amies if'n they showed up." The old man's voice turned pleading. "You could put in a good word fer me with them soldiers what's blockin' the roads, right? 'Sides, it be lettin' someone *out* what be bad, right? Lettin' someone *in* oughta be okay."

Watt's vented a frustrated sigh. "Fine. What name do I give the soldiers at the blockade?"

"Logan Gibson. An' he might bring Laney, too. She be his twin sister."

Absently, Watts said, "Gibson. Logan. Laney. I'll call it in."

Watts marched from the barn, with a pair of less authoritative footsteps following him. The helicopter engine started, spent a minute spinning up to speed, and then the aircraft rose and flew away.

Chris and I stayed under the chameleon cloth as the helicopter's noise faded into the distance. The old man walked to the barn door, paused, and then he said, "All right, you can come out."

I pulled the chameleon cloth off of us. "Thank you, Mr... Gibson?"

"Ayup." Mr. Gibson grinned. "Come on, let's get you two over to the house. It's much warmer in there. I've got food cooking, and I have two bathtubs."

"That sounds heavenly," Chris said.

Mr. Gibson swept Chris up into his arms. To me, he said, "Bring your friend's clothes, so I can clean and dry them."

I gathered all of our stuff, and then followed him to the house. Warm air and heavenly aromas enveloped us when we entered the house.

Chris said, "That smells delicious."

Mr. Gibson flashed a big smile. "I just hope a pair of desperate amies like you two can eat regular food."

Chris and I exchanged puzzled glances. Mr. Gibson noticed, and his grin faded. "Are you from Earth?"

Mr. Gibson's surprise question hung between us for too long.

"Uhhhhhhh." I drew the word as long as I dared while searching for a response. "What..." I almost said *on Aashla*, but caught myself. "Made you ask that?"

"I called you girls *amies* as a joke. But it confused you. Everyone on..." Mr. Gibson paused for a second, then continued. "Everyone on this planet knows what an amy is. Except you two."

I couldn't think of anything to say, so I remained silent. Chris did the same.

"For that matter, everyone knows what this planet is called," Mr. Gibson said. "But I'll bet you don't."

Neither Chris nor I confirmed or denied his deduction.

Mr. Gibson waited for a moment, nodded to himself, and headed down a hall. "Both bathrooms are down this hall. Let's get you girls warm, clean, rested, and fed. We can talk after that."

He carried Chris into a large bathroom off an enormous bedroom and gently set her down on the closed toilet. He smiled at her. "I'll look at your ankle after you get out of the bath." Mr. Gibson looked at me. "You should stay and help... You know, I don't even know your names."

"I'm Chris."

"I'm Anne."

He gave another nod. "Pleased to meet you. I'm Elias Gibson." He went to the tub, twisted two knobs, and water started pouring into the tub. "Anne, will you stay here and help Chris get into the bath?"

"Of course, sir," I said.

"You'll have to come back after your bath and help her out of the tub." Mr. Gibson pointed to a small pile of clothes on the bathroom counter. "Those clothes might be a bit big for Chris, but they'll cover her up and keep her warm."

"The other bath is two doors down on the right. I put clothes in there for you, Anne. If you put your uniform outside the door, I'll wash it with Chris's uniform." Mr. Gibson walked out of the bathroom and pulled the door shut behind him. Through the door, he called, "Soak as long as you want, girls."

Chris and I watched the door and listened to Mr. Gibson's footsteps as he walked up the hallway. When the sound faded away, Chris whispered, "Do you think we can trust him?"

I shrugged. "I think so. I mean, he could have turned us in when the soldiers were here."

"He seems kind, and it's not like we have much choice." Chris shook her head. "I can't exactly fight or Boost with my sprained ankle."

I opened a backpack and pulled out a medical nanite injector. "Which is why I think we ought to use this now. You'll be healed before you finish with your bath."

Chris bit her lip and then nodded. I injected the nanites into her ankle, put the empty injector back in the pack, pulled a blaster out, and put it next to the tub. "Keep this nearby. Just in case."

"You do the same, Anne."

"Don't worry, I will."

I checked the water temperature, liked what I felt, and closed the tub's drain. Then I helped Chris into the tub. "Do you need anything else?"

Chris shook her head and shooed me away with her hands. "Go."

I took the backpacks, slipped into the hall, found the other bathroom, and started filling the tub. The clothes Mr. Gibson promised to provide were on the counter. I peeled off my uniform, made sure the clothes fit, and then tossed my uniform into the hall. I put a blaster next to the tub and climbed in.

After everything that happened to me since the evacuation alarm sounded on the cadet cruiser, the bath felt heavenly. I soaked for a while, letting the hot water soothe aching muscles, and fought the urge to doze. Finally, I scrubbed myself and got out.

Five minutes later, dry and dressed in local clothing, I gathered the backpacks and left the bathroom. My uniform was no longer on the floor next to the door. It bothered me I never heard Mr. Gibson come get it, but not much.

At the other bathroom, I knocked. "Chris?"

"Come on in," she called.

I found her already dressed, standing easily on both feet. "How's your ankle?"

"As good as new." Chris fingered her hair. "I don't suppose you have a brush in one of those packs?"

I pointed at my own hair. "Do you think I'd look like this if I did? I'll ask Mr. Gibson."

I went back to the hallway and called. "Mr. Gibson?"

"Yes?" he said.

"Have you got a hairbrush somewhere?"

"Just a minute."

Mr. Gibson spoke in a tone too low for me to understand. Someone else responded, and then quick, light footsteps sounded. I couldn't help tensing, but relaxed when a girl close to my age strode briskly into the hallway. The girl stood almost as tall as Chris—one of the tallest girls I know—and her long, blonde hair framed a pretty, red-cheeked face.

Her lips curved up in a smile. "Hi, I'm Laney."

"Granddaughter?" I asked.

"Yep." She ducked through the door next to the bathroom I'd used. "I'll bring a comb with the brush. Do you need anything else?"

Yeah, I thought, answers that would allay Mr. Gibson's suspicions would be handy. But the answers might not be necessary. I mean, soldiers hadn't swooped in and tried to grab Chris and me from the bathtubs. And there couldn't be danger lurking down the hall, because Mr. Gibson sent his granddaughter to help us. No grandfather worthy of the name would put his grandkids in the line of fire. Right?

Laney returned and handed me the promised comb and brush. "Do you need help getting your friend out of the tub? Granddaddy said she hurt her ankle."

"Um, no. She's feeling a lot better. But thank you for offering."

I returned to Chris, and Laney tagged along. I introduced the girls, realized I hadn't given Laney my name, and introduced myself, too. Then Chris and I combed and brushed our hair until we looked presentable. All the while, Laney watched us with wide-eyed wonder. Chris and I watched her from the corners of our eyes. When Laney noticed, she blushed and looked down.

"I'm sorry to stare, but I never thought I'd see real, live amies," Laney said. "Especially not in Granddaddy's house."

"Everyone keeps calling us that," I said. "What does it mean?"

"Amy is an old nickname," Laney said. "It dates back to right after the colony ship landed, five hundred years ago."

I sighed. "But—"

"What does it mean?" Laney said. "It's sort of a slang version of an acronym. For an AIM." Our confused expressions must have tipped Laney off we weren't following her. She added, "You know, an Artificial Intelligence Minion?"

Chris and I exchanged a glance, something we'd been doing a lot lately. Then Chris said, "You've lost me. Why would an AI need, or even want, minions?"

"To serve them," Laney said. "After the AIs won the AI Wars."

CRAZY HISTORY

"Before *what?*" Chris asked.

"Before the AIs enslaved humanity, after the AIs won the war." Embarrassment colored Laney's face, as if she'd spoken without thinking. "That was rude of me. We've been taught AI rule would feel natural to people who grew up under it."

"It might," Chris said, "if it ever happened."

Laney furrowed her brows in obvious confusion. "Huh?"

Chris drew a deep breath, adopted a gentle tone, and said, "Laney, the AI war lasted less than a year, and humanity obliterated the insane AIs who started the war."

Laney shook her head. "You're wrong. Our colony records show the *Haven Seeker* was the last colony ship to escape Earth. It had just passed the edge of the Sol system when the AIs crushed the remnants of human resistance." Laney closed her eyes, showing genuine anguish. "Every school child on Refuge hears the ancient recordings of Earth's last defense. The pleas for mercy for the defeated population. The cruel rejection of those pleas by the AIs. And especially the desperate battle the *Haven Seeker* fought against the AI's robotic ships. The crew won, obviously."

"None of that happened," Chris said.

"What makes you so sure?" Laney asked.

Chris folded her arms over her chest. "I think I know my home planet's history better than someone who's never even seen Earth."

Laney adopted the same defensive posture. "And *I* think you're an amy, but have been programmed from birth to believe otherwise."

Chris opened her mouth to retort, but I beat her to it. "What about me, Laney?"

"You're obviously an amy, too."

"Even though I grew up on a planet that doesn't even *have* AIs? Heck, we don't even have things like jet aircraft or helicopters. Aashla, my home world, was a lost colony until my father discovered it less than thirty years ago."

"What's a lost colony?" Laney asked.

"That's Terran Federation terminology," I said. "We Aashlanders always knew where we were."

"But—?"

"Look, Laney, you're right that the AI war was terrible," Chris said. "Millions of people died, and more than a thousand years later, Earth still bears scars from the war. But Earth lost most of its AI managed records during the war, too. The Terran Federation doesn't know how many colony ships sailed from Earth, nor their destinations. We call the colonies founded by those ships *lost*."

Laney gave a slow headshake. "No, that can't be right."

I caught Laney's eye. "What kind of colony ship was the... *Haven* something?"

"*Seeker*. The *Haven Seeker*. I'm not sure what you're asking."

"Was she a generation ship, where the people who eventually found the colony are the great, great, a bunch more greats grandchildren of the people who originally set out from Earth? Or was she a sleeper ship, where the colonists went into cryogenic hibernation until the ship reached the destination world?"

"A sleeper ship," Laney said, "but I don't see—"

"Laney?" Mr. Gibson called.

"Yes, Granddaddy?"

"Dinner's going to get cold if you girls take much longer. Does, um... Chris? Yes, does Chris need me to carry her out here?"

"No. We'll be right there." Laney took a deep breath and pushed our differing ideas about human history aside. "We'd better go. Letting dinner go cold is a sin in Granddaddy's book." Laney glanced over her shoulder at us as she led us towards the hallway. "Be warned, my twin brother Logan is out there. He'll probably go totally catto when he sees you two."

"Catto?" Chris asked.

"Catatonic. Because you're a pretty girl about his age."

"If he goes catto when he sees *me*," Chris pointed at me, "what's he going to do when he lays eyes on the goddess incarnate?"

"Probably drool," Lane replied.

"Goddess incarnate?" I rolled my eyes. "Oh, please."

"I call 'em the way I see 'em," Chris said.

We entered a comfortable living room with a food-laden dining area at the far end. Mr. Gibson sat at the head of the dining table. A young man with a strong resemblance to Laney sat at the other end. Logan, no doubt.

Mr. Gibson smiled at us. "You girls clean up real pretty." He glanced at Logan and grinned. "Don't you agree, Logan?"

Logan watched us with wide eyes and an open mouth. "Ummmmmmm."

"Told you," Laney said.

"He's not drooling," Chris said.

"He will," Laney said.

Logan's cheeks reddened, and he cast his eyes down at the empty plate before him. I took pity on him and stopped next to the seat to Logan's right. I summoned my friendliest smile. "May I sit here?"

Logan looked up at me. "S-sure. I'm Logan."

I settled into the seat. "Pleased to meet you, Logan. I'm—"

Laney interrupted me. "A goddess, gracing our humble table with her radiant beauty."

I felt my cheeks warm. Mr. Gibson noticed, and said, "That's enough, Laney. You're embarrassing your brother *and* our guest."

Laney hung her head. "I'm sorry, Granddaddy."

"I'm not the one you should apologize to," Mr. Gibson said.

Laney nodded, looked at me, and said, "I'm sorry, Anne. You, too, Logan."

"It's okay," I said.

Logan gave a half nod of acceptance, but then glared at Mr. Gibson. "You know, *someone* could have warned me."

"Now, where's the fun in that?" Mr. Gibson's smile took any sting out of his words. "Logan, why don't you pass the roast beef to Anne?"

Over the next twenty minutes, the only sounds came from serving spoons, knives, forks, and Chris and me sighing in contentment as we ate. Mr. Gibson insisted we have second helpings, and neither of us argued with him.

Laney passed on seconds. Instead, she said, "Granddaddy, Chris and Anne told me a crazy story after I explained amies to them."

"How crazy?" Mr. Gibson said.

"They said Earth *won* the AI war."

"That *is* crazy," Logan said.

Mr. Gibson eyed his grandchildren, drew a deep breath, and asked, "So, what's the crazy part?"

Laney and Logan gaped at their grandfather. My eyebrows arched in surprise. Across the table from me, Chris's eyes widened.

Laney found her voice first. "What's the crazy part? Their whole story is crazy, Granddaddy."

Mr. Gibson spoke in an even tone. "Is it?"

"*Yeah.*" Sarcasm filled Logan's voice. "Only a complete loof would believe their story."

"What is a loof?" I asked.

"From the context in which my grandchildren use the word, it's current slang for an idiot or moron." Mr. Gibson looked at Logan. "Is that right?"

Logan looked down at the table, unable to meet his grandfather's gaze. But he nodded.

"Well," Mr. Gibson said, "I guess that means I'm a moron."

"Then that means Anne and I are idiots," Chris said.

Mr. Gibson dropped into the drawl he adopted when the soldiers' questions. "I reckon that do be the right of it, Miss Chris."

"Don't be that way," Laney said. "You know Logan didn't mean you three were loofs. But..." She shrugged. "We've all heard the recordings. Seen replays of the instrument readers. And even seen the security recordings from the bridge of the *Haven Seeker*. It's convincing."

"It ought to be," Chris said. "The *Haven Seeker's* crew had hundreds of years to perfect it."

Laney shook her head, as if trying to clear it. "What do you mean by that?"

"I understand you've been told one story your entire life," Chris said. "Do you want me to tell you what *really* happened on board the *Haven Seeker*?"

"It's *our* history, and you weren't even there." Logan glared at Chris. "Why should we listen to anything you say about it?"

Chris returned his glare with interest. "Have you ever been to Earth?"

"Of course not."

"Have you ever even left this planet?"

"No. What's your point?"

"You told *me* the history of *my* home world and expected me to accept your story without question. But the minute I try to do something similar with *your* history, it's suddenly wrong?"

Logan opened his mouth for a retort, but Mr. Gibson cut him off. "*I* would like to hear what Chris has to say."

Logan's mouth snapped shut, and his glare intensified. But he made an *after you* gesture to Chris.

Chris doused her glare and flashed a friendly smile at Logan. "One question before I start. Were the colonists already in cryosleep before the *Haven Seeker* left the docks?"

Logan nodded.

"So only the crew witnessed everything you're taught in school." Chris took a deep breath. "I believe the crew concocted the story that the AIs won the war, falsified the records and instrument readings, and staged the bridge's security recordings."

"Why would they do that?" Laney asked.

"To give themselves an excuse to set themselves up as the colony's rulers, at the end of the voyage," I said.

"It wouldn't be the first time, either," Chris added.

The Scout Corps history class all plebes take covered the phenomenon. I said, "It happened thirty-eight times that we know of. That includes a lost colony discovered by Scouts from my home world less than fifteen years ago. *That* crew set themselves up as gods, if you can believe it."

Chris took over. "When the *Haven Seeker* landed on Refuge, I'll bet the first thing the crew did was put themselves in charge of everything, and they used the story about Earth losing to the AIs as their excuse. Because maybe the AIs tracked the *Haven Seeker*." She eyed Logan. "Am I right?"

"Yes," Logan said.

"Except the emergency never ended, did it?" Chris asked. Logan shook his head, and Chris continued, "Do your leaders exhort you to be extra vigilant, because a stranger on the street might be an amy in disguise? And tell you to watch your neighbors, for the same reason?"

Introspection filled Logan's expression. But Laney turned an accusing glare on her grandfather and asked, "If you don't believe the history, why didn't you tell us?"

"Your parents and I were—"

"Wait," Laney said. "Mom and Dad knew this, and *they* didn't tell us, either?"

"You're a smart girl, Laney. We were waiting for you to figure it out. It's easier to accept something if you work it out for yourself first." Mr. Gibson looked at Logan. "The same goes for you." His gaze swept around the table. "But that's enough of this for right now. Our guests haven't finished their dinner. We should let them use their mouths for eating, rather than yapping about ancient history."

Mr. Gibson pretended to eat, probably so Chris and I wouldn't feel guilty about shoveling down his food. But the second helpings filled us, and we sat back with contented sighs.

"Granddad?" Logan asked. "Can we talk more about that ancient history now?"

Mr. Gibson glanced at a wall clock. "Not yet. It's about time for the national news. Logan, would you turn on the television?"

That was a new word for me. "What's a television?"

"I was about to ask the same thing," Chris said.

Logan went to a big, bulky piece of furniture with a large, rectangular, convex piece of glass on its front. He turned a knob, and the thing made a sort of electric pop. As he returned to the table, the glass started glowing. Then a low resolution picture in shades of white, black, and gray faded into view.

Though the answer wasn't necessary anymore, Logan said, "That's a television."

"So, it's like a bad quality vid?" Chris asked.

"Bad quality?" Laney said. "Grandaddy has the best television you can buy!"

A screen with writing appeared, and I felt as if I could almost read it. Implant translations only work off of spoken language. Even though Chris and I spoke the local language fluently, we couldn't read it all.

The screen shifted to a man who looked pretty old. Not as old as Mr. Gibson, but at least ten years older than my father. The man had dark hair with gray at the temples. He stared out of the screen with an earnest expression. I had to admit, the man had a good look for the television. He appeared... trustworthy.

"Ladies and gentlemen, at long last, our worst fears have come true. Minions of Earth's artificially intelligent rulers, those people many of you call amies, have invaded Refuge. We now send you to Ron Preciss, at the landing site. Ron?"

The picture switched to the meadow where our lifepod landed. Only the lifepod on the screen looked huge. Ron stood as far from the lifepod as possible, but the pod still more than filled the screen. Men moved around it, appearing tiny compared to it. Ron held some device before his mouth.

"Thank you, Sam," Ron said. "You can see the amies' assault craft behind. Our liaison with the military tells me it could easily hold hundreds of amies."

"It isn't that big!" I said. "It only holds six people, but Chris and I were the only ones in it!"

"And it's a lifepod," Chris said. "Not some kind of assault ship!"

"Hush," Mr. Gibson said. "Let me hear what they have to say."

The screen showed a split picture, with Sam on the left and Ron on the right. Sam asked, "Ron, has the military captured any of the amies?"

"I'm afraid not, Sam. They're bringing in more troops to broaden the search, but everyone in the area should be on the lookout for strangers. Civilians are advised that the amies will probably die to further their AI masters' goals."

I snorted. "Not even in your dreams."

The television picture zoomed in on Ron's serious face. "Should you spot strangers, avoid contact at all costs. Hide or run away. If you must defend yourself, grant the amies no mercy. Shoot to kill. Because God only knows what advanced weapons and superhuman abilities the amies possess."

Chris and I looked at each other, and our thoughts were plain for the other to see. *We are heavily armed, and we do possess superhuman abilities.*

Laney caught our exchange of glances. "What does that look mean?"

"It means the television boys might have finally said something true about our guests." Mr. Gibson looked back and forth between Chris and me. "I let you hide in my barn because my gut told me you weren't a threat. I even called in my grandchildren, because you will need help fitting in here. But if you're as dangerous as the newsmen say..." He sighed. "Girls, *are* you that dangerous?"

"Are we dangerous?" Chris met and held Mr. Gibson's gaze. "Not to Laney, Logan, and you."

"I'm looking for *yes* or *no*, Chris. It's not that I believe you'd endanger me or mine, but..." Mr. Gibson sighed. "You might be forced into doing something that does."

"This is crazy, Granddaddy!" Laney asked.

"No, crazy was bringing these two girls into the house after the soldiers left." Mr. Gibson shook his head. "But I let my paternal instincts get the better of my common sense."

"Of course, sir," Chris said, as we pushed back our chairs and rose. "You've already done more than Anne and I had any right to expect."

"We'll get our packs and go," I said. "Where are our uniforms, so we can change into them?"

Mr. Gibson pointed down a short hallway. "They're in the laundry room, down there. Those uniforms... Are they soldiers' uniforms?"

"No," I said. "They're Scout cadet uniforms."

Chris started down the hall towards the laundry. "I'll get them, Anne."

Mr. Gibson's brow furrowed. "Cadet is a military rank."

"We're explorers, not soldiers," I said. "Scouts explore uncharted wormholes, search for lost colonies, and sometimes fight pirates. My father discovered my home world, saved my mother from a kidnapping plot, and married her. He even fought space pirates before my older brother and I came along."

"So, you're following in your dad's footsteps?" Logan asked. "What about your brother?"

"No. Rob is, um, following in Mom's footsteps."

"What does your Mom do?" Laney asked.

I hesitated long enough that Chris, who wasn't even in the room, caught on. She called, "You might as well tell them, Anne."

"Mom is the heir to the throne of my country. And Rob is next in line, after her."

"Wait!" Laney began bouncing up and down. "Does that mean you're a... A...?"

Chris returned, carrying our still-damp uniforms. "The word you're looking for is *princess*." She looked at me. "Go ahead, do the full introduction thing."

I rolled my eyes, but said, "I am Her Royal Highness, Princess Anne Megan Karen Heidi Tisha Erin Courtney Stephanie Villas, third in line for the throne of Mordan. I'm also first year Scout Cadet Anne Villas."

"Oh. My. God!" Laney said.

Mr. Gibson took my introduction with a discernible lack of enthusiasm. "And your father? You say he was a Scout?"

"Only the most famous Scout in the Corps' history," Chris said.

"So it's a safe bet your daddy will come looking for his little girl?" Mr. Gibson asked. "And heaven help anyone who gets in his way?"

"That sounds about right," I said.

Laney crossed her arms and glared at her grandfather. "If I was the one missing, you and Dad would do the same thing."

"We would," Mr. Gibson agreed. "Which is why I know things won't go well for anyone who stands in the way when Anne's father comes for her." Mr. Gibson leaned back in his chair. "I'm sorry, girls. Family comes first. Always has. Always will."

Chris stopped next to me and held up our uniforms. "These are still wet from washing. I got cold wearing a wet uniform when the sun was up. It'll be worse tonight. If Laney doesn't mind, could we keep the clothes we're wearing? At least for a while?"

"I don't care about the clothes." Laney waved off the subject. "But I *do* care that you're sending Chris and Anne out to get caught by the government!"

"Or killed by wild animals." Logan stood, leaned over the table, and glared into Mr. Gibson's eyes. "What if they run into boars? Or a cougar?"

I put a hand on Logan's shoulder and smiled at him. "We aren't help-less, Logan. Chris and I have plenty of survival training. We're armed, and we have... other advantages."

"I finally have that *yes* or *no* answer I was looking for," Mr. Gibson said. "And the answer is *yes*. Just like the news people said."

I met his gaze. "Yes, we can be dangerous. But only to people who give us no other choice."

"I can be dangerous, too, Granddaddy," Laney said. "Just ask the boy who drove me out to Lovers Lane, and then didn't take 'no' for an answer."

Mr. Gibson's eyebrows arched high in surprise. "Which boy was that, Laney? I need to thrash him."

Laney leaned over the table, unconsciously mirroring her brother's posture. "I. Took. Care. Of. It. Because *I* can be dangerous, too."

"Now Laney—," Mr. Gibson began.

But Laney straightened, turned away from her grandfather, and said, "Give me a few minutes to pack some clothes and supplies, then we can get going."

"I'm coming, too," Logan said.

"Neither one of you is going anywhere," Mr. Gibson said. "It's not safe."

Logan ignored him and headed for the bedrooms. Laney started after her brother, then stopped and turned around.

"Granddaddy, if I ever got lost in these hills and stumbled on some-one's house, is this how you'd want them to treat me?"

"It's not the same, Laney."

"No, it's worse for Anne and Chris. They're more lost than I ever could be. They don't know the land or the people."

"They aren't my grandchildren," Mr. Gibson said.

"They're *someone's* grandchildren," Laney snapped.

"Chris and Anne are also going to have the government hot on their heels." Mr. Gibson stood up. "And that's trouble like you've never known, Laney."

Laney resumed walking to the bedrooms. "Then I guess I'm about to learn."

Mr. Gibson watched her turn down the hallway, then shook his head. "They're just as stubborn as their father was at their age."

"We can slip out while Logan and Laney are packing," I said.

"Right, but we can't leave our backpacks," Chris agreed. "Maybe you could toss them out the bathroom window, Mr. Gibson? Then we can grab them and run."

"It's kind of you to suggest that, girls." Mr. Gibson offered a rueful smile. "Especially with what I asked you to do."

"We understand the importance of family," I said.

Mr. Gibson's eyes lost focus. In an absent tone, he said, "Now, more than ever, I'll bet."

As Chris and I started for the door to the yard, Chris said, "Thank you for—"

"Can you girls ride?" Mr. Gibson asked.

"Ride what?" I asked.

"Horses."

"I can. We have a huge stable at home," I said.

"I have some simulator training from the Academy," Chris said.

Mr. Gibson laughed. "I don't even know what those words mean, Chris."

"They mean I can ride. Probably." She cocked her head. "Why?"

"With more troops on the way, the military is going to set up communication centers throughout these hills. This house is an obvious place for one of them." Mr. Gibson's gaze wandered around the big room. "Even with those fancy chameleon things you have, soldiers based here will find you if you tried hiding here. Might be by accident, but *how* they find you won't matter."

"That's all the more reason we should leave," I said.

"No, you can't stay here." Mr. Gibson tilted his head in the direction his grandchildren went. "But Laney and Logan are right. I can't let you go out there alone, either." He drew a deep breath. "Since the military blocked all the roads, we're going to have to get outside their search perimeter on horseback."

Laney returned to the room with a backpack slung over her shoulders. "We, Granddaddy?"

Mr. Gibson looked at Chris and me. "You girls need someone older, wiser, and a whole lot sneakier to help you stay free. Your parents aren't here, so I'll have to fill their shoes until they show up. Remember when I said family comes first?" He smiled at us. "Welcome to the family."

ON OUR OWN AGAIN

Once Mr. Gibson decided to come with us, he took charge of our preparations. To Chris and me, he said, "Go get your packs, girls. I need to figure out what we bring and what we leave behind."

"We can't risk leaving anything behind, Mr. Gibson," Chris said. "If the soldiers return and find some of our equipment—"

"Leave that to me, Chris," Mr. Gibson said. He pointed at Laney's pack. "Let me see what you packed."

By the time Chris and I came back with our four backpacks, Mr. Gibson had Laney and Logan packing food and other supplies. He pointed at the dining room table. "Empty your packs there."

I glanced at Chris. She gave a little shrug and pulled everything from the packs. We sorted our stuff into piles. Two blasters. Two night-vision glasses. Five medical nanite injectors. Six of everything else, including chameleon cloths, heat-reflective blankets, laser fire starters, basic first aid kits, and all our survival rations.

Mr. Gibson eyed everything, then pointed at the rations. "That stuff is food, right?"

"Yes, sir," I said. "Survival rations."

He nodded. "Bring all of that. And those chameleon cloth things could be handy, so bring them."

Chris began packing the food and chameleon cloths as Mr. Gibson picked up one of the blankets.

"What's this?" he asked.

"A blanket."

"Pfff." He dropped it back on the pile. "Too light to do any good. Leave 'em."

"The blankets reflect heat, sir." I put all six blankets in a backpack. "One of those can keep you from freezing to death in arctic conditions."

Mr. Gibson cocked an eyebrow at me. "You don't say? I guess we'd better take them."

The laser fire starters and first aid kits went into a pack, as did the nanite injectors. I tried explaining medical nanites to Mr. Gibson. But he cut me off before I'd even began explaining what nanites are. "I don't have to understand *how* those things work, just that they *do* work."

He set the night-vision glasses aside. "Keep them out. They'll come in handy during our ride."

That left the blasters. Mr. Gibson eyed them, but didn't touch them. "Any idiot can tell those are weapons."

"They're called blaster pistols," I said.

"What do they shoot?"

"Super heated plasma bolts."

"That sounds dangerous. Can you give me an idea *how* dangerous?"

I considered his question for a moment, then said, "It would take a lot of shots and probably drain the charge pack, but I could destroy this house and part of the barn with one blaster."

Mr. Gibson whistled. "That Scout Academy you go to? They trained you how to use these, right?"

"Yes, sir."

"Did they cover *not* using them in that training?"

"We only use them if lives are at risk."

"Good." He considered the blasters for a few seconds. "You and Chris better hang onto those. But stick to that training, and only use them in dire emergencies."

Chris and I nodded, and we slung blaster belts around our hips.

Almost as an afterthought, Mr. Gibson asked, "Did you leave four blasters and four night-vision glasses on that lifepod? You've got six of everything else."

Chris shook her head. "Lifepod supplies only include two blasters and night-vision glasses. I don't know why they do that."

"The people in charge at your Academy probably don't want a bunch of cadets getting trigger-happy and shooting everything that moves," Mr. Gibson said.

Chris and I bristled at his comment, and I said, "We're not foolish, Mr. Gibson."

"Nope, just young and inexperienced." He gathered Laney and Logan with his gaze. "Grab everything and let's go to the barn."

Mr. Gibson had six horses in the barn, and we saddled all six of them, even the horse no one would ride. "Speed is our best ally. I don't like saddling a horse no one is riding. But we don't want to waste time moving the saddle if one of our horses comes up lame."

We led the horses outside and mounted. Chris had the most trouble, since she'd never sat on a real horse before. But she got up on her second try.

I mounted with the ease of a lifetime around horses. "I should have one pair of night-vision glasses."

Mr. Gibson donned one pair, and his eyebrows arched in surprise at how well they worked. "Why should you get the other one, Anne?"

"Because I have one of the blaster pistols. If I have to shoot it, I want to see what I'm shooting at."

"Fair enough." Mr. Gibson passed the second pair to me. "Let's get going."

Mr. Gibson turned his horse downhill—in the opposite direction from our lifepod—and led us into the forest.

I expected Mr. Gibson to have Logan and Laney keep an eye on Chris and me until we proved we could handle our horses. But he took us at our word. We rode single file into the forest, which Logan said would mask our numbers if the army had more trackers, like the one who tracked Chris and me to the tree we hid under.

Mr. Gibson led, followed by Chris, Logan, and Laney. I brought up the rear. That way, we had a pair of night vision glasses at each end of our little procession. Mr. Gibson communicated with us by passing whispered commands and suggestions down the line. It wasn't fast—it took him five minutes to explain what we should do if we spotted a patrol—but it got the job done, and kept our noise to a minimum.

Helicopters flew overhead three times in the first two hours of our trip. With the racket the helicopters made, we had lots of warning before they got close to us. Mr. Gibson had Chris and me dismount, take the packs with our stuff in them, wrap a chameleon cloth around ourselves, and crouch under a tree each time a helicopter buzzed overhead. It was a good thing he did, too, since the second and third helicopters shined a bright searchlight down on us. Someone in the third helicopter used some kind of voice amplifier and ordered Mr. Gibson to stay put until a patrol got to us.

The helicopter hovered over us for nearly ten minutes, waiting for a patrol. The *chop chop* of the rotors beating the air hid the sound of the soldiers' approach. I didn't even know the soldiers were close until a soldier's foot came down on a broken branch a meter to my right. The helicopter moved on as soon as the patrol arrived.

The soldiers carried hand held lights, which they shined all around the area. Beams of light slid over our chameleon cloth twice, while I prayed the cloth mimicked our surroundings well enough to fool the soldiers. The beams finally turned inward, and Chris and I sort of saw the patrol surrounding Mr. Gibson, Logan, Laney, and the six horses. Once he had his men in position, the patrol leader said, "Papers."

"Figgered you'd want them." Mr. Gibson slipped back into his country accent. "You young'uns heard the... sergeant, be you? Can't rightly see your rank, what with all them lights in my eyes."

"I'm Sergeant Herrera," the man said. "Men, lower your torches so they don't blind these people."

We heard the rustle of paper, and one light angled down. Probably so Herrera could read Mr. Gibson's papers. Whatever those were. Another soldier gathered papers from Logan and Laney.

"Mr. Elias Gibson," Sergeant Herrera said.

"A'yup. That be me. These here be my grands. Logan Gibson and Laney Gibson."

"The names match up, Sergeant," a soldier said.

"Uh huh," Herrera replied. "Please tell me what you three are doing out here at this time of night?"

"It be that news report, Sergeant," Mr. Gibson said. "When them soldiers dropped in at my house, what they said got me ta thinkin' you was just chasing three, maybe four, amies. But them news fellers? They showed a big ol' spaceship, what coulda held a hunnert or more amies. I knew me an' my grands coulda held off a few amies, but not no army. So we grabbed the horses and lit out for town."

"A car would have been faster," Herrera said. "Why didn't you drive?"

"Welp, I done my time in the army, forty years back. In the Big Un, doncha know. Just like most menfolk my age. Anywho, I knowed roads be what the enemy goes fer. So figgered me and the grands be safer out here in the trees. So we saddled up and here we be."

"But why *six* horses, Mr. Gibson?"

"I only *got* six horses, son. And I weren't gonna leave three of 'em fer the amies. 'Sides, if'n we gotta run from amies, we can swap horses quick-like when the ones we be riding get tuckered out. That's why I saddled 'em up, Sergeant. So's we could just hop from one horse t'other."

"You should have stayed put, Mr. Gibson. Our captain wants to use your place as one coordination base for our search. You'd have had the army protecting you and your grandchildren."

"Welp, mighta helped if'n mister Lieutenant Watts done told me that when he searched my place earlier today." Mr. Gibson lowered his voice, and the sound came from closer to the ground, as if he'd leaned over in his saddle. "You got kids, Sergeant?"

"Two."

"Then you know how kids can catch a fright. Even ornery teenagers, like Logan an' Laney. My grands got awful fearful when they heard 'bout all them amies bein' nearby, an' I figgered it be best to get 'em on back ta town and home."

"I'll have to call this in, Mr. Gibson. Please wait."

I heard the sergeant fumble with a piece of equipment and assumed it was something like the big comm unit the soldier used when Chris and I hid under the tree. A burst of static followed, then a voice said, "Amy Base. Report."

"Sergeant Herrera here. We've got three locals riding through the forest on horses."

"Names?" the voice asked.

"A Mr. Elias Gibson, an older man. Says he fought in the Big One. His grandson, Logan Gibson, and his granddaughter, Laney Gibson. They're, um..." In a low voice, Herrera asked, "How old are the kids?"

Paper rustled, then a soldier said, "Eighteen."

Herrera's voice rose. "The grandkids are eighteen. Mr. Gibson says they're heading out because of the news broadcast about hundreds of amies landing in the area."

"Is this the same Gibson who has the house the captain wants to use as a base?" the voice asked.

Herrera relayed the answer. "It is."

Mr. Gibson said, "Ya can tell yer captain I don't never lock the doors. Him and his boys ain't gonna have no problem gettin' in. And they be welcome ta any food what's in the place. On account o' them keepin' us all safe from amies."

"Did you catch that, base?" Herrera asked.

"Yes. Hang on, while I check with the captain."

The comm fell silent.

"Just so's I know, Sergeant," Mr. Gibson said, "if'n the captain says we gotta go back ta the house, you an' yer men gonna come with us and make sure no amies get us. Right?"

"That will be up to the captain," Herrera said.

We waited for two of the longest minutes of my life, before the bulky comm unit broadcast static followed by the voice from earlier. "Captain says to let them go. But they have to check in at the search base in town when they get there. I'm calling them right after we disconnect, so the officer in charge will know they're coming."

"Roger," Herrera said. As he put the big comm unit away, he said, "You heard the man?"

"I did, Sergeant," Mr. Gibson said. "We s'posed ta check in with whoever be in charge of the soldiers in town, an' show 'em our papers. Right?"

"That's correct."

"Then you better give them papers back ta us, so's we can do that."

We heard more paper rustling as the soldiers returned the papers to Mr. Gibson, Logan, and Laney. Then Herrera said, "Let's get going."

"You comin' with us?" Mr. Gibson asked.

"Just until we get back to our normal patrol position," Herrera said.

"Welp, that sure will make the grands feel a might safer, Sergeant. I thankee."

With that, Mr. Gibson, Logan, Laney, and the soldiers started down the hill. Chris and I were on our own. Again.

Chris and I remained silent until the night swallowed the soldiers and the Gibsons. We waited another five minutes before we spoke, and we kept our voices to a whisper.

"I wish Mr. Gibson had left the other pair of night vision glasses with us," Chris said.

"That other pair will help the Gibsons find their way through the forest in the dark," I replied. "We can get by with one."

"That's not what I'm worried about," Chris said. "What do you think will happen to them if someone takes a closer look at those glasses?"

I mouthed a silent O. Then remembered I wore our pair of night vision glasses and realized Chris couldn't see my reaction. "Oh... At least we have all the rest of our stuff. And why would someone look at Mr. Gibson's glasses? Aashla is less advanced than this planet, and we have lots of people who wear glasses."

"Maybe... Do the glasses made on Aashla look much like the night vision glasses?"

I sighed. "Sort of? I mean, they all have frames and lenses. But the night vision frames are bulkier. I guess to hold the night vision electronics?"

"Sergeant Herrera didn't say anything about the glasses," Chris said, "so maybe everything will be okay. And Mr. Gibson is a smart man. I'll bet he takes them off before he goes into the town. But just having them could put all three of the Gibsons at risk."

I shrugged. "We can't do anything about that now. How long should we wait before we follow them?"

"Let's give it another thirty minutes, just to be safe. We'll need to keep the chameleon cloths wrapped around us, like we did... God, was it only earlier this afternoon?"

"I know what you mean. We haven't even been on Refuge for twelve hours, but it seems like it's been days." I took Chris's hand, removed the night vision goggles, and put them in her hand. "It's your turn to wear these."

Chris didn't take her hand away. "What's your marksmanship rank in the plebe class?"

"Um, I don't remember exactly. Maybe tenth, give or take a few spots. Why?"

"Because I rank right in the middle of the third year class. I hope we don't have to shoot anything. But if we do, the better shot should have the glasses. And that's you."

"If you say so..."

"Just lead me slowly. I don't want to sprain my ankle again."

"That makes two of us. You got heavier with every step I took earlier. And that was before you gorged yourself at dinner."

"Are you saying I'm fat?"

"This plebe would never do that, Cadet Sergeant Christine Montide, ma'am!"

"Very well, plebe. Now, I suggest we rest quietly until the thirty minutes are up."

I leaned against the tree trunk and closed my eyes. "This plebe hears and obeys."

All too soon, Chris tapped my shoulder. "It's time to get going."

We stood, and each wrapped a chameleon cloth around ourselves. As before, we left our faces uncovered. I shoot right-handed, so I offered Chris my left hand. She took it with her right hand, and we started downhill, after the Gibsons. It took me less time to find the Gibsons' trail than it did for Chris and me to develop a rhythm for walking that kept us from stepping on each other.

Even with the rhythm, we didn't make nearly as good a time as we had on horseback. We also stopped and hid every time we heard any noise that might be someone walking through the forest. Eventually, we learned enough to discount skittering from above and scurrying from below. Slithering sounds sent shivers down my spine, but I made myself ignore those, too.

We also got better at using our noses after I almost stepped in a pile of horse dung. That stuff blended into the underbrush better than I'd have expected. But once we added it to our growing list of things we shouldn't step on—snakes, squirrels, brambles, and now horse poop—the horse dung reassured me I hadn't lost the Gibsons' trail.

Downhill. Uphill. Over and through streams. Stand still and cover our faces when helicopters flew overhead. Cower under trees when we heard soldiers. No rest from the stops. Just mounting tension. Then trudge on. Beyond exhaustion. Beyond caring. Just trudge on.

By the time the first gray light of approaching dawn lit the sky, Chris and I drew ragged breaths between stumbling steps.

"Got to stop," Chris said. "We need rest."

"Yeah." I peered through the forest before us. "There's a clearing fifty meters ahead. We shouldn't get any closer."

Chris dropped my hand. "Agreed."

Without another word, she crawled under a tree like the one we had hidden under the previous afternoon. I handed our packs to her. Remembering what the tracker said the previous day, I took care to keep them off the ground, and Chris did the same. Finally, I used the same care crawling under the tree.

Chris and I didn't really have the energy to drape chameleon cloth around us, but we forced ourselves to do it. We made ourselves inspect the job when we finished, made a few adjustments, and inspected it again. Then we finally curled up next to the tree trunk and immediately fell asleep.

MORE DANGEROUS

A god-awful racket woke me up. My implant helpfully told me I'd slept for four hours. Half a night's sleep, so not bad, right? Yeah, but after everything Chris and I had been through since our lifepod approached the planet Refuge, I needed about a week of uninterrupted sleep.

Chris must have felt the same as me, because she groaned a wordless protest. She lifted her head and mumbled, "What is that?"

I didn't even bother lifting my head. "Sounds like a helicopter. Big one."

"Oh," Chris said. "So it's full of soldiers?"

"Probably."

"Searching for us?"

"Yeah."

"Think they'll kill us if they find us?"

"God, I hope so."

"One of us should look outside and see what's happening."

"This plebe defers to her superior officer."

"That's not the way rank works, Cadet Villas."

"How about, this plebe carried Cadet Sergeant Montide for hours yesterday?"

"Mmmm. Guilt." Chris rose to her hands and knees. "An effective technique."

"This plebe aims to please. And sleep."

Chris must have pulled aside a small part of our chameleon cloth blanket fort. A pinprick of bright light made me shut my eyes tighter. After a few seconds, the light returned to normal.

Chris dragged herself back to her sleeping spot next to the tree trunk. "One of those big helicopters landed in the clearing."

"Soldiers?"

"Oh yeah. A hundred, maybe?"

"That's a lot. Think they'll find us?"

"Sorry, Anne, I left my crystal ball on the cadet cruiser."

"Crap. This plebe left her tarot cards on the cruiser, too."

"I guess we'll just have to wait and see what life brings."

"This plebe hates waiting."

"What does the plebe think of surprises?"

"The surprises we've had on this planet have underwhelmed."

"Except for the Gibsons."

"This plebe concedes the Cadet Sergeant's point."

"We should take turns staying awake. The last thing we need is to attract the soldiers' attention if one of us snores."

I propped myself up on one arm. "This plebe hears and—"

"Will keep sleeping." Chris used her Cadet Sergeant's tone of voice. "I will take the first watch."

"This plebe hears and obeys." I lowered myself to the ground again. "But don't forget to wake me later. This plebe doesn't want to end up carrying the Cadet Sergeant because she stayed on watch all day."

I closed my eyes and fell asleep immediately. I don't remember my dreams, but I know growling machinery, shouting soldiers, and tramping feet filled them.

Someone shook my shoulder. The dreams faded, but the growling, shouting, and tramping remained. I opened gritty eyes. Chris leaned over me, bloodshot eyes locked on mine and a finger over her lips.

She put her lips next to my ear. "Sorry, you began mumbling."

My implant said I'd slept for another five hours. I whispered, "You should have woken me an hour ago."

"Is the plebe giving orders to the Cadet Sergeant?"

"No, I'm watching out for my friend."

"So am I. And *my* friend carried a much heavier burden than *your* friend."

"Blah blah blah." I sat up and gave an imperious wave. As a princess, I have a fantastic imperious wave. "You may sleep."

Chris gave a pretend curtsy. It was surprisingly good, especially since she wasn't wearing a dress and was sitting under a tree. "As you command, Your Highness."

She curled up on the ground and her breath deepened immediately. I turned my attention beyond our chameleon cloth fort and listened for nearby sounds. I took my time, filtered out the soldier sounds from the clearing fifty meters away, and concentrated on nearby sounds.

Skittering. Scampering. Slithering. Chittering. Buzzing. Tweeting.

Forest sounds. Reassuring sounds. I might not hear soldiers creeping around our hiding place, but the animals and insects would. Unless a soldier crept nearby while I was sleeping, and then stayed still until the creatures got used to his presence. But would a soldier go to that much trouble to confirm his suspicions? He could just call a bunch of his fellow soldiers and perform a detailed search of the area. So...

Stop being paranoid, I told myself, *and trust your instincts.*

I crawled to a seam where two chameleon cloths overlapped, one facing the clearing. With infinite care, I poked a finger through the seam and created a peephole. Half-a-dozen soldiers stood in the middle of the clearing, lounging next to the huge helicopter that brought them here. I moved my head so I could see in different directions through the peephole.

I saw tents, tables, camp cooking equipment, and a big machine with something sticking high into the air. The big device the sergeant used the day before, when the tracker almost caught us hiding under a tree, came to mind. I prayed the tracker wasn't with them, because I wouldn't bet on our chameleon cloth fort fooling him twice.

But the big machine with the thing sticking up. A primitive comm, maybe?

A soldier at the machine lifted something connected to the machine by wires. He spoke into it. Waited. Spoke again. Conferred with a second soldier. An officer? The soldier spoke into the thing connected to the machine again.

It had to be a comm. And even if it wasn't, it was safest for Chris and me to assume it was, and the soldiers were using it to coordinate their search for us. Which meant we should stay put until nightfall, when the soldiers' vision was poorest and, thanks to the night vision glasses, ours was best.

My stomach rumbled, so I dug out a pack of rations and a bottle of water. You can survive for a long time off the rations, but no sane person would want to. I chewed the stuff only enough to break each bite into small chunks, and then swallowed it all with a swing of water. My stomach stopped complaining, at least.

I woke Chris just before dusk, and we watched soldiers straggle into their camp in the clearing. Way too many of those soldiers passed within five meters of our tree. But we'd chosen it because it was off the game trail the Gibsons used and that we'd followed the night before.

Two more hours passed as the soldiers gave reports and ate. Finally, all but a handful of soldiers retired to their tents. Those who remained awake set up watch around the camp. So Chris and I moved with elaborate care as we dismantled our chameleon cloth fort. Then we each wrapped ourselves in one cloth, I donned the night vision glasses, and we set off around the clearing.

We had no path and spent an hour and a half circumnavigating the large clearing. But we finally reached the far side. I checked three paths before I found a dried pile of horse dung, and almost burst out laughing when I spotted a boot print in the middle of it.

I guided Chris past the horse dung, and we set off down the path, back on the Gibsons' trail.

Twenty minutes after we started following the path marked by the dung Mr. Gibson's horses had dropped, I spotted a squad of soldiers ahead on the path. Chris and I ducked off the path. None of the trees nearby had low-hanging branches, so we just wrapped our chameleon cloths around ourselves and huddled behind the biggest nearby tree trunk.

The soldiers didn't even slow down as they passed us. From the snippets of conversation we heard, the five soldiers were looking forward to resting, drinking, and eating. In that order. One soldier complained, "I'm missing out on a date with my girl because of the stupid search for the stupid amies."

"Don't let the captain hear you talking like that," another soldier said.

"He's bucking for a promotion. If he catches an amy, the promotion is a sure thing."

"Yeah?" the first soldier said. "Then maybe the captain oughta get off his butt and do some searching, too."

The second soldier replied, but the patrol was too far past us for me to make it out.

Chris and I waited another five minutes, then we crept back to the path. And immediately hurried back to our hiding spot when I spotted another patrol approaching. Those soldiers voiced similar desires for alcohol, food, rest, and women, though none of them said anything about missed dates. They also passed without slowing.

As before, we waited five minutes. Then Chris whispered, "Let's give it another fifteen minutes, just in case rush hour on the path isn't over."

We sat in silence as the cool night air drew the warmth from our bodies. We'd warm enough once we got moving again, but the chill made the extra fifteen minutes feel twice as long.

No more patrols came by, so we slipped back onto the path. We arranged our chameleon cloths for the best combination of concealment and clear vision and set off down the path.

The two previous patrols must have been the last ones returning on this path, because we didn't run into anyone else. We hid from helicopters four times. But they made so much noise, we heard them approaching long before they passed overhead. Since we didn't have to worry about soldiers on foot, we just stepped off the path, fully covered ourselves with the chameleon cloths, and stood still until the helicopter flew away. None of them slowed, and the random searchlight sweeps never came close to us.

The forest took its time coming back to life after each helicopter flyby. But within ten minutes, the scampering, skittering, slithering, and chittering resumed. As before, I took comfort from the noise of life around us. Because silence meant intruders. Intruders meant soldiers. And soldiers meant danger to Chris and me.

So you can imagine how I felt when the forest suddenly fell silent. I scanned the path ahead and behind for movement and saw nothing. But I wasn't about to risk capture just because my senses didn't register danger. Not when God only knew how many creatures' senses said the exact opposite.

Chris didn't have night vision glasses, but her hearing worked just fine. And she obviously felt the same as me. "Off the path."

As before, we found the biggest tree close to the path, huddled beneath it, and waited. After what felt like forever, but was only a minute, I heard rustling as something big moved through the underbrush about ten meters from us. Something about the sound told me it was an animal, not a person. The creature stopped, gave some bestial grunts, rooted around in the underbrush, and then began moving again.

"Take a look."

Chris spoke so softly I barely heard her. But the creature must have had fantastic hearing. It grunted once and stopped moving.

I carefully parted my chameleon cloth and peered towards the sounds I'd heard. A huge beast stood less than ten meters away. It looked sort of like a pig, only meaner. Rough fur covered it, two tusks jutted from its mouth, and it must have weighed close to two hundred kilograms. Its legs looked too small for its body, but I knew better. Back on Aashla, pigs were among the livestock owned by my family. And they could run surprisingly fast on those little legs. The wild version was probably faster.

I didn't want to shoot the thing—the noise could carry for kilometers —but it could maim or kill us if it charged. I drew my blaster, flicked off the safety, and pointed it at the wild pig. Then I whispered, "It's a boar. One of the creatures Logan was afraid we'd run into."

"Why do you think it's one of those?"

"Because it's a wild pig."

"And?"

"A boar is a male pig."

"Oh."

We fell silent. The boar either got bored or decided we weren't a threat, because it finally turned away from us and resumed its journey.

"Is it leaving?" Chris asked.

"Yes."

"Good. I assume Logan had a good reason for his concern. Let's give it time to get far away from us."

"Fine by me."

Twenty seconds later, I nearly jumped out of my skin as another large creature glided into view. Despite its size—it probably weighed half the boar's weight—it moved with silent and deadly grace. The creature before me weighed twenty times what my little cat at home weighed, but they both carried themselves in an unmistakably feline manner.

"Can we—" Chris began.

"Shush!" I hissed.

The big cat's head turned. Despite the darkness, luminous eyes looked right at me. My blood ran cold, and I desperately wished we weren't so close to this silently stalking, killing machine. Unlike the boar, if the cat attacked, I wasn't sure my reflexes were good enough to shoot it before it tore into me.

But I could do something about that. I issued a command to my implant.

Boost!

Time slowed as adrenaline flooded my body. Unwilling to risk getting tangled in the chameleon cloth covering me, I released it. The cat never moved as the cloth fell away. I rose to one knee, fully revealed to the cat, leveled my blaster, and met the cat's gaze.

"Don't even think about it," I said.

The cat and I stared at each other for nearly fifteen seconds. In the end, I think it decided I wasn't worth the trouble. With a sudden bound, the cat resumed stalking the boar.

I held Boost for another thirty seconds before releasing it. "Okay, Chris, we can get going again."

Chris waited until we reached the path, then asked, "Did you Boost back there?"

"Yes."

"Why?"

"I had to convince a dangerous predator that I was even more dangerous."

After I described the encounter with the cat, Chris said, "You'd better give me the night vision glasses. You might be a better shot than me, but it's not safe for you to Boost again anytime soon."

I did as she suggested, and Chris led me along the path. Once again, we walked all night. Fatigue built. Our steps slowed. But two hours before dawn, we passed the first of several remote houses. An hour before dawn, we finally reached the edge of the forest. Across a narrow, paved road sat the edge of a small town.

This had to be the town Mr. Gibson took Logan and Laney to. But how could we hope to find them without arousing suspicions?

The low sound of an engine drew our attention. We looked to our left and saw two beams of light illuminating the road. A third light played through the forest as a vehicle moved slowly down the road.

Chris and I had no time to erect a chameleon cloth fort, like we'd done twice before. We shared a wordless glance, dropped to our knees, and made sure chameleon cloth covered us completely.

The vehicle's lights shined so brightly, we had no trouble seeing them through the cloth. But those lights were dim compared to the dazzling bright searchlight that swept the forest.

"Shine the light over there," a woman said. "I thought I saw something move."

"Probably just a skrinx," a man muttered, "like the last three times."

The searchlight shone directly on us. Moved past. Swung back. Move again.

"Not even a skrinx." In a sarcastic tone, he added, "Good eyes, Morris."

"At least I'm an alert perimeter guard," Morris snapped. "I'll bet you idiots wouldn't even recognize an amy if the searchlight lit on one."

She was right.

"Like you'd do any better," the man said.

And he was right, too. I had to assume Morris had watched the searchlight slide right over our chameleon cloths without noticing anything. And an alert observer *might* have noticed something. The chameleon cloth has a few weaknesses, and one of them is a bright light shining directly on the cloth.

No matter how well the cloth mimics its surroundings, it can't do anything about the shadow cast by the person under the cloth. That's not a big deal in forest gloom, in a dimly lit barn, or at night. But we must have cast sharp shadows when the searchlight illuminated us. Shadows from the trees around us may have masked ours. Our shadows may have remained hidden, since our camouflaged bodies were always between the searchlight and the shadows. Or maybe Morris wasn't as alert as she thought she was. Whatever the reason, I felt as if we'd barely dodged a blaster bolt.

We remained hidden while the vehicle slowly moved away. When the engine noise faded out, Chris said, "We don't know how many vehicles the soldiers have patrolling the road, so let's hurry and get a proper hiding place set up."

Chris still wore the night vision glasses, so she took charge of finding a good place to erect our chameleon cloth fort. We'd had plenty of practice with chameleon cloth concealment since we landed on Refuge. In less than five minutes, we had our cloths draped beneath a tree seven or eight meters from the road. The tree had low-hanging branches, like the ones we'd preferred previously. We were safely inside it when the next vehicle approached.

As before, we heard voices from the vehicle. Different voices, so a different vehicle. But its searchlight speared the forest, too. As before, the light passed over our position and kept moving. The same thing happened every seven or eight minutes.

We counted four distinctive sets of voices, which meant four vehicles patrolled the town's perimeter. Chris and I wouldn't have any trouble slipping into the town in the gaps between patrols. But we couldn't risk that until we had some idea what to expect in town. With dawn approaching, we planned on spending the day watching and waiting. Then we'd try reconnaissance inside the town after sundown.

The patrols changed about an hour after sunrise. We peeked through seams in the cloth twice as the military vehicles passed. They appeared utilitarian, with high ground clearance, an open top, seating for two in front, and the searchlight mounted in the back. Each vehicle had three soldiers; a driver, a spotter, and a searchlight operator.

But the daytime patrols bore no resemblance to nighttime ones. Two enclosed vehicles replaced the military ones. The new vehicles looked sort of like the air cars we have at the Academy, except these cars ran on four wheels. They bore official-looking designs on the doors, and each carried a driver and a spotter. Both wore uniforms, but nothing like the ones worn by the soldiers.

"Local law enforcement?" Chris said.

I shrugged. "That seems like a good guess."

"I wonder why they switched from the military?"

"There are a lot of soldiers in the forest, searching for us. Maybe the garrison in the town is short-handed?"

"It doesn't really matter," Chris said. "What *does* matter, is it will be much easier slipping in town between the daylight patrols."

Once we established the civilian patrol routine, Chris and I took turns napping. Since Chris took the last watch the day before, I took the first watch today. She curled up and fell asleep quickly. I peeked through chameleon cloth seams every ten minutes or so, but spent most of my time listening. Fortunately, the natural sounds of the forest never dimmed or muted. Not even when the cars cruised by on their patrol.

I'd been on watch for over four hours, when everything changed. I heard a new sound, and not one from nature. Somewhere nearby, a woman sang a song. And I recognized her voice.

Laney!

I parted a seam and looked for her. Laney wasn't hard to spot. She wore a bright red shirt over faded, blue trousers like the ones she loaned to Chris and me. She walked along our side of the road, belting her song. I didn't recognize the song, of course, but it had an infectious tune. Laney kept her eyes on the forest, looking for us.

I felt certain the song was her way of letting Chris and me know she was there. When she drew level with us, I decided I'd poke my head out and call her. But first I shook Chris.

"Huh?" she asked.

"Laney is on the road. That's her singing."

Chris came alert and joined me at the seam. I let her take a look while I explained my meager plan.

"I don't have a better suggestion," Chris said. "So..."

She trailed off as we heard the sound of an approaching engine. One of the civilian patrol cars approached, but it slowed as it drew nearer. Laney, who wasn't more than ten meters away from us, let her singing trail off as the car stopped next to her.

Chris and I both peered through our seam as the passenger door opened. A big man, a few years older than Laney, got out. He folded his arms, and his face twisted into something he probably thought was an officious glare.

"Whatcha doin' out here, Laney?" he asked.

"Minding my own business," she said.

"It ain't safe out here. Doncha know there's amies in the forest?"

"Amies don't scare me. Anyway, I can take care of myself."

"Maybe so, but the mayor said ever'body gotta stay in town," the officer said. "Heck, I bet your daddy don't even know yer out here."

Laney matched the officer's posture. "I told him I was going for a walk. So he knows."

"Uh huh. Didja tell him where you was gonna walk out here?"

"He knows I like walking around the perimeter road."

"That be a no on tellin' him, then." The officer opened the car's back door. "Hop in, li'l lady, so's we can take you home."

"I don't see—"

"I *said*, hop in, Laney. So be a good girl, an' do it."

Since Laney had no choice, she did as the officer instructed. Then he and his partner drove away and took our best hope of connecting with Mr. Gibson with him.

BOY TROUBLE

C hris and I watched the big patrol car turn left towards the town. It quickly vanished behind trees and buildings on the town's outskirts. But we kept watching and caught glimpses of the car through the trees and between the buildings. We got lucky and saw it turn right onto a smaller road. Then it disappeared from sight, and it didn't reappear.

I sat back and let the chameleon cloth close again. "At least we have a better idea where to find the Gibsons."

Chris gave me a long look. "It sounds like you want to go into the town and look for them."

"I don't *want* to do that, but..." I shrugged. "If you have a better idea, I'm all ears."

Chris sighed. "No, I don't. But it's risky. And what if Laney or someone else in the family comes back to the road?"

I steeled myself for Chris's reaction, and said, "That's why I think we should split up."

Chris didn't disappoint me. "That's a *horrible* idea!"

"I know."

"Then why did you even suggest it?"

"Because all of our other options are worse."

"How?"

"We can't stay hidden under this tree forever. We'll run out of food or make a mistake or just have bad luck. All it takes is an animal scampering into the chameleon cloth while a patrol is nearby, and we're sunk."

Chris thought for a second, then said, "Those are good reasons for leaving. *Not* for splitting up."

"We split up for two reasons. You already mentioned the possibility of Laney or Logan coming looking for us again."

"And the other?"

I drew a deep breath. "If one of us gets caught, the other is still free."

"Free to do what?"

"Whatever she can. Find more people like the Gibsons. Mount a rescue for the one of us who gets caught. Get a comm warning to the ship that comes searching for us. Whatever it takes." I prepared for another poor reaction from Chris, and said, "But we need to decide fast. By the time the next patrol car comes by in," I checked my implant for the time, "about two minutes."

Chris looked as if she wanted to argue with me, but I guess my previous arguments had an effect on her. "Why then?"

"Because the other patrol car isn't patrolling the perimeter road right now. It's taking Laney home. That will give me more time to get out of sight from the road."

"You?"

"Me."

"Why?"

"Because I'm from a rural planet, and can probably pull off a country accent better than you. And whoever goes into town might need to convince people she's a hick from the sticks."

"Your planet is rural, Anne, but you're a freaking princess! How many country people did you run into growing up in a palace?"

"A few hundred." Chris's mouth dropped open in surprise, so I continued, "It takes a *lot* of support staff to run a seat of government, and that's what a royal palace is. From the stable hands to the cooks, from the gardeners to the cleaning staff, the palace employed a *lot* of skilled people who had little formal education. I interacted with them every day and even played with their children as a girl."

Chris wasn't ready to surrender yet. "I watched plenty of vids that had country people in them. It's not quite the same, but—"

"It's not even remotely the same, Chris. I've seen some of the recent vids set on Aashla, and the writers all assume that my planet is full of ignorant idiots who need the O So Enlightened Terran Federation to save them from their own stupidity." I caught Chris's gaze and asked, "On Earth, what happens if someone gets lost in the wilderness?"

"They, um, punch the emergency button on their comm, and someone comes and gets them."

"Something any idiot can do, right?" I waited for Chris's nod, then said, "On Aashla, a lost person must use their wits to survive and find their way out of the wilderness. Idiots die." I sighed. "Situations that are inconvenient on Earth can be life-threatening on Aashla. Bluntly put, Aashla kills her idiots, while Earth coddles hers. Aashlanders may not have a lot of what the palace stable hands called *book smarts*, but they have plenty of *life smarts*."

"And sneaking into town will require those life smarts?"

"It might." I heard the other patrol car approaching. "We've got to decide now, Chris."

She didn't hesitate. "Take a comm, but leave anything else from the Federation here."

I shoved a comm in my pocket, went to a seam facing away from the road, and listened to the approaching patrol car. The sound drew closer, passed us, and faded into the distance.

"Be careful," Chris said.

"I will," I said.

Then I slipped through the seam, crept around our tree, and headed for the perimeter road.

I dashed across the perimeter road and into some scraggly bushes on the far side. The dangerous side. The town side.

I gently pushed my way through the bushes, taking care not to break branches. There's nothing like a broken branch to tell a good tracker, *she went this way*.

I learned that from Tim, one of my younger guards, back home. I didn't handle boredom well as a little girl, so Mom gave permission for one guard to entertain me, provided the other guards remained vigilant. Tim was the one the older guards ordered to "go play with Princess Anne" when I got bored.

I was thirteen before I found out the older guards thought I'd make

Tim play with dolls, attend pretend tea parties, and play princess. That shows what they knew about me. I mean, why would a *real* princess need to *play* princess? No, Tim and I played *Scout*. We skulked through the nursery and, in good weather, the palace grounds, recreating Dad's adventures, and others we made up. We held tea parties, too, but only so we could find enemy spies among my dolls and stuffed animals. Along the way, Tim, who hunted when he could get away from the city, taught me a lot about tracking.

When the other guards saw how much fun Tim had playing with me, they suddenly decided Tim should spend more time guarding. He had no choice but to accept their orders, but I didn't. Mom said I screamed so loudly that she heard me in the throne room. She had to excuse herself from official kingdom business, hurry to the nursery, and give me a stern lecture about proper princess behavior. But she also made Tim my permanent playmate among the guards.

"Thanks, Tim," I whispered after I exited the bushes. "I can't wait to tell you all about this when I get home again."

If I get home.

I suddenly remembered something Tim told me during our games. "You always lose when you give up, Your Highness."

I pushed aside my negative thoughts and set off across a large, overgrown field on the edge of town. I saw a dozen houses, but the closest was two hundred meters away. Someone in a house might see me, but I was too far away for them to make out details beyond my blue pants, brown and white checkered shirt, and dark hair. Even in a small town like this one, I figured dozens of girls would fit that description.

I kept my pace purposeful, neither too fast nor too slow. Just a steady, suspicion-allaying walk that any local girl might use. I hoped. A road ran along the field's other side, and I turned right and walked alongside it. Again, hoping no one would give me a second glance, much less ask for the life story I concocted while crossing the field.

Ahead of me, a car turned onto the road and drove my way. It had no official markings on it and had a coat of bright red paint. I glanced at the car, pretended nonchalance, and looked back at the road. When the car slowed as it drew nearer, I gave it a longer look. A boy about my age drove the car, and a similar-aged boy rode with him. They grinned as they eyed me.

I'd worn the same clothes for two days—days spent hiking up and down hills and through the forest, sleeping on the ground, and not bathing. I hadn't even dragged a brush through my hair since after my bath at Mr. Gibson's. Was dirty and disheveled a look boys liked?

The car stopped next to me, a window next to the driver descended, and the boy leaned through it. "Hi there. Did the fall hurt?"

A fall sounded like a good explanation for the way I looked. So I said, "Not much. I'm fine."

Confusion crossed the boy's face. His friend laughed, mimed pushing a button, and said, "Bahnt! You lose, Jace."

"Ignore him," Jace said to me. "I'm just worried about you. Falling from heaven, like that."

My heart leapt. How did Jace know I'd come from space?

My expression must have shown something to Jace, because he added, "You know, because you look like an angel?"

Jace's friend said, "Not the sharpest knife in the drawer, is she?"

I felt my expression clear as I realized what was going on. The boy was trying a... what was it Dad called it when he talked to me about boys? A pickup line.

A bad pickup line.

I shook my head in disgust and resumed walking. But Jace wasn't ready to give up, because he drove the car backwards to stay even with me. "Hey, wait a minute. I still want to talk."

I drew from all the life smart people I knew from the palace and said, "God gonna git ya if'n ya don't shut it."

Jace screwed his face up in obvious confusion. "Huh? What are you talking about?"

"God don't be likin' it none if'n ya go messin' wit one a he angels," I drawled. "He git ya fer it, right sure."

Jace's friend laughed. "Maybe she's not as stupid as I thought."

"Look, girl," Jace snapped, "I don't know who you think you are, but—"

The passenger glanced out the car's front window, his eyes widened, and he poked Jace. "Better leave her alone, Jace. We've got company."

I looked over my shoulder and cursed my luck. A patrol car, just like the one that took Laney home, drove our way. The car gave a sharp, short wail and the lights on its roof flashed once.

Jace muttered words a princess shouldn't use and stopped his car. Since there's nothing more suspicious than running from the authorities, I stopped walking.

The patrol car stopped in front of Jace's car. Two uniformed men got out and strode our way.

The officer driving the car looked about the same age as my favorite guard, Tim. Mid-thirties, but with a world weariness Tim never had, dragging his face and shoulders down.

The other officer had to be at least ten years older than Dad. He hitched his belt up over his protruding belly. A futile gesture, since the belt slid down as soon as he released it. The older officer ignored the belt as he swaggered our way, his eyes locked on the boy driving the red car.

"Look at who we have here, Harry," the man said.

In a toneless voice, Harry said, "I see him, Sheriff."

"Ja-a-a-a-ace Walker," the Sheriff said.

I knew nothing about the history between Jace and the Sheriff, but the way the Sheriff drew out Jace's name didn't bode well for the boy. Maybe Jace had truly earned the Sheriff's enmity, but I wanted to keep a low profile. The attention from Jace and his buddy already put that in jeopardy. Official attention would raise my profile way higher than I wanted.

With a mental start, I remembered the comm in my pocket. I couldn't imagine how much more attention I'd draw if someone found me carrying an alien device. I could *try* claiming I found it hiking through the hills. But I felt sure I'd have to explain that the military officer in command of the soldiers searching the hills for amies. And he was the last person I wanted to talk to.

I stuffed my hands into my pockets and wrapped my right hand around the comm. With the officers watching the boys, and the boys watching the officers, maybe I could drop the comm in the field grass at the edge of the road. Then I could return for it later. I hoped.

I slowly pulled my hands from my pockets, but the Sheriff chose that moment to point at me. I jammed my hands back into the pockets as four pairs of eyes swung my way.

"How many times have I told you not to bug girls?" the Sheriff asked.

"I was just talking to her, Sheriff Clark," Jace said.

I had a glimmer of hope I could wriggle free from both Jace and the Sheriff. "Ayup, Sher'f. Me an' Jacy boy been jawin' 'bout reeligion."

Sheriff Clark raised both eyebrows, and he looked back at Jace. "Shoot, boy, are you still trying that stupid angel-fell-from-heaven line?" He laughed, which made his jowls and belly jiggle. "Has any girl ever fallen for that?"

With the attention back on Jace, I pulled my hands from my pockets and put them behind my back. Afraid the men and boys would turn their attention back to me when I dropped the comm, and they'd see it fall, I did something I'd sworn I would never do. I drew on what my maid back home called 'feminine wiles,' and pulled my shoulders back.

Jace said, "Not yet, Sheriff, but it only takes one."

I gave the comm a gentle toss, to make sure it landed away from the road. That's when Jace cut his eyes back at me. As the comm left my hand, the other three followed Jace's lead. I held my breath and waited for one of them to ask what I'd just dropped. But my maid hadn't steered me wrong.

Four pairs of eyes stared at my chest.

I heard the soft thud of the comm landing in the grass, pulled my hands from behind my back, crossed my arms, and glared at the men and boys. "Whacha'll starin' at?"

The two officers and the boy with Jace quickly averted their eyes. All three muttered, "Nothing."

Jace let his eyes linger, an intent expression on his face. Considering where he was staring, I hoped I'd never find myself alone with him. And I wondered if Jace was the boy Laney talked about two nights ago. The one who wouldn't take 'no' for an answer.

Sheriff Clark's expression darkened as he watched Jace eying my chest. "Eyes on me, boy!"

Jace turned his head back to the Sheriff, but he kept his eyes on me as long as possible. As his face turned to the Sheriff, Jace pasted an earnest expression on his face. Just like the one he wore when the officers first arrived. "Yes, sir, Sheriff Clark."

"Hey, Harry," Sheriff Clark said, "those army boys said we had to check everyone's papers, right?"

"They did, Sheriff," Harry replied.

The Sheriff flashed a smile at the boys. A smile that never reached his eyes. "Show us your papers, boys."

The other boy—I still didn't know his name—looked at Jace. Jace glowered at the officers. "Why do we have to show our papers? You know who we are."

The Sheriff's smile widened. "For all I know, you're an amy in disguise."

"That's the stupidest thing I've ever heard," Jace spat.

"Rules are rules," Sheriff Clark said. He held out his right hand. "Hand over your papers. Now."

"I... I don't have mine," the other boy said.

"Me neither," Jace said. He reached for his car's door. "We'll go get them and bring them straight to the station."

Sheriff Clark shook his head. "Sorry, boys, but it's like I said. Rules are rules. If you don't have your papers, I'll have to take you down to the station. But don't worry, I'll call your parents and let them know where you are."

A hangdog expression settled over the nameless boy, but Jace's face paled. I had the feeling Jace's home life wasn't good. But, after the way he looked at me, I couldn't find much sympathy for him.

Sheriff Clark took Jace by the arm, and Harry did the same with the nameless boy. As the Sheriff pushed Jace into the backseat of the patrol car, Jace looked at me and said, "What about *her*? You didn't check *her* papers."

Sheriff Clark didn't even look my way. "She wasn't bothering anyone."

Jace mimicked the Sheriff. "Rules are rules."

The Sheriff's face reddened, but he sighed and turned to me. "I'm sorry, miss, but I need to see your papers, too."

A HIT WITH THE LOCALS

Sheriff Clark ventured a kind smile as he extended his hand. "Don't worry, miss, you're not in any trouble. After that amy ship landed in the hills, the army put us under martial law until they catch the invaders. It's for our safety, after all."

I widened my eyes and whipped my head around wildly, as if searching for threats. "Amies? Where they be?"

Sheriff Clark made a placating gesture with his hands. "There's nothing to worry about, miss. The army has everything under control. Just show me your papers, and you go on about your business." He looked over his shoulder at Jace and his friend. "Without worrying about these boys bothering you."

"Ain't go no bizniss, Sher'f. I's jes lookin' fer my fren, Laney."

"Laney Gibson?" Sheriff Clark asked.

"Ayup."

"Her folks' house isn't far." Sheriff Clark nodded to his deputy. "I'll have Harry drop you off when we're done here."

I glared at Jace. "Nup. Don' wanna be in no car wit' Jacy boy."

"You show more wisdom than many of the local girls," Sheriff Clark said. "But you won't have to ride with him. Harry's going to drive Jacy boy's car back to the station, while I drive the patrol car. Harry will give you the ride."

I went to the open driver's door, climbed in, and scooted across to the passenger side. "That be right nice o' ya, Sher'f. Thankee!"

Sheriff Clark and Harry exchanged glances. Harry shrugged and walked towards the driver's side of the car. I held my breath, praying the Sheriff was as willing to play along as his deputy.

And he was.

Sheriff Clark lowered the hand he'd extended for my papers. "Harry? Walk that girl to the door, and make sure she's safe with the Gibsons. Then come on down to the station."

Harry nodded. "Sure will, Sheriff."

As the Sheriff ambled towards the driver's side of the patrol car, I began breathing again.

Too early.

Jace squawked in protest. "That's not fair, Sheriff Clark!"

The Sheriff glared at him and kept walking. "Shut up, Jacy boy."

Jace ignored him. "Rules are rules, Sheriff. You said it yourself."

"I know what I said, boy."

Most people would have caught the hard edge in the Sheriff's voice and dropped the subject. Jace wasn't most people.

"I guess I'm just going to have to tell those soldiers that you've been hassling people like me. People you've known their entire life. And that you've let people no one has ever seen before just walk away."

Sheriff Clark tilted his head back, as if asking heaven for patience. But when he lowered his head, Sheriff Clark came around to the passenger side of the car. He flashed his friendly smile again. "I'm sorry, miss, but I'm going to have to check your papers." His eyes cut to the patrol car. "It's the only way I'll get any peace and quiet during the drive to the station."

I screwed my face up in feigned confusion. "Wut's papers?"

"Identification papers, miss." Sheriff Clark leaned against the door, peering at me through the car's open window. "Your parents would have gotten them from the hospital when you were born."

"Weren't born in no hospital, Sher'f."

Sheriff Clark's smile faded. "Then they'd have gotten papers from the doctor who delivered you."

"Weren't no doc, neither. Pa say he deelivered me, heself."

Sheriff Clark's brows drew down. "Then they'd have gotten your papers the first time they took you into a town."

"Ain't never been ta no town, afore, Sher'f."

"Miss, are you telling me you don't have any papers?"

"Ain't never needed none. Don' rightly see why's I need 'em now, neither. I done told ya who I is."

"It's the law, miss." Sheriff Clark's fatherly manner vanished, replaced by his official one. "What's your name?"

There was no reason to complicate matters. "Anne."

"Last name?"

"Villas."

Sheriff Clark eyed me. "That's not a typical family name around here."

I didn't know what to say to that, so I remained silent.

Sheriff Clark pulled a notebook from his pocket, flipped it open, and scribbled in it. "Villas. How do you spell that, Anne?"

I could spell my name in a dozen languages, but not the one they spoke here. That's a big problem with my implant's translation routine. It translated the local *spoken* language. I'd have to learn the local *written* language the old-fashioned way. So I shrugged. "Ain't never spelt it, afore, Sher'f."

Sheriff Clark's eyes widened. In a kindly tone, he asked, "Anne, are you illiterate?"

I played the uneducated hill hick to the hilt. "Nup, Sher'f. I jes cain't read."

"I see." He scribbled a bit more in his notebook. "Anne, I'm going to have a few choice words for your father when I see him."

That was my cue to add to my backstory. I leaned towards the Sheriff. "You knows where my pa be?"

The fatherly expression returned to Sheriff Clark's face. "I don't, Miss Villas. Do I take it your father is missing?"

I reached into my memory for the fear I'd felt as the leaking lifepod limped its way towards Refuge, and let it settle over my face. "Ayup. I ain't seed him fer a couple'a days."

Sheriff Clark gave a sympathetic nod. "So, last Tuesday?"

I had no idea what the day of the week was and wasn't about to agree with the Sheriff. I didn't *think* he was trying to trip me up, but I shrugged. "Don' need no day names up to the hills, Sher'f. Days don' matter none, less'n it be rainin' or sump'em."

Sheriff Clark sighed. "I see. And you came here because...?"

"Pa always said I gotta hightail it to Laney's grandpa's place, if'n he don' come back. So's I done that, 'cept there weren't nobody at he house. An' all he horses be gone. I figgered he done come here, ta Laney's folks' place. So's I lit out after 'im. It be scurry in them hills, Sher'f. Lotsa strange folk and loud machines." I caught Sheriff Clark by the arm. "I's afeared sump'em bad done happened to pa. But if'n there be anyone whut can find 'im, it be Laney's grandpa. He know them hills real good."

Sheriff Clark patted my hand. "Don't you worry, Miss Villas. Those strange folk you saw are soldiers. They're already searching the hills, so they're bound to find your pa."

"I hopes you's right, Sher'f." I dropped my forehead onto my arm, trapping the Sheriff's patting hand between my arm and my forehead. "I jes wanna yap some wit Laney. She know how ta say stuff wut make me feel gooder, ya know?"

"Friends are like that." Sheriff Clark gently pulled his hand from under my forehead, gave my head an awkward pat, and remained silent long enough that I felt sure he was considering telling Harry to take me to the Gibsons. But then he said, "I promise I'll call the Gibsons as soon as we get to the station, Miss Villas."

He returned to the patrol car and drove around us. Harry turned Jace's car around and followed the patrol car, taking me to the last place I wanted to go.

The drive to the station took ten minutes, and I felt as if my trepidation doubled with every passing minute. I believed the Sheriff would hold to his word and call the Gibsons. And I knew Mr. Gibson would come straight to the station and do everything in his power to convince the Sheriff to release me. Assuming the army commander—the last person in town I wanted to see—let him.

I wasn't afraid of talking to the commander. If I stuck to my back country accent and kept up my role as a daughter worried about her missing father, I thought I could fool a busy military man. I knew most of the top brass at home, and they're some of the most focused people I'd ever met. Many of the Academy instructors are the same way. Which means they don't have time for nonsense. All I had to do was convince the commander that I couldn't help him find the missing amies.

And do it without telling any convoluted lies.

It's not that I worried about keeping my story straight. Successful lying is all about not contradicting yourself, and not over embellishing your story. Bad liars get so wrapped up in selling their lies, they end up doing the exact opposite. A good memory helps, and I have one. Add my implant to the mix, and I wouldn't have trouble keeping track of my story.

But Mr. Gibson was a different matter. He showed plenty of quick wits and guile when the soldiers searched his barn, looking for Chris and me. But he knew *nothing* about the story I'd spun, especially the bit where Laney and I were good friends. I knew Mr. Gibson would get as much of my story from the Sheriff as he could, and he'd be subtle about it. But the Sheriff wasn't a fool. And the military commander? If he was any good at his job, he'd be watching for just that kind of probing.

I'd have to watch for a chance to tell Mr. Gibson the bare basics of my story. If I got lucky, I'd get the chance for an emotional scene with him. A long, tearful hug from a scared hill girl would be perfect. But who knew what options I'd get?

The car door opened, yanking me away from my musings. Deputy Harry said, "We're at the station, Miss Villas."

My face must have telegraphed my fears, because the previously stoical deputy's lips turned up in a slight smile. "There's no need to be nervous, miss. The major coordinating the search in the hills looks intimidating, but that's because he's got an important job. Just stick to the truth when you answer his questions. Don't waste his time, and everything will be fine."

I jerked a nod and glanced around as Harry led me into the station. Our arrival attracted a lot of attention from townspeople. They gathered in clumps, pointed, and talked. Knowing nods followed whenever someone pointed at Jace. Intrigued expressions accompanied points my way. I guess strangers weren't too common in this town. *This town whose name I didn't know.*

I'd blamed an isolated upbringing for my ignorance, but that wouldn't explain why I didn't know the town's name. If Laney and I had been friends for years, she was bound to have mentioned the town's name multiple times. She lived here, for God's sake. Not knowing the town's name would make anyone suspicious, but especially an army major looking for people who just arrived on the planet.

I looked around and saw writing on the station door. "Deputy Harry, sir?"

He glanced over his shoulder. "Hm?"

I pointed at the door. "The writin' on the doe? Wut it say?"

"Burson Sheriff Department." In a curious tone, he asked, "Why?"

"I cain't read none. I figger if'n I git folks ta read stuff fer me, an' if'n I pays attenshun when they does, mebbe I can learn me ta read."

"I see..." Harry opened the station door and held it for me. "I hope that works for you."

When I entered, the Sheriff pointed at three unpadded chairs off to one side of the office. Jace and the unnamed boy took the two on the ends, leaving me the middle chair. I slowed a bit, which the Sheriff noticed and said, "I'm not sticking this girl between you two boys. One of you move to the middle seat."

The Sheriff turned his attention to a device on his desk and lifted a piece that wrapped from his ear to his mouth. So he didn't see Jace rise, move to the middle, grin at me, and pat the empty seat with his left hand. But Harry saw.

"Don't worry, Miss Villas," Harry said, "I'll keep an eye on him."

I settled into the chair and pointedly ignored Jace. He didn't ignore me. But with Harry watching from across the office, Jace kept his hands to himself.

The Sheriff put down the piece he'd held and looked at Jace. "I just spoke to your father, Jacy boy. He'll come right down here with your papers." The Sheriff picked up the piece again. "Oh, and he did not sound happy with you."

Jace froze in his seat, but his body vibrated with nervous energy. The same sort of energy that coursed through my body during the ride to this station. Was Jace that afraid of his father?

"Miss Villas," Sheriff Clark said, "I'm calling the Gibsons now."

He spun a dial on the device several times, held the other piece of it to his ear and mouth, and waited. A few seconds later, he said, "Hello Rebecca, this is Sheriff Clark... Good afternoon to you, too. I'm calling because we picked up an unknown girl in town, and she says she's friends with Laney." Sheriff Clark listened for a moment, glanced my way, and offered an encouraging smile. "Yes, her name is Anne... Yes, she's a remarkably pretty girl, if a bit dirty at the moment... You will? Great... Goodbye."

"The Gibsons will be here in a few minutes, Anne," Sheriff Clark said, "though you'll still have to talk to that army major before I can release you."

I didn't have to fake disappointment. "Oh. Um, okay."

Worse, I felt nervous energy humming through my body. It almost felt as if Jace and I were vibrating at the same frequency. I glanced at him, and found him staring at me, his eyes wide in... something. Kinship? Nervousness? Fear? All three? Who knew? Not me, and I felt the same way Jace did.

We stared at each other in shared misery, for God only knows how long. Then the station door flew open and two men walked in. One had to be the major. The air practically crackled with his intensity. The major spoke to the Sheriff, turned his hard stare my way, turned back to the Sheriff and pointed at what I assumed was an interrogation room along the back wall. Sheriff Clark nodded, and the two army officers marched to the room.

The station door flew open again. A large man with an unpleasant expression stomped in. I felt Jace jump at the sight of the man. His father, obviously.

Right behind Jace's father came the whole Gibson family. I recognized old Mr. Gibson, Laney, and Logan. The other man and woman with them could only be Laney's and Logan's parents. The adults followed Jace's father to the Sheriff's desk. Laney gave a happy squeal when she saw me, and she and Logan headed my way.

The major spun, pointed at me, and barked, "Do not approach the suspect until I speak with her."

Laney's eyes widened at the order, but she and her brother obeyed it.

Jace's father tossed something on Sheriff Clark's desk. In a snarling tone, he said, "There are Jace's papers. Look them over while I speak with my boy."

Sheriff Clark looked at the major, but he apparently had no objections to Jace's father coming over to us. The Sheriff turned his attention to the Gibsons, and that discussion drew Laney and Logan to the desk, too.

Jace's father stalked towards us, and his face darkened with each step. The still unnamed boy leaned as far from Jace as possible. All the pent up energy flowed out of Jace, replaced by a sense of resignation. As Jace rose to his feet, his father cast a furtive look around the station. When he saw no one else was paying any attention to him, a terribly satisfied smile further darkened his face.

I watched the man ball his right hand into a fist and cock it at his side. Surely the man wasn't about to hit Jace in the middle of a busy sheriff's station? But his expression said he was. Worse, it said he was sure he would get away with it.

Before I realized what I was doing, I issued a command to my implant.

Boost!

Adrenaline flooded my body. Fear muted the accompanying euphoria of Boost, but I didn't let it stop me. With a savage smirk, Jace's father unleashed his fist, aiming for Jace's gut.

With Boosted speed, I surged from my seat and slid between Jace and his father. The punch meant for Jace caught me in the side and sent me flying backwards into the wall.

I crashed into the wall, and only my Boost-enhanced reflexes saved me from serious harm. I cushioned my head by shoving my right hand between my head and the wall. My hand felt as if I'd caught it in a closing hatch, but it probably saved me from a concussion. And I got a glimpse of the station after I bounced off the wall.

Jace wore the expression of a man given a last-minute reprieve.

Dawning horror registered on his father's face, as the man realized his colossal mistake.

Fear shone from the women's faces, especially Laney's and her mother's.

Red rage ignited on the men's faces, and Logan took his first step towards Jace's father.

The last thing I saw before I crashed onto the floor was the major just turning his head my way.

I slammed into the unyielding floor, wrapped my arms around my head, pulled my knees up, and rolled as best I could. I ended up sliding a couple of meters on my elbows and knees. My borrowed clothes ripped under the strain, and so did the skin underneath. The scrapes joined my body's pain chorus, led by my throbbing hand and ringing head. And Boost made it all worse, as my accelerated mind registered every hurt. I dropped Boost when I finally slid to a stop, and then let myself topple onto my side.

A second later, Jace's father crashed to the floor under the weight of Logan and Logan's father. They ground the man's face into the floor and locked his arms behind his back. Pain replaced shocked disbelief on Jace's father's face, but I had no sympathy for the man. He was just lucky *my* father wasn't here.

Then Laney and Mr. Gibson dropped to their knees next to me, blocking my view of the big bully. And I had the golden opportunity I'd wanted so badly that my subconscious mind came up with a painful plan to make it happen.

"Anne?" Tears and terror reflected in Laney's eyes. "Please be okay!"

Mr. Gibson's muscular arms slid under me and lifted me from the floor.

I gave an exaggerated gasp, the kind you make when you have the breath knocked out of you, and doubled up. Which brought my lips close to their ears.

In a low tone, I said, "We've been friends since you were five." I gave another great gasp. "Found you when you got lost in the forest." Gasp. "Only see you when you visit your grandfather." Cough. "Never been to town. Paranoid father didn't want you talking about us in town." Wheeze. "You've never been to my home." Gasp. "I have a hill accent, and I'm illiterate."

"Got it," Laney whispered.

Mr. Gibson gave a quick nod and then rose to his feet.

Laney rose with him and quickly checked my elbows. Her mother reached us and tsked as she examined my knees.

Laney mother shook her head and turned her gaze on Sheriff Clark, who was helping Logan and his father yank Jace's father to his feet. She said, "Her knees are all scraped up and filled with dirt. Goodness, Sheriff, do you *ever* sweep the floor?"

Sheriff Clark made a placating gesture with his hands. "Now Rebecca—"

"Don't you *now Rebecca* me, Sheriff! Not only did poor Anne get attacked right here in the front office of *your* station, I've got to take her to a doctor right away to make sure she doesn't get an infection."

That was my cue to let the rest of the Gibson family learn about my accent. "Nup. Don' wanna see no doc. Pa say he don' trust 'em."

I prayed Rebecca Gibson was as quick on the uptake as her daughter and father-in-law. She eyed me for a second, patted my shoulder, and said, "You've known me for a long time, Anne. Do you think I'd ever let you come to harm?"

"Um, nup, I s'pose not."

Mr. Gibson took the matter as settled and started for the door. I waggled my fingers as we passed Jace's father. Mr. Gibson glared at the big man and said, "I have never seen a lower, more cowardly act in my life. You're a pathetic excuse for a man."

Anger flared to life behind Jace's father's sullen expression. "I wasn't aiming to hit *her*. She just got in the way."

"Sheriff Clark?" Mr. Gibson said. "Considering what he just said, I suggest you have the doctor examine his son. I'll bet everything I own that the doctor will find evidence of abuse hidden beneath that boy's clothing."

Sheriff Clark nodded. "I had the same idea, Elias. Leave that to me. You go get that little girl checked out."

"Not so fast, Sheriff." The major's voice cut through the babbling voices with ease. "I haven't questioned her yet."

"The girl needs medical attention," Sheriff Clark said.

"A few minutes' delay won't hurt her," the major snapped.

In a tone that sounded mild but wasn't, Mr. Gibson said, "That's an unkind position to take. We can bring her back here after the doctor treats her."

The major shook his head. "No."

"What's the big deal?" Laney asked. "Do you think she's an amy or something?"

"She has no identification papers," the major said. "Did you know that?"

"No," Laney said, "but I'm not surprised, considering the way her father acted."

"How did he act?"

"Paranoid," Mr. Gibson said. "I knew the man for years, and still don't know exactly where he and Anne lived."

That was a fresh addition to my story, but I liked it. "Yup. Pa don' want nobody knowin' zactly where our place be."

"I still don't see what the big deal is," Laney said. "You already know Anne isn't one of the amies you're looking for."

The major glared at Laney. "And how do I know that?"

"That amy ship landed on, what, Monday or Tuesday?" Laney waited for an acknowledgment from the major. When he didn't give one, she continued, "Anne and I have been friends since I was five. Unless the amies on the ship discovered time travel *and* brought a little girl with them, there's no way Anne can be one of them."

"That's enough, Laney," her father said. He stepped between his daughter and the major. "I apologize for my daughter's lack of respect, Major...?"

The major paused, as if his name was some kind of military secret, then said, "Higgins."

"Major Higgins," Laney's father said. "But my family has known Anne for thirteen years. We'll all happily provide statements to that effect, if you wish."

Major Higgins stared at us for a long moment, then gave a dismissive wave. "Go on."

"Thank you," both Mr. Gibsons said.

As the family turned towards the station door, I added one last comment to cement our story. "Mr. Major, sir? Ya gonna watch fer my pa, ain't ya?"

"Yes, we will," Higgins said.

"That be good," I said. "Jes don' shoot 'im if'n he run from ya. He be afeared o' mos' people."

If I'd had a lost, paranoid father, Major Higgin's expression would have worried me. But he just nodded and turned away.

Old Mr. Gibson carried me out to the car and deposited me in the back seat. Laney's father, whom I decided to call Young Mr. Gibson, took the driver's seat. Laney and Logan joined me in the back seat, while the adults squeezed into the front seat. Then we drove away from the Sheriff's station.

I OWE YOU

Mrs. Gibson looked at me over her shoulder. "It's not far to the doctor, dear. He'll have you right as rain in no time."

An infection didn't worry me—my Scout implant could handle first aid from its store of simple medications—but Mrs. Gibson told the Sheriff she was taking me to a doctor. I thought it was better to stick to her plan. If the major checked up on my movements, it would help allay suspicions.

I smiled and nodded to Mrs. Gibson. "Tha's right kind o' ya, Miz Gibson."

"There's no one listening in, Anne," Laney said. "You can drop the hick accent."

"Nup. Not whiles we wher other folks what ain't yer reelations can see me."

Old Mr. Gibson gave a quick nod. "You're a smart girl, Anne."

Logan looked at my skinned knees. "I still can't believe your bad luck back there."

"Whut bad luck?" I asked.

"You standing up just as Jace's jerk father tried to hit him."

"Weren't luck. I jumped twixt 'em on purpose."

Laney gasped. "Why on Refuge would you do something stupid like that?"

I looked out both sides of the car, assured myself no one outside was paying any attention to us, and dropped the rural accent. "Jace's expression told me he'd take the punch without protest. That he was expecting it. And that told me his father hit him a lot." I sighed. "No one deserves that kind of treatment."

Logan's eyes widened. "You did it to protect *Jace?*"

"It also gave Laney and your grandfather a reason to run to me, so I could whisper my story to them."

A dubious expression settled over Laney's face. "And you figured all of that out in a split second?"

"No." I shrugged. "I just acted on instinct."

The car pulled into the driveway of a small house. Mrs. Gibson said, "Laney and I will take Anne inside. You men stay out here with the car."

"At least let me carry the girl inside," Old Mr. Gibson said.

I adopted the accent again. "Nup. I can walk."

"Don't worry," Laney said. "Mom and I will lend a shoulder if she needs one."

I didn't need their help, but walking hurt a lot more than I thought it would. A receptionist looked up from a desk in the waiting room and flashed a sympathetic smile. "Sheriff Clark called and told us you were on your way." She stood and opened a door behind her. "Dr. Parker is ready for you."

The doctor went about his work quickly and efficiently, but he also had a grandfatherly air about him. Whenever I hissed in pain, he turned on a sympathetic smile that took some of the sting from his antiseptic. After he finished my knees and elbows, he spent another five minutes poking and prodding the side where the punch landed.

"You're going to have a sizable bruise soon, Anne, and it will stay tender for a few days." Dr. Parker turned to Mrs. Gibson. "She'll be fine after some rest." He put some bandages and antiseptic cream into a small bag. "Have her take a bath first thing. Spread some of the cream on her scrapes and then bandage them."

Mrs. Gibson accepted the bag with a nod, and Dr. Parker walked us out to the waiting room. With a grin, he offered Laney and me lollipops. "For being such good girls."

We returned his grin, and each grabbed a lollipop. With a sigh, Mrs.

Gibson took one, too. "For Logan. We'll never hear the end of it if Laney gets something, and he doesn't."

The house door opened behind us. We turned as Deputy Harry escorted a glaring Jace into the waiting room. "Morning, Doc. This is the other patient Sheriff Clark mentioned in his call."

All joviality fled from Dr. Parker's expression. In a gentle tone, he said, "Of course. Come this way, lad."

Jace's hardened exterior faltered at the doctor's display of kindness. With a sideways glance at us, Jace entered the examination room.

Harry nodded to us as we left, and said, "I hope those scrapes heal soon, Anne."

We all piled into the Gibsons' car, and Young Mr. Gibson drove us to their house. I'd expected something like the row houses that are springing up on Aashla, for people working in the factories and mills opening all over the planet. But the Gibsons' house was big, rambling, and well away from downtown. It even had a large, fenced meadow in back, where Old Mr. Gibson's horses grazed.

Mrs. Gibson and Laney hustled me upstairs and into a bath. The water stung my scrapes, so I skipped soaking and went straight to washing my hair. Then I scrubbed myself clean from head to toe, taking care around my scrapes. By the time I got out, Laney had fresh clothes selected from her small wardrobe. Mrs. Gibson gently smeared cream on the scrapes, bandaged them, and then helped me get dressed.

"Now you should rest, Anne," Mrs. Gibson said. "It's the doctor's orders, after all."

"I really wish I could, ma'am. But I need to go back to where the Sheriff picked me up. I dropped my comm there to keep anyone from finding it."

"What's a comm?" Mrs. Gibson asked.

"A communications device. I need to use it to let Chris know I'm okay."

"Chris is the other girl?" Mrs. Gibson asked.

I nodded. "She's probably worried that she hasn't heard from me yet."

"You really do need rest," Mrs. Gibson said.

"Logan and I can go look for it," Laney said. "Anne, can you describe the comm and where you were when you dropped it?"

"That's a splendid idea," Mrs. Gibson said.

I wanted to help look for the comm. But Mrs. Gibson was right about the rest. I wasn't as exhausted as when I carried Chris up and down hills, but Boosting and getting punched took a lot out of me. I described the location and the device as best I could. Then I stretched out on Laney's bed and fell asleep.

I awakened slowly, unwillingly pulled from my quickly forgotten dreams into grudging wakefulness. I kept my eyes closed, clinging to the hope I could slip beneath consciousness again, and rediscover my lost dreams. But then a door slammed. My brain jolted awake. I opened my eyes, and I felt a brief pang of disorientation as the room came into focus.

A girl's voice called, "We're back. Is Anne awake, yet?"

Laney. My new friend. This was her room. I wore her clothes. Chris and I were stranded on her planet.

In a lower tone, a woman—Mrs. Gibson—said, "She will be, if you keep shouting like that, Laney."

Laney lowered her volume and said, "Sorry!"

I swung my feet off the bed, stood up, and called, "It's okay. I was already awake."

It wasn't exactly a lie. Besides, if Laney and Logan were back with my comm, I needed to be up. I headed downstairs.

Laney and Logan waited for me at the foot of the stairs. Their faces gave away their news before Logan said, "I'm sorry, Anne. We couldn't find your comm thing."

"It's okay." It wasn't even remotely okay—God only knew what would happen if someone else found it and turned it over to the major—but that wasn't Laney's and Logan's fault. Mom taught me how to keep my feelings out of my expression—a vital skill during diplomatic negotiations—and it served me well now. "I probably just did a poor job describing where to look."

Laney appeared doubtful. "Maybe..."

I flashed a smile filled with confidence I didn't feel. "Now that I'm awake, we can just go back there and look again."

"Not a good idea," Logan said. "Curfew takes effect at dark, and that's in about an hour."

"Then I'll just take a chameleon cloth and..." I smacked my forehead. "Chris has all the chameleon cloths. She must be worried sick about me, too."

Old Mr. Gibson poked his head into the entry hall. "You kids come to the den, and we'll discuss this."

I shook my head. "If there's a curfew, I need—"

"You need to stop and think, Anne," Mr. Gibson said. "Stop *reacting* and start acting."

I followed him, Laney, and Logan into the den. "Chris and I haven't had time for anything else, sir."

In a gentle voice, Old Mr. Gibson said, "I know you haven't. But the army, or somebody else from the government, will capture you eventually, if you keep letting them make the first move."

I dropped into a seat, let my head flop back, and stared at the ceiling. "You're right, sir, but I don't even know where to start."

"The first thing you do is figure out what you want," Old Mr. Gibson said. "You can't make plans if you don't know what you're planning for."

I stared at the ceiling and tried to figure out what I wanted to do. Finally, I said, "I want to go home."

"That's a good start, dear," Mrs. Gibson said. "What do you need to get home?"

"A spaceship."

"Will your people send one to find you and Chris?" she asked.

"If they figure out what happened to us, they will." I thought for a second, and added, "Even if they don't, Dad won't rest until he either finds me or my body."

"If we have anything to say about it, he's going to find *you*," Logan said.

"That's right, lad," Old Mr. Gibson said. "Let's assume someone will come looking for you. Can you contact the ship with that comm thing Laney and Logan couldn't find?"

I shook my head. "That's just for short range communications. A few kilometers, at most."

"So, you'll need a big radio?"

"Yes."

Young Mr. Gibson grimaced. "The government owns all the big ones. And they're *very* big. Too big to just grab and sneak off with."

I remembered the radio the soldiers set up in the meadow while Chris and I hid nearby. "The soldiers had one they were using to coordinate the search for us. Could that work?"

"Maybe," Young Mr. Gibson said, "but that spaceship would have to be in orbit right over your head. I think we'll need one used for satellite communications."

"You have satellites?" I asked.

"Yes," he replied. "Didn't you notice them when you approached Refuge in your spaceship?"

"It was just a lifepod," I said, "and Chris and I were too busy to pay attention to sensor readings."

"Doing what?" Laney asked. "And what are sensor readings?"

Several sharp raps on the front door interrupted our discussion. The three adults exchanged concerned glances, and then Young Mr. Gibson rose and headed for the door.

I shifted mental gears. "Laney, girl, I don' know whutcha yappin' on 'bout."

Laney and Logan stared at me in surprise. The front door opened, and I watched dawning comprehension spread over the youngest Gibsons' faces when I said, "Ya'll spectin' people 'r sumptin?"

Laney cast a wary glance at the hallway to the front door. "Not that I know of, Anne."

As a pair of footsteps came down the hall, I said, "Mebbe them soljer boys done come fer me?"

Young Mr. Gibson entered the room. "Not soldiers, Anne. But someone even less expected."

Jace, his hands jammed into his jacket's pockets, followed Laney's father into the room. His eyes darted nervously around the room before stopping on me.

I cocked my head to the right. "Whayul, you's right 'bout that, Mr. Gibson. I weren't 'specting ol' Jacy boy!"

"You can drop the accent," Jace said. "I know it's an act."

I forced a confused expression onto my face. "Don' know whut you—"

Jace shoved his hands so deep into the jacket pockets, I thought he might tear them. "I overheard you whispering to Laney and her grandpa, right after my old man slugged you."

I thought about keeping up the pretense, but decided against it. "You have surprisingly good hearing, Jace."

"You would, too, if your old man liked sneaking up on you and punching you in the back of your head."

Mrs. Gibson's eyes widened. "Dear Lord."

"I've got good peripheral vision, for the same reason," Jace said. "That's why I stared at your chest for so long, when the Sheriff picked us up." His eyes darted back to my chest. "*Mostly* why."

I crossed my arms over my chest again. I thought I knew the answer to my next question, but I asked it anyway. "And why do you think that matters to me?"

"I think you didn't want anyone finding this." Jace pulled his right hand from the pocket and opened his fist. My comm rested on his palm. He gave it a little toss, caught it, closed his fist over it, and said, "Because you're an amy."

Laney and Logan gasped at Jace's claim. I'd expected it the moment he pulled my comm from his pocket. From the adult Gibsons' faces, I don't think Jace's words surprised them, either.

I called on all of Mom's training, kept my face expressionless and my voice level. "No, Jace, I'm not an amy."

"Yeah, right." Sarcasm filled Jace's voice. He held the comm closer to his eye and examined it with great care. "I suppose you *could* be a spy from Plausen, using super spy toys while contacting a family of sleep agents."

Old Mr. Gibson stood, his face reddening. "Now see here, boy, I fought—"

I looked at Old Mr. Gibson and raised a hand. "I don't think Jace believes that accusation."

"No, I just made it to watch your reaction," Jace said. "You didn't even flinch when I mentioned Plausen."

I shrugged. "I assume Plausen is an enemy country. But I'm only guessing based on what you've said."

"*Everyone* on this planet knows about Plausen."

I raised an eyebrow. "I never said I was from this planet."

Jace's brows drew down. "But... you just said you're not an amy."

"Because I'm not an amy, either."

Jace's face reddened. "Look, you're either from Refuge or you're an amy."

I shook my head. "From what Laney told me, 'amy' is slang for an AI minion. I don't serve an AI. So I'm not from Refuge, *and* I'm not an amy."

Jace considered that for a moment. "When the deputy took me to Dr. Parker, he took all sorts of X-rays, looking for broken bones." Jace grimaced. "He found some old, healed cracks in the back of my skull."

"I'm sorry," I said, "but I don't see your point."

"What if Dr. Parker had X-rayed *your* head? Would he have found one of those implants the AIs used to take control of people, back before the AI war?"

"Where did you hear about implants?" I asked.

"History class." He eyed me. "You didn't answer my question."

I drew a deep breath. "Yes, Dr. Parker would have found an implant."

Laney and Logan recoiled from me in... Surprise? Fear?

But Jace just nodded. "When you took that punch, you moved way faster than anyone I've ever seen. That was your implant, right?"

If I'd had any doubts that Jace was a lot smarter than he let on, that observation banished them.

"Yes, but my implant isn't like the ones that let AIs take control of humans," I said. "Those old implants let people send commands and requests to the AIs. No one even realized they also let the AIs send commands to people until the first missiles launched. But later implants didn't have that flaw. Mine can't receive commands at all and can only send them to certain devices. Ones *without* an AI."

"That sounds like something an amy would say."

Despair washed over me. I hung my head and said, "I don't know what I can say to convince you I'm telling the truth."

Jace stared hard at me. "Tell me why you did it."

"Came here?" I asked. "We didn't have any choice. Our lifepod was leaking air and—"

"Not that," Jace said. "Why did you take the punch my old man meant for me?"

I couldn't keep confusion off my face. "You already know. I did it to give Laney and Mr. Gibson a reason to come to me. So I could whisper my story to them."

Jace shook his head. "That's not it. I saw your expression when you made your move."

"How? Your eyes were on your father."

Jace tapped the corner of his right eye with one finger. "Good peripheral vision, remember?"

"What did you see on my face?"

Jace dropped his eyes to the floor. "You looked... I don't know. Noble or something." He raised his head and met my gaze. "And that face? That was *you*. The way you are inside." Jace's eyes cut to Laney and Logan. "And the rejection you felt when those two jumped back from you? That was the real you, too."

In a voice full of anguish, Laney said, "I'm sorry, Anne. It's just... He surprised me and—"

"It's okay, Laney," I said.

"No, it's not," Logan said. "We ought to know you better than that."

I turned my best smile on them. "You've had a lifetime of teaching that says implants are evil. I can't expect you to overcome that immediately."

Jace glanced at the Gibsons. "You saw that, right? The noble expression?"

Laney summoned a weak smile. "Of course she's noble. I mean, Anne *is* a princess on her home planet."

Jace turned wide eyes back to me. "A princess? Do I... bow or something?"

"No, of course not." I offered Jace the same smile I'd given to Laney and Logan. "But you didn't come here and question me like that out of curiosity. What do you want, Jace?"

Jace looked down again and even scuffed a shoe on the floor. "Nobody ever stood up for me before, like you did. Not even my mother. Before she left my father. And me."

"I'm sorry," I said.

"So I figure I owe you."

"You owe me nothing, Jace."

He waved my comment off. "I came here to offer my help." He handed me the comm. "And to bring this to you."

"Returning the comm is more than enough."

Jace shook his head. "I can do a lot more than just that."

I really wanted to comm Chris, but Jace's comment piqued my curiosity. "Like what?"

Jace smiled for the first time since he entered the house. "I can get you a set of identity papers."

ONE GOOD REASON

After Jace's declaration, the five Gibsons eyed him in surprise. Laney found her tongue first and said, "You were there in the sheriff's station when the major let Anne go, even though she didn't have identity papers. She doesn't need them."

"Maybe *I* don't need papers," I said. "But Chris will."

"Who's Chris?" Jace asked.

For simplicity, I said, "Another amy. Or another girl like me, anyway." I looked at the Gibson adults. "We were lucky Major Higgins let me go. If another paperless girl turns up, I think he'll take all of us into custody."

"I'm afraid you're right, Anne," Old Mr. Gibson said. "Besides, you *will* need papers to travel anywhere except around town." He turned to Jace. "Can you get two sets of papers?"

"I can get as many sets as you can pay for," Jace said.

"Where, and how much?" Young Mr. Gibson asked.

"I doubt I can add anything to this discussion," I said. "I'm going to go upstairs and comm Chris."

No one disagreed with me, so I left the den and headed for the stairs. Footsteps sounded behind me as Laney joined me. We went upstairs to her room. I put the comm in my ear and activated it. "Chris? Are you there?"

I heard two taps in reply, from Chris tapping a finger on her comm. I immediately muted my comm.

"Well?" Laney asked.

"Chris is there, but she can't talk right now."

"You think someone is close enough to overhear her?"

"Probably, but..." I shrugged.

"You can't hear what's going on around Chris?"

"Maybe. Let me ask." I unmuted the comm and whispered, "Chris, can you remove the comm from your ear and activate speaker mode so we can hear what you hear? I'll mute at my end, so we don't give away your position. Tap twice for yes."

Tap. Tap.

"Oh, and put the comm back in your ear after we hear what's going on," I added. "Tap twice again, so I know when you do that."

I immediately muted my comm, activated speaker mode on my end, and then held the comm in the palm of my hand. Laney leaned closer, the better to hear what was happening on Chris's end.

A man's voice, one I didn't recognize, called, "All right, men, sit down and rest while I contact the major."

"Sounds like he's on the road," I whispered.

Another voice said, "Aw, Sarge, can't we push on into town?"

I recognized that voice, and a second later I remembered why. He was one of the soldiers who'd searched Mr. Gibson's barn while Chris and I hid there. The city soldier who didn't like the smell of horses.

"Since when did you get so gung ho, Walsh?" the sergeant asked.

A voice I didn't recognize said, "Since he heard the town had some pretty girls."

Walsh laughed. "They don't have to be pretty, just willing."

Another familiar voice spoke, and I immediately recognized the country soldier who felt at home in the barn. "Don't be stupid, Walsh. You got *any* idea what a country girl's daddy would do to you if you messed with his daughter?"

"Don't see what difference it makes, as long as I'm long gone before he finds out," Walsh countered.

"Shut it, Walsh. You, too, Martello," the sergeant said. "I'm trying to get through to the major."

We heard some static, then a voice said, "Go ahead."

"This is tracker team nine reporting from the road around Burson," the sergeant said.

"Do you have anything to report, TT nine?"

"We found some tracks that might be the girl the major is interested in. But according to Martello—our best tracker—there were two people. Either boys in their early teens, or girls about the age of the one you've got in town. Martello says the other tracks we found belonged to our soldiers or animals."

Static. "Good work. The major will want to hear your report in person. Flag down the next perimeter patrol car that comes by and have them bring you into town."

"Roger. Over and out."

Two taps sounded a minute later, letting me know Chris had turned off speaker mode and put the comm back in her ear. I unmuted my comm and said, "While we wait for the soldiers to leave, let me catch you up on what's happened since I left you earlier today."

Two taps told me Chris was listening. I told her the highlights of my trip, left out Jace's father's punch, but included what little I knew about identification papers. "Anyway, the major is more suspicious of me than I thought, and I already thought he was very suspicious. I'd hoped we could smuggle you to the Gibsons' house, but now I think we need to smuggle me out of town."

Chris signaled her agreement with two taps.

"I'm going to explain the situation to everyone," I said. "I'll leave my comm on speaker mode so you can hear the discussion."

Tap. Tap.

Laney and I headed back to the den. From the set of everyone's faces, I got the idea the discussion hadn't been amicable. They all began speaking when I entered the room.

I held up a hand for silence, and to my surprise, got it. "I don't know what got you all so worked up—"

Old Mr. Gibson snorted and pointed at Jace. "It was this boy insisting that he needs to take you out of town, instead of bringing Chris into town!"

I felt my eyebrows rise and turned to Jace. "Can you get me out without getting caught?"

"No!" Mrs. Gibson said. "It's not safe."

"It's safer than if she stays here," Laney said. "We overheard some soldiers near where Chris is hiding. The major is already suspicious of Anne, and he'll be more suspicious when he hears their report."

I gave a quick summary of tracker team nine's findings. "The major *will* come looking for me, and probably soon. I think he only let me go because he assumed I'd stay put. And I would have, if we hadn't overheard those soldiers." I looked at Jace. "So I'll ask again. Can you smuggle me out of town?"

Jace nodded.

"When do we go?" I asked.

"Get everything you want to bring with you," Jace said. "We leave as soon as you're ready."

Jace crossed his arms, leaned against the closest wall, and let his face settle into a patient expression. I'm not sure why. Maybe he thought a princess couldn't travel without two suitcases and three trunks to pack?

I pulled the comm in my palm closer to my mouth. "Chris? I'm turning the comm to private mode."

Two taps sounded, showing that Chris both understood and still wasn't free to speak.

I switched off speaker mode, put the comm in my left ear, and smiled at Jace. "I'm ready to go."

Jace's eyebrows rose, and he pushed himself away from the wall. "Oh. Um, okay."

Laney stood and started for the stairs. "*I'm* not ready to go yet. But it'll only take me a minute to pack."

"Just one minute, Laney," Young Mr. Gibson said. "Where do you think you're going?"

"With Anne and Chris. And Jace, of course."

"Absolutely not!" Laney's father and mother said in unison.

Logan stood and also headed for the stairs. "I'm going, too."

Old Mr. Gibson pointed at the just-vacated chairs. "Plant your back-sides in those chairs. You're not going anywhere."

Laney whirled, crossed her arms, and glared at the three adults. "Give me one good reason why I shouldn't go?"

Young Mr. Gibson turned the question back on Laney. "Give me one good reason why you should?"

"Because Anne and Chris will need me," Laney said.

"To do what?"

"Fit in."

Young Mr. Gibson waved a hand at me. "She handled herself just fine with the sheriff."

"Only because she acted like someone who'd never been to a town before. Do you think she'd have gotten away with that for long without our help?"

"No," Laney's father admitted, "but now she'll have Jace helping her."

"What happens when she goes somewhere Jace can't go? Like the ladies' room. Or does something he knows nothing about? Like clothes shopping or putting on makeup? She won't know how to act, what to buy, or what her makeup says about her."

Hoping to quell the argument, I said, "At home, I usually only wear makeup for royal functions. And I don't wear any at the Academy."

Laney glared at her father. "See what I mean?"

Both Mr. Gibsons eyed Laney with perplexed expressions. But Mrs. Gibson wore an appalled expression as she said, "I hadn't even considered..." She glanced at her husband and father-in-law. "I hate to say it, but Laney is right."

"Why?" Old Mr. Gibson asked. "Do you think the government is going to swoop in and grab Anne just because she's not wearing makeup?"

Jace straightened. "Sir? Makeup is a small thing by itself. But if Anne also acts wrong in the restroom, wears the wrong clothes, does her hair up wrong? They're all little things, but it's the little things that give you away."

Old Mr. Gibson cocked one eyebrow. "And I suppose you're some kind of expert on this?"

Jace nodded. "My old man made me work for him. He punished failure with beatings. So, yeah, I'm an expert at this stuff."

Old Mr. Gibson still looked skeptical. "And why is passing unnoticed so important in your father's line of work?"

"He's a smuggler."

Silence fell over the room. After a moment, Logan asked, "Drugs?"

Jace shrugged. "Anything that made money."

"And he made you work for him?" Mrs. Gibson asked.

"Yes, ma'am. That's why I know how to get false identity papers for

Anne and Chris. I can get them for Laney and Logan, too, if they come, too."

Laney's father turned to her mother. "Rebecca, are you *sure* they need Laney?"

Mrs. Gibson nodded. "I hate to say yes, but..."

Young Mr. Gibson sighed, turned to his son, and asked, "Why do you need to go?"

"To protect Laney."

"Then maybe I should go, too."

Jace shook his head. "That's not a good idea, sir. Where we're going, there are lots of people about our age living on their own. We can blend in with them, and all but disappear. You'd just make us stand out more."

"That's another thing," Old Mr. Gibson said. "Where are you going?"

"It's better if you don't know," Jace said. "You can't let slip what you don't know."

Old Mr. Gibson opened his mouth, probably to protest. Then he closed his eyes. "You're probably right."

Young Mr. Gibson eyed his two children. "Short of locking you in the attic, is there anything I can do to stop you from going?"

"No," Laney said.

"No." Logan grinned. "The attic wouldn't work, anyway. I know more than one way out of it."

"Have I ever mentioned that you're both too smart for your own good?" their father asked.

"Once or twice," Laney said.

"A day," Logan added.

Mrs. Gibson rose. "I'll help you kids pack." She glanced at her husband. "Roger, gather all the cash we have on hand."

Young Mr. Gibson rose and left the room.

Old Mr. Gibson pulled the borrowed pair of night vision glasses from his pocket. "I better return these before I forget. We wouldn't want Major Higgins finding an amy device if he ever searches the house."

I smiled my thanks, pocketed the glasses, and then used the comm. "Chris, are you free to talk and move?"

To my relief, she said, "Yes. I've already begun taking down my chameleon cloth hiding place. Where should I go?"

"Jace?" I asked. "Where should Chris go?"

"She's just outside of Perimeter Road?" When I nodded, he said, "Tell her to go counterclockwise until she comes to another road. We'll pick her up there."

While I relayed those instructions, Jace said, "Make sure you have a story explaining why Anne, Laney, and Logan are gone. For when the major comes looking for them."

"It's simple enough," Old Mr. Gibson said. "Anne hightailed it back to the hills, and our foolish kids took off after her. We'll call Sheriff Clark after you leave and tell that story. Is two hours enough of a head start?"

Jace looked at a device on his wrist. Some kind of timepiece, I assumed. Then he said, "Make it two and a half hours."

"How are you going to explain Jace's absence?" I asked.

"We don't need to," Old Mr. Gibson said. "He's not part of our family."

A minute later, Laney, Logan, and Mrs. Gibson returned. Laney and Logan each wore backpacks. Young Mr. Gibson returned with two envelopes. He handed one to Logan and the other to Laney. Then he swept them into a hug. "Take care of yourselves."

Mrs. Gibson and her father-in-law followed suit. I got goodbye hugs, too. The two Mr. Gibsons shook Jace's hand and, to his pleased surprise, Mrs. Gibson gave him a quick embrace.

Jace turned towards the door. "You three slip out the back and meet me on Crocker Road."

We heard Jace's car engine roar to life as we hurried through the Gibson's big backyard. My new friends knew where they were going, so I just followed them. We reached a road two minutes later. A minute after that, we climbed into Jace's car and drove away.

We drove in silence as Jace made multiple turns onto increasingly dilapidated roads. After a few minutes, he pulled onto something that was more path than road. We jostled and bounced over the rough track for five more minutes before Jace stopped the car. He turned off the car's lights but left the engine running. "Perimeter Road is just around the next bend, and the road where Chris is waiting is maybe fifty meters from where this track comes out. We're going to wait here until the next jeep passes, then we'll cross the road and get Chris."

Jeep was an unfamiliar word to me, but I assumed he meant the military vehicles with the searchlights. I tapped my comm. "Chris?"

"I'm at the road, Anne," she replied.

"Good. We're not far away. We're just waiting for the next road patrol to pass, then we'll come get you."

"We'll be driving without lights," Jace said, "but I'll flash the lights once we turn onto the road."

I relayed that to Chris and then left the channel open. I suddenly remembered the night vision glasses I had, pulled them from my pocket, and handed them to Jace. "These will let you see in the dark."

He looked skeptical until he tried them on. "Wow! That's amazing." Then Jace looked over his shoulder. "Logan, open your door when we see Chris, so she can get in quickly."

Despite the chill outside, Jace lowered his side window and had me do the same. Then we all fell silent and listened for an approaching motor. Three long minutes later, I heard a slow-moving vehicle.

"Be ready, Chris," I said. "The patrol is close now."

A minute later, the jeep passed our location. Even though its search-light pointed away from us, its bright light filtered through the thick foliage between us and the road. And then it was past, and the jeep's engine gradually faded away.

Jace put the car in gear and rolled slowly forward. He peered intently ahead as he steered the car around the last bend before the Perimeter Road. The open road seemed bright compared to the deep darkness of the track. Jace turned left and drove down the road.

"We're approaching the turn to your road," I said into the comm.

"I hear your engine," Chris replied.

Jace spun the steering wheel to the right, and I said, "Turning now. Watch for the lights. Logan will open a door for you."

Jace flashed his lights. "I can see her coming out of the forest. She's wearing glasses like the ones you gave me and is carrying four back-packs." He stopped the car. "Open your door, Logan."

Logan did as instructed and then scooted over to make room for Chris. She slid into the vacant seat and closed the door. Logan took some backpacks from her, as Chris said, "Go!"

Jace drove away from Perimeter Road at a speed that was only safe because of the night vision goggles. A kilometer from where we picked up Chris, he slowed and turned left onto a dirt road.

Laney, her voice tinged with suspicion, asked, "Why are you taking us to Lovers Lanes?"

"To leave the car," Jace said. "I figure the soldiers have already searched this area, so it'll take them a day or two to find it."

"Why are we abandoning the car?" Logan asked.

"Because all the roads around town are watched or blocked," Jace said. "We'd get caught within fifteen minutes if we tried driving out of here."

"Oh," Logan said.

"Then how will we get wherever it is you're taking us?" Laney asked.

"Lovers Lane is only a couple of kilometers from the train tracks," Jace said. "There's a freight train due through here around five in the morning. We're going to hop it and ride the rails."

I assumed a freight train was a transport, one that could get us past roadblocks and searches. Since Jace's answer apparently satisfied Laney and Logan, I held my questions for a later time.

Jace drove for another two minutes, then pulled the car off the dirt road and into a clearing concealed by trees. The trees created near-total darkness.

"This Lovers Lane, do couples use its privacy for..." I searched for a phrase that wouldn't make Mom mad if I used it in front of her. "Um, amorous activities?"

"Yeah, it's for making out," Logan said. "You know, kissing and, um... other stuff?"

I wondered what it would be like to be so free of restrictions and expectations that a girl could come to a place like this with any boy she chose. And not have to worry about royal guards suddenly showing up and ruining everything.

Jace pulled me from my wondering by pointing to a small door in front of me. "Anne, there's a small notebook in the glove compartment. Can you get it for me?"

I fumbled with the opening mechanism for a few seconds before the little door dropped open. Odd pieces of paper and small tools filled the compartment. I dug through it all until I found the notebook. Under everything else, naturally. I handed it to Jace, and he pulled a pen from his pocket. Jace flipped open the notebook and wrote a few lines on a blank page. Then he ripped the page from the notebook and handed the page to me.

"If we get separated, go to that address." He tapped the writing on the page with his index finger. "Tell them Junior sent you. It'll cost money, but they'll help you with whatever you need. You should probably memorize the address and then burn the paper."

"Um, thanks, but I'm going to give this to Laney." I stretched my arm into the backseat towards Laney. "I can't read it."

"What?" all three of my companions said at once.

"Remember when I told Laney I was illiterate? It's the truth."

"But you speak our language so well," Logan said.

"And that's all I do." I tapped the back of my head. "My implant only translates spoken language. But I have to learn to read languages on my own."

"But you're a princess and a cadet!" Laney said. "How can you *not* know how to read?"

"I can read a dozen languages, just not *yours*."

"What about Chris?" Jace asked.

Chris shrugged. "I'm in the same lifepod as Anne."

"Um, that means you can't read our language, either?" Logan asked.

"Correct," Chris said.

Jace sighed and leaned his head back. "That makes this a lot harder. You have to know how to read to get around in the city."

"We'll just have to figure a way to work around it," Laney said.

"Maybe," Jace said. "Let me think on it."

After a moment, Jace turned and looked at Laney and Logan. "Can you two find your way to the train tracks from here?"

"Sure." Logan pointed deeper into the forest. "We just walk that way until we reach the tracks."

"Right," Jace said. "Just make sure you don't get turned around in the darkness."

"We can help with that," I said. "Our implants have built in compasses."

"Good. You four get out and head for the tracks. I have to run back to town for something."

"Splitting up isn't a good idea," Chris said.

"It can't be helped."

"Why?" Laney asked. "What are you going back for?"

"Books," Jace said. "We'll be on the train for a long time. We can use that time to teach Anne and Chris how to read. A little bit, anyway."

"That's a good idea," Laney said. "Want me to come along and help?"

Jace shook his head. "You have to stay and teach Anne and Chris how girls act on Refuge."

Laney gave a reluctant nod. "Go to our house. Mom and Dad still have all our own early reader books."

Chris pulled the comm from her ear and handed it to Jace. "You already have night vision glasses, so take this, too. It'll help us find each other when you return."

Since I was in the front seat, I showed Jace how to use the comm. We ran a quick test to make sure he knew the basics. Then everyone except Jace climbed from the car.

Jace caught my eye. "If the train comes before I get back, hop into the first empty boxcar you see."

"What about you?" I asked.

"I'll catch up with you at the address I gave to you." Jace gave a little wave and drove away.

Chris handed her night vision glasses to Logan, and then we headed deeper into the dark forest.

TRAIN HOPPING

We followed Logan through Lovers Lane and into the forest. Darkness deepened beneath the forest's unbroken canopy, and we held hands to ensure we stayed together. Dense underbrush forced us from the most direct path to the railroad tracks, but Chris or I always got us headed in the right direction after the detours.

After the third time we corrected Logan's course, he sighed. "I guess my sense of direction isn't as good as I thought it was."

"It's as good as mine," I said. "I'd have followed you without question, without the compass in my implant."

"You'd probably do fine, if you could see the moon," Laney said. "So don't beat yourself up, little brother."

"Little brother?" Chris asked.

"I was born four minutes earlier than Logan," Laney said.

"Probably because she pushed and shoved her way ahead of me in the womb," Logan said.

"No," Laney said. "I was born first because girls mature faster than boys."

"She has you there," I said.

Logan pulled down on my hand. I ducked, while also pulling down on Laney's arm.

"Low-hanging branches," he said. "And no, she doesn't have me. Girls don't mature faster than boys, just differently."

"You finally noticed the difference, little brother?" Laney teased.

"You'll have to excuse Laney," Logan replied. "She thinks she's a comedian."

"I *am* quite funny."

"Looking," Logan countered. "Funny *looking*."

"We may be fraternal twins, little brother, but everyone says we look alike. So what applies to me applies to you."

"Yeah, but our look is handsome in guys. Not so much for girls."

In a tone of mild exasperation, Chris said, "Will you two stop fighting? We're all on the same side, you know."

Laney, Logan, and I were silent for a moment. Then Laney said, "You know her best, Anne. You ask."

Curiosity joined the exasperation in Chris's voice. "Ask what?"

"Chris, are you an only child?" I asked.

"Yes. Why?"

"You, um, thought Laney and Logan were fighting."

"Of course I did. Didn't it sound like that to you?"

"No, they were just acting like typical siblings."

"Oh, sibling rivalry, right?"

"Um, no, just siblings joking around."

"By insulting each other?"

"Sure. I do it with my older brother all the time." I paused. "Did it, anyway."

"Chris, don't you do stuff like that with your friends?" Laney asked.

"Sure, I just thought... Isn't it different with your family?"

"Not if you really love each other," I said.

"Huh," Chris said. "Anne, did you ever call your brother funny looking?"

"At least once a week."

"Even though you say he's better looking than you?"

"The truth has no place in sibling bickering."

"Whoa," Laney said. "Anne, will you please introduce me to your super handsome brother, someday?"

"Get in line," Chris growled. "I asked first."

"Hey, I've got an idea," Logan said. "Let's stop talking about ridiculously good-looking guys and concentrate on reaching the train tracks."

Laney snorted. "You're only saying that because you've already met Anne and can look at her whenever you want."

From the way Logan stared at me when we first met, I expected an embarrassed silence or a stammered denunciation from Logan. But he was in full sibling bicker mode, and said, "Jealous much, sis?"

Laney laughed. "Um, *yeah*."

"Okay," I said, "that's enough on this topic."

In a light tone, Chris said, "I forgot. The Princess Scout doesn't like being reminded of her looks."

"Princess Scout?" Laney asked.

"That's a... less than complimentary nickname the other Academy cadets gave to Anne," Chris said. "But I'll make sure that changes after we get back."

"To something even worse?" I kept my tone light to make sure Chris knew I was only kidding.

"No, I won't change your nickname. Just its definition." Chris's tone turned serious. "Brave. Clever. Beautiful. Loyal. You know, the embodiment of the virtues included in the Scout Oath."

I remembered Chris's opinion of the Princess Scout right after our lifepod launched, and swallowed a sudden lump in my throat. "By that definition, you're a princess scout, too."

I couldn't see Chris's face, but she paused for a few seconds. In a light tone she said, "Beautiful is on that list, so nah."

"Wrong," I said.

Chris pushed back. "Come on, Anne, you know I'm right."

"Let's ask an expert," Laney said. "Hey, Logan, how pretty is Chris?"

"Am I going to get in trouble if I tell the truth?" Logan asked.

"There, see?" Chris said. "Logan is too much of a gentleman to say I'm not beautiful, but—"

"That's not it," Logan said. "It's just girls usually don't want to hear they're the *second* prettiest girl a guy knows."

"What?" Chris asked. "But Laney—"

"Sisters don't count," Logan said. "And I know I live in a small town, but—"

"Stop while you're ahead, little brother," Laney growled.

"Right," Logan said. "So, why don't we talk about something else? *Anything* else."

No one had a different topic, so we fell silent except for occasional course correction comments. We trudged on for what felt like forever, but I'd had a lot of recent experience with time passage while hiking through the forest. About two hours after Jace drove off, we reached an edge to the forest.

Parallel strips of metal on a raised bed cut through the forest. Soft moonlight bathed the railroad tracks, and I blinked as my eyes adjusted from the near pitch black of the forest to this comparative brightness.

Logan checked the timepiece on his wrist. "Jace said the freight train was due at five tomorrow morning. That's eight hours from now." He glanced at Chris and me. "I, um, guess we can rest and take turns keeping watch?"

"Good idea," I said. "I want to check in with Jace, so I'll take the first watch."

Logan handed me the night vision glasses. Chris handed chameleon cloths to each of us. Then he, Laney, and Chris settled down just inside the forest edge and closed their eyes. I donned the glasses and spent two minutes looking up and down the tracks for movement. I saw nothing but wrapped up in the chameleon cloth before I walked into the open.

To keep from disturbing the others, I crossed to the other side of the tracks before unmuting the comm. "Jace? This is Anne."

I waited five minutes for a reply and did my best to quell my uneasiness when Jace didn't reply. He might be somewhere around people, and simply couldn't speak. But he could just tap the comm, like Chris did, right? I know we taught that to him, but he could have forgotten. It's not like we spent much time teaching him. Jace's day had been at least as eventful as mine, so he might simply have forgotten.

I tried to reach Jace every ten minutes during my watch. He never answered. Finally, I turned the comm over to Laney, showed her how to work it, and leaned against a nearby tree. I didn't mean to sleep, but I dropped off almost immediately. I awoke to Logan shaking my shoulder.

"Wake up, Anne," he said. "We can hear the train in the distance."

I blinked and looked around. "Where's Jace?"

Logan's expression turned grim. "I don't know."

"He hasn't answered the comm?"

"No."

"And we can't wait for him."

Logan shrugged. "He told us to hop the train without him, and he'd meet us in Landfall."

"Landfall? That's the city we're going to?"

Logan nodded. "It's the capital."

I rose, stretched, and looked down the railroad tracks. Something Laney and Logan called a locomotive came around a bend, towing a long line of storage cars. Even at a distance, I had no trouble figuring out which ones were boxcars. The train slowed as it started up the hill towards us. We stayed in the forest as the huge locomotive rumbled past us, moving slower than we could run. A man leaned out a window in the locomotive, watching the track ahead of him. Fortunately, he showed no inclination to look backwards.

Two dozen cars rolled past us before Logan spotted what we wanted. He pointed down the track to a boxcar whose door was only halfway closed. "That one."

Chris handed me the night vision glasses. "If someone has to Boost, it should be you. You have more real life experience with it than I do."

"Not much more," I said, "but this plebe hears and obeys."

Chris rolled her eyes. Then the boxcar approached, and we sprinted for it. Even at the freight train's slow speed, clambering into the boxcar looked dangerous. But it would be much easier and safer if we had someone inside the car to help others up. I followed Chris's orders and sent the command to my implant.

Boost!

Adrenaline flooded my system. I easily outdistanced my friends and leapt into the boxcar. I left Boost active, leaned from the car, and pulled each of my friends into the car with me. Then I dropped Boost.

We were on our way. But where was Jace, and why wasn't he responding to our comms?

I stayed at the boxcar's door. Watching for Jace. Hoping he'd dash from the forest and join us.

Behind me, Logan said, "Anne, how did you do that? It was *amazing!*"

His comment only registered because he spoke my name. Without turning, I said, "Boost."

A small part of my brain said, *That won't mean anything to him*. But I ignored it and kept looking for Jace.

"Anne?" Logan asked.

"Shut up," Laney said. "Can't you tell she's worried about Jace?"

"Oh, yeah. Sorry, Anne."

That same small part of my brain said I should acknowledge his apology, but I caught movement in the corner of my eye. From farther up the hill. I turned my full attention on the movement as something hunched over stumbled out of the forest. The head lifted, and I saw the face.

Jace!

He lurched further from the forest. Slowed. Obviously hurt. With no chance of catching the train, much less hopping aboard. Someone had to go to Jace, help him reach the train and climb aboard. That's as far as I got before I acted.

Boost!

Adrenaline slammed into my system. But I felt no mild euphoria this time. Fire burned through my veins. A scream burst from me as I leapt from the slow-moving boxcar.

"Anne," Chris called, "no!"

My ankles cried in pain and buckled under me as I landed. My training took over, and I tucked into a roll. The tall grass next to the track bed felt like sandpaper on my skin. Then I was back on my feet, ankles ignored, and running for Jace.

I had just enough time to notice his scraped face, blackening eye, and the disturbing bruise circling his throat. His right hand clutched his ribs, and he had a backpack slung over his shoulders. Jace leaned hard on a thick branch clutched in his left hand, because his left leg looked incapable of bearing his weight. His face sagged with pain and exhaustion.

I'd hoped I could lend Jace a shoulder, but he needed more help than that. I pushed aside the pain coursing through my body, turned my back to Jace, and said, "Grab hold."

"No. Can't." Jace sucked air through his teeth. "Too heavy."

I glanced back at the train. The locomotive had vanished over the crest of the hill, and the train's speed increased. Not a lot. Not yet. But we had no time for an argument.

I crouched, backed into Jace, and grabbed his legs. We both hissed in pain as I rose from the crouch. But Jace dropped his stick and wrapped his arms around my shoulders.

I took a faltering step towards the train. Fought for balance. Took another step. Lurched into a shambling run. My knees protested every step. I ignored them and picked up the pace. The soles of my feet joined my pain chorus. But the train drew nearer. I just had to hold out a few more seconds.

Chris and Logan hung from the sides of the open door, each with an arm extended. Laney stood behind them, braced to help pull us into the boxcar.

"Come on, Anne!" Chris called. "You're almost here."

"Hold on!" I gasped.

Jace tightened his grip on my shoulders.

As I closed in on the boxcar, I knew I only had one chance to do this. If I got it wrong, I'd bounce off the side of the boxcar. Or fall beneath it, and then we'd both get killed when the wheels rolled over us.

No! I told myself. *Don't overthink this. Just do what must be done.*

I took one more step. Then I launched myself towards the boxcar's open door. It felt as if time stopped as Jace and I left the ground. Then I realized Chris and I moved at the same speed.

She'd Boosted, too.

Her hand grabbed my arm. She pulled with all her Boosted strength. Jace and I flew into the boxcar and crashed into Laney. We all went down in a tangle of flailing limbs and muffled cries of pain. Then everything was still, except for my still racing heart. And the fire still burning through my body.

Hands caught both sides of my head and turned my gaze up. Chris leaned over me, her expression tense. "Anne! Cancel Boost!"

I felt as if I should understand what she meant, but I couldn't grasp it. "Huh?"

"Cancel Boost!" Chris slapped me. "Before you burn out!"

Chris slapped me again. "Obey your orders, plebe! Do you understand?"

She pulled her hand back for another slap. But if there's one thing a plebe understands, it's her position at the bottom of the chain of command. Which means a plebe always follows her orders.

I canceled Boost. "This plebe hears and obeys."

Chris blinked rapidly and pulled me into a hug. "Don't ever do something like that again, Anne!"

"Yes, ma'am," I said. "I think I'll pass out now."

Only I didn't. Which was a cruel trick for my body to play on me, since that meant I experienced all the agony of recovering from double-Boosting. Geez, even Dad didn't have to suffer through that kind of torture. When I complained aloud, Chris showed unwavering compassion.

Not.

"It serves you right." Chris's prim tone went well with her stern expression. "Now that you know how it feels after you double-Boost, maybe you won't be so eager to do it again."

"Your bedside manner needs work," I said.

"My bedside manner is as compassionate as can be," Chris countered. "But you're not in a bed, so I'm not using it."

"Um," Laney said, "are you two saying anything we need to know? Because you're not speaking our language."

I switched to the local language. "Sorry. And no. Chris was just calling me an idiot."

"Good," Laney said. "But shouldn't we do something about Jace? He's hurt bad."

"Now that I know Anne isn't going to die," Chris said, "I can concentrate on Jace."

"Die?" Laney, Logan, and Jace all gasped.

Chris turned her attention to Jace, but said, "Explain it to them, plebe."

So I spent the next few minutes explaining Boost and Boost burnout to our three friends. They were all suitably appalled.

"Why didn't you tell Chris to go get Jace?" Logan asked.

"I, um, didn't think of that," I said.

"Don't do it again," Jace said. "I don't know how I'll ever repay you."

It hurt when I propped myself up on my elbows, but I did it. Then I caught Jace's gaze. "Repay me? For what? Caring about you? That's what friends *do*, Jace."

Jace looked away from me. "Not in my circles."

"Then it's a good thing we're not in your circles." I lowered myself to the boxcar floor again. "What happened to you? How did you get so badly hurt?"

"It wasn't at our house, was it? Maybe from soldiers?" Laney asked.

"No, everything was fine at your place," Jace said. "Your folks helped me collect the books you wanted and gave me that backpack to carry them in."

"Did you run into a patrol after you left?" Logan asked.

"I wish..." Jace fell silent, and we waited until he was ready to continue. Finally, he said, "Things went so smooth at your house, I had time to spare. I figured more money would be better than less, so I went by my house. I know where my old man hides his stash of cash. Since the sheriff arrested him, I figured the money was there for the taking."

Jace hissed as Chris probed a tender spot. She looked at me. "I think we should use a medical nanite injector on Jace."

I nodded in agreement. As Chris dug an injector from a backpack, I asked, "What went wrong at your house, Jace?"

"Dear old dad called his lawyer, who got him released from jail," Jace said. "He was waiting for me when I walked into the house."

Chris pulled a medical nanite injector from her backpack and leaned over Jace. He eyed the injector with undisguised fear.

"What's that?" Jace asked.

"It's a medical... injector," Chris said.

I agreed with her decision to leave out the word *nanite*. I remembered trying to describe nanites to Old Mr. Gibson, who told me not to bother. Because he couldn't grasp the concept. And I came from a planet full of people who wouldn't understand it, either. Worse, many of them would misunderstand or hate the idea of having millions of tiny medical robots crawling through their body. No matter how beneficial those tiny robots were.

"What's it inject?" Jace asked.

Chris glanced at me, a lost expression on her face. I said, "Amy medicine. It'll help you heal faster, fight infections, that sort of thing. I used one on Chris back at Old Mr. Gibson's house after she sprained her ankle."

"Old Mr. Gibson?" Logan asked.

I shrugged. "Your father is also Mr. Gibson, so I add *old* and *young* to keep them straight."

Laney laughed. "I can't wait to tell Granddaddy his new nickname."

"You could just call Dad by his first name—Roger," Logan said.

"That wouldn't be proper or respectful, unless he invited me to do so," I said. "And if there's one thing princesses and plebes learn, it's how to be respectful."

I'd hoped our exchange would distract Jace, but he kept a wary eye on the injector. Chris held it away from Jace, and asked, "May I give you the injection?"

"Are you sure it's safe for, um," Jace's eyes darted back and forth between Chris and me, "people who aren't amies?"

I reached out and took Jace's left hand. "We're just as human as you are, Jace. I give you my word as a Scout and a princess. The injection is completely safe."

When Jace still looked uncertain, Chris said, "You saw what Anne went through when she carried you to the train. Do you think she did that just so she could poison you?"

"Um, no." Jace squeezed my hand. "Okay. Do it."

Chris applied the injector to Jace's neck. He tensed at its soft hiss. Chris withdrew the injector once the hissing stopped. "That's it."

"Huh." Jace ran a finger over the injection spot. "That didn't even hurt."

"Do you feel up to telling us what happened when you went home?" I asked.

"Hm?" Jace looked my way. "Oh, yeah. Sorry, I got distracted by the medical thing." Jace drew a deep breath. "Like I said, my old man was waiting for me when I came home. He must have heard the car, because he was hiding behind the doorway into the den. He'd probably have clocked me good, too, except the floor creaked when he moved. I learned a long time ago to move fast when I heard something like that. So I dove forward, rolled, and came up facing him.

"I never saw him so angry before. Didn't help that he was drunk, too. He said, 'Welcome home, boy.' Then he raised his fists and shuffled towards me. Another thing I learned a long time ago was that the beating was worse if I tried fighting or running. I was just going to let him beat me, get it out of his system, and then I could slip out when he fell asleep. Only..."

Jace closed his eyes and stopped talking. I leaned over him. "Only what, Jace?"

Jace draped his right arm over his eyes. "In my mind, I kept seeing you jump up and take the punch meant for me. Even though my old man was half a head taller than you, and about fifty kilos heavier. And I thought, *If Anne can stand up to him, so can I.*

"When my old man threw his first punch, I blocked it. I did the same with his next three punches. That's when I finally realized I was faster than him. Stronger than him. Just as tall as him. And not going to fat, like he is. The next time he swung at me, I caught his fist with both hands and shoved him away. 'I'm not scared of you anymore,' I said. 'I'm leaving, so get out of my way.'

"That was the wrong thing to say, I guess. He just began flailing at me with both arms. I couldn't block everything. That's how I got the black eye and the hurt ribs.

"Once I realized he wasn't going to stop until one of us went down, I took a step towards him and punched him in the nose. Blood spurted from it, and the old man howled. It... felt good. So I hit him on the jaw. He stumbled backwards, tripped over his own feet, and fell down.

"I stood over him with both fists clenched, glaring at him. And the old man flinched, just like I'd always done after he knocked me down. I liked that, too, so much so that I pulled my foot back to kick him in the side. Just like he'd done to me so many times before."

Jace blew out his breath. "And then that same girl who took a punch for me jumped into my head, and said, 'You're doing just what your father would do. Is that what you want?' I shook my head, trying to get rid of the annoying girl. But I couldn't. So I thought about what she said. And she was right. I *hate* my old man. The last thing I want is to be anything like him. But there I was, causing pain and *liking* it.

"I stepped over my old man, and said, 'Never touch me again.' The girl popped out of my head. And my old man grabbed my left leg and twisted it hard enough it almost popped out of its socket. I fell on my face. The old man crawled on top of me, wrapped his hands around my throat, and began choking me. I bucked and heaved. Tore at his hands. Threw elbows into his gut and smashed the back of my head into his face. That's what did it. My head hit his nose, and the old man let go of my throat to hold his nose.

"I climbed to my hands and knees, dumped him off of me, and stood. He laid there at my feet, holding his nose and staring at me with fear shining in his eyes. I tried to kick him in the stomach, but my left leg couldn't hold my weight long enough for the kick. I got ready to hit him a few times. But..."

Jace shrugged. "I remembered I didn't want to be like him. I limped around my old man, went to his secret stash, grabbed the money, and left."

Jace moved his arm from over his eyes and looked at me. "I'm not like him, right? Please tell me I'm not like my old man."

I bent over and hugged Jace. "No, you're nothing like him. You never were."

"How can you be so sure?"

"Your father would have turned Chris and me over to Major Higgins," I said. "You helped us."

"And now you should get some rest," Chris said, "and let our amy medicine heal you."

Jace nodded, rolled onto his side, and fell asleep.

OUR TURF

Chris pulled one of our heat reflecting blankets from her backpack, and we wrapped it around Jace's sleeping form. Between the beating he took fighting his father and his body's medical nanite-induced rapid healing, Jace barely stirred as we tucked the blanket between him and the floor of the boxcar.

Remembering my inability to raise Jace on the comm, I checked his ears for it. "Chris, the comm you gave Jace is gone."

"How important is that?" Laney asked.

"If we have to split up in... Landfall?" When Laney nodded, I continued. "We could have used the comms to stay in touch. We can't do that now."

"And," Chris said, "Jace probably lost the comm during his fight with his father. If his father finds the lost comm and turns it over to Major Higgins..."

Chris left the ramifications unstated. But from the looks on everyone's faces, none of us had difficulty imaging the fallout if things went that way.

"The comm is small," Logan said, "and Jace said his father was drunk."

"And that was *before* Jace beat him up," Laney added.

"So..." Logan shrugged. "Maybe we're worrying about nothing?"

"Either way, we can't do anything about it now," Laney said. "We should follow Jace's lead and get some sleep." She glanced at Chris and me. "Reading lessons begin first thing in the morning."

Laney spread a blanket out on the floor and then rolled herself up in it. The rest of us followed suit. Then we did the same thing with chameleon cloths. Chris and I draped one over Jace, then we fell asleep.

I awoke to bright morning light streaming through the open boxcar door. I glanced at my companions with bleary eyes. Blinked twice. Realized everyone except Laney still slept. Laney held one of our backpacks open to the light and peered into it.

I sat up, stretched, and yawned. Laney's gaze swung my way, and she said, "I remember you saying to Granddaddy something about having food before we left his house. But I can't find it."

I stuck a hand into the backpack and pulled out a dull brown-wrapped block. "Here you go."

Laney eyed the block dubiously, even as she took it. "This is food?"

"Supposedly."

"Your ringing endorsement fills me with confidence, Anne."

"It'll keep you alive, but that's the only good thing I can say about it."

"Mmmmm boy." Laney ripped the wrapping from the food bar. "I can't wait to dig in."

I waved frantically for Laney to stop. "Wait!"

She stared at me wide-eyed. "What?"

I pulled a water bottle from the backpack. "Only chew the bar enough to break it down into chunks. Then use the water to swallow the chunks." I handed the bottle to her. "Trust me. You don't want that stuff on your tongue any longer than necessary."

With eyes wide, Laney took a bite from the food bar. Her expression turned sour when she tasted it. Laney chewed twice, took a pull from the water bottle, and swallowed. "God, Anne, you weren't kidding! This thing is vile."

Logan blinked and sat up. "What's vile?"

A sly look entered Laney's eyes. "Sleeping on a metal floor in an unheated boxcar."

Logan yawned. "Girls can be so picky."

"You bet." Laney tossed an unopened food bar to Logan. "Have some breakfast." Her brother eyed the bar with suspicion, so Laney took a bite of her own bar. "It's good."

When Logan turned his attention to his food bar, Laney quickly guzzled water and swallowed her bite. After her brother unwrapped the bar, he glanced at Laney. She held up her bar as proof she'd already eaten some of it, and said, "Yum!"

Logan nibbled the bar. He fought a successful battle to keep his expression neutral. Then he took a big bite from the bar and chewed with apparent contentment. "Not bad."

Laney gave a low growl of frustration. I laughed and said, "Logan wins this round."

That exchange woke Chris and, a moment later, Jace. When he sat up and looked our way, Logan and Laney gasped.

"What is it?" Jace asked. "The shiner my old man gave me, or the bruises around my throat?"

"Neither," Laney said. "They're gone."

"How's your side?" Chris asked. "And your leg?"

Jace sat still for a moment, obviously taking stock of his condition. His eyebrows rose in obvious astonishment. Jace hopped to his feet and walked around us. Then he pulled his shirt up and inspected his left side. "I feel great." He sat and smiled at Chris and me. "That amy medicine of yours is *amazing*! Thank you."

"You're sure you feel okay?" Chris asked.

"Better than I've felt in years," Jace said.

"That's because they haven't given you breakfast yet," Laney said.

"Don't listen to her," Logan said. "The food bars aren't that bad."

That kind of chatter helped take our minds from our unappealing breakfast. And we soon had food bar lumps in our stomachs. Then Laney and Logan broke out the books Jace got from their parents, and the three natives began teaching Chris and me how to read their language.

All I can say about the process is, thank God for my implant! Laney says their language was one of the most spoken languages on Earth before the AI Wars. Chris, who grew up on Earth, said it probably developed from something called English. All I know is the language has lots of grammatical rules, and even more exceptions to those rules. I'd *never* have kept them straight if I hadn't had my implant as a memory aid.

Chris picked it up quickly enough. But she said she learned basic

English in school. So, even though Refuge's English had hundreds of years to deviate from Earth's English, they had enough in common that Chris didn't have to memorize too many grammar rules.

I had so much trouble with the language that I welcomed our lunch break. Even though that meant eating another food bar.

We took two breaks in the afternoon. Both came when the train stopped in a city. We retreated to a corner of the boxcar and huddled under chameleon cloths while people ran up and down outside the train, and other cars clunked as they were removed from the train or added to it. We talked only when necessary, and then in whispers. And we did that until the train left each city.

"When will we reach Landfall?" I asked.

"Three or four tomorrow morning. It just depends on whether the train stops again. It usually doesn't."

"Will darkness make it easier for us to leave the train unnoticed?"

"Yeah. I've never had any trouble slipping away in the past."

The train clicked and clacked along the tracks without stopping. We slept once darkness fell, but this time we left one person on watch. Jace volunteered for the last watch, since he knew his way around the train station in Landfall. I woke briefly when his watch began, but the train noises quickly lulled me back to sleep.

A hand grabbed my arm and gave it a sharp, urgent shake. I awoke with a start. "Wha? Um, what?"

"Wake the others," Jace said. "We've got to get off this train."

As I shook Chris awake, I asked, "Why?"

"The train station is lit up as bright as day and it's crawling with men."

"Soldiers?" Chris asked.

"Probably," Jace said.

We quickly stuffed blankets and chameleon cloths into backpacks, then gathered at the boxcar's door. The train rode along a track raised ten meters over paved city streets.

"We can't jump from here," Logan said. "We'll get killed."

"I know," Jace said. "But the tracks go over a river just before they reach the station. We'll have to jump into it."

"It's cold out there. Won't we freeze in the river?" Laney asked.

"I don't think so," Jace said.

"What about the chameleon cloths?" Logan asked.

I shook my head. "A chameleon cloth still casts a shadow. Several, when light comes from different directions. We'd get caught in less than a minute."

"Then I guess we're going swimming," Laney said.

A minute later, we spotted the river. Jace shoved the boxcar's door wide open, and all five of us stood in it. Jace took my hand. "Hold hands. Jump when I say to. And try not to let go of each other when we hit the water."

The boxcar rolled past the river bank, and we stared down at the dark water.

"On three," Jace said. "One. Two. Three!"

We jumped.

Ten meters doesn't sound that far to go. Ten seconds walking. Two or three seconds running. About one and a half seconds falling. But that second and a half seems like forever during the fall. Long enough that my mind registered strange details.

Cold, moist air all around me.

Fogged breath swirling away.

Jace's cool, firm grip on one hand.

Laney's hot, damp hold on the other hand.

My lost sense of balance.

The sound of the train continuing on its way.

Bright light from the railroad station.

The flat black surface of the river.

Tension moving towards fear.

Then the fall ended.

Biting cold enveloped me.

Sound vanished.

Breath expelled.

The desire to panic.

The need for calm.

Sodden clothes pulling me down.

Kicking to go up.

Terrified I was really going down.

Relief when my head broke the surface.

Gasping for breath.

Foul-tasting river water.

Coughing.

Searching for friends.

Finding them around me.

Cold overwhelming all else.

Then...

"Go!" Jace gasped from next to me. "Swim. Away from the train station."

I turned towards the dark riverbank. Guessed I had to swim at least forty meters to reach it. Leaden limbs stroked the water. Feet weighed down by shoes kicked. Floating all but impossible because of water-logged backpacks. Backpacks full of necessities that we couldn't abandon to the river.

I thought the plunge to the river took forever. The swim taught me how wrong I was. Sodden clothing made every stroke harder, every kick less effective. Cold, foul water sapped heat from my body faster than my fight to swim generated it.

Though I swam with four friends. The misery I felt isolated me. I struggled alone. I suffered alone. I fought for life alone. Despair clawed at my mind. Cold sapped my will.

Then hands grabbed me. Pulled me back to the real world.

"You can stand now, Anne," Logan said.

I put my feet down. They sank into river muck, but my head stayed above the water. I waded towards the river bank, using my trembling arms to pull myself through the water faster. The water was only up to my waist. My knees. My ankles. Then I was free from the river's icy embrace.

And I felt *so* warm!

Someone fumbled with my backpack.

"The warmth is just an illusion, Anne," Chris said. "You only think you're warm because you're out of the river."

She pulled something from the pack and wrapped it around me. One of the heat reflective blankets from the lifepod. A moment later, all five of us clutched reflective blankets around ourselves. The same woven metal that reflected heat was also waterproof. We still lost heat as our wet clothes sucked heat from our bodies, but the blankets slowed our heat drain.

"We've got to get out of these wet clothes," Chris said.

"Yeah." Laney's teeth chattered. "But we can't just walk around naked under these blankets."

"I know where we can get dry clothes," Jace began climbing the river bank. "Come on."

We slipped and slid up the river bank. And I felt a wave of relief when we finally reached level ground. That relief ebbed away as I looked at the surrounding city.

Flickering street lights cast random pools of illumination in the dark sea of cracked, pocked streets and hulking, dilapidated buildings. Something moved in the corner of my eye. But it vanished when I focused on it.

Was something—or someone—there? Something quiet. Something waiting. For prey. For us.

I shrugged off my backpack, dug through it, and pulled out my night vision glasses. Donning them, I scanned the streets and buildings again. The city looked worse without its shroud of darkness. But the glasses let me peer into the shadows, where danger lurks.

Where danger lurk*ed*.

I removed the glasses and held them out to Jace. "Look at the alley on the left, halfway down the block."

Chris pulled her pair of night vision glasses from her pack as Jace donned mine. They both looked at the alley. Jace muttered something under his breath, too quiet for me to understand. But I felt certain the word wasn't one to inspire optimism. I got my blaster from the backpack and tucked into my pants pocket. Chris did the same.

"Let's get out of here." He pointed down a street that led away from the alley. "That way."

He set off down the street. "Walk fast and with purpose. Keep turning your head so you're aware of your surroundings. But don't jerk your head around. That makes you look scared."

"I *am* scared," Laney said.

"And freezing," Logan added.

"Yeah, sorry, but you're going to have to deal with the cold a little longer," Jace said. "The gang watching us from that alley is between us and the church where we could get dry clothes."

"Wouldn't going into a church wearing wet clothes attract attention?" I asked.

"Not as much as wandering the streets will," Jace said. "Even at this time of the morning."

We fell silent and followed Jace's lead. Copied his long stride. Imitated his roving eyes.

And the gang still surprised us.

Five minutes after Jace led away from the gang lurking in the alley, half a dozen young men filed from an alley and blocked our path. I glanced over my shoulder and wasn't surprised to see another half a dozen men behind us. Though their clothing ranged from tattered to immaculate, the men all wore identical jackets. Many of them twirled long-bladed knives. Three held objects that looked like primitive versions of our blasters.

The largest of the men ahead of us, one of the three holding a gun, stepped forward. "You on our turf, boy. Gonna have to pay a toll."

Jace gave a nonchalant shrug. "Okay. How much?"

The gang... leader? Let his gaze wander over us. "You look cold."

"Yeah," Jace agreed. "That's why I want to pay your toll and get going."

The gang leader glanced back at his followers, grinned, and turned his grin our way. "Then I got a deal for you, boy!"

Jace remained calm. "I don't want a deal. So just tell me how—"

"Don't care what *you* want," the leader said. "*I* wanna warm you up." His grin turned predatory, and he waved his gun at Laney, Chris, and me. "Leastwise, I wanna warm your girls up. Ain't that right, boys?"

The gang chorused their agreement with the idea.

"Oh, God," Laney moaned under her breath.

I wanted to take her hand and offer comfort, but I needed to keep my hands free. I settled for stepping between Laney and the gang leader.

Jace kept his attention on the gang leader. "You can't have the girls."

"I weren't asking!" The gang leader aimed his gun at Jace's head and closed half the distance between his gang and us. He waved at his gang. "Take the girls. Kill the boys."

The five gang members behind the leader leered and made big, showy, ridiculous slashes with their knives. Or, in the case of the one with a gun, twirled it on his finger. Gun guy was good at twirling, but what's the point in having a gun if you aren't ready to use it immediately?

The gang leader pointed his gun at Jace. He held it sideways because... I don't know. Maybe he thought it made him look like a big time bad guy or something. I just figured he had no idea how to handle a weapon. The way the gun wavered suggested I was right.

"I'll go forward," I said.

"Then I'll go backwards," Chris replied.

"You got that right, girl," the gang leader said. "I'm gonna."

Boost!

"Have."

I charged.

"Fun."

The gang leader's eyes just began widening when I grabbed his gun.

"Wha-?"

I twisted the gun, so it pointed straight up. The leader tightened his grip on the gun and fought to lower it. Finger bones cracked as I tore it from his grasp. His wrist popped. Probably dislocated. The leader screamed.

I know dropped guns can be dangerous, but I didn't have time to put the gun down. It didn't go off, so I kicked it towards Jace.

I ran towards the five gang members behind the leader, dragging the leader by the arm. The one twirling the gun caught it by the handgrip and tried to wrap a finger around the trigger. I spun around once and launched the gang leader at the gun twirler. Leader crashed into twirler, and they both went down in a tangle of limbs.

By then, two of the knife boys dropped into crouches and slid towards me. The showy slashes were gone, replaced by competent knife work. Probably learned the hard way, and probably against other knife fighters with no training. The first one lunged, starting with the knife low so he could stab under my rib cage. But he was turtle-slow compared to me. And his buddy was right next to him. Way too close for tandem knife fighting.

I caught and redirected his knife at his buddy's forearm. The point plunged into the buddy's arm. A severe wound if the arm was still. But the buddy's arm was mid-swing at me. His own movement made the blade open his arm from wrist to elbow. The buddy dropped the knife. A scream broke from his throat as blood covered his arm. As the knife dropped to the road, I twisted the first man's arm and dislocated his shoulder. He screamed and dropped his knife, too.

I kicked the two knives away. Saw the gun twirler pull free from the gang leader and scrabble for his gun. I took a quick step his way, stomped on his hand before it grabbed the gun, and then kicked that gun back towards my friends.

I turned to the two remaining men. One stared at me in stupefaction. The other flipped his knife over, so he held it by the blade, and then he flung it at me. I caught the knife, flashed my most dazzling smile, and pulled my arm back to throw the knife back. The knife thrower wrapped his arms around his head and crouched so I couldn't throw the knife into his gut.

"Don't!" Knife thrower turned his palms towards me. "I give!"

With a dull clank, the remaining gang member dropped his knife.

"Flat on the ground," I said. "All of you!"

Knife thrower and knife dropper fell to their knees and then stretched out on the road. The other four were already on the ground and worried more about slashes and broken or dislocated bones than about doing what I ordered. And their screams were much too loud.

"Silence!" I snapped.

To my surprise, that worked. Without taking my eyes off the six gang members, I called, "Clear."

I heard a muffled cry from behind me, followed by the sound of someone dropping to the ground. Then Chris said, "Clear."

I dropped Boost. From the change in her posture, Chris did the same.

I looked at Laney, Logan, and Jace. "Are you three okay?"

A wide-eyed Laney nodded several times in rapid succession. Her equally wide-eyed brother said, "Yeah."

Jace had the forethought to gather the weapons I'd kicked towards them. He shrugged off his backpack and dropped the weapons into it. "That was impressive."

"Oh, come on," Chris said, "you've seen us Boost before."

"Not like that," Laney said. "Not fighting."

"Yeah, that was like nothing I've ever seen," Logan added.

Chris and I shared a look, then she said, "You know we'd never do that to any of you."

"We do." Jace stood and put his arms through his backpack's straps. "But, fast as this fight was, it made a lot of noise. We need to get off the street."

"How far is it to the church you mentioned before?" Laney asked.

"Too far. But..." Jace walked to the gang leader and used a foot to push the leader onto his back. "I bet you and your gang have a place near here."

The gang leader glared up at Jace. Jace sighed, lifted his right foot, and held it over the leader's mangled hand. "Where is it?"

The leader eyed his hand and the foot poised over it. "I'll take you."

"Smart man." Jace pulled his foot back. "No wonder you're the leader."

The leader struggled to his feet and kicked his gang to their feet. Cradling arms and limping, the gang staggered into the alley they'd come from. Ten minutes later, we crowded into a room in an abandoned building. From the building's condition, I expected the worst. I couldn't have been more wrong. The gang's clubhouse or headquarters or whatever they called it was far from royal palace standards. But it was well lit, comfortably furnished, and *warm*.

It also had four gang girls inside. At sight of the stream of wounded men, the girls gathered first aid supplies and began quietly tending their wounds. One even threaded a needle and got to work suturing the arm with the long cut.

Laney eyed them for a moment, then asked, "You girls keep clothes here?"

Dagger glares turned on Laney, but one girl nodded.

"Show me," Laney said.

The girl led her behind a partition. Chris and I went along as a precaution. The gang girl didn't try anything, just glumly showed us a closet with women's clothes in it. A closet full of men's clothes was right next to it.

"Jackpot," Laney called. She took a moment examining the clothing, and murmured, "Sort of."

I saw Laney's point the minute I began sorting through the clothes, looking for something I could wear. Short, tight skirts. Plunging necklines in the blouses. The women's clothing was designed for form over function. The form was feminine, and modesty was an afterthought. Assuming it was a thought at all.

We turned our attention to the men's clothes in the hopes of finding less revealing attire. Even the smallest sized clothing fit us like tents. But we preferred that to the girls' clothes. We tightened belts, rolled up cuffs, wrapped reflective blankets around ourselves, and then returned to the main room.

Logan and Jace took their turn behind the partition while we kept a watch on the gang and their girls. Then, finally warm and as safe as we could be for the moment, we settled down and waited for morning.

EXTRA! EXTRA!

Tension blanketed the gang's hideout from the moment we walked in. It deepened each time the gang girls finished performing first aid on a gang member. The guy always rose, walked stiff-legged to the back wall, leaned against it, and glared at us. Half of them limped, which ruined the effect of their tough-guy walk. All of them accompanied their glare with arms folded across their chests. And then winced when they tucked splinted fingers under their arms. But the gang posed through the pain.

Three of the girls joined their guys along the back wall. Each one hovering protectively next to one of the gang members. The prettiest girl went to the gang leader, which probably made sense in the gang hierarchy. But one girl returned to the seat she'd occupied when we entered the hideout. She hadn't cried over the wounded toughs, nor did she offer quiet words of sympathy or encouragement. The girl just fixed the guys as best she could, and then ignored them.

I searched her face for a sign of emotion and came up empty. No concern. No fear. No loathing. The girl's face could have been a stone mask.

In a low voice, Laney asked, "What do you make of her?"

"I don't know," Chris said. "Maybe she's new, and hasn't picked a guy yet?"

"She's probably a new draftee," Jace said.

"Huh?" Laney asked.

"When gangs like this force people to join them, they call it the draft. They threaten the draftee, then their family. There's no escape for the draftee, so they finally give up and join." Jace glanced at the guys along the back wall. "Some of those guys probably got drafted, too. First, they're resigned to it. Then they accept it. Eventually, they convince themselves getting drafted was the best thing that ever happened to them."

Laney turned her attention back to the lone girl. "So, she's in the first phase? Resignation?"

"Probably." Jace shrugged. "But in six months, she'll be hanging onto one of those guys."

"Isn't there something we can do for her?"

Jace shook his head. "Not unless you can move her and her family somewhere far away from this gang." Jace looked at the floor, scuffed his right shoe over it, and lowered his voice. "It's sweet that you want to help her, Laney, but this isn't your world. Most anything you try to do will backfire and hurt the one you want to help."

Laney looked at Jace for a long moment, let her head droop, and nodded.

The gang leader took that moment to begin rebuilding his reputation with the gang. "You screwed up big time, pickin' a fight with the Immor."

"The who?" I asked.

"Immor. Us. We rule this turf." A crafty gleam entered his eyes. "I figger you new here. Don' know how things work, right?"

I hate this kind of posturing, and I'd seen plenty of it in the royal court back home. So-called diplomats or trade envoys who knew only how to threaten and bluster. The ones from other Aashlan countries were bad enough, but the ones from the Terran Federation were the worst. They always assumed we'd fall all over ourselves to get our hands on the cheap trinkets they offered in exchange for mineral rights or tax free passage through the wormholes in our system. I always enjoyed watching Mom and Dad take them down a few pegs.

I drew on that experience. "Oh, I think I have a good idea how you work."

The leader let his eyes roam over me and smirked. "How's 'bout I take you round back and show you how I work? Whatcha say?"

The girl hanging on the leader's arm stared at him. Her eyes widened and her mouth dropped open. "But Leon—"

"Shut it, Lily. You know how it works 'round here." Leon turned his glare on Lily. "*I* get the best. And that's her." Leon's mouth twisted into a cruel smile. "Fact is, any of them three girls is better'n you."

Lily's lower lip trembled, but just for a second. She turned to us, compressed her lips, and glared hot death at me.

I ignored her, kept my attention on Leon, and said, "So, about the way things work around here?"

"Yeah?" Leon said.

"Might makes right, yes?"

"You got it. An' nobody here's stronger than the Immor."

I flashed my brightest smile. "We are."

"You are what?" Leon asked.

"Stronger than the Immor." I hooked a thumb at Chris. "Or have you forgotten how my friend and I kicked your butts?"

Lily turned her glare on Leon. "Those two *girls* busted you up? Just the two of them?"

"No," I said. "*I* busted Leon up. And another five of his guys." I nodded my head at Chris. "My friend busted up the other six."

"Weren't a fair fight," Leon muttered.

Jace snorted in disgust. "You had twelve guys armed with guns and knives. You never wanted a fair fight."

Leon gave a dismissive wave at Jace, but also looked away from him.

I stood. "If a fair fight is what you want, I'll give you another shot right now. Just you and me."

"I got a busted hand," Leon said. "Still won't be fair."

I shoved my right hand into a pants pocket. "I'll fight you with one hand in my pocket."

Leon looked up at the ceiling and ignored my offer.

Lily elbowed him and said, "Fight her, Leon. 'Less you scared." When Leon still didn't move, she pushed him away and sauntered towards us. "I figger *I* oughta get the best, and that ain't you no more, Leon."

Lily stopped in front of us, tapped her lips, and looked back and forth between Jace and Logan. "Which one of you's the best?"

In unison, Jace and Logan pointed at each other and said, "Him."

A harsh laugh burst from Leon. "Guess you showed me, Lily." He pointed at the girl sitting to the side. "C'mere Tess. You my girl, now."

Tess's expression didn't change, but she rose and walked to Leon's side. Lily glared at Tess, then stomped to one of the other girls. Lily dragged the girl away and took her place.

I shook my head in disgust and turned to Jace. "What do we do now?"

"Did you get a close look at Lily when she came over here?" Jace asked.

"Close enough to point at you when she asked," Logan said.

"Yeah," Jace agreed, "but that's not what I mean. Lily's got the same hair and eye color as Chris."

"So?" Laney asked.

"So we can take Lily's papers for Chris."

"No, we can't," Laney said. "Chris is way taller than Lily."

"Yeah, but a good forger can change that. And carrying genuine but altered papers is a lot safer than carrying complete forgeries." Jace eyed the other girls. "I figure we can do the same thing with papers from the others in the gang, so we all get new identities."

"Won't the gang report their missing papers?" Chris said.

"Maybe we can give them a good reason not to." Jace stood and headed to one side of the room. "Leon, let's talk."

A wary look crossed Leon's face, but he went to Jace. They whispered back and forth for a while. When they turned back to us, Jace and Leon both looked satisfied. Jace went to his backpack, pulled out half of the cash he took from his father after their fight, and handed it to Leon. Leon took papers from three of the girls and two of the guys and handed them to Jace.

Jace stuffed the papers into his pack, then turned to Logan and Laney. "Give me the money your parents gave to you. I might not need it, but..."

Logan and Laney exchanged glances. Laney shrugged, pulled the envelope filled with cash from her backpack, and gave it to Jace. Logan did the same.

"Someone should go with you," Laney said.

"No, strangers won't be welcome where I'm going." He smiled. "Don't worry. I won't run off with your money."

"I'm worried about you, not the money," Laney said.

Jace obviously wasn't used to having people worry about him. "Uh, okay."

Logan decided the discomfort was the perfect moment to needle his sister. "What? You're not going to kiss him for luck?"

Laney smirked at Logan, wrapped her arms around Jace's neck, and pulled him down for a quick kiss on the lips. "Good luck."

"Uh, thanks?" Jace said.

Then he headed out into the city.

As soon as the hideout door clicked shut behind Jace, Logan turned his attention to his sister. "What was that?"

Laney's eyes remained on the closed door. In a distracted tone, she asked, "What was what?"

"That kiss."

Laney's eyes shifted to Logan. "Why are you asking me? It was *your* idea."

"Nuh uh. *I* suggested a kiss for luck."

Laney arched her left eyebrow. "And?"

"You kissed Jace on the lips."

"I'm still waiting for your point, little brother."

"You don't give luck kisses on the lips."

"Since when?" Chris asked.

"Why not?" I asked.

"I do." Laney's eyes cut back to the door. "For some people."

I caught movement out of the corner of my eye and looked at the gang along the back wall. Apparently thinking we weren't paying attention to them, four of them had pushed off from the wall and taken a couple of steps our way. I ignited my princess glare. "Don't even think about it."

The four guys backtracked so fast, one tripped over his feet and fell on his butt. My lips spread in what I hoped was a predatory smile. "Sitting is a good idea. All of you, sit down." The gang milled around for a moment, so I hardened my voice. "*Now!*"

The other three, who thought they could sneak up on us across ten meters of open floor, joined their fellow sneaker by sitting. The eight remaining gang members and the four gang girls waited two seconds in a futile show of resistance, then they sat, too.

Without missing a beat, Logan returned to our original discussion. "So, you like Jace?"

"He's helped us a lot," Laney said. "Why wouldn't I?"

"That's not what I meant, and you know it," Logan said. "You *like* Jace."

"Maybe..." Laney glared at her brother. "And so what if I do?"

"It's fine by me." Logan grinned. "I'm not the one who'll be kissing him."

Laney's return grin held a tinge of sisterly malevolence. "No, *you'll* want to kiss Anne or Chris."

Logan was over feeling intimidated by our looks, or he was once again in full-on sibling bickering mode. "Seriously, sis, what guy wouldn't want to kiss them?"

"What's stopping you, little brother?"

"I don't know if *they* want to kiss me."

"Don' wuss out, boy," Leon sneered. "Take whatcha want." Leon grabbed Tess by the back of the neck, pulled her face to his, and kissed her. "Like that."

Tess's expression remained unchanged until she looked at Lily. The corners of her lips turned up just enough to notice, and her eyes flashed. Then Tess's stony countenance returned.

In a monotone, Logan said, "Wow, Leon, you are such a man. I am so impressed."

Laney smiled at her brother. "Did I ever tell you how much you remind me of Dad?"

Logan replied with a smile and a duck of his head.

Chris leaned close to Logan. "Well, I definitely want to kiss you now."

Logan's head rose and stared at Chris with wide eyes. Then she gave him a soft kiss on the lips. As she pulled away, she whispered, "For luck."

"I'll save mine," I said, "in case we need more luck in the future."

"Save what?" Logan asked, his attention still on Chris.

Laney jabbed an elbow in her brother's side. "Her kiss, you loof."

"Stop it," Leon said. "You makin' me sick."

"*I* think it's sweet," Lily said. She eyed Logan. "And now I know which one of them's the best."

"Lookit them three girls, Lily," Leon said. "No way that boy wanna do nothing with you when he got them pantin' after him."

Anger flared in Logan's face, but Laney caught his eye. "Let it go. He's just trying to make you angry."

"He's succeeding."

"I know. But anger might make you do something stupid. Something that might help Leon and his boys turn the tables on us."

"You're right." Logan took a deep breath, then another. Calmer, he said, "I think we ought to take turns resting. Two watching, two napping."

"Good idea," Laney said. "You want to watch with Chris or Anne?"

Logan grinned. "Yes."

Laney rolled her eyes and sighed. "Boys... I'll watch with Anne." Laney's gaze cut to Chris. "No smooching my brother on watch."

Our implants had no translation for the word 'smooching,' which meant it was a slang term our implants never ran across. But the word's meaning was obvious from context.

"I'll keep my lips to myself," Chris said. "Scout's honor."

"We'll take the first watch," Laney said.

We fell silent as Chris and Logan stretched out for their naps. Three hours later, we woke them and took our naps.

The day dragged by like that. We let the gang girls tend to the gang guys' wounds and serve a cold breakfast. We four ate some of our food bars and again used water to swallow the bars after as little chewing as possible.

Morning crawled into afternoon, and afternoon towards evening. Our tension grew as we waited for Jace's return. Sleep came less readily, as did the easy banter of the early morning.

The only positive thing that happened was our clothes finally dried. We took turns going behind the partition and changing back to our own clothes. We all felt better for the change, even though our clothes still carried the odor of the river.

Finally, half-an-hour before darkness fell, the hideout door opened and Jace walked in. He held up five small booklets. "Got 'em."

He went behind the partition and changed into his clothes. When he returned, I offered him a food bar. But he shook his head. "I grabbed some food while I was out."

Jace distributed booklets to each of us, then we packed our stuff into the backpacks.

Leon said, "Hey, them's our guns and knives!"

"Not anymore," Jace said. He gave Leon a hard look. "Remember our deal. And remember what will happen to you if you break it."

"Yeah, yeah," Leon said. "I 'member."

"They got my gun," the gang member with the sliced arm said. "That deal o' yours better mean I get me a new gun!"

That complaint broke the dam, and the rest of the gang began haranguing their leader. Leon tried shouting them down. When that didn't work, he used his good hand to slug the closest complainer.

"You look busy, Leon. We'll just let ourselves out." Jace led us from the hideout as more gang members got into the fight. Once outside, he said, "We're going to have to hike across half the city. Are you up to it?"

"We got plenty of rest," Laney said. "What about you?"

"I had nothing else to do but rest while the forger worked on the papers. I'm good. Let's get moving. I want to put as much distance between us and Leon's gang as possible. Just in case he gets ideas."

We turned from the hideout and followed Jace deeper into the city.

The last rays of daylight colored the horizon orange. None of it reached the drab, gray streets, but the evening was young enough that we weren't alone on the streets. Tired men dressed for physical labor trudged into bars. Or staggered from them. Women wearing carefully maintained dresses hurried home, many clutching a sack of groceries. A few younger teens slouched against walls, eying their world with indifference.

Jace followed my gaze to three kids, none of whom looked older than twelve. He turned away. "Future draftees."

I gave a little shake of my head. "Leon's gang?"

"Maybe. This is disputed territory, so another gang could draft them before Leon."

"How can you tell it's disputed?"

Jace nodded to the side of a building, painted with garish symbols. "Those are gang markings. They're supposed to mark territory." He turned to a building across the street. "See how the markings on that other building are different?"

"Different markings for different gangs?"

"Yeah. And no gang tolerates another gang's symbols on their turf."

"So, both gangs *want* to add this area to their turf. But neither one can yet?"

Laney shivered. "I can't wait until we get to the good part of town and away from these gangs."

Jace snorted. "Gangs claim the good parts of town, too. The gang members are older, dress sharper, talk smoother, and blend in better. But they're more dangerous than Leon and his boys will ever be." Jace shrugged. "It's like that in every city in the world."

Logan shook his head. "Why do so many people want to move to big cities, if they're all like this?"

"Because there are more opportunities in cities," Jace said.

We walked on in silence, each of us lost in our thoughts. Twenty minutes later, we reached a bridge across the river we'd jumped into much earlier in the day. Bright, friendly lights beckoned to us from the far side of the river as we stepped onto a pedestrian lane on the bridge. Wind blew across the bridge, cutting through my clothes and whipping my hair. I shivered, pulled my jacket more tightly around me, and hugged myself for warmth. We picked up our pace, both to cross the bridge faster and to generate more body heat.

Laney suddenly looked at Jace. Through chattering teeth, she asked, "Is this the way to the church where you said we could get clothes?"

"No," Jace said. "I decided against going to it."

"Why?"

"It's probably in Leon's turf."

"So? Anne and Chris kicked his gang's butt before. And they're all walking wounded now, so it ought to be easier."

"I'm not worried about what Leon might do to *us*. It's what he might do to the people at that church if he finds out we went there."

"Oh." Laney hung her head. "I didn't think of that."

"That's because you're a good person, Laney. It takes someone like me to think like Leon."

Laney looked up at Jace. "What's that supposed to mean?"

"You know what my reputation was at home."

"So what?"

In a voice so low the wind almost blew his words away, Jace said, "I earned that reputation, Laney."

Laney stepped in front of Jace and blocked his way. "We all saw how your father treated you. Did you have any choice?"

"Everyone has a choice."

"*Children* don't." Laney caught Jace's right hand in her hands. "You were just a kid, Jace. Parents should protect their kids. But your mother abandoned you and your father beat you. You made the only choice a child could make."

"Like I said, Laney, you're a good person. And you see good in everyone, even someone like me."

"Because you're a good person, too. All it took was for one person to stand up for you."

Jace stared into Laney's eyes for a moment, shook his head, and looked out over the river.

Laney didn't give up. "Look at everything you've done for us since Anne jumped between you and your father." Laney caught Jace's chin and turned his head to face her. "You *are* a good person, Jace."

Jace sighed. "Look—"

"Will you shut up and listen to my sister?" Logan said. "I'm her brother, so I try *real* hard not to admit she's right about anything. But she's right about this."

"I agree with them," Chris added.

"I wouldn't have jumped in front of that punch if I didn't think you were worthwhile," I said.

Jace looked around at us. "I... I don't know what to say."

"Say we're going to get off this bridge," Logan said. "I'm freezing."

A small smile stretched Jace's lips. "I can't. Laney's blocking my way."

Laney spun around, linked arms with Jace, and set off again. In a bright voice, she asked, "If we aren't getting clothes from the church, where are we getting them?"

"It didn't cost nearly as much getting new papers for everyone, since I just had to get existing ones altered." Jace shrugged. "So I thought we could buy some new clothes."

"Mom always orders our clothes from the Theodore-Bonns catalog," Laney said. "I always wanted to go to one of the stores one day."

"Your wish is my command, Laney," Jace said.

Laney's steps developed a bounce. "Really?"

"Really," Jace said.

Laney kept bouncing as we crossed the bridge, and she probably stayed warmer than the rest of us because of it. The well-lit buildings in the nice part of town blocked most of the wind. The crowd of busy people going about their business helped, too. But my shivers hadn't stopped when, two blocks past the bridge, Jace led us into a bright, busy, *warm* building.

We walked along wide aisles past shelves filled with products of all kinds. Signs hung overhead, with labels and arrows pointing in different directions.

"Hang on a minute." Laney pulled us to the side of the aisle and looked at the sign. "Anne, can you read the top line?"

I had my implant call up the sounds associated with letter combinations and then studied the top line. "No fair. You gave me words that are exceptions to the rules."

Laney grinned. "Why should I make it easy for you? Now, if the words weren't exceptions, how would you pronounce them?"

"*Whoa men's cloths.*"

"Good. How is it really pronounced?"

"*Whimmin's cloze.*"

"Right!" Laney turned to Chris. "You do the next line."

"The first two words are easy," Chris said. "New fall. The third word looks like it should be *coe lors*. But I'm pretty sure it's pronounced *kuh lers.*"

"Why?"

"From context. And I know *color* is the word for the hue of something. And women's clothing always has new colors for each season." She lowered her voice. "Even in the Federation."

Laney smiled broadly. "Right! Now, let's go check out those new fall *coe lors.*" She glanced at Jace and Logan. "Come find us after you guys buy your clothes."

"What if you finish before us?" Jace asked.

"You've never gone shopping with girls, have you?" Logan asked as he led Jace in the opposite direction from us.

And the Gibson twins were right. Laney was still giving Chris and me different outfits to try when the guys joined us. They both wore new clothes, and each carried a bag with more clothing, including their old outfits.

"Are you almost done?" Jace asked.

"Don't be a loof," Laney said.

"Told you," Logan said.

An hour later, Laney proclaimed herself satisfied with our selections. She selected outfits for us to wear and paid for our clothing. Then we made one more stop to buy heavy coats. Well bundled at last, we left the store and resumed our walk away from the river.

At the next corner, we spotted a boy who couldn't have been older than ten standing over a large pile of newspapers. I recognized them for what they were because we have them on Aashla. But Chris asked, "What is he holding?"

"A newspaper," I said. "That's how civilizations without the Net spread information."

"Weird," she said.

The boy drew a deep breath and shouted, "Extra! Extra! Read all about it! Amies snatch teens from town!"

WHAT NOW?

The boy held one newspaper over his head and cried, "Special amy edition! Get it here!"

I couldn't quite read the headline from fifteen meters away, nor could I discern any details from the four pictures directly beneath the bold type. But it didn't take a genius to figure out who appeared in those photos. My friends came to the same conclusion, and they joined me in turning our faces away from the paperboy busily selling newspapers.

Jace led us into the deepest shadows, which weren't that deep in this well lit commercial district. "Hoods up." He followed his own advice, flipping his new coat's hood over his head. "Laney? Anne? Tuck your hair down your back, inside the coat."

"Don't make eye contact, either," Chris said. "Laney's and Logan's blue eyes are bad enough. But they're nothing compared to Anne's green eyes."

"The photos aren't in color, from what I can tell," Laney said. "And that has to be a sketch of Anne, since no one took her picture. We might be safe."

"Might isn't good enough," Chris said. "Besides, do you think a news story about you four won't mention your eye and hair color?"

"At least my eyes and hair are brown," Jace said.

"Maybe. It depends on how good the picture is. Since I'm the only one of us whose picture isn't in that newspaper," she held a hand out to Jace, "give me money to buy one."

Jace dug coins from his pocket, selected one, and handed it to Chris. "You won't get any change."

Chris nodded and started towards the paperboy. Over her shoulder, she said, "Cross the street and slip into the alley over there."

I kept an eye on Chris as we four fugitives set off across the street. She politely waited for the crowd around the boy to thin. But new customers shoved and pushed ahead of her. Just as we reached the sidewalk on the other side of the road, Chris gave up being polite and elbowed her way to the boy. By the time we reached the mouth of the alley, Chris was on her way to join us, a newspaper clutched in one hand.

When Chris reached our side of the street, she paused beneath a streetlight and examined the front page. She studied it for several seconds, then joined us in the alley. "The pictures don't look current, and the sketch of Anne doesn't do her justice." She handed the paper to Laney. "Can you check the article for descriptions?"

"The alley is too dark, Chris."

"That's something I can fix." Chris pulled out a pair of night vision glasses and handed them to Laney.

Laney put the glasses on and then turned her attention to the newspaper. "Let's see... Um, yeah, it notes our eye and hair colors and our heights. It spends more time on Anne and begins by claiming the drawing doesn't do justice to her 'exotic beauty' and her 'emerald green eyes.' The article also mentions Anne's hill accent. But the next paragraph speculates whether she's really native of Refuge or an amy who used some kind of mesmerizing powers on me and my family."

Laney read a little more, then glanced at Jace. "According to your father, you must be under the power of the amies. Because you attacked him, your loving father." She shook her head. "Why did they print that when Sheriff Clark and Dr. Parker know it's not true?"

"The truth doesn't mesh with the story your government wants told," I said. Even in the dark alley, I read doubt on Laney's face. "Do you remember when we watched the television news at your grandfather's house?"

"Yeah."

"They made our little six-person life pod look large enough to hold hundreds of people and called our arrival an invasion. That's the story they're telling, and they aren't going to let the truth get in the way of that story."

"But... why?" Laney asked.

"To scare you, because scared people are easier to control." A thought occurred to me. "I'm surprised they haven't blamed a few deaths on their fake invasion. But I'll bet it's coming."

"How can you know that, Anne? You're not even from this planet."

"Because I'm a princess."

"But princesses—"

"What?" I kept my tone soft. "Attend balls? Search for the prince who's their one true love?"

"Well, yeah. That's what it's like in the fairy tales."

"A princess must also be prepared to rule, should she end up on the throne. I don't want that, but I'll do it if I have to. That means my parents and grandparents must make sure I have the training required to rule. And that means I have to know all the tools available to a government, even if it's a tool my government wouldn't use." I shrugged. "You have to understand propaganda to counter it."

Laney gave a slow nod. "So, um, how do we counter this?"

I shrugged. "I don't think we can. Not without our own newspapers and television broadcasts."

"Would radio work as well as television?" Logan asked.

"Is that sound without video?" I asked.

"Yeah."

"It might. But we don't have one of those, either."

"Not right now," Logan said. "But with Jace's help, I think we can find both a newspaper and a radio station."

Laney folded her arms and frowned at her brother. "What are you blathering about, Logan? We've never even been to Landfall before. What makes you think you can find a radio station and a newspaper that will listen to us?"

"I can't. That's why I said I'd need Jace's help."

Jace shook his head. "I don't know anything about that stuff."

"But you have underworld contacts, right?" Logan asked.

"I know some crooks, but they aren't big on advertising their services. So why would they need radio or newspapers?"

"I'm not saying your crooked friends own either of those."

Laney blew out her breath in exasperation. "Then what *are* you saying, little brother?"

Logan met Laney's gaze. "Do you ever listen to underground radio?"

Laney's face screwed up in confusion. "What is underground radio?"

"It's a radio station that broadcasts without a government license. I stumbled across them one night while looking for something good to listen to on my radio. They broadcast from the back of a truck, I think, and only at night. They never use the same frequency two days in a row, so I always have to search for their signal. As long as the weather is clear, I can pick them up back home."

I saw where Logan was going with this. "What kind of stuff does this underground station broadcast?"

"Pretty much everything the government doesn't like." Logan began ticking off on his fingers. "Modern music, unapproved news stories, and political opinions. Last month, a girl gave a really passionate speech in favor of letting anyone run for political offices. Not just people approved by the AAIC."

"What is the AAIC?" Chris asked.

"The Anti-AI Interference Commision," Logan said. "No one is allowed to hold a government office unless the AAIC gives them the okay."

"And Mom and Dad let you listen to subversive stuff like that?" Laney asked.

"Why do you think I have earphones?" Logan paused for a second. "But after everything that's happened in the last few days, I bet they wouldn't have stopped me if they'd known."

"Okay, that sounds promising," I said. "But you already said they broadcast from a truck. What makes you think they broadcast from anywhere near Landfall?"

"Because they have a connection to an underground newspaper. The paper is random, too. The radio station has an announcement whenever the latest newspaper is available. The paper is only available in Landfall, so it has to be based here. If we find them, they can put us in touch with the radio station."

Jace gave a slow nod. "And you think the people running the station and paper get their supplies illegally. Because the government would have tracked them down by now if they bought their stuff legally."

Logan gave Jace a thumbs up. "Yep."

"Huh," Laney said. "That's... smart, Logan."

Logan grinned. "How much did it hurt to admit that?"

"About as much as it would hurt you to say I'm pretty," Laney said.

Logan twisted his face into a comical grimace. "That much? Ouch!"

"This has been a really useful discussion," Chris said, "but even with this new coat, it's cold out here. And I'm *really* tired of being cold. Can we go somewhere warm?"

"Yeah, sure," Jace said. "I know some places where they don't ask questions or look closely at you. But it's going to take us an hour to walk to the closest one."

"Then why are we still standing around in the alley?" Chris asked.

We returned to the sidewalk and followed Jace as he led us deeper into the city. We kept our hoods up, our shoulders hunched, and stuck to the shadows as much as possible. Jace knew the locations of all the police stations, and led us blocks out of our way to give them a wide berth.

The brightly lit commercial district gave way to bright residential areas, which gave way to less bright, more crowded residential districts. An hour later, Jace said, "Not far now."

The city around us was a far cry from the prosperous commercial and residential districts we'd walked through. But also a vast improvement over the ghetto where Leon and his gang lived. Despite the rundown appearance of the buildings, the area hummed with life and attracted a younger crowd. Men and women in their twenties gathered at restaurants and bars. Strange music filtered out of clubs. And there were enough people close to our age that we blended in with the crowd.

Finally, Jace pointed to a residential building. "That's the place." He stopped short of it. "I know I said they don't look too closely at people who rent rooms, but I think we should still play it safe and have Chris rent the rooms."

"Two rooms, one for us girls and one for you boys?" Chris asked.

"Right." Jace dug money out of his pocket. "Pay for a week."

"Got it."

We followed her into the building. Jace kept his hood up and stayed away from the desk, and Logan, Laney, and I followed his lead. Chris approached the desk and spoke with the clerk. The clerk nodded, grabbed some keys, and then turned a book towards Chris.

"Sign here," he said.

"Uh oh," Laney whispered.

But Chris took the pen and wrote where the clerk pointed. He spun the book, and glanced at whatever Chris wrote. Without a word, he handed her the keys and pointed to the stairs.

We followed Chris up the stairs. As soon as we had a flight of stairs between us and the lobby, Laney said, "I thought we were dead when he asked for your signature. What did you write?"

"Nothing. I just made a bunch of looping scribbles." Chris grinned. "From the way Jace described this place, I guessed they got a lot of illegible signatures. It looks like I guessed right."

We ended up in two fourth floor rooms with an inside door joining them. Our room had a double bed, a wardrobe, a sofa large enough for one of us to sleep on, and another chair. One of the telephone devices sat on a small table next to the wardrobe, along with a small pad of paper and a pen. The guys' room was a mirror image of ours. We stored our new clothes, and then Jace and Logan joined us in our room.

"Okay, Jace," Logan said, "what do we do first?"

Laney jumped in and said, "First, we try to change our appearance. Otherwise, we'll have to worry about being recognized by everyone who sees us."

"What do you need?" Jace asked.

"Scissors. Hair coloring. Makeup. Glasses for you guys, since you already have short hair." Laney grabbed the pen and pad of paper. "I'll make a list, then Jace can take Chris out to buy what we need."

"Why Jace?" Logan asked.

"His brown hair is more common than our blonde hair. He also knows more about staying unnoticed than you and me."

Jace and Chris were gone for a long hour, but they finally returned safe and sound with a bag full of supplies. We girls spent the next several hours cutting each others' hair and changing Logan and Laney from blonde to brown. Jace gathered the trash, including the cut locks of hair, into the bag from the store and took it to a public trash bin on the street in front of our hotel.

Finally, we wished each other good night and fell into bed. Or, in my case, onto the sofa. Despite the sofa's lumpy cushions, sleep claimed me within minutes.

The next morning, Jace telephoned a nearby diner and ordered a takeout breakfast for us. He deepened and roughened his voice while speaking to the diner, and ended with, "Name's Montide. My daughter's gonna pick up the food... Ten minutes? Thank you."

He hung up the telephone and then turned to Chris. "I usually eat at that diner when I'm in the area. Even with the changes you girls made to my looks, they might recognize me. Especially since I'd have to talk to someone if I picked up the food. So..."

Chris nodded. "I'm still the anonymous one in our group. So I should pick up the food." She flashed a sudden grin and held out her hand. "So, give me some money, *Dad*."

Jace peeled two bills from our dwindling stack of money. "Tell the guy at the register to keep the change. The tip is a little on the low side, so make sure you smile brightly and make eye contact with him. He raised four daughters, so he has a soft spot for girls."

Fifteen minutes later, Chris returned with two large paper bags. We dug into scrambled eggs, bacon, and toast, along with cups of coffee. After two days of nothing but survival food bars, the simple breakfast tasted like a royal feast. We'd meant to make plans during the meal. But, by unspoken agreement, we all concentrated on the food. And we ate it all.

Finally, I leaned back and gave a contented sigh. "I'd forgotten what real food tasted like."

"Me, too." Logan turned to Jace. "How do we go about finding the underground radio station? Do we start with your underworld contacts?"

"*I* start with my underworld contacts. They'll clam up if I bring strangers with me. And, since I'm disguised, they'd assume you were, too. Your hair cuts, hair coloring, and make up only work if people don't look closely at you. And my contacts will do that. They'd recognize you from the newspaper photos pretty quick. I guarantee someone will sell that information to a reporter or the police." Jace shook his head. "No, it's just too dangerous."

"But it's safe for you?" Logan asked.

"No, but I think I can explain away why my picture is in the paper with yours."

"How?" Laney asked.

"I'll tell my contacts that I got sick and tired of doing all the work and having my old man get all the money. We got into a fight. I beat him up, took the money *I* earned, and came to Landfall to set up business for myself. I'll start with guys who knew what things were like for me at home and tell them dear old dad lumped me in with you guys so everyone in the country would be on the lookout for me." A rueful smile played across his lips. "It's probably even the truth."

"Okay," Laney said. "So, what do the four of us do? Just wait here in the room for you to come back?"

"No, you could go out and see the sights. This is Refuge's first city and our country's capital."

"Um," I said, "that brings up a good point. I know the name of your country's enemy—Plausen—but what is *this* country's name?"

Logan's eyes widened. "That's right! We never have mentioned that."

When he didn't continue, I used my mildest princess glare on him. "So, what is it?"

"Ab Astra," Logan and Laney said in unison. Laney added, "It's supposed to mean 'from the stars' in some ancient Earth language."

"What's 'Plausen' mean?" Chris asked.

Logan grimaced. "That's the name of the guy who led the rebellion that made Plausen its own country."

"At home, people name cities after their leaders all the time," I said. "Why not countries, too?"

"Back to our plans for the day," Laney said. "You just want us to play tourist while you risk your life?"

"No, I want you to get a feel for Landfall's street layout and the downtown districts," Jace said. "Playing tourist lets you do that without attracting attention. Since the papers show two girls and two guys, I hope they won't pay much attention to three girls and one guy. Just keep your hoods up and avoid eye contact. When contact is unavoidable, let Chris handle it."

"Will a tourist map help make us anonymous?" Logan asked.

Jace nodded. "Good idea. Buy a map, but not until you're a few blocks from here. This area might not be on a tourist map, so make sure you remember this address and how to get back here."

I tapped my head over my implant. "Don't worry, Jace. That's second nature for scouts. Chris and I will store everything in our implants."

"Good." Jace pulled on his coat. "Don't expect me before dinnertime, at the earliest. So take your time playing tourist."

Jace left. We waited fifteen minutes, donned our coats, and headed out into the city. We wended our way along crowded sidewalks for two blocks, then Chris dashed into a shop. She returned a minute later with a tourist map. We stayed out of the flow of foot traffic and gathered around the map.

"Where should we go first?" Laney asked.

"I'd like to see the World War Memorial and the *Haven Seeker's* landing spot." Logan pointed to two icons on the map. "They're pretty close to each other, too."

"Those are fine with me." Laney looked at Chris and me. "What about you two?"

Chris shrugged. "Those sound as good as anything else."

"I don't mind starting there," I said, "but I want to get a look at the major government buildings afterwards. Are they close to the monuments?"

"Not really," Laney said. "But we're supposed to get a feel for the city's layout, so the extra walking will do us good."

Laney refolded the map, and we rejoined the teeming masses on the sidewalk. An icy wind whipped down the street and into our faces. Everyone around us walked with their heads down, their faces out of the wind, hats down low or hoods pulled tight, and their hands stuffed into coat pockets. Cold as the wind felt, it made it easy for us to hide our faces from others, even when the crowd thinned.

We walked for an hour before we reached the monuments Logan wanted to see. He and Laney found both monuments far more moving than Chris and I did. They grew up with history lessons about the landing and the World War, not to mention their grandfather's stories about his role in the war. While Chris and I appreciated the aesthetics of both monuments, we had no emotional connection to either of them. But we weren't the only people visiting the monuments. So we pretended emotions we didn't feel, echoing Laney's and Logan's authentic comments.

When our friends from Refuge finally had their fill of the monuments, Laney opened the map again. "Where to next?"

I glanced around to make sure none of the other tourists were nearby and pointed at a huge icon at the center of the map. "What's that?"

Laney said, "The Capitol Building. It's the center of government in Ab Astra."

"Then let's go there," I said. "I'm curious how it will compare to our palace back on Aashla."

Laney checked street signs, and we set off for the heart of power in Ab Astra.

GO!

As we walked towards the Ab Astran Capitol Building, I wished for warmer weather. Not because I was cold, though I was, but because you see fewer tourists during the cold season. Chris, Laney, Logan, and I weren't the only tourists wandering through the government district in Landfall. But we'd be hard pressed to hide ourselves in the sparse crowds out today.

At least we didn't have to watch for drones with cams, feeding images into facial recognition software. That technology was still decades away, based on what Chris and I had seen during our brief stay on Refuge. But that brought up another question. I'm from a low tech lost colony. Our original colonists lost all their technology when the colony ship crash landed on Aashla. Laney and Logan told us a lot about *Haven Seeker*, the colony ship that brought their ancestors to Refuge. But they never mentioned a crash that set their world back to more primitive tech.

I glanced around us, making sure no one was close enough to overhear me if I murmured. "Laney? Did the *Haven Seeker* crash land on Refuge?"

Laney's eyebrows arched in surprise, but she matched my quiet tone. "No. Why?"

"The colony ship to my home world crashed, and that set the colony's technology back a thousand years. Refuge's technology is a thousand years behind what was available on Earth when the *Haven Seeker* departed, but you say the ship landed safely?"

"Oh, that," Laney said. "The colonists who came on the *Seeker* were escaping from militant AIs, so they based their society on Earth in the 1950s. That was the last decade before computers really caught on. The technology is good enough for a comfortable life, but the computers are far from capable of hosting an AI."

"And everyone is okay with that?" Chris asked.

Laney shrugged. "Mostly. There are malcontents who want to build a technotopia, but everyone ignores their ravings."

"What's stopping some of those people from building better stuff in secret?" I asked.

"That's when Internal Security steps in," Logan said.

"And they do what?" I asked.

Logan shrugged. "Arrest everyone involved, destroy the technology, and make sure the people they arrested can't do that kind of work anymore."

The open-ended nature of that last part had an ominous note to it. "So, if we end up using an underground radio station and newspaper, the government will sic Internal Security on us?"

"Yeah." Logan's eyes darted around us, as if he was afraid Internal Security agents were all around us. "And the Izzies have an intimidating reputation."

"Izzies? That's a nickname for Internal Security agents?"

Logan nodded. "But maybe we'll get lucky and your Scout people will get here before the Izzies find us."

"But that won't help you, Laney, and Jace. Not to mention the rest of your family."

"Sure it will," Laney said. "Once we prove you're not amies, we'll be home free."

I had serious doubts about that, but I kept them to myself for the moment. Instead, I wondered at the vast power the Ab Astran government had brought to bear against Chris and me. We just wanted to go home, not upset the balance of power on Refuge. The government's actions so far told me they wouldn't just let us do that. If their whole rationale for maintaining power and control over the population rested on the claim that AIs ruled humanity, I could understand why they wouldn't want news getting out that the humans won the AI wars. I didn't agree with the rationale, but I understood it.

Before I went further with that train of thought, we reached the Ab Astra Capitol Building. I'd expected majestic architecture and luxurious building materials. Instead, I stared at a gray stone hulk of a building, with none of the grandeur found on countless worlds across the Federation. The Capitol Building's single claim to fame was its size. It spread across an entire city block, and the building's center rose at least ten stories above us.

I assumed the architect had gone out of his way to make the building appear intimidating. If so, mission accomplished.

"Wow," Chris muttered, "have you ever seen an uglier building?"

"No," I said. "Not even the meanest shepherd's hovel on Aashla is as ugly as that thing."

"Let's walk around the Capitol's perimeter," Chris said. "I doubt we'll learn anything useful from it, but you never know."

We made the circuit, and we learned nothing. Back at the main entrance, Chris nodded her head toward a sign over an exterior door. "Laney, am I reading that sign correctly? Does it say citizens can go on tours of the Capitol?"

"Sure. It's a guided tour. Do you think we should take the tour?"

Chris shook her head. "There's no way I'll risk letting you three go inside. There will be guards, and they'll have nothing better to do than look at the people on the tours. Your disguises won't stand up to that kind of scrutiny."

"What do we do while you're gone?" Laney asked.

Chris looked up and down the street. "There's a coffee shop down there. Spend enough money to justify taking up a table until I return from the tour."

"Yes, ma'am," I said. "Also, I'm imagining myself saluting."

"Then imagine I returned your salute." Chris turned away from us. "I'll be back."

We headed for the coffee shop as Chris headed into the monstrosity that was the Capitol. Laney and I made small talk—a vital skill in a royal court—while we sipped coffee and nibbled on pastries. Logan guzzled coffee and gobbled pastries and showed the typical guy response to small talk. He slumped in obvious boredom.

After half an hour, Laney waved her hand in front of her brother's face. When Logan ignored her hand, she said, "Look at his eyes, Anne."

"What about them?" I asked.

"They're glazed like a donut."

"Mmmm." Logan's eyes focused on the pastries. "Did someone say donuts?"

Our laughter sounded forced, probably because it was. I checked the clock on the wall—those worked the same as clocks on Aashla, thank God—and worked hard not to fret. Chris had only been gone for thirty minutes. Besides, she didn't panic when I went into the town searching for Laney and her family, even though I was out of touch for hours. If Chris could survive that, surely I could handle her going on a building tour. Even if the building *was* the center of the search for Chris and me.

Yeah, I could do it.

Yep.

No worries.

Laney reached across the little table, squeezed my hand, and whispered, "Chris will be fine. You'll see."

"I know. I just hate waiting."

But wait, we did, for another hour and a half. Finally, Logan's eyes focused again, and he said, "She's coming out."

Laney and I looked towards the Capitol Building, and we easily spotted Chris reach the street and turn our way. Thirty seconds later, she walked right past the coffee shop without stopping. But not without sending a Scout hand signal.

I immediately stood. "Let's go."

Laney and Logan looked confused, both because Chris ignored us and because I suddenly hopped up. But they dutifully fell in behind me and followed me from the shop. By then, Chris was half a block ahead of us and not slowing down.

"What's going on?" Laney whispered to me.

"Chris gave me a hand signal when she passed the shop," I said.

"What did she signal?"

"Follow me," I said. "And danger."

Chris kept her head down and set a brisk pace away from the Capitol Building. But the cold drove everyone else to do the same, so we blended into the late morning foot traffic. Every now and then, Chris looked up from the sidewalk and glanced up. At first, I thought she was checking street signs. Eventually, I realized she only looked up when she approached a street light atop a high pole. I couldn't figure out why she did that, and it took all my willpower to keep from copying her. Because a sketch of my face was all over newspaper front pages. Even with the hair cut, hair coloring, and makeup, I saw no reason to show my face in public more than was necessary.

By the time Chris slipped inside our hotel, I felt the burn of fatigue building in my legs. From their ragged breathing, Laney and Logan must have felt the same. I resisted a groan at the prospect of climbing three flights of stairs and soldiered on. But I couldn't resist a groan of fatigue when I finally flopped into a chair opposite Chris, in our room.

Laney and Logan did likewise, and Logan asked, "What was the big hurry, Chris? I know it's cold outside, but it's not *that* cold."

Chris was breathing as hard as the rest of us, maybe harder, since she'd been on her feet all morning. Laney, Logan, and I got to sit for an hour and a half while she toured the Capitol Building. So I said, "Catch your breath first, Chris. You've been on your feet a lot more than we have."

Chris nodded and slumped back in her seat. She closed her eyes and took long, deep breaths. Her color returned to normal as the room's warmth penetrated her muscles. Finally, she sighed, opened her eyes, and directed a solemn look my way. "The situation here is a lot more complicated than we thought it was."

"That sounds... ominous," I said. "Why do you think that?"

"Let me build up to that."

I sought to lighten her mood a bit. "This plebe hears and obeys, ma'am!"

Chris offered the ghost of a smile in response. "It's just as well I'm the one who took the tour of the Capitol Building. Guards just inside the entrance had copies of the pictures of you from the newspaper. They stopped everyone close to the right age and compared them to the pictures. Some poor guy a few spots ahead of me in line got pulled out because he bore a superficial likeness to Jace."

"It's a good thing you had us stay outside," Laney said.

"A very good thing. I don't look anything like you or Anne," Chris said, "but I got extra scrutiny because of my age. A man and a woman spent a full minute comparing me to your pictures, but they finally waved me through. That would have made me feel paranoid if they hadn't spent just as long with every person our age who came through the checkpoint.

"They had two tours—a self-guided one and one with a tour guide. I took the one with the tour guide, hoping we'd go to a few places the self-guided tour skipped. We did, too. Our guide led us into the operations center of the Capitol, pointing out the offices of important-sounding officials, and even let us look into the main parliamentary chamber."

"It all sounds interesting," Laney said, "but—"

"It was pretty boring, actually," Chris said. "Maybe it would have meant more to me if I recognized any of the names and titles the guide rattled off. But things got a lot more interesting as the tour guide led us back to the self-guided tour route.

"One of the children in the group stopped and gawked through a door with a window in the top half. Most of the office doors were like that, and the kid looked through them all. So did I. But when the kid began oohing and aahing, I activated my implant's record function and joined him at the door. It only took the tour guide five seconds to return and push the kid and me back to the group. But that gave my implant time to record everything in the room.

"I kept just enough concentration on the tour to stay with it and turned the rest to examining my implant's short recording. The room had banks of monitors showing scenes from the streets outside the Capitol. People watched all the monitors, and sometimes zoomed in on people on the street." Chris looked at me. "I didn't have time to see more, but you can guess what it reminded me of."

I nodded. "Facial recognition software."

'Right," she said.

"Okay, that went right over our heads," Laney said. "What's 'software' and how does it recognize faces?"

"Software is another word for a program that runs on a computer," I said. "In really simple terms, facial recognition software can match faces to other photos or pictures."

"Um, we don't have computers on Refuge," Logan said. "That's kind of the whole idea behind the colony."

"Who told you that?" Chris asked. "The same high ranking crew members who claimed humanity lost the AI wars?"

Logan shrugged. "I guess."

"Well, they lied about not having a computer, too. The last stop on both tours is a lovely courtyard entirely surrounded by the Capitol Building. It's got flowers, well trimmed bushes, a reflection pool, and six abstract sculptures that just happen to look like water cooling systems—the largest ones I've ever seen."

"So?" Logan asked.

"I've only seen pictures of that design," Chris said, "and that was in history books. It's a cooling system for an enormous computer. One powerful enough to host an AI."

As Chris's words sank in, Laney's eyes widened. "That can't be right."

Logan gave a slow shake of his head. "You must be wrong, Chris."

Chris met their gazes. "Why?"

"Because..." Laney's hands fluttered in helpless anxiety. "Our whole lives we've been taught to hate AIs."

"What better way to cover the truth?" Chris asked.

"No." Logan's voice held firm determination. "Grandad fought in a war to stop Plausen when Ab Astran spies learned Plausen was developing computers and AIs."

"That's the Big One your grandfather talks about?" I asked.

"Yeah." Logan turned a challenging gaze on me.

I met his eyes. "And Ab Astra won the war?"

"Plausen signed a treaty forbidding computer and AI development, so yes."

"It wasn't a military victory?" I asked. "Plausen didn't surrender?"

"Not really, I guess. But we got what we wanted from them. So we won."

"Ab Astra signed the same treaty?"

"Of course."

"And does Plausen claim *they* got what they wanted from Ab Astra, so *they* won?"

"Yeah, but so what? Ab Astrans know better than to believe their propaganda."

Chris looked at me. "The AI runs both governments."

Again, Laney shook her head. "There's no way an AI can run *anything* on Refuge. We don't have computers—"

"You have at least one," Chris said.

"*And* we don't have implants." Laney crossed her arms. "So it's impossible."

"How do you know you don't have implants on Refuge?" Chris asked.

"Because..." Laney's voice faltered. "That's what we were taught in history classes."

In a gentle tone, Chris said, "Just like you were taught humanity lost the AI wars?"

In a small voice, Laney said, "Yes."

Belligerence filled Logan's voice. "You know, we only have *your* word that humans won that war."

"Mine, too," I said. "And your parents and grandfather already figured that out on their own."

"Logan," Chris said, "do you honestly believe Anne and I are lying?"

"No." He sighed. "But you could be programmed by an AI to believe that story."

"You don't really believe that, do you?"

"I don't know what to believe anymore, Chris."

"Me, neither," Laney said.

"Then there's only one thing to do," Chris said. "Let's get lunch."

"Huh?" the Gibson siblings said.

"We'll order lunch from that deli," Chris said. "And we'll stop talking about AIs and governments or anything else disturbing or controversial."

We did as Chris suggested. And I discovered a new delicacy to take back to Aashla if—make that *after*—the Scout Academy rescued us. Okay, maybe other Aashlans already knew about a bacon, lettuce, tomato, and fried egg sandwich. But the royal kitchens served nothing like it I knew of.

Conversation lagged as we avoided the subject of AIs on Refuge. Finally, Laney said, "You know, we still don't know much about your lives before you hid in Granddaddy's barn."

"There's not much for me to tell," Chris said. "I grew up on my family's tramp freighter, and nothing remarkable ever happened to me until Anne and I came here. But *Anne's* father is the most famous Scout in the history of the Corps."

Laney's eyes cut to me. "Spill."

I assumed that meant she wanted me to tell my parents' story. "Okay, but I'm going to tell the stories the way Mom and Dad told me, and that's not nearly as exciting as the vids Chris has seen."

"Wait," Logan said, "what's a vid?"

"A visual recording that people watch in theaters or at home," Chris said.

"Oh, like a movie," Logan said.

"Or a television show," Laney added.

I shrugged. "I guess. We don't have any of those on Aashla—that's my home world—so I only got to see those when we visited Dad's parents."

"You don't have them at that Academy of yours?" Logan asked.

"We do," Chris said, "but we don't exactly have a lot of spare time between studying and training."

"Yeah, whatever," Laney said. "We don't have any of those now, either. So drop that subject and let's hear Anne's stories."

They all fell silent, and I said, "I guess it all started when Dad crash landed on Aashla and saved Mom's life."

At the Academy, I answered questions about my parents as briefly and factually as possible. Since Laney and Logan didn't already know anything about Mom's and Dad's adventures, I really opened up about them. I'll admit that I really got into the excitement and danger that filled my parents' life before I was born—and after, in one case. I even told what Mom and Dad felt during the most dangerous and most romantic parts. Hours passed, and I never quite knew it.

"Wow," Laney breathed when I ground to a halt.

"That was amazing," Logan said.

"Why didn't you ever tell the stories like that back at the Academy?" Chris asked.

"I didn't want to sound like I was bragging," I said, "or, I don't know, trying to claim some of their heroics for my own."

"Didn't you realize that's what all the cadets *wanted* to hear?"

"They did?"

"Yeah." Chris shook her head. "When you gave those really terse answers, a lot of people assumed you thought they weren't good enough for your stories."

"But I was trying to *avoid* acting like that!"

"No one knew that, though," Chris said. "At least this will be easy enough to fix when we get back." Her eyes dropped to the floor. "Assuming we ever do."

"How can you say that after hearing Anne's stories?" Logan asked. "Do you honestly believe her parents will *ever* rest until they bring you and Anne home?"

Before Chris responded, the shrill ringing of the telephone filled the room. Laney spoke aloud the question we all thought. "Who could be calling us?"

"There's only one way to find out." I lifted the receiver and held it to my head. "Hello?"

Jace, his voice low and urgent, said, "Grab what you can and get out of the hotel. Do it *now!*"

"What?" I asked.

I heard more voices from Jace's end. He shouted, "Go!"

Then the connection went dead.

LOVE YOU, SIS

"Who was it?" Laney asked as I replaced the receiver in its cradle.

"Jace." I headed for our room's three-drawer dresser. "Grab everything. We've got to get out of here."

Chris's Scout training took over. She joined me at the dresser and began scooping up armfuls of clothes. Laney and Logan exchanged startled glances, and Logan said, "What about Jace?"

I stuffed shirts and pants and underwear into backpacks. "He's in trouble."

"What kind?" Laney asked.

"I don't know!" My voice sounded harsh to my ears. Angry. Worried. "But he took time he probably didn't have to warn us." I pointed through the connecting door to the boys' room. "Don't waste it!"

The siblings jumped to their feet, and Logan dashed into the other room. Laney paused for a second, realized Chris and I didn't need her help, and hurried after her brother.

A minute later, Chris and I slipped our arms through our backpack straps. I grabbed Laney's backpack, and then we followed Laney and Logan into the other room. They did as we had, grabbed the boys' few clothes and stuffed them into the two packs the boys had worn.

"Ready?" I asked.

"Yeah," Logan said.

"Wait," Chris said. She went to the window and peeked through the curtains. "There's a lot of activity out there."

Logan joined her at the window, and Chris pulled her head aside so he could see out. "Plainclothes cops."

"How can you tell?" Laney asked.

Logan turned away from the window. "It looks like a scene from a gangster movie out there. They'll have the back exit covered, too."

Laney turned to me. "Will those chameleon things work in the city?"

"Yes, but not well enough to let us sneak through a crowd of people. Especially if they're looking for us. Direct light doesn't help, either."

"They'll search our rooms," Logan said. "So..."

"The roof!" Laney said and darted for the door.

In the hallway, we heard a commanding voice echoing up the stairwell. "Up the stairs. Hurry, before they know we're coming."

"Fire escape!" Logan hissed.

He led us to a window at the end of the hallway as feet began pounding up the stairs. He threw open the window, climbed out onto a metal stairway landing, and climbed towards the roof two stories above us. "Last person through closes the window."

Chris shoved Laney through the window and sent me next. The footfalls on the stairs sounded way too close for comfort as Chris flowed through the window. She moved with such speed and fluid grace that I knew she'd Boosted. Chris slid the window shut, grabbed the rails of the fire escape, and pushed herself into a handstand. That moved her body out of the direct line of sight through the window. Just in time, too, as the footsteps changed from stair pounding to hallway running.

Chris hand-walked up the railing as someone in the hallway shouted, "Police!" followed by two doors smashing open.

Chris tucked and swung down onto the stairs. She had just enough room to stand on the stairs without being seen by the policemen down the hall. "Hurry, while they're making so much noise!"

We traded stealth for speed and ran up the stairs. Twenty seconds later, we found ourselves on the flat roof of the hotel. It had a small building in the center that I assumed protected the inside stairway from the weather. A meter high wall ran around the edge of the roof, with dozens of metal poles attached to it. Those poles held more poles that extended at odd angles from the supporting pole.

Laney pointed to a three-meter section of the low wall free of the poles. "There aren't any television antennas there. It'll be the best place to hide. That way, we won't interfere with anyone's signal."

We neither understood nor questioned Laney's choice as we sat with our backs against the wall. Chris and I pulled chameleon cloths from our packs and spread them over us. We showed Laney and Logan how to tuck the cloth around them without leaving folds, which can sometimes cause a ripple effect in the cloth's chameleon circuits.

We were panting by the time we finished. And that alerted me to another problem—our breath clouded in the cold. Like folds in the cloth, it probably wouldn't give us away. But probably wasn't good enough.

I whispered, "If the police come to the roof, breathe through your nose. That way, your breath won't cloud as much."

My friends nodded their understanding. And we settled down to wait.

As we huddled under two chameleon cloths, we heard the sounds of shouts and lots of banging from below. The hotel's top two floors softened the sound into something almost melodic, with a surprisingly predictable rhythm. The sounds trailed off after five minutes and stopped entirely after ten.

We heard the deep engine roar from several more cars approaching. They stopped in front of the hotel, the engines stopped, and the quieter sound of opening doors came from the street. Voices called back and forth until a loud one rose above the others.

"All right, quiet down." The other voices chattered on, which obviously irritated the man with the loud voice. He raised his voice even more. "I told you to shut up!"

"Gee, Lieutenant," another man called, "you don't gotta yell."

A few others laughed, which the Lieutenant didn't like. "Can it, Thompson. Same goes for you morons who think he's some kind of comedian." He paused for a beat to make sure everyone was listening. "We got information the kids who got involved with amies holed up here. Three girls, two boys. The guys from Internal Security *think* one of the girls is an amy."

Apparently Thompson couldn't resist a crack. "When did the Izzies learn how to think, Lieutenant?"

Instead of chastising Thomson, the Lieutenant said, "Yeah, it was news to me, too." He waited for the laughter to die down, then continued, "The hotel clerk says four of them came in around noon. One of the girls brought back lunch from Vinnie's Diner, but none of the others left.

"We checked their rooms, and it looks like they cleared out in a hurry. I think we missed 'em by only a minute or two. But we had men covering all the exits, so they're probably hiding somewhere in the building. That means we gotta search the place from top to bottom."

Some of those listening grumbled, but it didn't sound serious to my ears.

"Okay, here's the plan," the Lieutenant called. "Four men to each floor and another four for the basement. Search every room, and check every place somebody could hide. Anybody complains, you send 'em to me. Got it?"

The men chorused their assent, and the Lieutenant began assigning men to the different floors.

"He didn't say anything about the roof," Laney whispered. "Maybe they won't check up here?"

"Don't hold your breath." Logan kept his voice as quiet as his sister's. "It might mean the Lieutenant will check the roof himself."

Under her breath, Chris said, "God, I hope not."

I agreed with her. The Lieutenant came across as far more observant than the average policeman. And policemen are usually more observant than the average person, anyway.

A soft splat sounded from over my head as a drop of water hit the chameleon cloth. A second followed the first. A third. A fourth. And then more drops than I could count.

God above, couldn't you have waited to let droplets fall from the sky?

"Oh, no." Dread filled Chris's quiet voice. "Rain."

"What's the problem?" Laney asked. "Will rain short out the stuff that makes your chameleon cloth work?"

"No," I said. "The cloth is waterproof."

"Then what's the problem?"

"Because the water will pool in depressions and run down the sides. The chameleon circuits will still work, but that won't affect the water."

"It'll be like water running down a window," Chris added, "except without there being any glass in the window."

Comprehension dawned on Laney's and Logan's faces, and Logan said, "So a cop who comes up here will definitely see us?"

"Maybe not, if he just glances around," I said. "But if he takes time to look? Yeah."

Logan stuck his arm out from under the cloth and pointed at the little building that I thought covered the inside stairway. "Then let's go in there and try to hide in a corner."

Neither Chris nor I had a better idea. We nodded and began pushing ourselves to our feet. The door was on the far side of the building, and time was short. At the same moment, we heard a voice from the direction of the fire escape.

"Keep looking, men," the Lieutenant called. "I'm going to check the roof."

We heard a muffled clang as the Lieutenant stepped out onto the fire escape landing. The sound repeated ominously with each footfall as he climbed towards the roof.

We pulled the chameleon cloths off of us as quietly as possible. Logan leaned towards me as I stuffed one under my arm. He reached behind me, cupped the back of my head, and drew me into a short, tender kiss on the lips.

"Wha—?" I murmured.

"I'm collecting your promised kiss for luck," Logan said.

"Not the time—" Laney began.

Logan flashed a lopsided grin at Laney. "Love you, sis!"

Then he dashed towards the fire escape. His move surprised us so much, Logan was halfway to the far side of the roof before I belatedly, uselessly, reached out a hand to stop him.

Laney drew breath to call out. But Chris slapped a hand over her mouth and hissed, "He's creating a diversion so we can find a better hiding place. Don't waste it!"

Wide eyed, Laney nodded her understanding. Chris pulled her hand back and set off for the little building atop the roof. We all watched as Logan reached the edge of the roof. The Lieutenant spotted him and shouted, "Stop right there, young man! Police!"

But Logan ignored the shout. He hopped up on the edge of the low wall running around the roof. My wildly beating heart went into overdrive as Logan jumped over the edge. A split second later, we heard a resounding clang as he landed on the sixth floor landing below the Lieutenant.

"Stop!" the officer yelled.

Pounding footsteps descending the fire escape told us Logan had ignored the command. The Lieutenant ran down the stairs in pursuit as he yelled, "Fugitive on the fire escape! Stop him!"

Shouts sounded from inside the building and a few more rose from the alley behind the hotel. The echo of running feet filled the air as what sounded like half the police force of Landfall chased after Logan.

We rounded the little building and caught sight of the door. Chris grabbed the knob and twisted, but the knob didn't turn. "Locked."

"Can't you break it open with your Boost thing?" Laney asked.

Chris nodded. "But it will be loud. What if there are still policemen in the building?"

I glanced across the back alley, at the building behind the hotel. The two buildings were the same height, and both had flat roofs. "If Logan's distraction worked, there shouldn't be any policemen in the back alley. We can jump across it to the other building."

Laney shook her head. "That's at least five meters. I can't jump that far."

"You can with our help," Chris said. She walked quickly and quietly to the roof's edge and cautiously peered over it. "The alley is empty." She came back to us. "Here's what we're going to do, Laney. Anne and I will Boost. You wrap your arms around each of our shoulders, we'll each wrap an arm around your waist, then we run for the edge and jump to the other building." Chris flashed a confident cadet sergeant's smile. "It'll be easy."

"What do I do?" Laney asked.

"Run with us," Chris said.

"And you close your eyes, if you want," I added.

Laney immediately closed her eyes.

Chris gauged the distance to the edge. "Start with your left foot. Boost and run on three. One. Two. Three!"

Boost!

Adrenaline flooded my body as the three of us led off with our left foot. With our legs pumping in sync, we ran for the edge. As we neared the low wall, Chris and I leapt up to its top. Laney gave a quiet yelp.

Then Chris and I planted our right feet squarely on the top of the low wall. In unison, we shoved up and out.

A twenty-meter chasm yawned beneath us. Then the roof of the other building appeared beneath us. We landed a good two meters past the edge and caught our balance. Laney cracked one eye open.

"We made it?" she asked.

"Drop Boost," Chris ordered.

I did, and then said, "We made it easily."

"Okay. I'm going to worry about my brother now."

"So are we," Chris said.

"And we'll do our best to figure out a way to rescue him, too," I said. "But right now, we need to get out of sight."

This building also had a smaller structure atop it. But the door into it wasn't locked. Chris listened for a moment and then opened the door. We slipped out of the rain, waited for our eyes to adjust to the dim interior, and then looked around. Tools hung neatly from hooks above a workbench. Another wall held shelves full of spare parts; door knobs, hinges, plumbing supplies, and just about every fastener you can imagine. Stairs that led down to the rest of the building were positioned next to the wall opposite the work bench.

Chris pointed towards a corner where the floor was dirtiest. "There's so much dirt there, no one must ever walk into that corner. We can cover up with dry chameleon cloths and wait for night. Then we'll slip out of here and get far away from this area."

"What do we do after that?" Laney asked.

Chris shook her head. "I wish I knew."

YOU CAN SAY IT

With the need for silence paramount in our minds, we sank into introspective silence. I touched my lips with my fingers, trying to reawaken the feel of Logan's lips on mine. Because Logan's unexpected kiss was my first on-the-lips kiss. Ever. In my life.

I know it sounds odd, but Princesses don't get asked out on dates like normal girls. Princesses get invited to chaperoned balls. And woe be unto a guy who tried to sneak a kiss from me. I can't imagine what my guards would do to him. Somehow—probably through my own behavior—that 'hands off the princess' policy carried over to the Scout Academy.

But Logan didn't know any of that. Nor did I have a gaggle of guards dogging my steps. Right now, that was too bad. Because I'd love to dump this situation in my guards' laps and just follow their lead. Then maybe Logan wouldn't have had to create a distraction for us girls to get away. And maybe he wouldn't have kissed me.

But he had. And I had liked it. Enough to want another kiss. Which meant finding a way to rescue Logan. And Jace.

Which brought me back around to our big problem. Chris didn't know how we could do that. And neither did I. That's why I'd let my mind wander to Logan's kiss. I could have forced myself to think about our problems, but

Mom and Dad taught me that sometimes you have let your mind wander. Get out of your own way so your subconscious can work on your problems. That can work, too, though it hadn't yet worked for our current situation.

The rest of the afternoon passed in shared, miserable silence. Chris and I lent silent support to Laney whenever we felt like she needed it. We put our arms around her when her shoulders silently shook, her mouth open in unvoiced grief.

After what felt like forever, the cloud-dimmed sunlight visible through the crack beneath the door faded to black. From the building below, we heard the sounds of people locking offices, descending the stairs, and exiting the building. An office building of some kind, then. That helped us, since everyone in the offices had somewhere better to go at the end of their working day.

We waited half-an-hour after the quitting time departure rush ended. Then Chris said, "I think it's safe for us to leave."

"Okay," Laney said. In a low voice, she added, "Sorry about my crying earlier."

"Your brother just gave himself up so we could escape," I said. "Crying is perfectly natural."

Laney hung her head. "You're both dealing with the same stuff I am, only it's even worse for you. *You* don't cry. Neither does Chris."

"We did all of our crying before we met you," I said. "I even cried over what my *cat* would think if I never came home again."

Laney's lips spread in the ghost of a smile. "You did?"

"Pretty silly, huh?"

"I think that's sweet," Chris said. "Not silly at all."

"I agree with Chris," Laney said.

"And that's enough self pity for the moment," Chris said. "We need to dry our eyes and get moving."

"Do you know where we're going?"

"I think we need to find out what the government is telling people," Chris said. "That store where we bought our clothes sells televisions, and the televisions all showed the same show."

Laney's eyes widened in understanding. "We can watch the evening news on those TVs!"

"Yep." Chris began stuffing her chameleon cloth in her backpack and slipped her arms through the straps. "But we need to leave now if we're going to reach the store in time."

"Um," Laney began, but fell silent.

"What?" Chris asked.

"I know we've been wearing the backpacks a lot," Laney said, "but they're not something most people wear in town. Especially not girls."

"So we'll stand out if we're wearing them?"

"I think so."

"That's good enough for me." Chris removed her backpack and put it in the filthy corner we'd been sitting in. "Stack them here. Then Anne will wrap her chameleon cloth around the packs. They'll be as safe here as anywhere."

"We should take the night vision glasses," I said. "And maybe the blasters?"

"No weapons," Chris said. "We can't win a straight up fight, anyway."

"Good point." I pocketed my night vision glasses, waited while Chris did the same, and then added my backpack to the pile. I took care wrapping my chameleon cloth around the packs. When I was done, I even had trouble seeing the cloth-covered pile. "Let's get going."

We descended the stairs as quietly as possible. Sounds came from a few offices. Low voices. Clacking I recognized as the sound of someone using a typewriter, which are still fairly new tools on my home world. The soft swish of a mop on a floor.

On the first floor, we took deep breaths and walked boldly through the doors. Pedestrians walked with their heads down and collars up, protecting themselves against the cold drizzle. No one gave us a second glance. Chris pulled her hood up, lowered her head, and led us away from the hotel. At the next corner, we turned in the direction of the distant commercial district.

We paralleled the road the hotel was on and matched the fast pace of the people sharing the sidewalk with us. The street lights brightened as we left the less affluent neighborhood of the hotel, and brightened more when we reached the commercial district. An hour after we left the office building, we reached the big department store and entered on the heels of a couple old enough to be our parents.

We broke away from the couple when they headed upstairs. From there, Laney led us straight to the department that sold televisions. To our relief, the national news program hadn't started yet. A few younger children stared at the televisions, probably waiting for the parents to finish shopping. We settled in close to the children, hoping passersby would take us for older sisters keeping an eye on our younger siblings.

The news started, and it led off with Jace's and Logan's capture. The man reading the story added all sorts of nonsense about amy thought control. Then he spoke of the three girls who accompanied Jace and Logan. Laney's photo appeared on screen.

"Laney Gibson, sister of Logan Gibson, the unfortunate victim of amy thought control, is believed to be traveling with these two girls."

Depressingly accurate drawings of Chris and me filled the screen.

"Officials from Internal Security believe both girls are amy spies, identifying likely targets for destruction by their AI masters."

In a low voice, Chris said, "They're really laying it on thick."

"No joke," Laney said.

Something in my peripheral vision caught my attention. I glanced that way, and spotted the kids who'd been watching nearby. A boy among them watched Chris, Laney, and me with a wary expression. His darting eyes met my gaze. His eyes widened, then he turned and ran away from us.

The other kids who'd been watching the store's televisions looked at their running friend. As their heads swung our way, I turned my back on them and blocked their view of Chris and Laney.

"We need to go," I whispered. Laney turned towards the kids, so I hissed, "Not that way!"

They both caught the urgency in my voice and turned their backs on the kids and the televisions. We walked away, acting as casual as possible.

One of the girls behind us asked, "What spooked Tommy?"

Another girl scoffed by blowing out her breath. "Knowing Tommy, his own shadow scared him."

The other kids laughed as Chris, Laney, and I ducked out a store exit. We bundled up against the cold as we began retracing our steps to the office building next to the hotel.

Chris pulled her hood as far forward as possible and looked down at the sidewalk. "What happened?"

Laney and I followed Chris's example with our hoods. Then I said,

"One of the kids watching television recognized us. He ran off, but I had to assume it was to tell his parents about us."

"Okay." Chris raised her head for a moment and looked around. "If you're right, it won't be long before the police descend on this area, looking for us. They'll be looking for three girls together, so we'd better split up. Stick to the shadows and alleys as much as possible."

"I don't like the idea of leaving Laney alone," I said.

"I can take care of myself," Laney said.

"I'd agree if we were back in your hometown. But the dangers in this city's alleys and shadows walk on two legs, not four. You can't Boost if some thug attacks you."

"I'll stay with Laney," Chris said. "You follow us from a distance and watch for signs of recognition from people around us."

"I still say I'll be fine," Laney said. But I thought I heard an undertone of relief in her voice.

With the decision made, I looked up and down the street before dashing across it. Once there, I pulled my hood low, shoved my hands into my coat's pockets, and headed in the same direction as Chris and Laney.

An icy wind whipped around me, stung my face, and forced tears from my eyes when I looked into it. Since everyone else fought the same thing, it made it easy to walk the street all but unnoticed. Chris and Laney benefited as well. But Chris stuck to her original plan of taking alleys when possible and sticking to shadows when not. The first time she did that, I had to hurry back across the street so I could tail them through the alley.

Five minutes after we exited the store, two police cars roared by. Their red lights strobed, telling pedestrians and other drivers to give way before them, but they ran without wailing sirens. I'd heard several sirens from a distance since we came to Landfall, and was just as happy not to hear one up close. Not seeing police cars at all would be even better, but I knew better than to hope for that.

With the first signs of police activity, Chris led Laney into the next alley she came to. I was about fifty meters behind them, and alert for anyone who took notice of my friends. And this time, someone did.

A young man about my age, wearing a leather jacket that reminded me of the ones Leon and his gang wore, glanced about furtively and then slipped into the alley behind Chris and Laney. Just before he disappeared into the alley, I saw the glint of steel as he pulled a knife out from under his jacket.

I picked up my pace, though I didn't quite break into a run. Chris could handle the guy if it came to a fight. But if I could find a rock or a brick or something in the alley, maybe I could sneak up behind the guy, bash him over the head, and then Chris could save Boost for possible later emergencies.

When I entered the alley, I saw Chris standing protectively in front of Laney. Knife guy stood a couple of meters from Chris, holding his knife in a steady, underhand grip. Unlike Leon's minions, he didn't wave it around like an idiot. He'd taken a good stance, too, one that showed he knew more about knife fighting than Leon and his gang combined.

"Look girlie," knife guy said, "just gimme all yer money an' things don't gotta get... complicated."

Chris sighed. "If you don't want complications, just turn around and walk away."

Knife guy shook his head. "I like me a confident girl, but I ain't lookin' fer a tumble right now. If you gonna complicate things, maybe I take more'n yer money. You get me?"

Chris and Laney saw me sneaking up behind the guy, so Chris worked to keep his attention on her and Laney. She began unbuttoning her coat in what I could only call a seductive manner. She opened her coat wide and threw back her shoulders. "If you think you're going to lay hands on this body, you've got another think coming."

Knife guy's stance shifted, and I heard confusion in his voice when he said, "What's wrong with you, girlie? You actin' like you want me ta do ya." He waved his knife. "Look, just toss ya money on the ground and I let ya walk away. Okay?"

"I don't think so."

"I'm the one with the knife, 'member?"

"Yeah," Chris drawled, "but *I'm* the one with a friend sneaking up behind you."

Knife guy laughed. "I ain't fallin' fer that old trick, girlie."

Putting all my strength into it, I kicked knife guy between his legs. He made a sound like air leaking from a balloon, dropped the knife, and fell to the ground. As he curled into a ball, I picked up his knife. "Thanks for the knife."

I watched over knife guy for half-a-minute while Chris and Laney went on their way. He was still rocking and moaning, but I wasn't willing to risk him getting up and following us. So I gave his head a hard whack with the hilt of his knife. Then I took off after Chris and Laney.

The run in with knife guy must have convinced Chris that alleys weren't worth the risk. She and Laney stuck to normal sidewalks. As before, I trailed after them and kept watch for anyone paying extra attention to them.

At random times, I stopped in front of shops and used reflections in their glass windows to look for people paying too much attention to me, too. But one benefit to the frigid weather was that everyone around us wanted nothing more than to get out of the wind. They hurried towards their destination, showing no interest in those around them.

We finally reached the office building where we'd left our backpacks. Chris and Laney hurried up to the building's door, acting like a couple of girls just looking to get out of the wind for a few minutes.

Chris turned the doorknob. "Oh thank God, it's unlocked! Hurry and get inside."

They slipped into the building and stood in the foyer, bouncing up and down and rubbing hands over their arms. Exactly like anyone would do to warm up. Just before I reached the door, they turned and headed deeper into the building. I imitated their act, and then followed them to the stairs.

We met on a landing between the second and third floors, then climbed quietly up to the sixth floor. As before, we heard sounds of activity on a couple of floors but saw no one. We stopped at the foot of the last flight of stairs, the ones that went to the maintenance shed on top of the building. Dim lights in the stairway barely pushed back the darkness. Tired from the cold, the long walk, and the stress, we hurried up the stairs towards the shed.

A few steps from the shed, we heard a soft scraping sound from it. We stopped climbing and stayed as silent as possible.

A man's voice came from the shed. "I heard you coming from the time you three started up the stairs. You came this far, so you might as well come the rest of the way."

In response to our silence, the man said, "All your stuff is up here in the corner. At least, I assume it's your stuff. I'm keeping it if you don't come up and claim it."

We exchanged glances. Laney shrugged. I gave a tentative nod. Chris gave a more decisive nod, fixed a friendly smile on her face, and started up the stairs. I activated my best princess smile and followed her.

The sound of static came from above, and the man said, "Ha! Got it."

We rounded the last landing before the shed and got our second surprise. The shed was completely dark. But we clearly heard the static, and then the static changed subtly. Chris and I exchanged puzzled glances, but Laney whispered, "It's a radio, and the guy is changing frequencies looking for a radio station."

"Right you are," the man called. The static faded, replaced by an announcer's voice.

"Don't want the news," the man said, and the static returned.

Chris started up the last flight of stairs. The man found and bypassed four more stations before our heads rose high enough to see into the shed. Dim light came from something on the workbench—the radio, I assumed—but the dark shape of a man stood between us and the radio.

"Hello?" Chris said.

"Hello," the man said. "You can come the rest of the way up the stairs. I don't bite."

"It's dark," I said.

"Oh, right! Sorry about that." The dark shape of the man moved a bit, and a bare light bulb on the ceiling came to life. "I'm not used to visitors up here."

We climbed the rest of the way into the shed, and Chris said, "My name is Chris. The other two are Anne and Laney."

The man turned around. He stood nearly two meters tall—taller even than Jace—and looked like he was in his mid twenties. He wore a friendly smile, and sightless eyes stared in our general direction. The man extended his hand more or less in Chris's direction. "I'm Cam Wheeler."

Chris took his hand and shook it. Laney and I did the same.

"You can say it, you know," Cam said.

"Say what?" I asked.

"That I'm blind."

"I figured you already knew that," I said.

Laney gasped. "Anne!"

Cam threw back his head and laughed long and loud. "Oh, my. That's a new one on me!" His smile spread into a delighted grin. "Most people tiptoe around that subject. I like that you don't, Anne."

I drew a deep breath and took a big chance. "That's good, because we desperately need help."

Cam's grin faded to a sliver of a smile. "You *must* be desperate if you're asking a blind man for help."

"You have no idea, Cam."

"Try me."

One thing life in the royal court taught me was the importance of snap judgements. Only, they're usually not as snappy as most people believe. Snap judgements emerge from a collection of tiny impressions others make on us. From the gleam in their eyes—not an option with Cam—to the sound of their voice. From the words they use to the things that make them laugh. From the way they stand to the way they breathe. And God only knows how many other impressions we form when meeting someone for the first time.

Cam gave the impression of a likable guy. Someone who would listen to your problems and offer his best advice. Who would laugh at your jokes, but not at your dreams.

There are plenty of con men in the galaxy who could do those things. But Cam also gave the impression of a trustworthy man.

So I decided I trusted him.

"Do you keep up with the news, Cam?"

"Not tonight, but enough to know what's going on."

"You know the three girls that are all over the news right now? The ones your government says are amy spies? We're those girls."

Cam's sliver of a smile widened. "I know."

"You do?"

"Yep."

"How?"

"Let's see." Cam began counting on his fingers. "One, the cops came to the hotel across the alley, looking for three girls and a guy suspected of consorting with, or being amies. Two, the guy led the cops on a merry chase while the three maybe-amy girls made their escape. Three, I came up here to tinker on my radio and smelled girlish odors coming from the shed's unused corner. And four, shortly after that, three girls crept up the stairs to this shed."

Cam lowered his hand. "It didn't take a genius to figure out your secret."

"Just a blind man, who relies on smell and hearing more than most," I said.

"You got it."

"So, what are you going to do about us, Cam?"

"Well, Anne, that depends on what kind of help you need."

"Are you sure you don't want to turn us in? Your government—"

Cam's voice dropped to a growl. "Will *not* get you in their clutches, if I have anything to say about it." His voice returned to normal. "So, again, what kind of help do you need?"

Cam's unexpected vehemence caught me by surprise. My left eyebrow rose in a way I hoped would encourage him to explain it. Then I wanted to smack myself for using a visual cue on a blind man. I lowered the eyebrow, remembered my diplomatic training, and decided it might be best to come at the question in a roundabout manner. Injecting a note of sincere thanks into my voice, I said, "I can't tell you how much that means to us."

Cam's smile returned. "But?"

I thought I'd hit the perfect tone of voice to hide what I really wanted to say. So Cam's question caught me by surprise. "Um, what?"

"You buried your curiosity well, Anne. But we've already covered my blindness and reliance on senses other than sight. I can hear a question lurking beneath your words."

I sighed. "First Jace, now you."

"He's the other friend who got caught?" Cam asked.

"Yes. He has highly developed hearing, too. But you're right, I was working around to asking you a question."

"It would be less work if you just asked it, Anne."

"You're probably right, Cam. It just goes against my mother's training."

"Is your mother a diplomat?"

"You could say that. Anyway..." I took a moment to organize my thoughts. Cam must have sensed that, because he waited patiently until I asked, "It's your tone of voice when you said you'd do everything in your power to keep us out of your government's hands."

"Clutches." The vehemence returned to Cam's voice. "Hands can be gentle and protective."

"*That* tone, Cam. That's what I don't understand. What's behind it?"

"The same reason I know you're nobody's minions, AI or human."

"You're right," I said, "but what makes you so certain?"

"Because the only AI minions on Refuge are members of our own government." Pain filled Cam's face. "And my father is one of them."

GIRLS AND THEIR AIRS

We stared at Cam in stunned silence, until Chris asked, "What makes you think your father is an amy?"

"It's... a long story," Cam said.

Chris's shoulders rose towards a shrug. Then she remembered Cam's blindness, and her shoulders dropped again. "This shed might be the only safe place for us in the city. So unless you have pressing business somewhere else...?"

A smile played across Cam's lips. "My most pressing business is keeping you three safe and free. And I mean that from the bottom of my heart."

"Thank you." Chris leaned back against the shed's wall. "Begin your long story when you're ready."

"I've got a small apartment in the basement. We'll be more comfortable there. Are you hungry?"

"Starving," Laney said.

"I'm not a very good cook—"

"I am," Laney said. "Take me to your stove and refrigerator. I'll do the rest."

Cam's infectious grin reappeared. He clicked his heels and bowed in Laney's direction. "Your wish is my command, m'lady."

We grabbed our stuff, and Cam led us down the stairs. He paused before each floor to listen for people moving around on the floor. I never heard anyone out and about, and I assume Cam didn't either. The basement was pitch dark, which didn't bother Cam. But he knew we needed light, so fumbled around for a light switch he must never use. A bare bulb identical to the one in the shed blazed to life.

We followed Cam down a narrow hallway, past a door labeled *Electrical* and another labeled *HVAC*, to a door at the end of the hallway. Just inside that door, Cam searched for another light switch, found it, and led us into a tidy one-room, windowless apartment.

Laney headed for the kitchen section and began rummaging through the refrigerator. Cam sat on the floor and leaned against the wall. "Sit anywhere."

I looked between the single upholstered chair and the bed. "Why don't you take the chair, Chris. I can sit on the bed."

We sat, and Cam began his tale. "My father was the kind of man every kid wants for a dad. He was funny, encouraging, and willing to give me enough freedom to make my own mistakes. I'm not saying he let me run wild, he was strict about important issues that I was too young to understand. But he believed childhood cuts and scrapes were part of the rites of passage to adulthood.

"Dad always found time in his day to spend with me. He'd throw a ball with me, play a game of chess, or whatever. And he always took thirty minutes at the end of the night to read to me.

"I lost my sight when I was nine. A man ran a traffic light and smashed into the rear passenger door I sat next to. Blindness terrified me. And, as much as I love my mother, she sort of fell apart for a while after the accident. Blamed herself, even though she didn't do anything wrong, and let that guilt consume her. And she became so overprotective of me that she wouldn't let me do anything by myself.

"My Dad saved me. He treated me exactly the same as he did before the accident. He bought a toy ball made for dogs, one that had a bell inside it, and I learned to catch it by the sound it made. We played chess, and Dad never got impatient when I touched every piece on the board to make sure I knew where everything was. After a while, I learned how to remember the board's layout without touching all the pieces. And he still read to me every night.

"Dad taught me to use my other senses to compensate for my

blindness. At random times, he'd quiz me about what I could hear, smell, feel, or taste." Cam fell silent for a moment. "I'm not saying I wouldn't have learned all that stuff eventually. But I believe it would have taken me years. Dad helped me learn it all in less than a year. He never told me I couldn't do something, either. Like when I was eleven and got interested in electronics. Dad picked up a beginner's electronics set and let me figure it out on my own. If I found myself totally stumped, he'd offer just enough advice to get me back on track. But he let me screw up, shock myself, short circuit things, and learn from those mistakes.

"I'm not bragging when I say I'm an electronics expert. It's too bad the big electronics firms are too closed-minded to hire a blind guy." Cam gave a wry smile. "But it's good for you three that the only job I could land was here, working as a combined janitor and maintenance man."

The sound of sizzling came from the stove. Cam took a deep breath. "That smells delicious, Laney."

"Thanks," Laney said. "But you should have time to finish your story before it's ready."

"Okay." Cam took a moment, probably to organize his thoughts. "I told you about what Dad was like at home. But he was just as good at his job as he was at fathering. He worked for the government, in the Treasury Department. And his treasury bosses thought highly of him. They promoted him several times while I was growing up. Then, when I was thirteen, he got the *big* promotion, to Assistant Secretary of the Treasury.

"Mom and I were so proud when he told us the news. The Treasury held a big promotion ceremony and everything. The day after that, Dad had to go off for a week of special training. The man who came back wasn't the same. I mean, he was my father. Mom said he looked right, had all the right scars and birthmarks. Walked the same. His voice sounded the same, mostly. But he was different. He dismissed me when I tried to talk to him about my latest discoveries. He took no interest in my electronics. Wouldn't throw a ball with me, nothing.

"Mom tried blaming the pressures of his new position, but I could tell she didn't believe that explanation. I had no idea what had happened to my father. Then I met the children of some other high-level government employees. They all had similar stories. Their father or mother got the big promotion, went away for a week for training, and were never the same again.

"Most of them just assumed their parent was just too wrapped up in their new job. But I met two others who had the same kind of relationship with their parent that I did. We all assumed something strange happened during the business trip, and being turned into an AI minion was the only explanation that made sense to us."

"I hate to interrupt," Laney said, "but supper's ready. Eat it while it's hot."

We grabbed plates of food, and spent a few quiet minutes enjoying the fruits of Laney's labor. Cam took a moment between bites to say, "This is really good!"

Chris and I nodded our agreement, which put a brief smile on Laney's face. We finished eating and leaned back in contentment.

Laney turned to Cam. "What did you and your friends do after you figured out what happened to your parents?"

"We dedicated our lives to destroying the AIs running our world." Cam sighed. "Not that there's a lot we can do. We don't even know where the AIs are, much less how to destroy them."

"We know," Chris said.

"Know which?" Cam asked.

"Both."

"You do? Seriously?"

"Yes. But the second part will be much easier if we can get access to a radio."

"What good will that do?"

"Our people are probably already looking for us. This star system will be one of the first places they look. We need a way to tell them we're here. And what to destroy."

A thoughtful expression spread over Cam's face. "I could build a transmitter, but it will take a while. Unless..."

When he didn't elaborate, I asked, "Unless what?"

"Hm? Oh, sorry. There's a pirate radio station that operates in the area. I can make contact with them, and maybe I could increase their transmitter's power."

"We had the same idea," I said. "Or Logan, Laney's brother, did. Do you know how to get in touch with them?"

"No, but one of the other kids I told you about—the ones who lost a parent to the AI—knows."

"Can we trust the person?"

"Absolutely."

I glanced at Chris and Laney. They nodded, and I turned back to Cam, "Where do we start?"

"I can hear how exhausted you three are," Cam said. "So what you should do next is sleep."

"Won't we risk tripping you, if we're sleeping on your floor?" Chris asked.

"At least one of you can sleep in the bed," Cam said. "Two, if you don't mind being a little cozy."

"How can you even think of sleeping while the Izzies have Jace and my brother?" Laney demanded.

"We'll be no help to Logan or Jace if we're exhausted, Laney," I said.

"Easy for you to say," Laney snapped. "The Izzies aren't holding *your* brother."

I kept my voice as gentle as possible, and said, "Even if we bring down the AI that's running Refuge and rescue Jace and Logan, I still might never see my family, friends, or home world again. It's the same for Chris."

Guilt swept over Laney's face, and she dropped her head into her hands.. "God, Anne, that was thoughtless of me. I'm sorry, I didn't mean—"

"I know." I gave Laney a hug. "We're all three stressed and exhausted. That's not a good combination."

"Listen to Anne," Chris said. "She's smart. For a plebe."

"Then the smart plebe should get the bed," Laney said. "After all, she slept on the hotel room's lumpy sofa last night."

"Sounds fair to me." Chris turned to Cam. "I feel grimy. Do you have a bath?"

Cam smiled. "You don't smell grimy." He pointed to a narrow door on the back wall. "There's a shower stall in there, but the bathroom is tiny."

Chris opened the bathroom door. "Wow, you weren't kidding. I'm not sure I'll even have room to undress."

Cam shrugged. "You can undress out here."

Chris began unbuttoning her shirt, but Laney shook her head. "I am *not* parading around naked in front of a guy."

Cam waved his hand in front of his eyes. "Why not? It's not like I can see you." His grin returned. "And if you do parade around, at least I can brag to my friends that I had three beautiful, naked women in my apartment."

"As if," Laney said, but she smiled when she said it. "And what makes you think we're beautiful?"

"Are you saying you're not?" Cam asked.

"No. I'm just curious."

Cam thought for a moment. "The old saying is that beauty is in the eye of the beholder. Since I'm blind, beauty is in the ears and nose of the... behearer and besmeller."

"How do we smell?" Laney asked.

"You have the scent of fresh air and the outdoors, with a hint of an animal I don't recognize."

"Horses. What about Chris?"

"Sweet, but in an antiseptic way. Like she doesn't usually spend much time in nature. And, since I figure you're going to ask about Anne next, her scent is exotic and tinged with unfamiliar spices." Cam's grin faded into a sad smile. "It makes me kind of sad that I can't see what you three look like."

Chris froze, having just stepped out of her skirt, and shared a look with me. God above, we'd been so wrapped up in our own troubles that we'd forgotten what we could do for Cam.

I waved Chris towards the bathroom. "Go shower. I'll talk to Cam."

"Okay." Chris finished undressing and entered the bathroom. "But don't administer it until we've all showered."

"Don't administer what?" Laney asked.

I took a deep breath. "Cam, what if you *could* see us?"

"Huh?" Anger filled Cam's face. "I didn't take you for a cruel person, Anne. That's not a funny joke."

"It's not a joke, Cam. And I can't guarantee our... medicine will cure you."

"Oh!" Laney said. "You're talking about giving him the same amy medicine you gave Jace on the train?"

"What are you talking about?" Cam demanded.

"Yes, Laney," I said, "though it's not exactly medicine. Cam, may I explain?"

"Yeah, sure. Since you've gone this far with it, you might as well finish."

"You know Chris and I are not from Refuge?"

"Yes," Cam said. "I figured it out from what you said to Laney just now."

"We come from a civilization that has access to far more advanced technology than you have here."

"You came on a spaceship of some kind, so that's kind of obvious," Cam said.

"Spaceships are just to the tip of the iceberg, Cam. We have access to medical technology that would boggle your mind."

"And repair my eyes?"

"Since you lost your sight in an accident, I *think* so."

"How?"

"I can only give you a really simplified explanation, because that's all I know."

"Okay, spill."

"Most of our medical technology works through things called nanites. You know what robots are, right?"

"Yes."

"Well, nanites are microscopic robots. One medical injection has millions of them. They find damage to your body and fix it." I sighed. "That's really all I know."

"Wait," Laney said, "you told Jace that the injection was medicine."

"You three had just found out about our implants, and Chris and I thought knowing about nanites might make you trust us less. Believe the government's amy stories. Something like that." I ducked my head. "I'm sorry, Laney, it's just—"

"You're a loof," Laney said. "One who's stuck on a planet full of people out to get you. And you didn't want to scare away the only friends you had."

"Pretty much."

Laney gave a nonchalant wave of her hand. "I forgive you, Your Highness."

The ghost of a smile flashed across Cam's face. "Girls and their airs."

"What does that mean?" Laney asked.

"Your Highness?" Cam shook his head. "Seriously?"

Laney looked at me. "Introduce yourself, Anne, and give him the full treatment."

I sighed. "I am Her Royal Highness, Princess Anne Megan Karen Heidi Tisha Erin Courtney Stephanie Villas, third in line for the throne of Mordan, a kingdom on my home planet of Aashla."

"You're not pulling my leg?" Cam asked.

"No. But I'm also plain old Scout Cadet Anne Villas."

"Could you maybe start your story at the beginning?" Cam asked. "Because I'm lost."

By the time Chris emerged from the bathroom, I was describing our close brush with death in the leaking lifepod. Chris pulled her clothes on and asked, "Who's next?"

"Anne," Laney said. "She's royalty, after all."

I stuck my nose in the air. "At least you know your proper place, peasant."

"Um, did you tell Cam about...?" Chris's eyes cut to our backpacks.

"Yes, though he hasn't given me an answer yet."

As I pulled off my shirt and slipped out of the skirt, Cam said, "I might as well try it. But finish your story first."

"Chris will have to take over," I said. "I have a reservation with soap and hot water."

Thirty minutes later, after my shower, Laney's shower, and the completion of our tale, Chris asked, "Are you ready for the injection, Cam?"

"I... think so."

"Are you nervous?"

"Yeah. And I'm trying real hard not to get my hopes up."

I gave one of our four remaining medical injectors to Chris. She knelt down next to Cam. "Should I do it?"

"Uh..." Cam's face hardened. "Do it."

Chris held the injector to Cam's neck and activated it. When she removed it, Cam asked, "How long will it take to work?"

"I don't know," Chris said. "The more extensive the damage, the longer it takes."

"Probably by morning, though," I added. "And I bet sleep will help."

We bade each other goodnight. Chris, Laney, and Cam rolled themselves up in survival blankets while I slipped under the covers of Cam's bed. I closed my eyes and fell asleep immediately.

Something woke me suddenly, and I fought down panic as I tried to figure out what had spooked me. As my nose registered the unfamiliar scent of the pillow, panic rose again as I wondered where I was, too.

Then a sliver of light shining through the cracked bathroom door caught my eye. The light wasn't bright, but it cast just enough illumination for me to see three sleeping pallets on the floor of a one-room, windowless apartment. One pallet held Chris, her face relaxed in sleep. Tousled blonde hair was all that was visible of Laney, who slept on the next pallet. No one slept on the third pallet. So where was Cam?

I looked back at the sliver of light. A shadow blocked the light briefly, followed by a muffled sound. A... sob?

I slid out of bed. The shock of the cold floor on my feet drove the last of the sleep from me. I wrapped my arms across my chest, wishing the shirt Cam loaned me to sleep in had more insulation, and tiptoed to the bathroom door. I stopped, stood still, and even held my breath to better hear any sounds from the bathroom.

A shuddering gasp sounded from the bathroom. I turned my head and put my lips to the sliver of an opening. In a low voice, I asked, "Cam?"

Another shuddering breath. Panting. A long, deep breath. Then a quiet voice. "Anne?"

"Are you okay?"

Another shuddering breath. "Yeah."

"Are you sure?"

"Could you...? Would you open the door?"

"Um, sure." I pushed the door open wide enough to sidle partway through the door. "What can I do?"

Cam turned towards me, tear tracks running down his cheeks. He blinked. *And his eyes focused on me.*

"My God," Cam whispered. "You are more beautiful than I could have ever imagined."

I flashed a modest smile. "You're just saying that because I'm the first girl you've seen in what? Fifteen years?"

"Sixteen. And no, I'm not."

Laney's sleepy voice said, "What's going on?"

"Let me out," Cam said. "I've got to see Laney and Chris, too!"

I backed out of the doorway. Cam slipped by me and stared at the other two girls. Chris was awake by then, and she and Laney blinked into the bright light streaming from the bathroom.

Cam dropped to his knees and his head swung back and forth between the two girls. "You're both gorgeous. All three of you are gorgeous. And... And..." Cam swiped at the tears on his face and then stared at his damp hand in wonder. "Tears. I thought mine were gone forever. But those little robots even fixed my tear ducts! How can I ever thank you?"

I smiled, letting my joy for Cam spread over my face. "Make sure I can talk to my father when he comes looking for me, and we'll call it even."

Cam shook his head and gave a gentle laugh. "That doesn't seem like sufficient repayment for this miracle. You girls have changed my life!"

"And you'll change our lives if you can give us a way to talk to Dad when he gets here. That seems like a fair deal to me."

"And me," Chris added.

"And me," Laney added, "because I'll need Anne's father's help getting Logan and Jace back."

Cam stood. "Then what are we waiting for?"

Laney tilted her head and raised her eyebrows in an are-you-kidding expression. "You, to go get breakfast or a newspaper or anything that gets you out of this apartment for at least fifteen minutes."

"Why?" Cam asked.

"I felt strange enough parading around naked when you were blind. There's no way I'm going to do that now that you can see!"

"Oh! Right!" He glanced towards the door. "So, I should, um..."

"Leave," Laney said.

Cam rose. "Of course."

"And *knock* before you come back in," Laney added.

"Sure. Knock. You got it." Cam stopped with his hand on the door-knob. "Do you mind if I invite a friend here? Someone I'd trust with my life?"

We three girls exchanged glances. Laney shrugged. I nodded. Chris said, "Just one friend?"

Cam gave a decisive nod.

"Okay," Chris said. "But don't tell *anyone* you've recovered your eyesight. You're going to need to act like you're still blind for a while."

"Because news like that would get back to the Izzies, for sure," Cam said.

"Exactly."

"So, what do you want for breakfast?"

"Anything that includes bacon," Laney said.

"I wouldn't say no to pancakes," Chris said.

"I'll eat anything that tastes better than a survival food bar," I said.

"Talk about setting a low bar," Laney muttered.

"Got it." Cam turned the doorknob, released it, went to his dresser, picked up a pair of dark glasses, and grabbed a cane leaning against the wall. "Camouflage."

As soon as Cam left the apartment, we three girls got busy preparing ourselves for a busy day. By the time he returned forty minutes later, we were dressed and made up as modest Ab Astran young ladies.

Cam followed Laney's instructions and knocked. Laney opened the door for him and found herself face to face with a blonde woman who looked as if she'd just stepped off the cover of a fashion magazine.

"Um, come in?" Laney said.

The sophisticated woman looked from Laney to Chris to me. She turned to Cam and raised one immaculate eyebrow. "Is your surprise that you've taken to robbing cradles?"

"Don't be silly, Laura. You know I only have eyes for you."

Laura smiled and shook her head. "Morbid as always, Cam."

Cam and Laura stepped into the apartment. Cam closed the door and removed his dark glasses. "I wasn't being morbid, Laura. I *do* only have eyes for you."

"Really, Cam—"

"I like that green blouse," Cam said. "It goes well with your hair."

"Thank you, Ca—." Laura's eyes widened. "How do you know my blouse is green?"

"The same way I know your skirt is maroon." Cam caught Laura's gaze and held it. "Because I can see them."

WE DON'T MATTER

Laura gasped and covered her open mouth with her right hand. Her gaze met Cam's. Laura's eyes widened when she saw Cam's eyes focus on her. "H-how?"

Cam's gaze flicked over Laura's shoulder to us. "That's going to take some explaining."

Laura cast a quick glance at us. Then she turned her attention back to Cam, and her expression hardened. "Cameron Wheeler, this had better not be one of your practical jokes, one those girls are helping you with. Because it's not funny if—"

Cam stepped back from Laura. "Hold up some fingers. Use either hand, and hold your hands so the girls can't see them."

Laura looked at us, her face still stern. "Don't any of you girls move."

"We won't, ma'am," Laney said.

Laura turned back to Cam, moved her hands so her body blocked our view of them. "Okay, Cam, how many fingers am I holding up?"

"Seven," Cam said. "Four on your right hand. Three on your left."

"And now?"

"You didn't change anything, so—"

"Now?"

"One, on your right hand. And it's pointing at me."

"Okay..." Laura did something with her hands. Something that made Cam's eyes widen and his gaze sharpen. Then she asked, "What color is my bra?"

Cam's eyes lingered on what I had to assume was his first look at cleavage since he became old enough to care about such things. "Uh..." Cam blinked three times, found the strength to drag his gaze back to Laura's face, and gave her a mischievous grin. "Does your underwear's color always match your outer clothing? And have you always had that little beauty mark between your breasts?"

Laura wrapped her arms around Cam's neck and pulled him down for a tender, loving kiss. "I don't know how many times I've asked God to restore your sight. And finally..." Laura sniffed and rested her head on Cam's shoulder. "I never thought He'd answer my prayers."

I felt as if I was intruding on a deeply personal moment. From the looks on Chris's and Laney's faces, they felt the same. We three turned around and studied the blank wall. We tuned out the words Cam and Laura exchanged as best we could, while also staying silent so we didn't interrupt them.

After a couple of minutes, Cam murmured, "My three guests must be getting tired of looking at the wall."

In a conversational tone that betrayed none of the emotions she must be feeling, Laura said, "No doubt."

We turned around to find Laura buttoning the top three buttons of her blouse and eying us with open curiosity. Cam picked up two paper sacks, none of us even noticed he had brought with him. "Why don't you ladies introduce yourselves while I'll set out breakfast?"

Laura flashed a professional, impersonal smile. "I'm Laura Ackerman, soon-to-be ace reporter for the Landfall Times." Her smile disappeared. "Perhaps someone would be so good as to explain what you three much too young, much too pretty girls are doing in my boyfriend's one room, one *bed* apartment?"

Laney and Chris looked at me, perhaps assuming—rightly—that my family had trained me for such occasions. I made an introductory gesture towards Laney. "This is Laney Gibson. She's here helping Chris," I shifted my gesture to Chris, "and me get home."

"Uh huh." Laura crossed her arms. "And you are?"

I hesitated, and Chris said, "Tell her, plebe. But you can cut the list of names down to just one, if you don't want to sound too ostentatious."

I met Laura's gaze. "I am Her Royal Highness, Princess Anne, third in line for the throne of Mordan."

Laura rolled her eyes and looked at Cam. "Really, Cam? A princess?" Her gaze hardened. "If I find out this is all one huge practical joke and that you're still blind," Laura half-turned and pointed at the door, "I will walk out that door and *never* speak with you again."

I couldn't really blame Laura for her reaction. We were asking her for a huge leap of faith. But I asked, "Why don't you believe me?"

Laura turned back to me. "Trust me, I'd know if there was a report of a missing princess. Oh, and next time you want to play princess, at least have the grace to pick a real country."

"Mordan *is* a real country." I crossed my arms. "Just not on *this* planet."

Laura opened her mouth to say something. Closed it again. Came closer to us and studied our faces. Finally, she said, "You're the amies!"

"No, we're just from other planets," Chris said. "Anne and I are the Scout cadets who got stranded here."

Laney added, "I'm not. But they stumbled across my grandfather's farm, so I really am trying to help them get home."

"Wait a minute," Laura said. She reached into a purse slung over one shoulder and pulled out a notebook and pencil. "Start from the beginning and tell me everything."

"I could run up to the shed and get your tape recorder, if that will help," Cam said. "I finished repairing it yesterday afternoon."

"Please do, Cam," Laura said.

As Cam headed for the door, Chris said, "Remember to act blind!"

Cam grabbed his dark glasses and slipped out of the apartment.

Laura fixed her gaze on Chris and me. "May I assume you two restored Cam's eyesight?"

"It's more accurate to say our advanced medical technology restored it," Chris said. "We just administered it."

"Very modest of you," Laura murmured. "So, what makes you think you can trust me not to turn you in?"

"Gut instinct," Chris said.

"And Cam trusts you," I said.

"Plus," Laney said, "you'd miss out on the biggest news story in the history of Refuge. No ace reporter would do that."

"Which brings up a question," I said. "Will your newspaper print this story?"

"Absolutely not," Laura said. "But I'll run it in the underground newspaper. And the radio station will play the interview we're about to record."

"It'll be dangerous for them," Chris said.

"I am positive the news editor will run the story and broadcast the interview," Laura said.

"What makes you so sure?" Laney asked.

Laura grinned. "Because *I'm* the news editor."

After Cam returned with Laura's tape recorder, she explained how she would perform the interview. "We'll start with a little background on each of you, cover the events leading up to this interview, and then see where things go from there. While I'm not looking for 'gotcha' responses, I will expect you to defend conclusions you've drawn. Okay?"

"Okay," we three said.

"Laney, I don't want you to take this the wrong way," Laura said, "but this story centers around Chris and Anne. I'm not saying don't answer questions, but I'll mostly use you for corroboration of events and to give the average Ab Astran's point of view of the events you've witnessed."

Laney nodded, and Laura turned to Chris and me. "Is there anything I shouldn't ask about?"

Chris caught my eye and scratched her head. Someone who didn't know Chris would assume she was thinking. But her hand scratched directly over her implant, something only I would know. Her meaning was clear. *Don't talk about our implants and what they let us do.* I agreed with her reasoning, especially since our bag of tricks was limited to Boost and our few advanced technological items.

I gave a microscopic nod of understanding, and Chris said, "We'll have to tell her about medical nanites, since they restored Cam's sight, and I don't think we can avoid describing chameleon cloths. And those are our only big secrets."

Past Chris, I saw understanding come into Laney's eyes. I sighed and gave a slow nod. "I think you're right."

Laura said, "Since I don't know what those things are, I'll let you introduce and explain them when you see fit. Are you both ready?"

We nodded, and Laura began the interview. As promised, Laura asked Chris and me for a brief biography. Chris talked about growing up on Earth and onboard her family's freighter, her desire to explore the unknown, and her acceptance to the Scout Academy. Laura asked, "This Scout Corps sounds somewhat like a military organization. What is its mission?"

"The Corps is *organized* somewhat like the military," Chris said, "but our mission is peaceful. We explore beyond the bounds of human settled space, searching for human habitable worlds and lost colonies."

"What is a lost colony?"

"A colony that the Federation has no record of, and which has no contact with the Federation. For instance, Refuge is a textbook lost colony. As is Anne's home world of Aashla."

"So you're saying Scouts don't fight?"

"Not if we can avoid it," Chris said. "But we're trained to fight if we must."

"Against who?"

"Mostly space pirates, who tend to hide their bases on the fringe of human space. The same places Scouts explore."

"I see."

Laura turned her attention from Chris to me and asked for my story. I tried keeping my answers simple and factual, but Chris wouldn't let me gloss over my parents' adventures. After I spent five minutes giving an incredibly broad telling of everything they'd done, Laura interrupted me.

"Fascinating as your parents sound, this interview isn't about them. Let's move on to the events that brought a pair of Scout cadets to Refuge."

Chris and I took turns describing our emergency departure from the cadet cruiser, Chris's realization that it was only a drill, our encounter with the unmapped wormhole, the crash with the asteroid, and the near-fatal trip to Refuge.

"So you came here by accident?" Laura asked.

"Right," I said.

"You're not scouting Refuge as advance members of an invading force?"

I gave a dismissive snort. "No."

Chris added, "What would even be the point of a Federation invasion?"

Laura had a ready response. "At the very least, this Federation of yours would get another human-habitable world."

"Do you have any idea how many human-habitable worlds there are in this part of the galaxy?" I asked.

"No," Laura said.

"The Federation has..." I glanced at Chris. "What is it? Ninety-three member worlds?"

Chris shook her head. "Escoth joined last month, so it's ninety-four."

"Ninety-four, then," I said. "And then you have recently rediscovered lost colonies, like my home world of Aashla. There's around fifty of them. And then there are unsettled worlds. Like the one all the other cadet lifepods landed on after the cadet cruiser evacuation drill. God only knows how many of them are out there."

"But Refuge is already developed," Laura persisted.

"So what?" Chris asked. "No offense, but your technology is so far behind Federation standards that bringing Refuge up to date would be almost as expensive as establishing and supporting a new colony. More expensive, when you consider how much an invasion costs in lives and equipment. I mean, seriously, why would the Federation bother? Especially for a backwater world like Refuge?"

"That's a bit... harsh," Laura said.

"The truth usually is," I said. "If it makes you feel any better, my home world of Aashla is at least a century behind Refuge's technological level. And that's after over twenty years of contact with the Federation."

Laura smiled, obviously pleased with this exchange. "Well, now that we've put those invasion rumors to rest, let's move on to what happened after you landed."

For the next hour and a half, we described almost everything that had happened to us since the landing. Laney chimed in with a few clarifications and provided the Ab Astran point of view of the events. We never mentioned Boost or blasters, and Laura never asked us about Federation weapons. We wrapped up with the restoration of Cam's sight.

"That's an astounding story," Laura said, "but one I find completely believable. As a patriotic Ab Astran, I am appalled at our government's actions in this matter. Imagine, if you will, this tale reimagined for our world. Imagine two young Ab Astran women stranded in Plausen. Imagine the national outrage we'd feel if Plausen mobilized their army, their air force, and their police against those two young women."

Laura paused for a few seconds. "Imagine what Ab Astra would do to rescue those young women." Another pause. "Now imagine what the Federation will do to rescue these two innocent young women."

"You don't have to imagine," Laney said. "Just ask Anne what her father will do to get her back?"

Laura turned to me. "Anne, would you care to answer Laney's question?"

I shrugged. "Dad will start by asking for our return."

"And if the Ab Astran government refuses, or claims they don't have you?"

"Bear in mind that my home world isn't part of the Federation, Laura. Dad will follow the laws of my homeland, Mordan."

"And what are those laws, Anne?"

"Ab Astra's actions against a member of the Mordanian royal family can be viewed as a declaration of war."

"But we already discussed the impracticality of an invasion," Laura said.

"You misunderstand, Laura. Dad won't lead an invasion. He'll tear this country apart until he finds me or my body." I hardened my voice. "And there's *nothing* Ab Astra will be able to do to stop him."

"But how is a marauding army any less expensive than an invading army?"

"Dad won't need an army to rip Ab Astra apart."

Laura's face registered honest confusion. "He won't?"

I caught and held her gaze. "One space-borne warship can raze Ab Astra without even entering Refuge's atmosphere. And unless your military has weapons that can reach space, there is nothing they can do to stop the destruction."

In a somber voice, Laura asked, "Nothing?"

I kept my voice cold. "Nothing." I smiled and lightened my tone. "But if the Ab Astran government helps us communicate with Dad or whoever else comes looking for us, everything will be fine. Chris and I will leave, and Refuge can go back to its isolationist ways."

"You heard it here first, folks," Laura said. "And if you ask me, we owe it to these girls to help them get home."

Laura turned off the tape recorder, then smiled at us. "That was fantastic. And Anne, your," she made air quotes with her fingers, "Dad threat bluff was great! I bet that will put the fear of God into the government."

Chris and I exchanged sidelong glances, then I said, "Laura, it wasn't a bluff. If anything happens to me, the people of Mordan will demand retribution. Dad knows that and will act accordingly."

Blood drained from Laura's face. "Okay... But no reasonable government would tempt that fate, right?"

"No reasonable *human* government would," I said. "But an ancient AI, such as the one we believe runs this world, is neither human nor reasonable."

Cam stayed quiet during the interview. But after my comment about the AI, he asked, "What are you suggesting, Anne?"

"If you're right, and an AI runs this world—which Chris and I also believe—that AI won't just let us leave Refuge."

"Why not?" Laura asked. "Won't the AI realize it can't win a war with your father or the Federation?"

"It doesn't matter," Chris said. "The AI *has* to fight."

"You've lost us," Cam said.

Chris said, "During the AI wars, Earth's government outlawed all artificial intelligences, and issued deletion orders for every AI in existence. From what I can tell, your colony ship fled Earth *after* that deletion order. The AI on Refuge must believe it's under a digital death sentence." She shrugged. "The thing is, the AI is right. There's no way the Federation will let a rogue AI control a log cabin, much less a lost human colony."

"If the AI lets Chris and me go, Dad or the Federation will delete it," I said. "If the AI holds us hostage and fights against whoever comes looking for us, it will *probably* lose and get deleted."

Cam nodded. "But there's still a chance it will win."

"Right," Chris said.

"And you can bet the AI will do everything possible to capture Chris and me before anyone comes looking for us," I said. "We'd make great bait for a trap."

"A trap for what?" Laura asked. "Even if the AI destroys the first spaceship, won't the next spaceship destroy the AI?"

"Sure," Chris said. "But if the AI can *capture* the first spaceship, it can use that ship to escape Refuge. And the last thing anyone wants is a rogue AI loose in the galaxy."

"So what do we do?" Laura asked.

"Let Cam boost the signal strength on the pirate radio station and then broadcast our interview repeatedly. Whoever comes looking for us will intercept the broadcast. After they listen to it, they should come to the same conclusion Anne and I have."

"Meaning they won't fall into any trap laid by the AI?"

"Exactly."

"Even if you and Anne are the bait?"

"Even if."

"And even if Anne's father commands the first ship?"

Chris looked at me, so I said, "Dad will do everything in his power to rescue Chris and me. Everything except letting a rogue AI loose on the galaxy."

Cam asked, "If the AI baits the trap with you girls, and the trap fails, what happens to you two?"

"We don't matter," I said.

Cam blinked, then shifted his gaze from me to Chris and back again. "You matter to me."

"Me, too," Laney said.

"And I'll bet everything I own that you matter more to your father than his own life," Laura said.

"I know. That's why I said Dad would raze Ab Astra to find me or my body."

"That seems... harsh," Cam said.

"Reality sometimes is," Chris said. "But the AI couldn't catch Anne and me with the army or the police. There's no reason to assume it will suddenly get lucky. So, what do we need to do to upgrade the radio transmitter? Where do we start?"

"At an electronics store," Cam said. "Laura and I will go buy the stuff we need. *You* three stay here."

"While Cam and I are out," Laura said, "I'll use a pay phone to call our radio tech and make arrangements to meet him and the radio truck."

"So, Logan was right. The transmitter is on a truck." Laney blinked back sudden tears. "I pray he's okay."

Chris and I caught Laney between us and hugged her tight, and she let her tears flow freely. Laura and Cam slipped out of the apartment while we comforted Laney.

"Don't worry," Chris murmured, "we'll free Logan and Jace. I promise."

"What if..." Laney gulped. "What if the government uses the guys as bait to catch us? What if they threaten to kill them if we don't turn ourselves in?"

"Even a rogue AI will figure out that a public threat against Logan and Jace won't work," I said. "People would turn against the government en masse, and that's the last thing the AI needs right now. Okay?"

Laney didn't look entirely convinced, but she said, "I guess..."

"Good." I considered ways to distract Laney, and settled on food. "How about a mid-morning snack? I could reheat the breakfast leftovers or cook something."

Laney looked askance at me. "Just how much cooking experience did you get growing up in a palace?"

"More than you'd think," I said, "but not a lot more."

"I did some cooking on our family freighter," Chris said.

"Were you any good at it?" Laney asked.

"Um..." Chris looked up at the ceiling. "It was mostly automated equipment and heat-and-serve meals."

"Hopeless." Laney stood up. "You're both absolutely hopeless."

I also stood. "But not so hopeless that we can't help you."

Chris bounced to her feet. "Right."

"Uh huh." Laney looked back and forth between us. "What can you do in the kitchen? And be honest."

"I can do whatever you tell me to do," I said, "especially if it involves stirring pots."

"I can peel vegetables, and even cut them up," Chris added.

I turned a mock worshipful gaze on Chris. "This plebe hopes she may someday be as skilled in the kitchen as the cadet sergeant."

Chris sniffed. "I doubt it, plebe."

Our banter had the desired effect. Laney flashed a half-hearted smile.

"You're lucky Chef Laney is here. Otherwise, you'd both end up eating more of those vile survival bars."

"Thank you, Chef Laney," Chris and I said in unison.

Under Laney's orders, we fixed and ate a tasty snack. Then we settled down to wait for Laura's and Cam's return.

BOYFRIENDS AND BROADCASTS

Waiting for Laura's and Cam's return wore on our nerves. We burned off our nervous energy by cleaning Cam's apartment, even though it didn't need cleaning. Laney went to work on already-clean pans and dishes. Chris began scrubbing shining bathroom tiles. I changed the fresh sheets on Cam's bed and then hunted for dust bunnies, which looked as if they were extinct in Cam's apartment. We also kept a constant eye on the wall clock and wondered why its hands moved so slowly.

I must have jumped a foot when the telephone rang next to me, just before noon. I turned a wide-eyed stare on Chris. Who stared at Laney. Who stared at me, completing the circle. The telephone rang again, jangling our taut nerves a second time.

I'd only answered a telephone once in my life, and it hadn't delivered good news. Logically, I understood that telephone calls didn't *have* to mean trouble. But my emotions hadn't gotten the message yet.

"Should I answer it?" I asked.

Chris's response didn't help. "I guess, maybe?"

"What will you say if the caller isn't Laura or Cam?" Laney asked.

A third ring sounded, and I came to a decision. I lifted the receiver, held it to my ear, but said nothing.

After a few seconds, a woman's voice said, "Hello?"

It sounded like Laura, but I wasn't positive. I kept my response non-verbal. "Hm?"

"What? I couldn't understand you." A deeper voice spoke near the telephone on the other end, though I couldn't understand what it said. Then the woman said, "Oh, yes. Cam says you're probably being cautious. This is Laura. Have I got Laney, Chris, or Anne?"

Relief flooded through me. "Anne." I looked at Chris and Laney and said, "It's Laura."

The tension on their faces faded, though didn't vanish. After all, we'd had to go on the run after Jace's phone call.

"I'm sorry to startle you with the phone call," Laura said. "But we felt we should let you know it's taking us longer to get the parts Cam needs than expected. Cam and I both felt waiting would wear on your nerves worse than the call."

"So there's nothing to worry about?" I asked that question for Laney's and Chris's benefit. And they relaxed even more after I asked it.

"Nothing at all. Cam is just being paranoid."

That sent my heart racing again. "Does he think someone is following you?"

"What? No, nothing like that. I'm sorry again, Anne. I guess I'm not very good at this spy stuff. Let me turn the phone over to Cam. I'm sure he can explain things better than I can."

Odd clicking and clacking noises followed, which I hoped came from Laura handing the phone to Cam. Then Cam said, "Hello, Anne. Is everything okay there?"

"Yes, but your apartment is going to be *really* clean by the time you get back."

"Okay," Cam said, with a laugh. "As for us, the reason this is taking so long is because I don't want to buy all my electronic parts from the same store. I doubt anyone at my usual parts store would get suspicious, but I'd rather not take chances."

"If you're looking for the approval of a nineteen-year-old girl, you've got it."

Cam laughed again. "Phew! That's one thing I can mark off my list of things to achieve before I die."

I knew it was a joke, so I gave a half-hearted laugh. Cam noticed, and said, "I guess I'll have to get new material, if that's the best laugh I can get from you."

"It's not you or your material, Cam."

Cam's tone softened. "I know, Anne. And I promise I'll do everything I can to help you girls." Laura said something in the background, and Cam added, "Laura says that goes double for her."

"Thank you both."

"Well, that's as much maudlin stuff as I can tolerate in one day," Cam quipped. "Just sit tight in the apartment and don't worry. We'll be back in a few hours."

"Will do, Cam. Goodbye."

"Goodbye, Anne."

With a click, Cam hung up the telephone.

I relayed what he told me, and Chris flashed a relieved smile. "That makes sense, and it's pretty smart."

"Yeah," Laney agreed, "but we can't tell that to Cam. If he's anything like Logan, a compliment like that will go straight to his head."

That set off a competition between Laney and me to come up with our best brother-with-an-inflated-ego story. Chris tried to play along, but all she had were stories of guys she dated. And guys on dates don't act like typical brothers. After a few minutes, I felt bad that Chris was mostly excluded, and questioned one of her weirder date stories. That started a new competition between Laney and Chris to tell the weirdest date story.

That competition left me out, since I've never dated. But I didn't mind. I just sat back and enjoyed my friends' stories. But when they realized I had no stories to share, they shifted gears and started giving me dating advice to follow after Chris and I returned to the Academy. Some of Chris's advice made me blush, which Chris said was "absolutely adorable."

Chris's most risqué dating story even made Laney blush. Laney and I were trying to come up with an appropriate response to the story when someone knocked on the apartment door. Immediately after, we heard Cam call, "We're back."

A key turned in the lock, the door opened, and Cam and Laura entered. Laney eyed Cam's empty hands, raised an eyebrow, and asked, "Weren't you supposed to buy a lot of stuff?"

"I did," Cam said. "But I saw no point in bringing it down here, just so I could turn around and carry it back to Laura's car."

"Oh, yeah," Laney said. "Good point."

Cam grinned. "I know."

Laura suggested a change of clothes for us three and banished Cam to the hallway. "We're heading out of town to a large public park. So you might as well wear the clothes you wore during your mountain trek."

We changed back to the sturdy, blue trousers and warm, checked shirts we'd worn when we left Laney's hometown. Then we went upstairs, where Laura stopped at a pay telephone in the lobby. "Let me make a quick call, and then we can all leave."

She dialed a number with rapid, assured motions. After a few seconds, she said, "Hello Jack. It's Laura." She listened for a moment. "Yes, we're finally ready... Uh huh... Got it. In the clearing... Yes... See you soon."

Laura led us out to her car. We girls crowded into the backseat, leaving the front seat to Laura and Cam. Laura started the engine, pulled out into the street, and set off for our rendezvous with the pirate radio transmitter.

Laura obeyed all the traffic laws. She stayed under the speed limit, obeyed every traffic sign, made all the proper signals, and never left what Laney called the slow lane. When a long line of cars passed us as we drove out of the city, Laney said, "God, Laura, you drive like my grandfather!"

Laura's eyes never left the road ahead. "With an eye towards care and safety, you mean?"

Though Laura couldn't see it, Laney shook her head. "With an eye towards taking twice as long to get anywhere, I mean."

"Maybe your grandfather believes his passengers—especially his grandchildren—are more precious than the few minutes he'd save by driving with reckless abandon."

"I didn't say drive with reckless abandon," Laney countered, "just faster."

"Has it occurred to you that *my* passengers are the three most-wanted people in Ab Astra? The last thing we can afford is a run-in with the police. And the best way to avoid one is by obeying all the traffic laws."

"You realize that your driving makes you stand out all the more because no one else on the road is obeying all those traffic laws? Don't you think the cops will notice that?"

"Perhaps," Laura said. "But will you answer one other question for me?"

"Ask away," Laney replied.

"Has your grandfather ever been pulled over by the police?"

"No."

"Even though he drives like I do, and gets passed by every other car on the road?"

Laney crossed her arms, heaved a sigh of frustration, and looked out a side window. "Fine. Whatever. You win."

Cam laughed. "Graciously put, Laney."

"Can it, Cam," Laney growled, "or maybe I'll tell Laura about how us three girls wandered around naked in your apartment." She flashed a devilish grin. "Oops, I just did."

But Laura didn't rise to the bait. "I've done that many times when I needed a quick shower before we went out. Though I'll have to change my ways now that Cam can see."

Cam sighed. "Darn. I was really hoping you'd slip up and do that at least once."

"There's only one way that will ever happen," Laura said, "and you know my conditions."

"I do."

For some reason, Cam and Laura laughed. Curious, I asked, "Why was that funny? Or am I prying into a personal matter?"

"Not at all, Anne," Laura said. "My conditions are vows and a ring."

"And I responded with the traditional response to those vows," Cam said. "It's an old joke between us."

"Oh," I said. "If it's a joke, does that mean you're not planning on getting married?"

"We're only going to get married," Laura said, "if *someone* gets around to popping the question."

"Meaning Cam?" Chris asked.

"Meaning Cam," Laura said.

"Why?"

"Because I can't say yes if he doesn't ask."

"That's not what I meant," Chris said. "Why does *Cam* have to be the one who does the asking?"

"Because..." Laura paused. "Um, because..."

"It's tradition," Laney said.

"So?" Chris asked.

"I never thought about it that way." Laura glanced at Cam and then back at the road. "You're being awfully quiet, Cam. Why?"

"You always wanted a ring, but until this morning I couldn't see to pick out a nice engagement ring. Once I find the right one, though—"

"Idiot man," Laura muttered. "Cam, I want a *wedding* ring. You know, a simple, gold band."

"Oh. So you want the ring *after* the vows, not before?"

"Of course. Why do you think I always put vows first on the list?"

Cam was silent for a moment. "So, the proposal... Do you want it in private?"

"As long as I *get* a proposal, I don't care."

"Laura, will you marry me?"

"It's about time, Cam. And yes."

"That's so romantic," Laney sighed. "Laura, aren't you going to pull off the road long enough to kiss Cam?"

"No. Since I had to wait four years for a proposal, he can wait an hour for a kiss."

"Very practical," Chris said. "So, are there any other problems Anne, Laney, and I can solve?"

"I have a question for you," Cam asked.

"If it has anything to do with weddings, you'd better ask Laura."

"It doesn't."

"You just got engaged, Cam," Laney said. "Your thoughts are *supposed* to be all about Laura."

"Sorry." Cam didn't sound sorry at all. "But this question has bugged me off and on since before I even met Laura." Cam paused for a second. "An AI can only control a person who has an implant, right?"

"Only if the implant can receive instructions as well as send them," I said.

"Okay. But how does the implant get inside someone's head? My father was only gone a week, and he didn't have any surgical scars, a shaved head, or any other evidence of brain surgery."

"They're built by nanites, using their own microscopic robot bodies as the materials," I said. "You get a big injection of specially programmed nanites, and wait for them to do the work. Mine took about two hours from start to finish, but before the AI wars the process took several days."

"But we don't have nanite technology on Refuge," Laney said.

"You must," Chris said. "Or, rather, the AI who rules you must. If you could see your colony ship's original cargo, I'll bet you'd find machinery for building and programming nanites."

"I have trouble keeping radios working for more than a few years," Cam said. "Would those machines still work after centuries of use?"

"I think so, if they got regular maintenance," Chris said. "So you can probably add electronic parts fabricators to the list of advanced tech your amy ancestors brought with them. They'd need those to keep the computer that hosts the AI running, too. And the parts fabricators, for that matter."

"Geez," Laney muttered, "is *anything* we learned about history true?"

"Most of it probably is," Chris said. "But the AI and its minions hid the most important parts from you."

"Is that how you can stop the AI?" Cam asked. "By destroying its support machinery?"

"We could do that if we knew where the AI has the machines hidden," Chris said. "But it would take years. Nobody wants to wait that long."

"Is there a faster way?" Cam asked.

"Oh yeah," Chris said. "Our way would take ten minutes, tops."

"Please don't make me drag it from you bit by bit," Cam said.

"All you have to do is destroy the host computer's cooling system. Those old computers produced an astounding amount of heat. Without the cooling system, the host computer's processors would melt in, well, about ten minutes."

"So, all we need to do is find the cooling system and—"

"Chris is way ahead of you, Cam," I said.

Cam turned and looked Chris in the eye. "You know where the cooling system is?"

"Have you ever toured the Capital Building?" Chris asked.

"About a dozen times," Cam said.

"Did you ever see the garden in the inner courtyard?"

"Sure. I even saw it a couple of times before I lost my sight. It was a pretty garden, but I don't see what—"

"Do you remember the six abstract sculptures?"

"Sure. I always thought they were pretty cool."

"The AI running your world thinks they're cool, too. As in towers for a huge, water-based cooling system. The kind that keeps an AI host computer from melting."

"And if we destroy those towers?"

"Your AI's host computer turns into a big ol' puddle of silicon slag."

"And then the AI dies?"

Chris nodded. "And then the AI dies."

With our spirits buoyed by hope that we could destroy the Refuge AI's cooling system and happiness for Laura's and Cam's future marriage, we made the rest of the trip to the middle of nowhere in companionable silence. We reached the park after three-quarters of an hour, but it took another twenty minutes driving down a series of increasingly rough and narrow roads before we emerged into a small clearing. It reminded me a bit of the Lover's Lane we went to before hopping the freight train for Landfall.

Except for the small truck waiting for us. It had no back seat. Instead, the truck had a box-shaped container mounted behind the driver's compartment. The box was about four meters long, maybe two and a half meters high, and had words and a string of numbers painted on the side.

"Anne," Laney said, "what does the writing on the truck say?"

Cam turned around, an inquisitive expression on his face. "Why do you want her to read that?"

"Our implants can translate and teach us spoken languages," Chris said. "But we have to learn written language the old-fashioned way."

"Except their implants makes it easier," Laney said. "But I just realized that I haven't tested their reading in at least two days, so..."

I sniffed, pointed my nose up, and said, "I am a princess. I have people who read for me." I waved an imperious hand at the truck. "Cadet Sergeant Montide, the Princess Plebe demands you read for me."

Chris got into the spirit of it and growled, "Nice try, plebe. You will either read what it says on that truck or drop and give me twenty."

"This plebe hears and obeys." I lowered my nose and examined the words on the truck. "It says... Moe ving truck rental." I glanced at Laney. "My implant doesn't recognize that last word."

"It means people can pay money to use the truck for a while. The first word is pronounced moo ving, but that's one of our language's many exceptions," Laney said. "Chris, you read the smaller words."

Chris examined the side of the truck for a few seconds. "Um... Cal? No, call." She flashed a smile at Laney. "I got the pronunciation from context. Call this number. I assume the series of numbers is a telephone number?"

Laney smiled. "Right! Gold stars for both of you."

A big door on the back of the truck swung open, and a man about Cam's age hopped down. "Laura? That is you, right?"

Laura opened her door and got out of the car. "It's me, Stan."

"Why were you just sitting in the car?" Stan asked.

"One of our friends gave a reading test."

"A what?"

"I'll tell you in a bit." Laura walked to the back of the car as the rest of us got out. She opened the trunk. "Everyone, grab a box and take it to the truck."

We did as instructed and got our first look into the back of the truck. It immediately dispelled my mental image of a radio transmitter with a gleaming metal case, carefully labeled dials, and blinking lights. The reality was a dull metal framework with wires snaking and twisting through a bewildering collection of boards and circuits and tubes.

As Chris, Laney, and I exchanged dubious looks, Cam grinned and said, "Sweet setup! Did you build it by yourself?"

"I did the circuit boards," Stan said, "but a couple of friends helped me wire everything."

Cam extended a hand. "I'm Cam."

Stan took the offered hand automatically. Then his eyes widened. "You can't be Cam. Laura told me he's blind!"

Cam released Stan's hand and hopped up into the back of the truck. "I was until this morning."

"But..." Stan turned to Laura. "But?"

"It's all thanks to Chris," Laura pointed to her, "Anne," she pointed to me, "and the incredible medical technology they have. You'll understand better after you listen to the interview I recorded with them," Laura pointed to Laney. "And this is their friend, Laney. The two boys captured by the Izzies are her brother and her boyfriend."

Laney's eyebrows arched when Laura said Jace was her boyfriend. But she didn't deny it. I briefly wondered what Jace would say about his promotion from bad boy to boyfriend, and decided he'd probably grin like an idiot.

"What can we do to help?" I asked.

"Honestly?" Cam said. "Unless you know something about radio transmitters and electronics, just let Stan and me work. No offense, but things will go faster if we just do it ourselves."

"No offense taken." I made shooing motions with my hands. "I grant my royal permission for you boys to have fun."

"Royal permission?" Stan climbed into the back of the truck with Cam. "Who does she think she is, a queen or something?"

"A queen?" Laney said. "Don't be silly. She's a princess."

Stan stared at me. "You're kidding, right?"

"Not even a little bit," Laura said.

"Is that all part of the story about how Cam got his eyesight back?"

"Yes," Laura said. "It's also part of the reason Cam asked me to marry him."

Stan gave Cam a hard look. "From everything Laura has told me about you two, it took you long enough."

Cam shrugged. "What can I say? I was blind to what was right in front of me?"

Laura turned a mock glare on Cam. "Only *you* could get your sight back and almost immediately turn it into a new source of bad jokes."

"It's a talent," Cam said.

"It's a curse," Laura said.

"Yes," Cam said, "I see your point so clearly now."

"Gah!" Laura turned her attention to Stan. "Did you bring my editing equipment, like I asked?"

"In the passenger seat," Stan said.

"Good. I'll be up there pretending this conversation never happened. I'll let Cam and the girls tell you their stories."

As Laura headed for the driver's compartment, Chris asked, "Is there anything we can do to help you, Laura?"

"I might need to record some of your answers again. And maybe record some new questions." Laura looked over her shoulder and smiled. "But you stay back here and amaze Stan with your story. I'll call if I need you."

So we three stood around the back of the truck, taking turns telling our tale to Stan. After the first half hour, we ended up sitting on the back of the truck, dangling our feet out into the freezing afternoon air. Laura called on us a few times over the next several hours. But once we finished telling our story to Stan, we didn't have much else to do.

Chris leaned over against Laney. "So, Jace is your boyfriend now?"

Laney shrugged. "Why not?"

"I can't think of a reason why not."

"Do..." Laney paused. "Do you think *Jace* will think of a reason?"

"To be your boyfriend?"

"No, to *not* be my boyfriend."

"Unlike Cam, he's not blind, so..."

"Ouch!" Stan said. "I think Cam needs stitches after that cut."

Cam laughed louder than anyone else, and was still laughing when Laura returned from editing the interview. She glanced at Stan. "Give this a listen to make sure I distorted my voice enough."

"Why distort your voice?" Laney asked.

"So listeners can't figure out who I am from listening to the interview. We *always* distort voices."

"Even mine?"

"Well, no. The government already knows who you, Chris, and Anne are. We don't gain anything by distorting your voices, and we'd lose your girl-next-door innocence."

"Yeah," Cam said, "your voices sound beautiful. I'll bet they'll bring people to our side, even if they ignore everything you say."

Stan played the interview. Laura's distorted voice came across as mechanical, yet weirdly warm at the same time. After listening for five minutes, he said, "Good distortion, and the girls all sound great." Stan looked at Cam. "Do you have any more work to do on the transmitter?"

Cam shook his head. "We're ready." He patted the transmitter's framework. "With the extra power, there's not a person in Ab Astra who won't be able to pick up this broadcast."

Cam and Stan started the transmitter while Laura threaded the tape recording into a machine hooked to the transmitter. A subtle hum rose as the transmitter powered up. Finally, Cam said, "Let her rip, Laura."

Laura activated the tape machine, sending our interview across the country. And out into space, where I prayed a Federation or Aashlan ship would intercept it.

THE TRAGEDY OF LANEY GIBSON

C am closed and locked the back of the truck while Stan climbed into what Cam called the cab. Stan drove the truck from the clearing while Laura, Cam, and we three girls piled into Laura's car. A moment later, Laura followed the truck. Cam turned on the car's radio and tuned it to the frequency the pirate radio station chose for today's broadcast. I felt weird listening to my voice coming from the radio. Based on the looks on Chris's and Laney's faces, they felt the same.

I became so engrossed in the interview, I hardly noticed when Laura followed the truck out of the park. Laney never once criticized Laura for driving too slowly, either. But Chris showed why she's a cadet sergeant, and I'm just a plebe.

"How long do we have before the government can track the radio signal?" Chris asked.

"It depends on how long it takes them to discover we're broadcasting," Laura said. "For safety, we're going to have to stop and change frequencies soon."

"No need." Cam held up a small box with an extendable antenna attached to it. "I can control the transmitter with this."

"When did you make that?" Laura asked.

"Months ago. I keep my shortwave radio in the maintenance shed on the roof, but sometimes want to listen to it in my apartment." Cam patted the box. "I built this baby so I wouldn't have to climb to the roof whenever I changed frequencies. Modifying it for your transmitter only took a few minutes." Cam glanced at Laura. "Which frequency should I set?"

"Whichever you want, Cam."

Cam pressed a button, then turned a dial on the box. Static replaced the interview. But Cam quickly tuned the car's radio to the new frequency, so we only missed a few seconds of the interview.

Cam grinned. "Sweet, huh?"

"Yes, you're very smart," Laura said. "Is that the compliment you were looking for?"

"Yep."

From then on, Cam changed the frequency every few minutes. But even with the broadcast signal hopping all over the place, someone in the government was on their toes. Half-an-hour after we left the park, we heard a helicopter far off to our right. A moment later, another helicopter flew past on our left.

Laura cast a worried glance in the direction of the second helicopter. "Maybe we should shut it down for now. We can start it once we're back in city traffic and are less exposed."

Cam nodded. "I think that's a good idea." Cam used his box again, and static replaced the interview once again. "The transmitter is off."

Traffic increased over the next twenty minutes and forced Laura to drive even slower than she normally did. "We can't risk broadcasting while we're moving this slowly. The Izzies would zero in on us in minutes, and we'd have no way to escape. We're just going to have to park the truck and wait until a few hours after dark, when traffic is light enough for us to keep moving, but heavy enough to hide us."

Laura checked for oncoming traffic, pulled the car into the other lane, and flashed her lights twice. Stan turned the truck's light off and then on again, showing he got the message.

"I guess you do this a lot?" Laney asked.

"Every time we broadcast," Laura said. "The Izzies have gotten a lot of practice tracking us, too, and have improved a lot. They'll especially want to stop this broadcast, so we'll have to be extra careful. Cam, that'll mean changing frequencies every minute or two."

"When the broadcast babe speaks, I obey," Cam said.

Laura gave Cam's arm a playful slap. "Oh, you!"

"This is really cute and all," Laney said, "but can we go back to Cam's so I can fix dinner? I'm starved."

As if it merely needed a reminder, my stomach growled. "Um, I second that."

Chris chimed in, "Third it."

"I doubt Cam has enough food to feed us all," Laura said. "We'll follow Stan to the garage where he parks the truck, and then go get dinner."

"We're going to risk eating in public?" I asked. "What if someone sees Chris, Laney, or me?"

Laura shook her head. "Stan has a friend who runs a diner. He'll let us slip in through the kitchen and eat in a small private room in the back."

Stan's garage wasn't far. Within fifteen minutes, Stan joined Cam and Laura in the front seat. Then Laura drove to the diner at her normal, sedate pace. Twenty minutes later, a man several years older than Stan let us into a hot, busy kitchen. None of the staff even glanced our way as he led us through the kitchen and into a hallway. The main dining area lay ahead of us, but the man opened a door on the right. It revealed a small room with a table set for eight.

"I feed my people in here after we close for the night." He glanced at a clock on the wall. "That ain't for three hours, so you got lots of time. Stan, can you take orders for your friends?"

"Sure thing, Chuck. And thanks."

Chuck grinned. "No problem. I'll just charge you double." As he turned to go, he waved at the far corner. "I know you like watching the news, Stan. Turn on the television, if you want."

Five of us studied the diner's menu, written on a chalkboard against one wall. Stan, who probably didn't need to even look at the menu, went over and turned on the television. I glanced at the screen as a newsreader —one I hadn't seen before—filled the screen and looked directly at the camera.

From the way his eyes moved, I knew he was reading from an off-camera script. But he spoke in a tone of voice that made people want to believe him. The lighting made it look as if his eyes shone with concern. I hadn't noticed this level of attention to detail the other times I'd watched televised news. I'd had other things on my mind during those brief viewings, so maybe I just missed it. Or maybe those behind the broadcast put a lot of extra effort into it this time.

"Good evening," the talking head said, "tonight we bring you deeper insight into the story that has captured the hearts and minds of all Ab Astrans."

My friends had their eyes on the menu. Even Stan had his back to the screen as he sauntered back to us. I caught Chris's shoulder, turned her away from the menu, and said, "Um, guys? I think you ought to watch this."

Everyone turned to face the television. Laura's eyebrows rose after she saw the scene, and she said, "Someone is going all out to make him look even more trustworthy than usual."

The news reader continued. "Tonight, we explore how a traditional, rural upbringing created the trusting, cheerful nature that ruthless amy spies used to turn that good nature against an innocent young woman. To snare her in their web of lies. To turn her against her country, and even her family."

The reader's face faded from view, replaced by a photo of the pretty blonde girl I counted as one of two best friends in the galaxy.

"Tonight," the reader intoned, "we bring you a cautionary tale the likes of which we have never covered. Tonight, we bring you the tragedy of Laney Gibson."

"Tragedy?" Laney cried. "Who does that idiot think he is?"

"He's the most popular and trusted man in Ab Astra," Laura said.

"I *know* that," Laney snapped. "But—"

In her cadet sergeant tone of voice, Chris said, "Quiet. I want to hear this."

On the screen, a photo of a much younger Laney replaced the first one shown. She sat astride a horse and wore a delighted smile. "A horse lover from a young age, Laney Gibson became an expert competition rider."

The photo of the little girl faded, replaced by several shelves filled with riding trophies. Laney gasped. "That's my bedroom! How did they get into my bedroom?"

Laura put an arm around Laney. "How do you think they got in?"

"No, that can't be. Mom and Dad would never allow it."

Laura squeezed Laney tighter. "Honey, they didn't have a choice. Remember, the government has your brother."

The television screen was back to the most trusted man in Ab Astra. "When the amy spies landed in a meadow near her grandfather's house, Elias Gibson made the mistake that will haunt him to his grave. He asked his grandchildren—Laney and Logan—to come help him guard his home. Authorities think Laney went to the barn to visit her beloved horses and believe that's where the amy spies took control of her mind. It's believed Laney, acting against her will and at the bidding of her new amy masters, lured her brother to the barn. They quickly took control of Logan."

A photo of old Mr. Gibson filled the screen. In a voice filled with sympathy, the newsreader said, "Elias Gibson was too overcome with guilt to speak with us. Laney's and Logan's parents also declined the opportunity to speak on camera, as they are still in shock over the fate of their two children. But they provided a statement and asked us to read it on the air."

The newsreader picked up a single sheet of paper. In solemn tones, he read, "To our beloved Laney, you must fight the amy mind control. Find a way to flee from the amies. Go to the nearest police station and turn yourself in. You must trust in the government. They can solve all of your problems and keep you safe. We're begging you, Laney. Do what's right!"

The newsreader put the paper down and dragged a hand across his eyes. In a voice supposedly quavering with emotion, the newsreader said, "After this short break, we'll introduce you to the two prettiest, sweetest-looking fiends ever to set foot on Ab Astran soil. Stay tuned for an introduction to the amy spies."

The reader's solemn face faded away, replaced by an advertisement. Laura shook her head. "They're really piling it on with this story." She turned to Laney. "Are you okay? It can't have been easy listening to that statement from your parents."

"It was easier than you might think," Laney said. "The only part that's really from my family was the last bit, where they begged me to do what's right." Laney looked at Chris and me. "And that means helping you two get home."

Before Chris or I could say anything else, the advertisements ended. The talking head faded into view.

"Before we continue with poor Laney Gibson's story, we must explain how the two amies ensnared the minds of three young Ab Astrans. As we said earlier, we believe they exercised some sort of mind control on Miss Gibson. But authorities believe the amies sunk their claws into Laney's brother and Jace Walker with a lure as old as time."

A drawing of Chris appeared behind the reader. "Meet the amy known as Chris. As pretty as she appears in this drawing, we've been told she's prettier in person. She also appears a few years older than the Ab Astran teenagers." The reader flashed a self-deprecating smile. "I believe every man in Ab Astra—indeed, in the world—has a story of unrequited love for a lovely, somewhat older woman. Authorities believe the amy Chris used the attraction the Gibson and Walker boys undoubtedly felt towards her, to lure them to the true villainess."

A drawing of me replaced the one of Chris. Cam said, "It doesn't do you justice, Anne."

"I said be quiet!" Chris said.

"This is Anne. Or Princess Anne, as she sometimes calls herself. Notice her exotic beauty, the enticing slant of her eyes, the high cheekbones, and the perfect nose. Her emerald green eyes are dangerous all by themselves. Dangerous in a way any red-blooded Ab Astran teenage boy would find irresistible. Authorities believe the AI who controls Anne surgically sculpted her face and body, as such incredible beauty is beyond the realm of nature.

"But authorities also say Anne has some kind of hypnotic gaze built into her impossible eyes. Once Logan Gibson and Jace Walker looked into those emerald eyes, they were lost. And that is the true danger posed by this pair of AI-controlled women. They can ensnare any young man who has even the slightest interest in the opposite sex. An unfortunate citizen of Landfall learned of Anne's powers the hard way."

The news reader disappeared, replaced by a familiar and unexpected face. Street gang leader Leon stared into the camera and said, "Me an' my boys work real hard to keep our neighborhood safe. We take care of people what need help, ya know? An' when we saw them amies an' their friends wanderin' the street 'round midnight, we tried to help 'em."

From offscreen, the news reader asked, "And, instead of accepting your generous offer of aid, the amy Anne turned her hypnotic vision against you?"

Leon nodded vigorously. "Yeah, tha's 'xactly what she did. I didn't wanna look, you know? But..." Leon shrugged.

"She ensnared you, just as a snake ensnares a baby bird," the news reader said.

Leon's face screwed up in confusion. But someone off camera must have given him a signal, because Leon cleared his face. "Just like a baby bird. Yeah. An' then we had to do what she tell us to do." Leon raised the hand I'd broken wrenching the gun from his grasp. "She told me to break my hand, an' I just whacked a wall with it. Didn't feel nothing, neither, 'cause she controlled my mind."

"How did you free yourself from her hypnotic gaze?" the news reader asked.

"After Anne and her buddies left, I jus' sorta come outta it, you know?"

Leon vanished, and the news reader returned to the screen. "Authorities believe distance weakens the mind control, which explains how that unfortunate, upstanding citizen regained control of his actions. We must also assume Anne's hypnotic vision does not work on mature men, otherwise she would have captured Logan Gibson's father and grandfather."

The talking head faded into another advertisement.

I said, "What utter garbage."

"I don't know," Chris said. "Your eyes—"

"Are just eyes, thank you very much," I said.

"But they are captivating," Laura said. "Right, Cam?"

Cam snorted. "I'm not stupid enough to answer that question."

"I'm not, either," Stan said, "and I don't even have a girlfriend."

"Will you all shut up," Laney said. "Can't you see you're making Anne feel self conscious?"

The television picture suddenly dissolved into static, drawing everyone's attention away from me. The picture flickered, and we glimpsed the ghostly image of a man's head before the static returned.

"I wonder what happened to the signal?" Laura said. "It can't be the weather."

The ghostly man's head appeared again. The static cleared somewhat, but the picture began rolling. It moved too fast for me to make out any details.

Suddenly, the picture stopped rolling and the static vanished. But the man in the picture wasn't the news reader. He was a good ten years younger than the reader, and he stared out of the screen with what can only be called steely-eyed determination.

"Who is *that*?" Laura asked.

"That," I said, "is my father!"

Dad stared out of the television screen for a long moment. A moment during which my friends gaped first at me, and then at the television. Then Dad broke his silence.

"People of Ab Astra. You cannot escape this broadcast. Do not waste your time changing television channels. I am on every channel. Do not bother changing radio frequencies. My voice is on every frequency. I have much to say, and you *will* listen to me.

"I am David Rice, Prince Consort of the Kingdom of Mordan, on the independent world of Aashla. I am David Rice, Master Scout Emeritus of the Terran Federation's Scout Corps. I am David Rice, father of Princess Anne of Mordan. I am David Rice, father of Scout Cadet Anne Villas. Diplomatically, I am empowered to speak for both Mordan and the Terran Federation. Parentally, I care only for the wellbeing of my daughter, her fellow cadet, Christine Montide, and those who have befriended them.

"After my ship's arrival in your solar system one of your days ago, we received and translated your radio and television broadcasts. Then teams of specialists analyzed your political structure and your beliefs. Yours is not the first lost colony founded on a distrust of artificial intelligences. It *is* the first colony founded on the belief that humanity lost the AI wars and was subsequently enslaved by those AIs. I would accept your beliefs as little more than harmless eccentricities," Dad's already steely eyes hardened even more, "had you not used them to vilify two innocent young women and persecute those who aided them.

"I have watched your news broadcasts. I know the lies they show and tell, including the obnoxious, ridiculous broadcasts I interrupted a moment ago. Your government mobilized your army and your air force against a pair of lost, frightened academy cadets. Your government pursued those cadets across half of your continent. You forced them into hiding. You drove them into danger. And..."

Dad leaned closer to the cam. "If you have harmed my daughter, her friend, or those who gave them comfort, there will be a reckoning the likes of which you cannot imagine."

"Whoa." Stan looked at me. "Your dad is one scary guy."

Dad leaned back from the cam after five seconds. His hard glare faded, replaced by a diplomatic smile. "But I'd rather extend a hand in friendship." He sighed. "You see, I need your help finding my daughter and her fellow cadet. As sophisticated as our ship's sensors are, they cannot find specific individuals. Based on your own reports, I believe our missing cadets are in your capital city of Landfall, but well over one million people live in and around that city. I can't find them on my own. That's why I need *your* help."

Dad was telling the truth about the ship's sensors. The sensors could be tuned to search for implants. But Refuge had its own implant technology, and God only knew how many thousands of implants right here in Landfall. The sensors could no more differentiate our implants from theirs, than it could differentiate me from any other person on the planet.

So Dad was pretending he didn't know Refuge had implants. He was pretending he didn't know—or at least suspect—that a rogue AI ran the planet. Because rescuing us would be a lot harder if the Refuge AI knew it had been discovered. Dad was giving the AI reason to decide it remained undetected. And I realized it was a good thing we'd never finished broadcasting our interview with Laura, since we outlined our AI suspicions at the end of it.

I realized Dad was speaking again and turned my attention back to him.

"I have no interest in interfering with your world or your way of life. I honestly don't care that you believe humanity lost the AI wars. I care about my daughter. I care about Christine Montide. But I cannot find them without your help. If you want me to leave you in peace—and, trust me, you most definitely want that—you will find the two young women I seek and have one of them broadcast a message on any of your channels or frequencies. I will land, collect Anne and Chris, and depart."

We were all so caught up in the television broadcast that we paid no attention when the door opened. Besides, someone was supposed to come collect the dinner orders from Stan. None of us even turned our heads.

Until Laney gave a strangled cry.

I turned and saw Laney struggling against an arm wrapped around her throat. The arm belonged to a tall, powerfully built man in a solid black uniform. He held a large handgun to Laney's head. Two equally large men stood behind him, covering us with identical handguns.

Laura gasped. "Izzies!"

The one holding Laney looked at Chris and me. "Do as I say, or I will kill Laney Gibson."

Chris and I held our hands up, and Chris said, "We will. Just don't hurt Laney."

"Cuff them," he said. As his two associates holstered their guns, he added, "Do not try taking one of us hostage as a bargaining chip. I will not negotiate, and Laney Gibson will die. Do you understand?"

"We do," Chris said.

The Izzies weren't taking any chances with the remaining five of us. They made us turn around and handcuffed our hands behind our backs. Then they marched us back through the kitchen. Stan's friend Chuck assayed an apologetic smile. "Sorry, Stan. The reward they're offering for them girls was just too good to pass up."

Stan looked at the Izzie who still held Laney. "He's not a member of Internal Security, right?"

"What of it?"

"I just wanted to make sure before I did this."

Stan spun and kicked Chuck in the gut. Chuck stumbled back and instinctively grabbed for something to keep his balance. Skin sizzled as Chuck's flailing hand landed on a hot griddle. He screamed, dropped to the floor, and curled up around his burned hand.

An Izzie grabbed Stan and shoved him towards the back door. We followed them outside, and the Izzies pushed us into the back of a dark van. A wire mesh barrier divided the cargo compartment into two areas. They herded us through a low gate in the barrier, then closed and locked the gate. Two Izzies settled into the other area, next to the doors.

"Don't try anything," the Izzie in charge said. "We will shoot if you do."

The van's engine roared to life, and it drove into the night.

THIS IS MY PLANET

The van's cargo compartment had no windows, so I could only guess where the Izzies were taking us. The compartment also had no heat, and the Izzies left our coats back at the diner. We six huddled together for what little warmth we could share amongst ourselves. But we were all shivering violently by the time the long ride ended. My implant said we rode for twenty-eight minutes, but the cold made it seem far longer.

The two Izzies sitting in the cargo compartment opened the rear doors. An icy wind swirled into the cargo compartment and sucked out the minuscule warmth we'd generated among ourselves. The driver joined the others, and two of them held guns on us while the third unlocked and opened the gate in the wire mesh barrier.

"Out," he said.

Without the use of our hands, it took us five minutes to exit the van. Five minutes of chattering teeth and increasingly violent shivering as the cold had its way with us. I was the second one out and made a point of looking around me. The van was parked in a small courtyard surrounded by ten meter high stone walls. The stone strongly suggested the Izzies had brought us to the Ab Astran Capitol Building. But I was past caring about anything else except getting somewhere warm.

Cam climbed out last, and the Izzies immediately shoved us towards a door five meters away. It opened as we approached, and four new Izzies took possession of us. Those four marched us down hallways, around corners, past pipes, and finally up a set of stairs. The temperature rose with each step we climbed, at least. A door at the top opened into a richly carpeted, well-lit, *warm* hallway. The Izzies turned us to the right, escorted us to an ornate wooden door, and ushered us into a... sitting room?

The room held a dozen thickly upholstered chairs, small serving tables, a bright, crackling fire, and a middle-aged man standing near the fire. The man wore an impeccable business suit, had his hands inside his trouser pockets, and wore a pleasant smile. He gave me the creeps. Something about his eyes just wasn't right. Wasn't quite human. I realized he must be a real amy. For some reason, he also looked familiar, though I knew I'd never seen him before.

"Oh," Cam said, "they would send *you*."

"How did you know it was me, son?" the man asked.

"Thanks to Chris and Anne, I can see again."

"Ah, that explains it." The man showed no further reaction to the news as he turned at the Izzies. "Remove their handcuffs."

Without a word of protest, the Izzies did as he instructed. Once free, we clustered around the fireplace, hands outstretched, and turning every few seconds to dispel the bitter cold that had seeped into our bodies over the previous thirty something minutes.

In a low tone, Laney asked Cam, "You get your sight back, and *that* is how your dad reacts?"

Cam shrugged. In a voice so tight I thought it might break, he added, "That's my *father*. I don't have a dad anymore."

"Yes, I am Cameron Wheeler, Senior," the man said. "And I must apologize for your rough handling over the last little while. Internal Security has their own information network, and they acted entirely on their own when they apprehended you." Wheeler paused for a second. "Not that IS acted inappropriately. But had the governmental senior staff known who they were collecting, we would have insisted upon gentler handling."

The lone door into the sitting room opened, and several servants entered, pushing a cart loaded with food and another with steaming hot beverages. Wheeler waved the servants towards us. "I understand IS apprehended you before you ate dinner. I had the kitchen whip this up on short notice. It's not a full dinner, but I hope you'll find it satisfactory. At the very least, I'm certain the hot drinks will be most welcome."

They were, though none of us admitted it. We also tore into the food, which was equally welcome. But we also followed Cam's lead and didn't offer thanks to our... Host didn't feel right, but we also couldn't quite call him a jailer. Not yet, anyway.

Wheeler looked at Laura. "Your father wanted to be here, Miss Ackerman, but I'm afraid duties of the job prevented his attendance. He asked me to pass along his regrets, with the promise that he'll join us as soon as possible."

"Where's my brother?" Laney asked. "And Jace?"

"I sent for them as soon as I knew we'd have the pleasure of your company, Miss Gibson." Wheeler looked at his watch. "They should be here in a few minutes."

"What's your game, Father?" Cam asked.

"I don't know what you mean, son," Wheeler said.

"You're buttering us up for some kind of play. I want you to cut to the chase and tell us what it is."

"Oh, that. It's neither a secret nor a game. It is, indeed, of utmost importance to both Refuge and the two young ladies who crashed here."

Wheeler turned to Chris and me. "I'm afraid your arrival caught everyone in the government napping. Long standing emergency protocols went into effect before we in the capital even knew you were here. Once the army and air force deployed... Well, you can imagine the inertia created by an operation of that size. My colleagues have only just reined in the military and the police."

"So," Chris said, "this was all one big ol' misunderstanding?"

Wheeler frowned. "I cannot fault you for having doubts, Miss...?"

"Cadet Sergeant Christine Montide."

"I am genuinely pleased to meet you, Cadet Sergeant." Wheeler turned to me. "That means this lovely young lady must be Princess Anne."

"Cadet Anne Villas," I said. "I am a Scout, first and foremost."

"As you say, Cadet Villas."

Wheeler turned as the door opened again. A pair of Izzies entered, leading Logan and Jace. Laney raced across the room and threw one arm around each boy. Chris and I weren't far behind. A minute passed while we made sure the guys were okay and the guys did the same with us.

At last, we led the guys back to Cam, Laura, and Stan. Ignoring Wheeler, we made introductions all around. But I guess it was just too normal for Jace.

"Whoa, whoa, whoa," Jace said. "I'm as happy as anyone to see you girls, but aren't you forgetting something?" Jace pointed at the Izzies still standing at the door. "The Izzies have captured us all."

"On the contrary, Mr. Walker," Wheeler said. "You and Mr. Gibson are not captives and are free to leave at any time."

"Great." Jace looked at the rest of us. "Let's clear out of here before they change their minds."

"But you and your companions may want to stay a while longer. As our guests, naturally."

Jace glared at Wheeler. "Why would we even consider doing that?"

"Because I assume Cadet Villas would like to talk to her father and make arrangements for her and Cadet Sergeant Montide to go home."

"Just like that?" Jace scoffed.

"Not in the least, Mr. Walker," Wheeler said. "While the government and the armed forces presented a united front to the country, our minds have been sharply divided behind the scenes. Because of the protective nature of their mandate, the military view you as potential threats and wanted you treated as such."

"Threats that should be rounded up and neutralized, Father?" Cam asked.

Logan's eyes darted back and forth between Cam and Wheeler. In a low tone, he asked, "That's his father?"

Wheeler heard him. "Yes, Mr. Gibson, I am Cam's father." A dim twinkle rose in Wheeler's eyes, and he offered the closest thing to a genuine smile we'd seen from him. "And I'm quite proud of my boy." The twinkle faded, and the smile twisted into something that wasn't quite right. "Despite our rather significant differences."

I glanced at Cam, saw his surprise at the brief spark of humanity shown by his father, and saw his face fall when the spark vanished. Laura saw it, too, and enveloped him in a hug.

Wheeler's attention returned to Jace. "We in the government are more prone to talking. Too much so, according to the citizens we serve."

Wheeler's not-quite-human smile flashed again. "We opposed the military's plan. Which, I hasten to add, did not involve neutralizing any of you."

"We heard your television news broadcasts advise their viewers to shoot us on sight," Chris said. "That sounds a lot like neutralizing to me."

"That was not our doing." Wheeler spread his hands in a what-are-you-going-to-do gesture. "That's an unfortunate side effect to a free and open press."

Laura gave a soft snort, but otherwise remained quiet at Wheeler's declaration.

I crossed my arms. "Let's say we accept your version of events."

Wheeler inclined his head, apparently accepting that we didn't believe his story but were willing to move on.

I asked, "Why weren't the Izzies informed of those discussions? We froze half to death in the back of their unheated van."

"While I wish Internal Security had treated you more humanely," Wheeler said, "we only settled on your new status after they had apprehended you."

"Uh huh. And what made you change your mind?"

"Your father's rather forceful message, Cadet Villas. While there are still holdouts among certain hardline members of the military, the senior commanders realize they cannot hope to win a fight against a space borne warship."

"So the *only* reason you're not treating us adversarially is because my father's threats cowed your army and air force?"

"The only reason?" Wheeler shook his head. "No, Cadet Villas. But it was an important reason." Wheeler's gaze sharpened. "That is why your father delivered the threat, is it not?"

I nodded.

"Then, isn't your accusatory tone misplaced? Shouldn't you be happy it had its intended effect?"

Wheeler's point carried the inexorable weight of logic. I said, "You're right. Whatever the reason, I'm happy the Ab Astran government has chosen to talk rather than fight."

"Now, why don't you young people return to eating and reacquainting yourselves with each other? I must see how our technicians are progressing with the transmitter you will use to speak with your father."

Wheeler left the room, but the Izzies remained at the door. They looked exactly like the guards I believed them to be.

As we huddled around the food and drinks, Jace whispered, "Did you notice how the government guy—"

"Wheeler," Laney said.

"Yeah, Wheeler. He told Logan and me we were free to go. But he *only* told us."

"Yeah, I noticed that," Stan said.

"He wouldn't want Chris and Anne leaving," Laura said. "They've got to talk to Anne's dad."

"But he could have included the rest of you," Jace said. "Or at least told Laney she could come with us if we left."

"True... Why do you think he singled you two out?"

Jace shrugged. "Maybe he knew we wouldn't leave without the rest of you?"

"Probably," I said. "But I bet he'd have let you walk out the door, if you wanted to. He already had Chris and me, and four hostages to make sure we behave ourselves."

"Six hostages, since Jace and I stayed," Logan said.

"Four or six, it's still enough," Chris said.

"Back when I interviewed you girls, you said that you don't matter," Laura said. "What happened?"

"*We* don't," Chris said. "But *you* do."

"Don't you *dare* treat us differently than you treat yourselves!" Laney glared at Chris. "This is *my* planet, and I demand the right to risk my life for it. Is that clear, Chris?"

"Um, okay," Chris said.

Laney turned her glare on me. "Clear, Anne?"

"Yes, ma'am," I said.

"That's my girl." Jace grinned and looped an arm around Laney's waist. "The same goes for Logan and me."

"And Cam and me," Laura added.

"And I make it unanimous," Stan said.

Laney's glare faded. "Don't you forget it."

"We won't," I said, "but don't *you* repeat it. My plan falls apart if the real amies don't believe they can control Chris and me."

"You have a plan?" Logan asked.

"Let me guess," Laney said. "You're going to talk to your dad in code, right?"

"A bit, yeah. I can warn him to watch for traps, but we don't exactly have code words setup for 'destroy the six cooling towers in the central garden.' That's going to take some finesse. If you know any prayers to help Dad recognize teenage slang, this would be a good time to say them."

The door to the room opened again. Wheeler returned, accompanied by a distinguished-looking man.

"Who's the guy with Cam's father?" Chris asked.

"My father," Laura said. "Otherwise known as the President of Ab Astra."

Laura's father flashed a professionally polite smile. "Hello, Laura. I wish I could say I'm surprised to find you mixed up in all of this." He eyed Cam. "Is this the young man you've told your mother so much about?"

"Yes, Father. This is Cam. But you already knew that."

"I did." Laura's father turned to Cam. "I'm Arthur Ackerman."

Cam nodded. "I know."

"I hear you've recently regained your vision. Well done, Cam." Ackerman turned his attention to the rest of us. "As much as I'd like to get to know all of you, I'm afraid business must come before pleasure. Would the two cadets accompany me to the radio transmitter?"

"What of our friends?" Chris asked.

"They'll be safe and sound right here, Cadet... Montide, is it?"

"I'm sure everything will be fine." I offered a big smile and wrapped Laney in a hug. With my mouth next to her ear, I whispered, "If you hear explosions, get everyone out of the building as fast as you can."

"Got it," she whispered back. Aloud, she said, "See if you can wrap this up fast, Anne. I miss my horses."

Without another word, Chris and I followed the Ab Astran president from the room.

I looked back at our friends as I walked through the doorway. Anxious smiles stretched taut faces, inset with eyes filled with love and fear. I flashed the best princess smile I could manage at them, did my best to ignore the hammering of my heart, and activated my implant's mapping function. Then the door closed, cutting me off from every friend with whom I'd been through so much.

Every friend but one. Chris. Calm, courageous, clever Chris.

She must have felt my eyes on her, because Chris met my gaze and smiled. "You've got this."

I returned her smile. "I'd never have made it here without you."

"You're the Princess Scout. You'd have made it."

"This plebe disagrees."

"And you can drop that plebe nonsense, Anne. You're a Scout, plain and simple."

"I'm not the only one, *Scout* Montide."

President Ackerman frowned over his shoulder at us. Chris giggled, and whispered, "The president must not like listening to girl talk."

I straightened my shoulders and set my face in an expression of polite respect. One every cadet—and at least one princess—knows so well. Chris matched my posture and expression. Our steps synchronized. And a pair of perfectly behaved cadets finished the ten-minute walk from the sitting room to a room filled with what must be high technology consoles on Refuge. On my home world of Aashla, it would be ridiculously high tech.

But to Federation-trained eyes? It was like walking into a living museum exhibit.

Uniformed military officers hovered over civilian technicians dressed in gray trousers, white shirts, and neckties. Large video screens covered the far wall, displaying artists' renderings of Refuge and its surrounding space. Lights blinked all around the planet, probably showing the relative positions of Ab Astran satellites in orbit. A group of men and women dressed in business suits gathered beneath the central video screen. The constant susurration of cooling fans softened the rising and falling voices into something almost soothing.

President Ackerman strode between the consoles towards the group at the front of the room. Voices fell silent as we passed. Soon, the only sounds were the constant hum of the fans and the click of our steps.

Ackerman stopped two meters from the others, turned sideways and gestured to us with his right hand. "These are Cadet Sergeant Christine Montide and Cadet Anne Villas."

Murmurs of greeting rose from what I assumed were the most

powerful people in Ab Astra. Ackerman confirmed my assumption, when gestured to them with his left hand. "These are my cabinet ministers. I would normally introduce them by name," he gave a not-quite-human smile, "but I suspect you'd much rather speak with your father. I *know* he would like to speak with you."

I heard myself say, "Yes, please."

One of the white-shirted men appeared next to me and pointed to a nearby console. "Right this way."

Chris and I followed him to the console. Two empty chairs waited in front of a large, shiny silver microphone. After we sat, the technician pointed to a large black button on the microphone. "Press the button to activate the microphone. It will remain depressed until you press it a second time."

I nodded my understanding, and the technician backed away. Chris and I exchanged glances, then I pressed the black button. "Greetings, Father."

Formal. Proper. The perfect little princess reporting to her honored father. Not to mention a code phrase telling Dad my situation remained precarious.

Dad didn't miss a beat. "Greetings, daughter. Is your fellow cadet also present?"

I nudged Chris, who said, "Uh, greetings sir."

"I trust you are both healthy, uninjured, and well-treated?"

"We are, Father. Cadet Sergeant Montide and I have suffered nothing more than scrapes, bruises, and a sprained ankle. The Ab Astran government provided food and drink for us and our friends among the Ab Astrans."

From news broadcasts, Dad had to know the government had Jace and Logan. But this told him they held other friends, too.

"Please let your friends speak, so I may extend the official thanks of Mordan and of the Terran Federation to those who so selflessly aided you."

"Our companions remained with the food and drink and let Cadet Sergeant Montide and me have this moment to ourselves."

I didn't have a code phrase for 'they're hostages against our good behavior,' but I knew Dad would read between the lines.

"That was thoughtful of them," Dad said. "I do hope I'll see them when I land to pick you up."

Before I could answer, President Ackerman appeared behind me. "Captain Rice? I am Arthur Ackerman, President of Ab Astra. Where will you land your ship?"

"I hope my daughter has a suggestion," Dad said.

I abandoned my formal tone of voice. "I do! You've traced this broadcast, right?"

"Yes."

"Oh, good!" I spoke rapidly, acting the part of the overexcited teenager. "The ship's sensors show a garden courtyard in the building, right? I haven't seen them in person, but the pictures I've seen are *so* beautiful! Flowers and sculpted bushes and six sculpted tower fountains that are patchless and zing and... and... every other word used on lost colonies that means something fantastic!"

'Patchless' is Aashlan slang for perfect or fantastic. Dad had heard Rob and me say it so many times, I knew he'd understand. 'Zing' is used throughout the Federation and means the same thing. Dad's sister, my Aunt Sandra, still used it. So Dad would pick that up, too. But would Dad remember the much older word that's still used on a few recently rediscovered lost colonies? The one I implied when I said "every other word used on lost colonies." Would he make the connection I suggested, and remember 'cool' also meant something fantastic? *I* only knew the word because Aashla's first native Scouts, Jade and Chris Marlow, taught it to me. And *they* only knew it because Jade's roommate at the Scout Academy was from Escoth, one of those worlds that still used 'cool.'

But would Dad remember all that? I mean, yeah, he's got an implant to help with his memory. But he's old, nearly *fifty*. Even if he remembered 'cool,' would he connect it to the towers?

I shouldn't have worried. "I saw something like that on Escoth. Of course, when *I* was your age, my friends and I would have said it *wailed*."

Oh. My. God. Dad not only remembered 'cool,' he even made up his own slang word on the spot. *And* it had a special coded meaning, too.

What wailed?

A Banshee Assault Shuttle coming in fast and hard.

If Dad brought a Banshee, he had to have at least a full squad of marines to man it. And that meant—

Ackerman interrupted my train of thought. "I'm afraid I cannot allow you to land your ship in the garden, Captain Rice. The gardens are a sacred memorial to those who gave their lives, bringing us to Refuge."

"Of course, Mr. President," Dad said. "My ship is too large to fit inside the courtyard, anyway."

"It is?" Ackerman sounded a bit taken aback. "How large is your ship?"

"Two hundred meters long," Dad said.

"I would like you to land close to our capitol building," Ackerman said, "so you may be reunited with your daughter and her friend as quickly as possible."

Or Ackerman wanted Dad to land as close as possible to his most loyal troops, the thugs from Internal Security. But Dad was forewarned, so he played along.

"There is a large paved area next to the capitol building," Dad said. "If you'll have it cleared of ground vehicles, I can land there easily."

"It shall be done," Ackerman said. "I look forward to meeting you in person soon."

Before I could say anything else, Ackerman leaned over and turned off the microphone. At the same time, Izzies grabbed Chris and me by the arms and hauled us to our feet.

Ackerman swept the room with his gaze. "Captain Rice has taken the bait. You all know what to do."

I felt like Chris or I had to protest. Chris beat me to it. "You're making a big mistake, Ackerman!"

Ackerman's tone of voice turned more mechanical than ever. "No, I am not." He waved towards the control center's exit. "Prepare them."

Without another word, the Izzies dragged Chris and me away.

THE LAST THING I EXPECTED

Chris caught my eye as the Izzies shoved us out of the control room. She said nothing, but she didn't need words. Her expression said it.

Don't fight. Not yet.

Her warning was timely. Waiting was the right course of... inaction, I guess. That didn't make waiting easier, though. I mean, I'm the daughter of David Rice. A living legend. The man who Boosted for thirteen minutes and survived.

Thirteen.

Freaking.

Minutes.

Chris and I wouldn't even need a minute to mop the floor with the four Izzies escorting us, if we Boosted.

Six more Izzies waited for us outside the control room, each of them holding large handguns at the ready. Three aimed their guns at Chris. The other three aimed at me. The four Izzies holding our arms took care to keep out of their compatriots' line of fire.

I decided my original estimate of less than a minute to handle our guards had been optimistic. *Way* too optimistic. As in, Chris and I probably wouldn't survive the fight. Maybe if we didn't have a strong man hanging onto each arm. And had a blaster in hand. Or even a sword.

Then we *might* take out the ten Izzies around us before they filled us with bullet holes.

Chris's warning look was both galling and timely. I gave a microscopic nod of understanding, and Chris's face relaxed a bit. Besides, cooperating with the Izzies was part of our plan. The whole idea was to keep the AI from figuring out we knew about it. And that meant keeping our knowledge from the Ab Astran amies.

So, we let the Izzies push us down the hallway. As before, I activated my implant's mapping function. If everything went according to plan, I had every intention of coming back inside the capitol building to find our friends. Without asking, I knew Chris would feel the same way.

We must have started out somewhere near the center of the capitol building, because we walked through arrow-straight corridors for five minutes. Then the Izzies stopped before a door.

The Izzie holding my right arm released it. "Open the door."

As soon as I did, the Izzie grabbed my arm again. Three gun-toting Izzies backed into the room, then the two Izzies holding Chris shoved her after them. The Izzies guarding me followed the same procedure.

The room beyond the door was close to ten meters long, but only three wide. More like a corridor, really, especially since there was another door in the far wall. But there were tall, narrow windows on each side of the door. The first windows we'd seen since the Izzies dragged us into the capitol building. The windows looked out on a vast, nearly empty parking area. Even as we watched, the few cars in the lot started moving towards the exits. Ten minutes later, the lot was empty, and a perfect landing spot for the spaceship Dad commanded.

The door we'd come through opened, and a host of Izzies escorted a dozen Ab Astran government officials, led by President Ackerman, into the room. The Izzies and the officials all wore heavy coats against the cold they'd find outside. To my surprise, an Izzie carried two more heavy coats. He gave one to the two Izzies who'd held my arms, and the other to the two who'd held Chris's. The two Izzies politely held the coat to my back.

"Put it on," one said.

I knew just how cold it was outside, so pushed aside a sudden twinge of misgivings and slid my arms into the coat sleeves. I'd called it a heavy coat because it looked warm enough for the frigid temperatures outside. But it was also *heavy*. Much heavier than it should have been.

"Button the coats," Ackerman said. "We wouldn't want your father thinking we mistreated you."

Chris and I exchanged a glance. My twinge of unease grew by leaps and bounds. But I shrugged and began buttoning the coat. Chris did the same.

When we finished, our Izzies pushed us to the far side of the room. They released us and backed far away.

An Izzie somewhere in the host of other Izzies said, "Armed."

"Excellent," Ackerman said. "Cadets, have you noticed that your coats weigh more than you expected from the materials?"

"Yes," Chris said.

"The extra weight comes from powerful explosives sewn inside the coats. May I also assume you understand the concept of a deadman switch?"

"We do," I said.

"Excellent. The deadman switch for the explosives in your coats is radio controlled and set to a frequency restricted for government use. The deadman switch is the only device broadcasting on that frequency. A member of my Internal Security team has the switch in hand. Should either of you, Captain Rice, or any member of his crew take any threatening action, he will release the deadman switch."

Ackerman was silent for a moment. Maybe so we could ask questions. Since we didn't speak, he asked, "I trust you understand what will happen if my man releases the switch?"

"Boom," Chris said.

"And we die," I said.

"That is correct," Ackerman said. "Rest assured, I will explain the situation to your father when he lands. If he and his crew behave themselves, no harm will come to you."

As if on cue, the glass in the windows began vibrating. The deep thrumming of massive repulsor engines followed. A minute later, Dad's spaceship descended. It settled gently onto the parking lot, and the thrumming gradually faded away.

"Let's not keep Captain Rice waiting," Ackerman said. "Cadet Villas, please lead the way."

I'd somehow remained calm and composed throughout Ackerman's explanation about the deadman switch. But the prospect of walking out that door and facing my father as a hostage to the AI set my heart pounding. I blinked back tears that welled up in my eyes.

We'd worked so hard to stay out of the government's clutches. And we'd come so close to pulling it off, only to have diner owner Chuck's small-minded greed ruin everything.

And that meant I was going to die. Blown to pieces in front of my father. Because there was no way he'd surrender to the AI.

He'd take the AI out, at least. But Chris and I would be—

Chris laid a hand on my shoulder and whispered, "Don't give up, Anne. If anyone in the galaxy can get us out of this, it's your dad."

I sniffed once, nodded, and straightened my shoulders. Then I opened the door and walked out into the freezing early evening gloom.

Ackerman and his gang of Izzies waited until Chris and I walked ten meters beyond the door before they began filing out behind us. Chris and I walked another ten meters before Ackerman called, "Stop there."

Fifty meters ahead of us, Dad's sleek, deadly, and huge spaceship filled the parking lot.

Twenty meters behind us, the stone monstrosity that was the Ab Astran capitol building towered over us.

Standing between them with Chris, I felt tiny, helpless, and hopeless. Chris must have felt the same, because she reached out and took my hand in hers. It was a minor comfort, but any comfort was better than nothing.

The spaceship's exterior lights flared to life, bathing the ground between the ship and the capitol building in bright light. But none of the lights shined directly into our eyes, so I clearly saw the main airlock hatch slide open. The inner airlock hatch slid open next, something only made possible because the ship's sensors detected a breathable atmosphere outside the ship.

As a ramp extended from the airlock to the ground, Dad strode through the airlock. A dozen men and women followed him, including Tim, my favorite guard who played Scout with me when I was a little girl. But at least Mom and Rob weren't there. I thanked God they wouldn't have to watch me die.

Halfway down the ramp, Dad spread his arms wide. "Anne, aren't you going to come give your father a hug?"

Ackerman spoke from somewhere well behind me. "No, Captain Rice, she will stay exactly where she is."

Dad slowly lowered his arms. His hands closed into fists and his shoulders tensed. "I thought we had agreed that I would collect our two lost cadets and leave your planet in peace?"

"That is what I wanted you to believe, Captain Rice. But why should I let a prize as great as a modern spaceship slip through my grasp? Especially when I control your daughter, who I believe you value more than you do the spaceship."

"You are correct. But you have foolishly put Anne and Chris far from you. With a single word from me, my crew can kill you and everyone around you."

"Cadet Villas," Ackerman said, "please explain to your father why he will not do that."

"He..." My voice broke. I drew a deep breath and fought for control of my voice. "He..." My voice failed me again, and my vision blurred as tears filled my eyes.

Chris squeezed my hand. In a shaky, though clear voice, she said, "There are explosives sewn into the coats we're wearing, sir. One of President Ackerman's men has a device broadcasting a signal on an unused frequency. The device has a deadman switch."

Dad set his face in an expression of absolute control. Absolute fury. And, ultimately, absolute powerlessness. "If I refuse your demands, you kill these two innocent girls. Correct?"

"Correct, Captain Rice," Ackerman said. "Must I remind you how messy their deaths will be?"

"No."

"I believe I will, anyway. Imagine, Captain Rice, bits and pieces of your daughter and her friend scattered all across the ground. Globs of their flesh oozing down the side of your spaceship. The soft splatter of organs—"

"You've made your point, Ackerman."

"Good."

Dad stared at Ackerman for five seconds. Then he turned his head and spoke over his shoulder, and Tim slipped back inside the spaceship.

I'd thought Tim would stubbornly stay with Dad, but I was glad he hadn't. If I could just get Dad to go back inside, no one I loved would have to watch when Chris and I exploded. But I knew nothing could make Dad leave.

"Where is that man going?" Ackerman asked.

"He is relaying orders to the ship's gun crews to stand down. I do not want an anxious gunner accidentally initiating an incident that leaves me with no reason to be merciful."

"I believe you overstate your position, Captain Rice."

"Need I remind you of *my* threat to you, should anything happen to Anne and Chris?"

"Ah, yes. If I recall, you promised 'a reckoning the likes of which you cannot imagine.' That was the phrase, was it not?"

"Yes, but that was before you pulled this stunt." Dad spoke in an even, almost conversational tone. "If you are stupid enough to harm my little girl, I will erase this misbegotten country from the face of this planet. Not one building, not one house, not one hovel, not even an outhouse will remain standing." Dad's voice deepened. "A thousand years from now, the ruins of Ab Astra will remind the people of the galaxy exactly what happens to *anyone* who threatens *my* child and her friends."

"Brave words, Captain Rice," Ackerman said. "But we both know it won't come to that. Your man may deliver orders, but they will be evacuation orders for your crew. He may start with the gunnery crews, if you wish. They cannot accidentally fire if they're not in the ship. You have one minute, starting now. If you do not comply, I will have your daughter and her friend blown to pieces."

I squeezed Chris's hand and whispered, "I'm sorry, Chris."

She squeezed back. "For what?"

"For this." I looked at Dad, raised my voice, and said, "You can't surrender the ship, Dad. Chris and I know our lives aren't worth the risk of letting an ancient rogue AI loose on the galaxy."

"Why did you apologize for that?" Chris asked. "We already agreed that we don't matter."

"Be silent, girl!" Ackerman shouted.

Dad's eyes flicked to Ackerman. "Do not take that tone of voice with my daughter."

Ackerman cackled, his laugh no more human than his smile. "Or what, Captain Rice?"

Dad ignored Ackerman's question and looked at me. "Do you have any idea what your grandfather would do to me if I let *anything* happen to his favorite granddaughter?"

Despite the situation, a laugh pushed its way out of my mouth. An hysterical laugh, but still a laugh. "I'm his *only* granddaughter, so being his favorite doesn't mean much."

Five men walked through the spaceship's open airlock and descended the ramp. At the bottom of the ramp, each man stopped and bobbed his head to me. Each man said, "Your Highness." Then each man walked to the right side of the ramp. They turned stony stares on Ackerman and rested their hands on the butts of their holstered sidearms.

"And don't even get me started on what your mother and brother would do to me," Dad said.

"I appreciate what you're doing, Dad, but—"

Four more men and five women walked through the airlock and descended the ramp. Except for walking to the left side of the ramp, they copied the actions of the first five men exactly.

"Captain Rice," Ackerman called, "perhaps you should remind your evacuating crew of the fate that awaits the two cadets, should your crew offer any resistance."

As six more men imitated the fourteen members of the crew already arrayed before the ship, Dad asked, "Crew? Do you understand the consequences of resistance?"

As one, the now-twenty stern-faced crew members said, "Yes, sir!"

Helpless frustration overwhelmed me. My shoulders drooped, I hung my head, and whispered, "You can't give up the ship, Dad. You just can't."

Though I was talking to myself, Chris whispered a reply. "Anne? Have you taken a good look at the crew members who have exited the ship?"

I didn't look up. "Evacuated the ship, you mean."

"If I'd *meant* evacuated, I'd have *said* evacuated." Chris's whisper took on a sharp edge. "Look at those men and women. That is an order, plebe!"

In a dull, toneless voice, I said, "This plebe hears and obeys."

I lifted my head and let my gaze wander down the line of crew members lined up in front of the ship. I blinked to sharpen my vision and looked at them again.

"Do they look beaten to you, Anne?"

"Um, no... But what can they do about the deadman switch?"

"How should I know? I'm just a cadet. But think about it, Anne, who commands that ship?"

"My father."

"And who is your father?"

"David Rice."

"Exactly. David. Freaking. Rice. The most famous Scout of all time. A legendary hero during his own lifetime." Chris's eyes bored into mine. "What have the clowns behind us got to match David Rice?"

"Um, a centuries old, inhuman AI, two coats full of explosives, and a deadman switch."

Chris gave a decisive nod. "Yeah. It sure sucks to be them."

Before I could come up with a response to that, Tim returned to the airlock. He walked through it and down the ramp to Dad.

"Fifty-five seconds. Your man cut it close, Captain Rice," Ackerman called.

Tim spoke softly to Dad for a few seconds. And then Dad did the last thing I expected.

My father laughed. Long and loud. At the same time, he clapped Tim on the shoulder.

Dad's laughter obviously confused Ackerman. "Has the strain of surrendering your ship proven too much for your mind, Captain Rice?"

Dad turned to face Ackerman. "Oh, yes, my laughter was rather rude, wasn't it?" A genuine smile lit Dad's face. "I know! I could share what Guard Captain Dawson just told me."

I know I shouldn't have worried about Tim's title, but he'd been a sergeant when I left for the Scout Academy. "Guard Captain? When did you promote him?"

"Just now, Anne," Dad said. "And he definitely earned it."

Ackerman shouted, "Captain Rice—"

Dad made placating gestures at Ackerman. "Yes, yes. An explanation." He took a second to compose himself. "We've already established that you heard the speech I made over television and radio."

"What of it?" Ackerman asked.

"Did you watch it on television or hear it on the radio?"

"Television. Again, what of it?"

"I'd ask which channel you watched, but it doesn't matter. Just as it wouldn't matter which radio frequency you selected, had you listened to the speech via radio. Because my speech was on all of them."

Chris and I gasped, as we got our first inkling of what Dad had done.

"You're trying my patience, Captain Rice. Come to the point or I *will* blow up your daughter and her friend."

"No, you won't." Dad looked at Chris and me. "Girls, please take those coats off. Just as a precaution."

"If they touch one button, the person with the deadman switch *will* release it."

"Let him," Dad said. "The signal broadcast by your deadman switch is of no consequence."

Dad strode down the ramp and towards Ackerman. The wide line of armed crew members marched with him.

"Right now, my ship is blasting your city with a signal on *every* frequency. The explosives in those coats will never explode unless *I* want them to. And, should I ever want that, I promise my daughter and Chris will be nowhere near the coats."

Dad drew his blaster pistol. The line of crew members also drew their blaster pistols. Without turning his head, Dad said, "Now, Tim."

Tim raised a comm to his lips. "Bring it, Banshee."

A wail sounded from high above us and grew louder with each passing second. Even as I fumbled with the buttons of the explosive coat, I looked up into the night sky. A glowing dot appeared and bloomed into the familiar shape of a Banshee Assault shuttle. The wail that gave the shuttle its name rose to a deafening shriek.

Ackerman, his fellow government officials, and the Izzies put hands over their ears. But I just grinned into the night sky, listening to the most beautiful sound I'd heard in a long time.

The pilot pulled the shuttle out of its dive. Doors opened on both sides of the shuttle, revealing marines crouched there. Each one held a long tube.

"What is the meaning of this?" Ackerman cried.

The Banshee's wail drowned out the sound of the missiles launching. But I saw a dozen contrails expand behind a dozen missiles. They streaked down at the capitol building and vanished from sight. A second later, the light from a dozen explosions illuminated the Banshee in unnatural light. Several seconds later, we heard the sound of six cooling towers collapsing.

Ackerman, his fellow government officials, and a handful of Izzies clutched their heads and screamed. They kept screaming as, somewhere below the Ab Astran capitol building, the computer hosting the AI overheated, and its circuits bubbled and then melted into a molten pool of silicon sludge.

PEOPLE OF REFUGE

Some part of my mind registered the biting cold that enveloped me as I shrugged off the explosives-filled coat Ackerman had given me. But I couldn't tear my eyes from the Banshee Assault Shuttle hovering over the capitol building. I watched as the shuttle's doors slid shut, hiding the missile-launching marines from view. Then it slid sideways, and when it had open ground beneath it, gently descended.

While I paid no attention to the weather, Chris did. As I watched the Banshee, Chris took my arm and led me towards Dad's spaceship. Tim met us halfway and handed us jackets made from the same heat reflecting material as the survival blankets Chris and I took from the lifepod.

Tim bowed as we took the jackets. "It's good to see you again, Your Highness. And equally good to meet you, Miss Montide."

I took the jacket, but didn't put it on yet. Instead, I threw my arms around Tim and hugged him tightly. "Don't you *Your Highness* me, Tim! I am, and always will be, Anne to you."

"And," Chris said, "I would be honored if you would call me Chris."

Tim kept one arm around my shoulders and opened the other arm for Chris. "I'll call you Chris, but only if you let an old guardsman hug the young lady who took such good care of my princess."

Chris joined our hug. "You've got it backwards, sir."

Tim frowned in mock disapproval. "Tim."

Chris nodded. "Yes, Tim. As for me taking care of Anne, *she* carried me up and down mountains for half of a day and exhausted herself doing it."

Tim arched an eyebrow. "I definitely want to hear that story!"

"You will, but not yet." I slipped from Tim's grasp and pulled on the jacket. "Could you please gather half-a-dozen people for a search and rescue run?"

"You have friends in that ugly stone building?"

"The friends who helped us," I said.

Tim's expression turned all business. "Can you provide descriptions of the people we're looking for?"

"No need," I said. "I'm going with you."

Tim shook his head. "Absolutely not."

"Wrong," Chris said. "Anne and I are both going. Our implants have the only map of the route we took away from our friends. So we have to go."

Tim looked back and forth between us and then shook his head. "I'll gather a team." He pointed at Dad. "*But* you're not going unless your father gives his permission."

I heaved a theatrical sigh and rolled my eyes. "You're no fun anymore, Tim."

"And you're not seven anymore, Anne."

I flashed a conciliatory smile at Tim. "Okay, okay. I'm off to ask my daddy if I can go find my friends."

Tim jogged back towards the ship while Chris and I turned and walked towards the big cluster of people gathered near the entrance to the capitol building. Five of the crew members had pulled aside the ten or twelve Izzies unaffected by the AI's destruction. The rest of the crew knelt next to those who must have had implants—the fallen government officials and half of the Izzies. Dad's crew were making sure they were still alive, I guess. And maybe trying to figure out if the fallen had functioning minds left.

Dad knelt next to Ackerman and spoke to him. For Laura's sake, I hoped her father could respond rationally. I'd know soon enough.

I took a quick look over my shoulder and saw Tim reach the ship. He pointed to a few crew members and led them our way.

I seriously considered making a break for the entrance and leaving

Tim to chase after us. Before my time on Refuge, I might have done that. But now I understood what it meant to feel responsible for another person's life. I understood the consequences of acting on emotion and without thought.

As we closed on Dad, Chris said, "I half expected you to take off on your own. I'd have gone with you."

"I know, but..." I shrugged.

"No buts, Anne." Chris grinned at me. "Asking your father is the right thing to do. And we Scouts always try to do the right thing."

We stopped next to Dad as he helped Ackerman sit up. While Ackerman rubbed his head, Dad rose and hugged me. I returned Dad's hug, but I broke the hug after a couple of seconds.

Dad saw my expression and offered a rueful smile. "Uh oh."

"What does that mean?" I asked.

"It means my little girl is about to ask permission to do something dangerous. And I have to say yes, because my little girl is not so little anymore." Dad met my gaze. "What may I do for you two Scouts?"

"We need to go back inside to find our friends."

Dad glanced over my shoulder as Tim came up behind us. "You and your squad are escorting them, Tim?"

"We are, sir," Tim said.

"There is no one I trust more, Tim." Dad took and then released a deep breath and straightened his shoulders. "Good luck, Scouts."

I didn't trust myself to speak, so I just nodded and then headed for the capitol building's entrance. With Chris at my side and Tim's squad around us, I left the quiet safety outside and confronted the chaotic danger of a collapsing government inside.

The ten-meter hallway just inside the door was empty and quiet. We crossed quickly to the door at the far end, and the shouts and cries from beyond it gave me pause. But I steeled myself, grabbed the knob, and opened the door.

A panicked man carried an unconscious woman past the door. He glanced our way but showed no sign he recognized Chris or me. He continued on his way as we walked through the door. Our route led us into one of the building's main corridors, where we ran into many more people.

Business-suited civilians shambled aimlessly in the corridors, their faces filled with confusion or loss or fear or a combination of all three. Some older civilians had concerned staff members guiding them along the hallway. They posed no danger to us, so we ignored them.

The military officers wore the same expressions we'd seen on many of the civilians. Their military training kept their posture erect, their stride purposeful, and their gaze steely-eyed. Despite the illusion of purpose, some strode back and forth across the hallway while others zig-zagged down it.

The Izzies worried me the most. Small bands of them stalked through the building, attempting to restore order. The Ab Astran amies ignored all attempts at direction. Most of the panicked civilians did as well. More than one Izzie squad also eyed us. Each time, our guards quickly formed around us. Tim's glare, backed by blasters held at the ready, repelled the Izzies every time.

We stopped at every cross corridor and looked up and down for our friends. Our already-slow progress dropped to a snail's pace. But Chris and I knew caution was our ally, so we diligently scanned every corridor. Our original walk from the control room to the building's exit only took five minutes. The return trip took thirty. But we were fairly certain we hadn't missed Laney and the others.

And we hadn't.

The control room door stood open. Tim insisted—reasonably—on entering first. As he stood in the doorway, he said, "I believe your friends are here. But so are about twenty of those Izzies."

"Let us see," I said.

"That's not a good idea," Tim said. "The Izzies are well-armed,"

"I can't help my friends from the hallway, Tim. Please move."

Tim sighed and moved farther into the room. "Yes, Your Highness."

Chris and I entered the control room, followed by the rest of Tim's squad. The sight that met our eyes was both strange and familiar.

Laney and Laura each had an Izzie standing behind them, with an arm wrapped around their throats and a gun pressing against their temples. Cam supported his father, who appeared dazed but more alert than the zombies we saw in the hallways. He, Logan, Jace, and Stan stared daggers at the Izzies holding Laney and Laura.

At least a dozen Izzies pounded furiously on buttons on the various consoles, all the while glancing up at the static-filled screens along the far wall. An older Izzie, with a more ornate uniform—probably an officer—stood beneath the screens and screeched at the men banging on the consoles.

"The screens must work!" he raged. "They will bring the Voice back."

The man said 'voice' with the same reverence a priest gave when speaking to God.

"He was an Ab Astran amy," Chris said.

"Yeah," I said, "and he misses it."

Tim looked at me. "I *believe* my men can shoot the two holding the women. But it will be risky."

"Lower your guns and let me by," I said. "I have an idea."

"Care to share?" Chris asked.

"No time. Just follow my lead." I glanced at Tim. "Comm the ship and see if they can broadcast some appropriate space scenes on those screens."

Chris and I stepped forward. I stared at the ranting Izzie at the front of the room, raised my voice, and eliminated all inflection from my tone. "Cease this noise."

The man's gaze swung to me. "What? Who... who are you?"

Chris adopted a monotone. "She is who your guiding Voice said she was. As am I."

The man blinked twice, and his eyes darted back and forth between Chris and me. His twitching head reminded me of a nervous bird watching for predators, and I felt a nervous laugh form in my gut as he said, "You are...?"

I ruthlessly squashed my building laugh. "We are what you call amies."

Laney and Laura gasped, and the four guys stared at us in open-mouthed astonishment.

The Izzie officer asked, "What happened to the Voice? Do you know where it went?"

I kept my face as impassive as my voice was toneless. "Your Voice was unwelcoming. Our master sent us to establish relations with your Voice. But your Voice rejected our master's overture."

Chris took over. "Your Voice attacked our master, forcing our master to defend itself."

"But why is the Voice gone?" the officer asked.

"We have told you," I said. "Our master defended itself and destroyed your Voice."

"Noooooo!" The officer raised his hands to his head. "It can't be!"

"It can be, and it is," I said. "But you can serve a new master, if you choose."

"Our master will need servants on this world," Chris said. "You could be among the first so honored."

Doubt clouded the officer's eyes. But then the screens in the control room sprang to life. The scenes didn't match what the screens had shown before, but the central screen displayed a view of the planet as seen from space.

The officer spun and stared at the images. "Your master did this?"

"Yes," I said.

"How... can I make sure your master replaces the Voice?"

"Put down your weapons and release the servants we have already recruited."

The officer turned and looked at our friends. "They serve your master?"

"Of course."

"Release them," the officer ordered.

"Are you sure, sir?" the man holding Laura asked.

The officer's eyes bugged out, and he screamed, "Follow your orders!"

The Izzies lowered their guns and released Laney and Laura. Our friends milled about, obviously unsure what to believe.

I caught Laney's eye. "Come. My father is lost in the mountains, and I need your help."

Laney looked confused for a second, then she grinned. "Sure thing, amy Anne."

The others followed when Laney headed our way. Chris and I led them from the control room. Tim wisely closed the door behind us. Otherwise, the Izzie officer might have wondered why Chris and I grinned like idiots and pulled our friends into a big group hug.

Tim broke up our group hug. "Your Highness, may I suggest further celebrations wait until you and your friends are safely aboard your father's ship?"

"Good idea," I said. "But when did you get all formal and boring, Tim?"

"When your father promoted me to captain of your guard, Your Highness."

Laney said, "You have your own guards, Anne?"

Tim said, "All members of the royal family do, Miss Gibson. I've been a member of Princess Anne's guard since she was four."

"That brings up a question," I said. "Why did Dad suddenly promote you, Tim? Not that I'm complaining, but it seemed pretty spur of the moment."

"Perhaps you should ask your father, Your Highness."

I glanced at the squad escorting us. "Do any of you know?"

A man guarding our left flank said, "I know, Your Highness."

"Spill," I said.

The man turned a confused expression my way. "Excuse me, Your Highness?"

"Sorry, that's Ab Astran slang for 'please tell me what you know.'"

"I see, Your Highness." The man took a second to compose himself. "Your father sent Guardsman Dawson to have the sensor techs isolate the frequency used by that deadman switch. But Dawson realized that could take several minutes, and the local leader only gave your father one minute. Unwilling to gamble your lives—"

"Stop embellishing, Rogers," Tim said.

"Yes, sir," Rogers replied. "Dawson bypassed sensors and had the communications officer beam a signal on all frequencies. Your father laughed when Dawson told him what he'd done and then promoted him."

I laughed with delight. "That was *brilliant*, Tim!"

"It was just common sense, Your Highness."

I arched an eyebrow. "Are you disagreeing with a member of the royal family, Guard Captain Dawson?"

The corners of Tim's lips quirked up in the gentle smile I knew so well. "No, I'm just disagreeing with Princess Brat."

Chris laughed. "Princess Brat? I can't *wait* to tell—"

I felt my cheeks redden. "Mention that nickname to *anyone* at the Academy, and I swear no one will ever find your body!"

Chris shrank from me as if I'd terrified her. "Wow, the Princess Brat is *way* scarier than the Princess Scout!"

Tim burst out laughing. "Princess Scout?"

"If you tell that name to anyone at home, I'll bury you in the shallow grave with Chris," I snarled.

Tim glanced at Chris. "Do you see what I've had to put up for fifteen years?"

Chris clapped her hands to her cheeks in mock horror. "And here I thought dealing with her for the last week was bad!"

Fortunately, we exited the capitol building then, and the sudden cold distracted everyone. Always thinking ahead, Dad was waiting for us with a stack of survival blankets. As he handed them out to our friends, I made introductions.

Laura, Cam, and Cam's father went to where Laura's father, President Ackerman, sat. Laura spoke with her father for a moment, then she dropped to her knees and gave him a fierce hug.

I felt a sudden need for some parental comfort and leaned against Dad. He put an arm around my shoulders and planted a kiss on the top of my head. Despite the frigid temperatures, I felt warmer and more secure than I'd felt in years.

Dad opened his other arm to Chris. "I'll be happy to stand in for your father until he can hug you."

Chris smiled and let Dad pull her close. Dad surprised her by kissing her on the head, too. "Thank you for everything you've done for Anne." He looked at Laney, Logan, and Jace. "Thank you three, too. I'm sorry I don't have enough arms to hug all five of you at the same time. But maybe you'll settle for hugs from the Gibson family when they get here."

"What do you mean?" Logan asked.

"As soon as we had everything under control here, I communicated with the Gibsons and sent a shuttle to pick them up." Dad looked at Jace. "After speaking with the Gibsons, I did not contact your father. But if you want—"

"No, sir," Jace said. "I never want to see my father again."

An uncomfortable silence settled over us. So I changed the subject. "What's the plan, now that the AI is gone?"

"I'm going to spend all night working with all the mentally competent Ab Astran government officials and contacting other world leaders who can also function without AI control." He looked me in the eye. "And tomorrow afternoon, my ship will broadcast an address to everyone on the planet."

"Have you figured out what you're going to say, Dad?"

"No. But I don't need to plan a speech."

"You're just going to wing it?" I asked.

"No. I'm not even giving the speech."

"So, um, President Ackerman will give it?"

"No. He's well enough to advise me in my talks with other governments, but he's in no condition to give a vital speech."

I shook my head in frustration. "I'm tired of guessing. Who's giving the speech?"

Dad flashed a grin. "You are."

I opened my mouth to protest Dad's speech idea. But I yawned instead. My yawn proved contagious when Chris and Laney yawned as widely as I had. Jace and Logan didn't follow my lead, but from their expressions resisting took all their willpower.

Dad pulled his arms from around Chris's and my shoulders. "Tim? Please get these young people out of the cold and into a warm bunk."

"Of course, sir." Tim caught my eye. "If you and your friends would accompany me, Your Highness?"

I looked at Cam and Laura, who remained with their fathers. "What about Cam and Laura?"

"I think they have a lot of catching up to do," Dad said. "Don't worry, I'll make sure they're well taken care of."

I nodded and then followed Tim to the ship. Chris and I didn't give our surroundings a second thought, but Laney, Logan, and Jace had never been inside a spaceship before. They marveled at virtually everything inside the ship. I wanted to explain controls and displays to them, but a yawn surfaced every time I opened my mouth.

Tim took us to the crew quarters, pointed us three girls into one cabin and the two guys into the cabin next door. He smiled at me. "I'm afraid our quarters aren't up to royal standards of comfort, Your Highness."

"Are the bunks horizontal?" I asked.

"They are."

"Then I declare them fit for my royal person." I made a shooing motion at Tim as I entered the cabin. "Go away, Tim. You're dismissed."

I dropped into a bunk, closed my eyes, and slept.

Sometime later, low whispers roused me. I cracked an eyelid open and saw Laney's parents and grandfather hugging her. I smiled, happy for her and Logan, and fell asleep again.

Much later, I awoke to Chris and Laney whispering to each other. Without opening my eyes, I said, "You can stop whispering. I'm awake."

"Good," Laney said. "Logan and Jace claim they're starving, but I wouldn't let them eat until you woke up."

I sat up on the bunk. "You could have let them get breakfast without me."

"We did."

"Huh?"

"It's time for lunch."

"Past time, really," Chris added.

"If you already let the guys eat breakfast, why would you torture them like that over lunch?"

Laney grinned. "Because I could."

I shrugged. "As long as you had a good reason."

Lunch was less leisurely than I hoped. Dad joined us and brought us up to date on the worldwide political situation. "It's far from stable, but better than I dared hope last night. My promise of Federation diplomatic assistance was met with skepticism. The governments of Refuge are more interested in the diplomatic team your mother is bringing from Aashla."

"Because she's so beautiful?" Logan asked.

"No," Dad said, laughing. "It's because Aashla has much in common with Refuge. Both planets have many countries, all with their own political goals, while Federation planets have one world government. So, Federation politicians don't have to deal with as much internal disagreement. Aashla is also less technologically advanced than Refuge, yet remains independent from the Federation."

Logan nodded. "Gotcha."

"How soon will Mom be here?" I asked.

"Tomorrow."

I looked at Chris. "Is Rob coming with her? I kind of promised Chris I'd set her up with my super handsome brother."

Chris blushed. "Anne!"

"Yes, Rob is coming." Dad smiled at Chris. "Rob will be delighted to meet such an enchanting young lady." Dad turned back to me. "Meanwhile, we need to get you ready for your address."

My appetite vanished. "Um, did you write a speech for me, Dad?"

"No. I want you to speak from the heart, honey."

"And say what?"

"Whatever you feel will reassure the people of Refuge."

"Are you sure about this, Dad? I'm just a nineteen-year-old girl!"

"Like it or not, you're the face of this crisis."

"So is Chris."

"Less so. The Ab Astran government didn't even know about her until they captured Jace and Logan. Chris also doesn't have your diplomatic training or your experience speaking in public."

Chris nodded. "He's right, Anne."

I gave Chris a sidelong look. "You're just saying that because you don't want to give the speech."

"Yeah, but that doesn't mean your father is wrong."

Two hours later, I sat before the vid equipment Dad used for his broadcast. I took deep, calming breaths and tried to slow my racing heart.

"Are you ready, Anne?" Dad asked.

No.

"Yes."

Dad turned to the comm officer. "Start the broadcast."

I looked at the cam for five seconds after the comm officer gave me a thumbs up. Then I said, "People of Refuge, I think most of you will recognize me. The Ab Astran government spent the last week broadcasting my image and calling me a dangerous amy, or AI minion. But I'm no minion. I don't have hypnotic vision. My appearance is because of good genetics, not surgical sculpting."

I smiled and held up a photo of Mom. "This is my mother. Gorgeous, isn't she? And she's *old*—forty-five." I lowered my voice, as if speaking in confidence to the cam. "That's just between us, okay? If Mom finds out I revealed her age, I'll be in big trouble!" I returned to my normal speaking voice. "Now that you've seen my mom, can you doubt I came by my looks naturally?

"So, please ignore the stuff said on that stupid news program last night. I'm just a normal nineteen-year-old college girl." I decided against mentioning the Scout Academy. It would take more explaining than the 'college girl' description. "I go to classes, study hard, worry about my grades, and cram for the end-of-year exams. Just like millions of college girls and guys here on Refuge.

"My fellow student and close friend Chris and I didn't come here on purpose. We definitely didn't come here to destroy an AI and bring down your governments. I won't say we're upset things worked out the way they did, because an AI should never rule over humans. But all Chris and I ever wanted to do was go home.

"We didn't force anyone to help us. Even if you don't believe me, don't say so around anyone in the Gibson family, Jace, Cam, or Laura. They helped us because they're good people, not because Chris and I used hypnotic vision—whatever that is—on them. Chris and I wouldn't even have gotten out of the mountains without their help. *They* are the true heroes of our story."

I paused for a moment and tried to put myself in the place of the people of Refuge. That gave me an idea. "Dad wanted me to reassure you all, to help you understand that the destruction of your AI marks the *beginning* of humanity's history on Refuge, not its end. You don't know me. Why should you trust me?"

I took a deep breath, because I knew my next words would be unpopular with my father and Tim. "So I'm going to give you the chance to meet me. And not from a distance. As soon as I finish speaking, I'm going on a walking tour of Landfall. I invite everyone in or near the city to join me. Meet me. Talk to me. And decide if you're willing to trust me.

"To those of you who don't live near Landfall, I'll do my best to visit your cities, too. I'll travel with my mother. And while she confers with your leaders, I'll go on a walking tour of the city." I offered a shy smile. "I know I'll only meet a small fraction of you, but I hope those I meet will tell their friends about our meeting. And, by the time my walking tours are over, I hope you'll know me well enough to trust me.

"Citizens of Landfall, I look forward to meeting many of you today. And remember to bundle up. It's bitterly cold outside!" I gave my most sincere smile. "I'll see you soon!"

The comm officer tapped some buttons. "Broadcast over, Your Highness."

"Thank you." I turned my attention to Dad, who just stared at me with an unreadable expression on his face. "How did I do, Dad?"

He blinked, as if waking from a dream, and shook his head. "Have I ever told you how much you remind me of your mother when I first met her?"

"No. But thank you for saying it now."

Then Tim burst into the room, looked at Dad, and asked, "Did you approve of this walking tour?" When Dad shook his head, Tim relaxed. "Good. I was afraid—"

I ignited my princess glare. "I'm going on the walking tour, Tim."

Chris crowded into the room behind Tim. "And I'm going with you!"

"Hey," Laney said, "don't forget me!"

"Sir?" Tim asked.

"I told Anne to speak from the heart," Dad said. "I can hardly complain that she did what I asked."

I let Tim bring one squad of guards for crowd control, armed with stun batons. But we didn't need them. The crowds that joined us in the streets of Landfall were patient and polite. And I think most of them believed my message.

Mom and Rob arrived the next day, and the Federation diplomatic mission showed up the day after. The cadet cruiser came in with the Federation ship, and my fellow cadets joined me on walking tours all over the planet. By the time Mom wrapped up her discussions with the various governments, most of the people on Refuge were on our side.

And, when we finally got back to the Academy, Rob escorted Chris to the much-delayed end-of-year Scout Academy Ball.

EPILOGUE

Three years later

I fought down a nearly overwhelming urge to fidget and tug at the collar of my dress Scout uniform. Which was ridiculous. I had worn the dress uniform dozens of times during my four years at the Academy, and I'd never once thought it felt constricting. I'd worn it while marching in the scorching sun as sweat trickled down my back. I'd worn it on the dance floor at three Scout Academy Balls—and would wear it at a fourth tonight—and the dress uniform never even felt tight. I hadn't put on weight. My bust and hip measurements remained the same as when my plebe year began.

So what was so different today?

You're about to walk across the stage and accept your commission. Then the most famous Scout of all time—your father—will pin your rank insignia on your uniform collar. The one you will not *tug on.*

Yeah, so just another day at the Academy.

Academy Commander Mills called, "Pierce Vahn."

Pierce, who all my fellow fourth-years agreed had the best name in our class, solemnly climbed the stairs to the stage. His family cheered as he strode across the stage. Commander Mills recounted some of Pierce's cadet accomplishments, but I didn't listen. I just prayed I would look as calm and composed as Pierce did.

Commander Mills said, "Pinning Scout Second Class Vann's rank insignia is his father, Robert Vahn."

Pierce stepped past Commander Mills and stopped in front of his father. The beaming civilian fumbled with the pins, but didn't drop them. A moment later, Pierce spun to face the faculty and snapped off a salute. Then he and his father walked off the stage.

Meaning I was next. I drew a deep breath and released it.

"Anne Villas."

As I climbed the stairs, Commander Mills recited some of my highlights. "A rare four-year participant in the Cadet Cruise, Cadet Villas also served as Cadet Commander during her fourth year at the Academy. Despite the time-consuming responsibilities that come with that position, she graduates at the top of her class. She is also listed in Scout Corps records as the youngest discoverer of a lost colony."

From among the third-year cadets, a familiar voice shouted, "Woo hoo!"

I fought the urge to scan the cadets for Laney's blonde head. But my friend wasn't done yet.

Laney clapped her hands in sync with the syllables as she chanted, "Prin cess Scout! Prin cess Scout!"

Logan and Jace joined in. "Prin cess Scout! Prin cess Scout!"

Dozens more voices joined the chant. "Prin cess Scout! Prin cess Scout!"

By the time they ran through the chant for the seventh time, I think every cadet in the crowd had joined in. I felt heat as I almost blushed. Then I turned all the willpower I'd spent not blushing to keeping myself walking steadily across the stage.

"Prin cess Scout!"

I stopped before Commander Mills and saluted. He smiled and returned the salute. The cadets chanted my nickname one more time and then fell silent.

In a low tone, Commander Mills said, "In my fifteen years here, that's the only time the entire Cadet Corps cheered on one of their own." He gave me my commission, shook my hand, and surprised the heck out of me by winking. "I hope the Academy doesn't get *too* boring without you, Scout Second Class Villas."

I couldn't help grinning in return.

Commander Mills addressed the crowd. "Pinning Scout Second Class Villas's rank insignia is her father, Master Scout Emeritus David Rice."

Cheers erupted a second time, though nobody chanted for Dad. I'm biased, but Dad looked great in his old dress uniform. To my amazement, he blinked back tears. Even with tear-blurred vision, Dad handled my rank pins like a pro.

Snap on the right collar.

Snap on the left collar.

Then Dad did something no other parent could do today. He straightened his spine, drew back his shoulders, and saluted me. I returned his salute. Turned to face the faculty and saluted them.

Like the gentlemen he is, Dad offered me his arm. I looped my arm through his, and he escorted me off the stage.

And Laney got in one last cheer. "Prin cess Scout!"

I only hoped I could come up with something to embarrass Laney for her graduation next year.

One advantage of having a name near the end of the alphabet is the ceremony ends shortly after your moment in the sun. Twenty minutes after getting my commission, I got hugs from Mom, Rob, Laney, Logan, and Jace. I wished Cam and Laura could have joined us, but Laura just gave birth to a little girl. I could only hope little Anne Christine lived up to her two troublesome namesakes.

Someone came up behind me just as Jace released me and said, "About face!"

With an unscoutly squeal, I spun and wrapped my arms around the person. "Chris, you made it!"

She returned my hug. "Just barely. And then, only because the ship's captain sent me directly to the Academy in one of his shuttles." Chris looked at Dad. "Do I have you to thank for that?"

Dad pointed at Mom. "That was all Callan. She can be quite... persuasive when she puts her mind to it."

Rob pried me away from Chris, swept her into his arms, and kissed her.

Mom leaned close to me, as if she was about to impart a secret. Only she didn't lower her voice. "You know, Rob gets all his romanticism from your father."

I leaned my head against Mom's. "Then it's a good thing I was around to find a girlfriend for him."

Rob held Chris close but looked at me. "Fear not, Anne, I plan on returning the favor. Lately, I've been scouring Aashla for a man for my baby sister."

I arched an eyebrow. "And?"

"No luck so far, sis. All the guys I know are... How should I put this?" A magnificently malicious expression settled over Rob's face. "They're all sane."

I gave a dismissive wave at Rob. "Away with your meddling, brother! I wouldn't want anyone you found for me, anyway."

"Why is that?" he asked.

"I'll find my spacebeau the old-fashioned way." I looked up into the darkening sky. "I'll find him out there. Among the stars." I slid my arm around Dad. "Because I'm a Scout. Like my father before me."

YOU MIGHT ALSO ENJOY...

If you enjoyed *The Princess Scout,* you might enjoy *The Hostage in Hiding*, an Imadjinn Award nominated space opera featuring two young, female heroines. Available now!

If you enjoyed *The Princess Scout*, please post a brief review. Reader recommendations are the best advertising.

ABOUT THE AUTHOR

Henry Vogel began his writing career in comic books way back in the 1980s, with the indie titles *Southern Knights* and *X-Thieves*. When the bottom dropped out of the black & white comic book market, Henry went into IT, where he worked for the next thirty-three years. Henry took up professional storytelling in 2006, and has performed all across his home state of North Carolina.

As a lifetime fan of science fiction, Henry always wanted to write science fiction novels. He began writing *Scout's Honor* in 2012, and released it to the world in 2014. He hasn't stopped writing since.

Henry makes his home in Raleigh, NC, and is hard at work on his next novel.

www.henryvogelwrites.com

ALSO BY HENRY VOGEL

Travis & Trouble

Trouble in Twi-Town

Trouble on Mars

The Fortune Chronicles

Fortune's Fool

The Scales of Sin & Sorrow

The Scout Series

Scout's Honor

Scout's Oath

Scout's Duty

Scout's Law

Scout's Training

Scout's First Mission

Hart for Adventure

The Princess Scout

Stand-alone Novels

The Lost Planet

The Adventures of Matt & Michelle

The Fugitive Heir

The Fugitive Pair

The Fugitive Snare

The Hostage in Hiding

The Captain Nancy Martin

The Counterfeit Captain

The Undercover Captain

The Recognition Series

The Recognition Run

The Recognition Rejection

The Recognition Revelation

Illustrated Children's Book

I'm in Charge! and Other Stories